The Nine Dragons

Justin Scott

The Nine Dragons

A Novel of Hong Kong 1997

BANTAM BOOKS   New York   Toronto   London   Sydney   Auckland

To Gloria Hoye,
My love, my beauty, my friend

THE NINE DRAGONS
A BANTAM BOOK/JUNE 1991

Copyright © 1991 by Justin Scott.

BOOK DESIGN BY JAYA DAYAL

Library of Congress Cataloging-in-Publication Data

Scott, Justin.
The nine dragons : a novel of Hong Kong, 1997 / Justin Scott.
p.   cm.
ISBN 0-553-07329-X
I. Title.   II. Title: 9 dragons.
PS3569.C644N5   1991
813'.54 — dc20   90-25090
CIP

Published simultaneously in the United States and Canada

Bantam Books are published by Bantam Books,
a division of Bantam Doubleday Dell Publishing
Group, Inc. Its trademark, consisting of the words
"Bantam Books" and the portrayal of a rooster, is
Registered in U.S. Patent and Trademark Office and
in other countries. Marca Registrada.
Bantam Books, 666 Fifth Avenue,
New York, New York 10103.

Printed in the United States of America

BVG   0 9 8 7 6 5 4 3 2 1

"If you can't swing a deal in Hong Kong it can't be done."

—A BANKER

"Everyone in Hong Kong has a secret."

—A LAWYER

"The East Is Red."

—MAO ZEDONG

Home Free

1973

T HE LITTLE GIRL felt a surge of water lift them from below. Terrified, she imagined the great body of the shark circling under them. She struggled in her father's arms. He begged her not to splash, whispered that it would not bite them if they were still. Something terrible brushed her foot.

It was night in 1973, a brutal Year of the Ox. Behind them, the China coast was dark. Soldiers and double barbed-wire fences prevented escapes by land from the Communist People's Republic. Tai Pang Bay was the only way out. Ahead, across the water, a faint red glow marked the electric lights of the free British Crown Colony of Hong Kong, which clung to the rugged Kowloon peninsula and a few small islands in the sea.

Her father thought the shark had gone. He swam a slow side-stroke, never breaking the surface, and whispering to her in a voice cracked with fear. She held his belt and trailed behind him, glancing fearfully over her shoulder.

He had been a teacher before the Red Guards beat him for being an *"enemy without a gun."* He had waited for his wounds to heal so he wouldn't spill blood in the sea, and he had studied the sharks, concluding that swimmers who splashed made noises like the dying fish that sharks attacked. Tonight he had put his theory to the test, hoisting his daughter in his arms and wading into the dark.

He swam for hours, resting when he had to on an inflated pig bladder, round as a balloon, which helped them float. At last they passed the four-second flashing channel light he had been navigating by. Now he kept his course by looking back. A strong current moved in their favor, but the waves were rough. She felt him swallow deeply and knew the wounds inside his body were bleeding again.

Another surge lifted them like a giant hand.

Helpless within sight of the steep jagged hills of Kowloon, they drifted on the current and waited for the beast to attack. It passed close. Its tail knifed beside her. The flashing light showed blood trickling from her father's mouth. Instinctively she licked it away.

Slowly, the current bore them closer to shore. She heard waves breaking. Father began swimming again. At last the sand was slanting under their feet.

Dogs bayed. Slivers of light skipped along the beach. They ran into the brushy hills, climbed inland until dawn, and hid all day in a bridge culvert while British Gurkha troops roared overhead on the road. She half-slept, dreaming of her mother's face, which kept dissolving into darkness. Her father's skin was burning. Delirious, he kept pressing his forehead to the ground, giving thanks to Tin Hau— goddess of the sea, Queen of Heaven—who had delivered them from the shark.

That night they ventured onto the road. Headlights blinded them, but it was only a farm truck delivering ducks and cabbage to the city. The driver let them ride in back for their last piece of jade, and dropped them in the dense slum of Mong Kok.

The little girl held on to her father with one hand and with the other clasped Auntie Chen's address on a scrap of paper. Wide-eyed, she led him through a market where the air was thick with the mouthwatering scent of hot oil. Nine years old, thin as sticks, she was a child of bone-poor China. She had never seen so much food, nor so many things to buy.

Snakes drowsed in wire cages. The winter monsoon sweeping down from the Chinese Mainland had thickened their blood. Across the narrow alley a pig shivered. It lay on its side in the gutter, legs bound tightly, one eye staring up at a thin blue ribbon of sky pinched by leaning tenements. The buildings sprouted bamboo poles hung with shop signs, bedding, and laundry drying in the shade. Shirts for sale dangled from fire escapes, and the narrow space echoed shuffling feet, shouts of determined Cantonese, and the steady thump of a stamping machine in a ground-floor factory.

A man squatting on his heels, tying hairy-legged freshwater crabs with strands of grass, thrust one of the struggling creatures at her. Claws and legs flailed the air, but she had seen too much to be afraid and simply stared back at him. He laughed and tossed her an orange.

She ran to the hawker selling pork buns and offered to trade. He extended a pork bun wrapped in paper, but she saw the orange's value in his eyes and demanded four.

"*Yih.*" Two.

They settled on three.

The taste of food made her even hungrier. When she took her father's hand she felt him trembling. He looked like a ghost the wind would blow away. "Not much farther," she said, and he shambled after her as if she knew where they were going.

The address on the paper began to melt before her eyes. She asked directions of a Hakka woman selling salt fish. Her mother's flat was along this lane, the old woman thought.

"*Xiao yie,*" cried a most familiar voice. Little daughter. An old woman dragging a string bag of vegetables scooped her up in powerful arms. Tin Hau herself could not have been more wonderful, and the child felt her limbs collapse in a spasm of relief.

"Chen-*gwoo!*" Auntie Chen.

In China, in better days, Auntie Chen had been the little girl's nanny, or *amah*. Auntie Chen's family had sold her as a child to Father's family. She had raised the little girl's father and had cared for the little girl during her mother's frequent absences. When loyal servants drew the special ire of the Red Guards, Father had given her money to flee to Hong Kong.

Carrying the little girl and supporting Father, Auntie Chen took them up dark flights of stairs to a tiny flat. Then she brought a Chinese ambulance attendant, who examined Father and prescribed a visit to the clinic. Father was afraid without identity papers. The ambulance man said that the British had a "touch base" or home-free refugee policy that permitted people who had made it to stay. But Father was done taking chances.

Auntie Chen promised to find an herbal doctor in the morning. After Father had fallen into a twitching sleep, the little girl asked where her mother was.

Auntie Chen's mouth hardened with distaste. "Go to sleep. You're home with me."

"Isn't she in Hong Kong?"

"Of course she's in Hong Kong. Where else could she go?"

Auntie Chen's flat had a window facing a brick wall and a hanging electric light bulb. By its glare and leaping shadows she did piece-work, assembling artificial flowers from leaves, petals, and stems sold by the man who bought back the finished flowers. Father's cousins, who had escaped earlier, tracked them down quickly and brought rice and old clothes. But Father was strong enough to help Auntie Chen tie flowers and had twice taken the little girl to the beautiful Tin Hau Temple in Public Square Street where they burned joss sticks to thank the sea goddess for their lives, before Mother finally appeared.

She was even prettier than the little girl remembered, with a warm smell of perfume and cigarette smoke, and deep black Shang-hainese eyes, dark as caves and just as mysterious. Mother took her for a ride on the Star Ferry. In one astonishing afternoon she saw the giant ships in the harbor, the towering buildings ablaze in the sun-light, and her first *gweilos*—ghost people from the West. They were deathly pale and frighteningly huge, some twice as tall as Father. But Mother was not afraid; when a giant in a white uniform spoke to her, she chatted back freely in her broken English, confusing the words *little sister* for *daughter*.

Soon, to Father's dismay, Mother was drifting in and out of the flat much as she had in China. On the mattress the little girl shared with Auntie Chen behind a draped sheet, she awakened to their ar-guments—Father baffled, Mother ripe with new slang.

Where do you go?

You have to know the right people in Hong Kong to get ahead.

Who is this friend?

Lost everything. Just like us. Started from scratch. Now he's hit the big time.

The little girl heard her father suck in his breath, summoning his courage as he had the night he picked her up and waded into the dark. She held her own breath, fearing the answer to a question she could not understand.

Do you sleep with him?

Of course not. He'll help start a business. Blue jeans. They're the right bet at the right time.

But I'm a teacher.

Look where that got you. Thank God you taught the child English. At least she'll have a chance.

Mother came home one day with momentous news that would change the little girl's life forever. Mother's friend had fixed a place in a local Catholic mission school—an elite school where Chinese children could study English. A warm morning found her running down the lane in a faded blue skirt a half-size too large, a thin white blouse Auntie Chen had scrubbed and ironed, and carrying a knapsack to bring books home in.

"*Out* of those puddles!" Auntie Chen puffed after her. Mother had gone again and Father had to work. Along the lane where the ground shook she stopped at the open wall of the toy factory to watch her father operate the stamping machine that pounded toy trucks out of hot metal. His arms were thin as bone. For the first time she felt anger. He worked two jobs, the factory and cooking in a restaurant, because Mother would not work even one.

Auntie Chen led her from the lane onto wider and wider streets, where hundreds of gigantic colored signs loomed over the sidewalks. They squeezed into the queue for the bus. An enormous gleaming car parked in the bus space and a uniformed driver opened the door. A broad-shouldered, red-faced gweilo climbed out, trailed by a little girl with yellow hair in braids.

The gweilo had a thick bushy mustache and piercing blue eyes that raked in every feature of the street. And yet when this terrifying apparition growled deep in its throat, "Come along, Your Majesty — let's have a gander at this clinic Mum's got me writing checks for," the pale child seized his hairy hand as happily as the little girl ran to her own father.

Startled by the unexpected connection to the rich gweilos, she stared openly. A gweilo woman — a *gweipo* — tall and tawny as a tiger, bounded from the car. Laughing loudly, she took her daughter's other hand. And for a shining moment all the people on the sidewalk and even the cars in the street seemed to stop, and the family stood together, a golden trio gazing proudly upon their Hong Kong. The mother noticed the gaping little girl. "Duncan, darling, look at that adorable child."

Fiery blue eyes pinned her to the pavement. "Dose of Shanghainese there. You'll never see a pure Cantonese that fine." He laughed. "Going to be a heartbreaker when she grows up."

Their blond child returned the little girl's stare with steady blue eyes — bluer than the father's — as if she, too, wondered what a "heartbreaker" was.

"Victoria? Come along now."

"She's squinting, Mummy."

"She's not *squinting*. She's Chinese."

"No, Mummy. She needs glasses, like Samantha at riding school."

The gweipo mother bent down. Her enormous face hung over the little girl like the moon. "By golly, you may be right, Victoria. Good lass." She rose again to her astonishing height and addressed Auntie Chen in a loud, clear tone.

"I say! This child needs eyeglasses. Now I want you to tell her teachers. The schools have programs — they'll pay. Do you understand me?"

The old amah's face had turned as blank and smooth as a glazed urn.

"Good Christ, what the devil's Chinese for eyeglasses?"

"*Ngaan geng*," the little girl whispered to Auntie Chen. "The lady says I need eyeglasses."

"*Ngaan geng?*" said Auntie Chen. "Ask the female barbarian if we should buy a motorcar too. *Ngaan geng?*"

"The school will—"

"That's the wrong word," interrupted the golden-haired Victoria. "Eyeglasses are *yaen gein. Yaen gein.*"

The little girl corrected her politely. "You speak excellent Mandarin. Unfortunately, my poor amah is Cantonese."

Victoria's father laughed. "She's got you there, Your Majesty. So much for those Chinese lessons. Let's hope you do better on the horse."

Victoria appeared to collapse from within when her father laughed at her. Her pink cheeks flushed dark as blood, and the little girl could almost feel the hurt welling from her eyes. In an instant, however, she straightened up and set her jaw and shocked the little girl with a bold, angry retort to her own father. "*Mandarin* is the official language of China, Daddy."

"We don't live in China. We live in Hong Kong."

The mother shot her husband a reproachful glance and comforted her daughter with a brisk pat on her shoulder. "Many different Chinese languages are spoken on the Mainland. They speak Shanghainese in Shanghai, Fukienese in Fukien Province. Here in Hong Kong *our* Chinese speak Cantonese, because they originally came from Canton. But *English* is the official language of Hong Kong. Has been for donkey's years. And *you,*" she said, looming over the little girl again, "speak English. Jolly good."

She fished inside her handbag, which had a rich gold clasp. "Here. You take my card and tell your teacher Tai-Tai says you need eyeglasses. Do you know what eyeglasses are?"

The little girl was struck dumb. *Tai-Tai!* A *taipan*'s wife. The queen of a mighty British trading *hong*. She was as likely to meet Tin Hau.

"Do you?"

"Yes."

"Take this card. Give it to your teacher."

Sally Farquhar Mackintosh, it read in flowing script. *Peak House.*

"There's your bus. Run along."

Auntie Chen dragged her aboard and the gweilo Taipan laughed again. "Good show, Mother. Come along, Victoria. Mum's done another good deed for the day."

Victoria and the little girl looked back. Their eyes met just before the bus lurched away. Victoria tossed her head, flinging her gold braids like sunlight and exposing her ears. The little girl gasped with envy. She was wearing beautiful jade earrings, a dangly pair of bright-green dragons. Then she reached up without even looking and found her mother's hand.

At school that first day, the little girl sat bolt upright with a pencil in one hand and paper under the other and listened to every word her English teacher said. It was hard; the accents in the classroom were different from her father's. It was very important to be a good student, the teacher said. Good students were rewarded with something called scholarships. These scholarships allowed good students to attend technical college or even, if they were very very good, university. They might, when they grew up, receive a job in the British Civil Service, which administered Hong Kong. Good students studied hard and obeyed their teachers and prayed to God.

And now, so that God and the Civil Service would know who they were, the teacher would bestow upon each student a proper English name. She named the child at the head of row one: Anthony. After Bennett came Carolyn. By Deborah, the little girl had seen the pattern. Quick with numbers, she calculated in a glance that her new name would begin with the letter V. The coincidence was fate, a gift from Tin Hau. Thus prepared when the teacher reached her, she did something wholly uncharacteristic. She drew some of her courage from the kindness shown to her on the street, and some from the headmistress's respectful acceptance of the tai-tai's card and promise of an immediate eye examination. But most of her courage came from a hopeless wish that she had a mother like the girl with the gold braids and dragon earrings.

"Vivian," the teacher named her.

"Could I be Victoria?"

"I *beg* your pardon? What did you say? *Stand up when you speak to me!*"

The little girl jumped from her desk. In terror she whispered, "Could I be Victoria?"

"Vict*ollia.*" The teacher mocked the child's accent. "Vict*ollia* is the name of a great British queen. You are not a British queen. You are a little Chinese child. Sit *down*, Vivian."

She dragged her new name home like a dirty doll's head she had found in the street. She was sure they wouldn't let her keep it. Mother was still away. "If you touch vermilion," Auntie Chen hissed, "you get red fingers."

Vivian's father hushed the old amah. He repeated the new name, tasting it on his tongue. "Vivian. A fine name," he said at last, staring at the plastic flower in his fingers. "A fine name for a new home."

She did not tell him about Victoria—the first secret she'd kept from him. Still, he noticed she was troubled. "You still have your own names. This is just one more."

She curled up in his lap, knowing he had to leave soon for his cooking job, and opened the ancient textbook the teacher had given her. She was ahead of the other children because he had taught her to read as well as speak. Now she read to him the first English words she had learned in school:

" 'Hong Kong is a small fishing harbor on the south coast of China.' "

"How could this be?" she asked. Hong Kong was a city of giant buildings, roaring roads, and ten thousand ships. Hadn't she and Father seen its red glow all the way from China?

Father turned to what they called their library. By then a corner of the little room had begun to fill up with materials to read and learn by: old books from relatives who cooked and cleaned in gweilo homes; glossy magazines her mother had left behind; a treasure trove of discarded fact sheets published by the Hong Kong Tourist Association. He unfolded a visitors' map from the Peninsula Hotel, where his cousin's elder son waited tables in the lobby.

What was Tsim Sha Tsui? They had walked the Nathan Road gazing wide-eyed at the district's restaurants, clubs, and expensive shops. But the Cantonese meaning of Tsim Sha Tsui was "sharp, sandy spit"—the sort of name a fisherman would choose. And look at Shek-O on the east end of Hong Kong Island where rich taipans played golf. Here was a picture of the sea beating the rocks. What did Shek-O mean in Cantonese? It didn't mean "rich taipans play golf," did it?

"No," she giggled. It meant "rocky beach." Another fisherman's name. "I don't understand." She did understand, but she wanted him to keep talking to her. "What about Kowloon? Kowloon means 'nine dragons.' Fishermen don't catch dragons."

"Well . . . Once upon a time, the last Sung emperor—a little boy, no bigger than you—was chased by the Mongols all the way to Hong Kong. There were eight hills on Kowloon then, and the little boy emperor said to his tutor, 'Look! Eight dragons.'

" 'No, Your Majesty,' the tutor corrected him. 'Emperors are dragons too. So here are *nine* dragons.' "

"What happened to the little boy? Why was he last?"

"When the Mongols discovered his hiding place, his tutor picked him up in his arms and jumped into the sea."

Vivian covered her ears.

Cursing himself for a fool, her father gently moved her hands and gave the legend a new ending. "They swam across the strait—where the Star Ferry goes today—all the way to Hong Kong Island, where they lived happily ever after."

"I don't understand," she said suspiciously. "What does it mean?"

He had to leave for work, so he settled on the one truth he had discovered to be consistent in his own short life. "What it means, Vivian, is that things change too fast in China to stop them."

"But this isn't China," she echoed the British Taipan. "We live in Hong Kong."

A broad smile brightened her father's face—the smile of a man unexpectedly on firm ground—and for a moment he was not a machine operator and not a cook and not a penniless refugee, but a scholar of the Middle Kingdom, which had, with only the briefest interludes, ruled the world for four thousand years.

"Hong Kong is China," he said. "Your China."

BOOK ONE

The Red Junk

1

July 1996

V ICKY MACKINTOSH hit Hong Kong at her usual top speed, first off the plane.

A reporter for the *Tatler* gossip magazine ran after her, wondering what had brought Duncan Mackintosh's daughter back to Honkers.

"Business with the Taipan."

She flashed a pretty smile for his camera and hurried on, a small woman with shoulder-length blond hair, a slim-waisted hourglass figure, and a self-contained blue-eyed gaze good for masking lavish dreams and private doubts. She was wearing a bright T-shirt and loose slacks, lively earrings, and a striking gold pendant—a coiled dragon with a big jade eye.

Cheklapkok Airport, still under construction out on Lantau Island in the middle of the harbor, was a madhouse. A Peking flight had arrived moments ahead of Vicky's, and hordes of bureaucrats from the People's Republic of China were mobbing the taxis, jumping queues, and shoving ordinary citizens with their shoddy plastic briefcases. Mandarin invective hurled at blank-faced Cantonese taxi drivers provoked a second, thinner smile from her: a timely reminder of why she was trying to establish for her family a U.S. beachhead in the Manhattan hotel business before the PRC smothered Hong Kong.

"Missy!" her mother's driver called. The huge old Daimler glistened amid the chaos like a rock in a running sea. The driver held the door and she dived into the air conditioning.

"Welcome home, Missy."

"Thank God and heaven for you, Ah Ping. Where's Mother?"

"Tai-Tai say morning coffee in Peninsula."

"Good Christ—I'm supposed to be meeting Hugo. Hurry!"

Ah Ping lead-footed the car onto the Kowloon Bridge. Vicky punched numbers into the telephone. Desperate for a private moment with her brother, she finally ran him down at his office. It was nine-thirty in the morning, half a day ahead of New York and ten degrees hotter; a humid July Saturday in 1996, one year before Great Britain had to surrender the city to China.

"Mother's ambushed me. Let's make it eleven-thirty instead."

"Why don't we just talk on the boat?"

"What do you mean?"

"We're sailing to Manila this afternoon."

"*Sailing?* But I'm here to restructure the hotel."

"Restructure? Is that like coming home to borrow pots of money?"

"The second-born restructure. The firstborn stay home and grovel."

She and Hugo had become fast friends working together, although her brother, eight years older and off at Gordonstoun and then in the army while she was growing up, remained blissfully ignorant of their one-sided competition for their father's approval.

"I can't believe I just flew eighteen hours to go sailing."

"Vicky. Maybe the old boy outsmarted himself. It's four days to the Philippines. Dad's your captive audience."

"True. Good point . . . Wait a minute! It's typhoon season. Is he daft?"

"The Taipan says we have a clear slot," Hugo answered in the deadpan tone he reserved for relaying their father's orders. "Needless to say, Fiona insists we fly the girls over to meet us. Something's cooking down below the Marianas."

Vicky lowered the tinted window to check the sky. It was blue, above the harbor mist, but some very high thin clouds were capping it with a steely glaze. Here and there, mare's-tails indicated winds aloft, hinting at movement in the east. It looked like a dicey time to cross the China Sea.

"I've got to talk to you first, Hugo." *Before* they all went sailing and Hugo the heir fell under the Taipan's spell. Her brother agreed to meet at eleven-thirty in the Yacht Club bar. And Vicky, mindful that her mother would look smashing, got busy with the limousine's makeup mirror.

Typical of her father's highhanded ways, she seethed. And he would never forget it if she lost the hotel. Forgive, yes. But she would carry the mark of failure in his eyes forever. Never mind that MacF had come like babes into the woods into New York's cutthroat hotel scene and paid too much for a beautiful old building in a neighborhood one long block west of perfect. Never mind that for one brief season the Golden had been the best in town. *Les Dames d'Escoffier*, the Manhattan club for women in the food-and-wine trade, had thrown a black-tie bash to honor her "elegant" contribution to the New York hotel industry—*elegant* being *Les Dames'* shorthand for Vicky's success in negotiating labor-union permission to import highly skilled staff from Hong Kong.

Never mind, because a bold move to leverage her success into purchasing the legendary Plaza had fallen over a cliff in the economy. Never mind that one woman's *bold* was another man's *impetuous*. She should have seen it coming.

She caught Ah Ping watching her in the rearview mirror.

"How are things, Ah Ping?"

"Very bad, Missy. They say PRC troops cross border if more riots."

Hong Kong had always churned out the hottest gossip in Asia, and the old Chinese driver, a notorious rumormonger, relished tales of doom and gloom. Vicky countered with a nutty story she had heard at the airport.

"I hear that the PRC's going to ask Great Britain to stay on after Turnover to run the Civil Service." The reversion in 1997 was called "Turnover" in Vicky's parlance; "Changeover," "Changing the flag," or simply " '97" in Ah Ping's.

"I hear that too," Ah Ping said, heartily embracing the contradiction and proceeding to spin an even wilder tale: Two-Way Wong—Sir John Wong Li, CBE—Hong Kong's richest billionaire shipowner and most voracious property developer, was going to landfill the Causeway Bay Typhoon Shelter where the Royal Hong Kong Yacht Club had moored its boats since the Opium Wars.

"How is my mother?" she interrupted, edging closer to the main event.

"Tai-Tai fine, Missy."

Vicky caught the careful tone, afraid it meant her mother was drinking again. "And Hugo and Peter?"

"Brothers fine. Master Peter has new girl."

"Yes, I know. Mary Lee." Peter had written rhapsodically.

"Fine family, Lees."

"And my father?" she asked at last as Ah Ping guided the Daimler to a majestic stop in the Peninsula Hotel's motor court. "How is my father?"

"Taipan fine, feel new strength," answered the old man, glancing slyly in the rearview mirror. Before she could ask what that meant, the Peninsula's doormen—boys dressed in white-and-gold yacht uniforms—rushed to help her from the car.

"Welcome home, Missy." They grinned. "Tai-Tai waiting."

Vicky spied her mother's table across the Pen's vast gold-and-cream vaulted lobby. She started toward her, then shrank behind an ornate pillar. Apparently Sally Farquhar Mackintosh had assumed it would take her daughter longer to escape the mess at the airport—time for a ten A.M. sherry or two.

Vicky waited, heart pounding, mind blanking, unable to confront her, stealing glances to see if the waiters had cleared her glass. Three were in attendance because her mother cut a truly imperial figure. Everything about Sally Mackintosh, from the way she crossed her long legs, to the set of her shoulders and the tilt of her head, suggested that this rather grand beauty of indeterminate years

had a gunboat waiting in the harbor in case the natives turned
snippy.

She was blond and suntanned, much taller than Vicky, with sun
wrinkles around her eyes and a regal downturn at the tip of her
nose. Larger than life, she had a gift for diminishing her accoutre-
ments so that her red nail polish and masses of gold jewelry — rings,
diamond bracelets, a big airy link chain, earrings, and a Rolex —
looked quiet and basic.

Empty at last, the glass was whisked away.

Vicky ran to her. A kiss and a quick embrace while Sally fumbled with a breath mint, a rush of words for the flight, the traffic,
the sticky heat. Then sudden silence as mother and daughter post-
poned, by unspoken agreement, enormous issues like drinking, marriage, divorce, and no grandchildren. Vicky had written about breaking
up with her boyfriend. Sally wanted to know the details. But Vicky
joked that she intended to live alone the rest of her life, and steered
her mother into homey gossip over a pot of green tea.

Turnover loomed. Friends had packed it in and gone "home"
to England. Love affairs were enjoying renewed popularity, and
"everyone" was buying houses in the south of France. The husband
of one of Vicky's school friends had climbed "to the top of the
heap" when hired to manage an old Anglo trading hong the Chinese
had taken over. "Your father calls him the gelded Taipan," Sally
announced in a full voice that turned heads.

Being with her mother at her ebullient best made Vicky feel like
a gull soaring on a thermal updraft. But the waiters kept hovering,
expecting another order for the bar.

"How's Dad?"

"Busy as ever," Sally answered noncommittally. She reflected a
moment. "Dashing about like a man of forty. He's quite remarkable,
you know."

"I know. . . . Any reaction to my . . . return? Other than this
surprise cruise?"

"Delighted, of course," her mother replied. "He misses you off
in New York as much as I do."

Was that code? Would he order her back to Hong Kong? Her mother stayed steadfastly out of the business of the family's hong, even when it involved her own children's positions with the company, but surely she would know if he were giving up on New York.

"Let's whiz 'round to the boat, darling. Dad wants to get going."

On the drive to the Cross Harbour Tunnel they passed a row of burned-out shops whose blackened fronts glared accusingly at the street. Ammunition, Vicky thought, for her argument to maintain their base in New York, but she was shaken by the sight of the raw destruction.

"Just a mini-riot," her mother assured her. "Nothing the police couldn't handle." She glanced at the Chinese picking through the ashes and reflected good-naturedly, "Poor buggers'll miss the Union Jack when it's gone."

"I'd think they regard us as sort of irrelevant by now."

"Irrelevant?" Sally Mackintosh arched a splendid eyebrow. "British Hong Kong's the last bit of China where the Chinese haven't been allowed to run amok. No knock in the night here, no warlords, no secret police, no famine. Food in their bellies and a chance to get rich. Isn't that true, Ah Ping?"

"Yes, Tai-Tai."

"You see? Not to worry. It'll sort itself out. Hong Kong is the richest Chinese city in the world. The PRC can't afford to destroy it. Hong Kong's their window on the West, their banker, their technology tutor. Besides, Peking knows damned well it can't feed another six million unproductive mouths. No, the real danger of Turnover is we'll bore ourselves to death talking about it."

Then why, Vicky wondered aloud when they emerged from the tunnel, was the Causeway Bay Typhoon Shelter—which the Royal Hong Kong Yacht Club shared with a floating city of Tanka fishermen, boatboys, and smugglers—so crowded? It was a dense anchorage nearly half a mile long, squeezed between thirty-story buildings on the shore and a stone breakwater that shielded it from Victoria Harbour. Every inch of its surface sprouted yacht and junk masts swaying in the wakes of sampans. Boats were even slotted between the stanchions of a highway that jumped the eastern end.

Many Tanka who had moved ashore over the years were returning to their boats, her mother admitted. If the PRC reneged on its
promise not to interfere in Hong Kong's internal affairs, the sea
offered the boat people, at least, a ready escape.

"Sounds grim."

Her mother laughed. "Depends who you listen to. Wally Hearst,
one of the new China traders your father's invited sailing, claims it's
the Mainlanders who should be quaking in their sandals—what with
six million hard-working Hongkongers poised at the border to
stampede at the scent of fresh meat."

On the South China Sea, seventy miles southeast of Hong Kong, a
Thai fishing boat captain surveyed the sky and decided he didn't
like those broadening mare's-tails one bit. He debated running for
Hong Kong, where he would find storm shelter in Victoria Harbour. But if a police or PRC patrol boarded, they would discover
his arsenal and draw the obvious conclusion that the fisherman was
a pirate when opportunity arose.

Then his quandary deepened. Out of the east came a great
Chinese junk. She was enormous and defenseless, lumbering before
the wind under scalloped red sails. Her cargo might be nothing more
valuable than salt fish, but she could be smuggling gold or opium.
Either way, there might be women.

Greed overcame his fear of the weather. Engines roared and the
fishing boat dug in her stern and made speed for the victim. His
sailors gathered on the bow with their guns, the captain on the bridge
with the grenade launcher.

The junk's hull was salt-blackened and draped with a protective
necklace of automobile tires. As the Thais swung alongside to board
the bigger boat, a fat Chinese called down, pleading with a frightened, broken-toothed smile. The captain tipped the grenade launcher
toward him and he ducked like a turtle. The Thai sailors laughed.
Fore and aft, they twirled grappling hooks as the corridor of water
between the two hulls dwindled.

Suddenly, tongues of flame shot from among the tires. The Thai sailors screamed in shock and terror as gunfire exploded all around them. Bullets pounded their bodies, flapping their loose clothing, knocking weapons from their hands, smearing their faces with blood. The captain raised his launcher. Twenty rounds blew him off the bridge into the sea.

The fat Chinese shouted. The shooting stopped as suddenly as it had begun. He cast a cold eye on the carnage, then heaved a heavy satchel onto the low stern of the fishing boat. For a moment the loudest sound was the creak of her rigging as the junk veered away. Then a thunderous explosion blew the bottom out of the Thai boat. Bow pointing to the sky, she sank in the wake of the red junk, which continued west before the wind.

2

<hr />

SEVERE, AND REMARKABLY YOUNG, the antiquities scholar from Beijing's Palace Museum was struggling hard not to be awed by Hong Kong. He ignored the tantalizing views from Two-Way Wong's office atop World Oceans House. Two-Way—Sir John Wong Li, CBE—thought it an act of singleminded determination, for the city was pure spectacle this hazy morning, rimming the harbor like a silver ring hammered around a turquoise stone.

Two-Way Wong himself often stood in the window, rejoicing at how he had risen above the filth. For seven decades he had triumphed over his fellow Chinese, over beggars, prostitutes, opium sellers, gangsters, warlords, and revolutionaries, over Japanese invaders, over the British and the other gweilos from the West. He had killed many, some with his hands, some with a nod. Others he had absorbed. Most he had corrupted.

He had no doubt he deserved Hong Kong.

His gaze, flickering over the blue-green harbor and Kowloon, settled on Kai Tak, where, amid the bustle of workmen racing to complete the vast Exposition project in time for '97, Duncan Mackintosh's Expo Golden Hotel stood dark and silent. Work on the British Taipan's super-luxury hotel, he recalled with a smile, had been going very slowly.

Two-Way's visitor found the views within the chairman's office even more seductive. For how many were as qualified as the second assistant curator of the Palace of Abstinence's Hall of Bronzes to appreciate a private collection that spanned two millennia of Chinese craft? Wherever he looked were ancient carved ivory, antique screens, and carpets of a beauty that many a provincial museum could only dream about. Try as he might to restrain his eyes, they kept swiveling back to a splendid cabinet that was certainly Yüan dynasty. The translucent porcelain bowl sitting on it had turned his mouth as dry as paper.

"Is it hot in the North?" Two-Way asked politely as his servants brought green tea in covered cups. Crippled since childhood, when a beggar broke his legs to make him a better beggar, he granted all audiences from behind his desk, a polished slab of salt-blackened teak.

"Yes, hot," came the stiff reply.

"Dry and dusty, too, I'd imagine."

Observing the young curator closely, he led him from an extended discussion of the weather down a labyrinth of courteous inquiries about the health of his superiors at the museum. The boy looked at first sight like a typical Beijing *biaoshu*, a bumpkin from the North. Stiff suit and stiffer necktie, chopped-seaweed haircut, thick eyeglasses in plastic frames. His protruding front teeth had probably earned him the name Watermelon Scraper at school.

But there was fire behind the shoddy glasses. A zealot. Two-Way had battled them all his life. Thirty years ago, during the Cultural Revolution, this one would have rampaged through the streets, brandishing Mao's *Little Red Book*. He would have smashed the same porcelain bowl he was drooling over this afternoon. Twenty years before that, he'd have been a blank-faced revolutionary stalking Shanghai's alleys or digging tank traps in the country.

The curator began to fidget. Two-Way rambled on, indulging an old man's prerogative. His attack was well under way before the young man saw it coming. ". . . grateful you could make time in your schedule to visit a simple businessman. I am told you have difficulties with your collections."

"Well, no. Not at all. I mean, not all the collections."

Two-Way waited. He had stopped smiling. His long, handsome face looked hard as bone. The curator, who glared back in sudden confusion, discovered himself the target of a fierce and scornful gaze.

"It is your collection. Sir."

"My *contribution*," Two-Way corrected.

"The musical bells."

"My musical bells."

At that the young man hesitated. His silence was tantamount to insolence and Two-Way wondered if the scholar was building the nerve to remind him that the priceless set of Eastern Chou dynasty bronze bells had vanished under mysterious circumstances thirty years ago from a Shanghai museum during a Red Guards riot. No one had been so crude as to question how they had fallen recently into Two-Way's hands, as he had immediately donated the priceless antiquities to the People's Republic. The bells hung now in the Forbidden City's Palace of Abstinence, an irony not lost on Two-Way.

Sadly, this overeducated young man had discovered a problem with one of the bells. Two-Way's agents, having caught wind of his allegations, had arranged permission for the curator to travel to Hong Kong on official museum business, to mask this private meeting.

"Is there a problem with my contribution?" Two-Way asked silkily.

The young man took a deep breath. "One of your musical bells is a forgery."

"A forgery?" Two-Way echoed.

"A fake. Cast recently. Probably right here in Hong Kong."

"Please explain," said Two-Way, stroking his long chin while his eyes held rock-steady on the young man's face. "How can you be so sure it is a forgery? You are a very young fellow and no one else has called it a forgery. How could you see what your elders cannot? How old are you?"

"Twenty-two."

"How do you know better than scholars who have spent their lives studying ancient bronzes?"

"I am but a poor scholar," the curator demurred, indicating he had learned good manners and modesty somewhere along the way. "But my teacher was the most learned in China."

"Your teacher says my bells are forgeries?"

"My teacher died five years ago."

"When you were only seventeen?"

"But since I was six when he was released from prison after the chaos—"

"The Cultural Revolution."

"After the Cultural Revolution, yes. He was released from prison and he came to live with my family. He had been beaten by the Red Guards and he was going blind. I became his eyes. He discovered I had a . . . talent . . . for his work. So much was destroyed. So much was lost. But when the Red Guards were finally gone, some treasures were unearthed and his skills were in great demand. Brave people had hidden bits and pieces. We had to catalogue them to save the little China has left. To be his eyes, he taught my eye."

Two-Way had warmer memories of the time: Mao had died in 1976. The Gang of Four were arrested. It had been the beginning of the end of the Communist Party's total power and—as chaotic economic reforms and the backlash Beijing massacre further eroded the crumbling faith—the opening of boundless opportunity for visionaries like himself. As for the curator's story of a boy and an old man, frailer connections than this one had kept knowledge alive.

"So you are quite sure one of the bells is a forgery."

"A fake. Beyond any doubt."

"That is terrible," said Two-Way. His expression darkened. "Naturally I made the assumption when I donated my bells that your museum would protect my collection. Now you suggest that someone removed one of my bells and put a fake in its place."

The young man turned ashen. "No. No! Of course not."

"Then what *do* you suggest? How did you lose it?"

"That did not happen. That is not true."

"Well, what happened to my bells?"

The curator was very brave and very foolish. "That bell was switched before it came to Beijing."

"*Before?* . . . Ahh, now I understand. You are suggesting my collection is tainted, its value therefore less. And of course, I understand, I understand, its presence taints your entire collection. If the curators of the Palace Museum can't screen out a fake, then what sort of a museum are you? You may get away with that on the Mainland, but the rest of the world has higher standards. Well, I'm very sorry. I regret the inconvenience. I will take back my collection immediately."

"What?" the young man gasped.

"But I warn you, young fellow"—and now his face again looked stripped to bone—"if I find out that fake was switched by *your* people, I will take my case to the highest authorities."

"No. No. You do not understand, sir. I'm not saying—"

"You cannot keep a fake in the Beijing Museum."

"We can't give your collection back."

"I'll *take* it back. I will not have some bumbling curator drag my good name through the gutter."

Stricken, the young hero stared at his shoes.

An English clock made for the Ching Emperor Hsien-feng ticked steadily in a corner. After a long while Two-Way spoke gently. "Perhaps there is another way."

"I see no way."

"Would it help if I promised never to undermine the reputation of your museum?"

"What do you mean?" he asked warily.

"I will tell no one. I'll keep this to myself."

"But the fake—"

"If you promise the same, perhaps, with luck, no one else will notice. . . . As I understand it, no one but you did notice. You are a very fine expert."

"No, no, a very poor expert."

"A fine expert, for so young a fellow," Two-Way insisted. "Did anyone else notice?"

"No," the young man said scornfully. "Even when I told my boss, he said I was wrong. But it's so terrible—our country has been looted for so long. We must protect what we have left."

"Not to worry about your boss," Two-Way assured him grimly. "He will not be a problem. The fact is, it fooled them all. Which leaves you with a problem, doesn't it?"

"What do you mean?"

"The other experts will be very embarrassed if it comes out either that they lost my contribution or, worse, that they were fooled from the start. And especially embarrassed if you, their subordinate, discovered they were wrong. This would not be good for you, would it?"

Two-Way waited patiently while fear and righteous indignation raged in the young man's face. At last he conceded, abjectly, "It is a very good forgery."

"The best, I am sure," Two-Way agreed, adding magnanimously, "Someday a fellow as talented as you will rise to a position where he can expose fakes. Particularly if he learns to deal with his superiors. Patience. Until then, patience. Yes?"

"Yes," he agreed, after too long a moment.

Two-Way sighed. Perhaps his young opponent was not a total fool. But in case he woke up brave one morning, Two-Way would leave him a couple of reminders of how the world worked. He pressed a wireless pager hidden in his pocket. His beautiful English receptionist entered quietly and crossed several carpets between the door and his desk.

"Excuse me, Sir John. Comrade Jiang is here from Beijing."

"My old friend. Show him in." He turned to his guest. "Your boss, Executive Director Jiang Hua."

The curator jumped to his feet. "Jiang Hua is *here*?"

"Old Hua will dream up any excuse to escape your miserable summer dust," Two-Way explained with a conspiratorial chuckle. "At our age, young man, one's lungs turn dry as paper. Hong Kong's damp heat is a blessing. Ah! I see what's troubling you. You need some reason why you're here. What if I tell Old Hua you've come asking for more bells?"

"It's better if I don't stay."

Two-Way shrugged innocently, as if he didn't know that an unscheduled private meeting with the heroically generous Wong Li could be misconstrued by the curator's superiors as an attempt to take credit for future donations. Posts in the sands of Sinkiang Province awaited such temerity.

When Two-Way Wong saw that an angry fire still burned in the young man's eye, despite his fear, he delivered the second, blunter warning he had taken pains to prepare. Picking up the business card the curator had presented upon introduction, he held it to the light streaming over his shoulder.

"What a literary name you have," he remarked. "You're obviously not the first scholar in your family."

"We are poor scholars," the curator demurred, with another nervous look at the door.

"But there is real art to your name."

The second character of the young curator's name represented the generation into which he was born and would be instantly recognized by anyone who knew his family, while the third, chosen by a learned relative, was an artfully formed character which could be translated as "Wise Eyes." And, like the best of names, it had proved prophetic.

Two-Way Wong, in fact, could read just enough Chinese to skim a newspaper. In *his* China, sixty years ago, English had doubled his power. But having had little Wise Eyes thoroughly investigated, he knew more about the young curator than the learned grandfather who had chosen his clever name.

"In fact," he said, pretending to make the connection his agents had already traced, "doesn't your father's third brother's younger son conduct research in Guangzhou?"

"You *know* him? He's a doctor. We went to school together."

"We did business with his laboratory," Two-Way explained. "In fact he has just been transferred to an infectious unit. AIDS viruses. Dangerous work. He must be careful not to be exposed, accidentally. Mustn't he?"

The young curator turned pale. "He knows the danger."

Two-Way's fierce eyes glowed like onyx. "If he knows the danger, there is no danger. Is there?"

The boy's mouth set in a hard line. He might never bend, thought

Two-Way. Wise Eyes would return to haunt him. He glanced across his office where an elevator door concealed an empty shaft. Eight hundred feet down yawned a garbage Dumpster.

A simple end to a small problem, perhaps, but ever mindful of the power of restraint, he decided to allow him another test. . . .

The receptionist led young Wise Eyes away. Two-Way picked up a telephone, which was answered on the first ring, and said, "He's your decision. Enjoy yourself."

Then Two-Way Wong rose painfully from the great wooden slab of his desk and shuffled across the carpet toward the inlaid Yüan cabinet.

Opening its doors caused lights to shine inside.

The Chou bell hung from a silk cord. It was fifteen inches high, cast of bronze, with a dull green patina. Dragons reared back-to-back on top, their intertwined tails forming the loop for the cord. Its surface was richly decorated.

Two-Way picked up a bamboo gong.

The bell was 2,500 years old, cast twenty-five centuries before he was born. The set to which it belonged had made music for rituals performed while Confucius taught and Lao-tzu compiled the *Tao-te Ching*, five centuries before Buddha and Christ had walked the earth.

He struck it and struck again at another point.

Two different notes resounded. Clear and sweet, they hung in the air. It was a pity he could not have kept all the bells, he thought. As it was, he'd eaten his cake and still had it as well, for his vision demanded that he be known as a great friend of China.

Two-Way Wong turned his back on the treasure and shuffled toward the windows. His feet splayed in nearly opposite directions—the source of his nickname, it was mistakenly assumed by those who had not done business with him. Sixty-five years ago the beggar's purpose had been to maim when he broke the child's legs. Grotesquely twisted children stood a slightly better chance of sympathy in Shanghai's alleys, and Two-Way knew now that had the beggar not put him out to beg he would certainly have starved to death, which was an orphan's fate in Warlord China. There had been no malice in it, and his subsequent treatment of the beggar had been almost as dispassionate.

Reaching the windows, he caught his breath. He was otherwise strong and healthy, but the badly knitted bones had developed arthritis in recent years and the pain could be stunning. His many sons and daughters from his many wives beseeched him to use the latest Japanese wheelchairs they were always bringing him, but he refused, for the same reason that he had stopped taking opium. The pain was a reminder that one who failed to dominate, ultimately failed to survive.

The sights that greeted him at the glass never failed to delight.

"Sir John," his receptionist interrupted softly. "Mr. Wu of the PRC Labor Committee is on the telephone."

He commenced a long, slow shuffle to his desk. The Englishwoman watched, fighting the impulse to take the old boy's arm and help him. That was forbidden. You had to hand it to the Chinese, she thought as he gestured her to leave him. At his age your average English managing director had long since retired to Dorset.

When his receptionist had gone, Two-Way Wong spoke to the hidden microphones, and his personal secretary appeared instantly from an interior door.

"A businessman named Alfred Ching is attempting to raise money to buy Cathay Tower," Two-Way told the young man. "Set the price very high. And see to it that he meets with success in New York, Toronto, Vancouver, and Los Angeles."

"Is Alfred Ching to know the source of his good joss, Master?"

"No."

Two-Way's confidant hesitated. "Master?"

"What is it?"

"Alfred Ching is no fool. He's made a success of everything he's turned his hand to."

"He'll expect to make a success of Cathay Tower too. Alfred Ching is young. And he is hungry."

•   •   •

Wise Eyes waited, seething, at a rear freight elevator. Wong Li's receptionist had explained with hand signals and broken Chinese how to find the street from the underground garage, so he could avoid Director Jiang.

Nothing had worked out as he had expected. Wong Li was corrupt beyond imagining. Far from acting contrite, much less admitting his guilt, the Hong Kong capitalist had wriggled out of every charge. He had stolen. He had lied. And when confronted with his crimes he had counterattacked with vicious threats. Wise Eyes was appalled and sickened by his own powerlessness.

He was accustomed to the dead blanket of bureaucratic corruption on the Mainland. It was the primary fact in an official's life. But to find such power and evil in the hands of a single person was totally beyond his experience and left him sick with despair. Yet he had to do something. Perhaps some of the younger curators could be persuaded to approach Jiang Hua's deputy. . . . A consensus of the group would be most compelling. Director Jiang would have to act.

The elevator came at last, and Wise Eyes boarded feeling much better. A consensus. That was the right way.

The elevator plummeted, making his ears pop. Suddenly, it whined to a halt.

The boy panicked. Wong Li had betrayed him. Director Jiang would misinterpret his reason for visiting the Hong Kong Taipan and would destroy his career. Shrinking back when the doors slid apart, he was greeted not by Director Jiang but by a loud bang and a pretty girl in a short skirt.

"Hold the door, please?" she called in Cantonese, bending over to retrieve the metal folding table she had dropped. When he failed to act, not comprehending the southern language, she glanced over her shoulder at his sober northern face and asked again in high-school Mandarin.

It was said that neither heaven nor hell possessed terrors to compare with the sound of a Cantonese attempting to speak Mandarin. But this one was so lovely, who would notice? Perhaps she came from another southern province, for after the shrieks he had heard on the airport bus, her voice was almost melodious. As the doors started to close, he stopped them with his body.

"Thank you, thank you," she said, hauling the table into the elevator. "Down?"

The curator gaped again. Dressed all in white, she looked like a nurse or technician. Her face was the most beautiful he had ever seen.

"Down?" she repeated.

"What? Yes. Yes. Down."

"Then let go the door."

He let the door go and they started down together. She misinterpreted his stare. "It's my table," she explained cheerfully. "I'm a masseuse and acupuncturist. When I make office visits I bring my table. Their desks are so low it hurts my back."

"Your eyes are blue," he mumbled in astonishment.

"I'm Eurasian. Two of my great-grandmothers were German."

Of course. Germans had built beer breweries in the last days of the emperor. Except for her eyes she looked pure Chinese.

"And you must be from Beijing?"

"How did you know?"

"You look so serious." The elevator stopped and the door opened on the underground garage. She hauled the table out and groaned, "My car is all the way on the other side."

"You have a car?"

"My clients are everywhere. It helps me get around. Could you help me carry this?"

He hefted the table, which was quite light, and followed her through the rows of cars. She wore high heels, which clicked musically on the gray concrete. Muscles rippled in her calves. Twice she glanced back at him with a heart-stopping smile.

"Not much farther . . . There I am."

It was a shiny little Korean car, rather like the one Director Jiang was driven about in, but bright red, not sober black.

Attempting to understand, he stated a question. "Your employer permits you to drive this car."

"*I'm* my employer. It's *my* car. It's an awful bother, let me tell

you. The taxes are impossible and parking is—well, parking. . . .
You know how old people ask, 'Have you eaten?' In Hong Kong,
you should ask, 'Have you parked?' "

This confused him further; in his experience all people greeted
each other with the traditional "Have you eaten?" Could Hong Kong
be so wealthy that no one cared about food?

"That's a joke," she explained. "Don't people laugh in Beijing?"
And with that she loosed one of those earsplitting Cantonese howls:
"*Aieeyaaa!* It will be dull when you lot take over. Hang on. I'll open
the trunk."

He helped her fit her table into the trunk and stood by awkwardly as she got behind the wheel and started the engine. "Thanks
for your help." She started to back up. "Drop you?"

"What?"

"You were nice to help. Let me drive you where you are going."

"All the way to the airport?"

"Hop in. My next client lives near the bridge."

It was the first time in his life he had ridden in a private car,
and he found himself enjoying mightily the way she made it leap
at openings in the traffic. On rare occasions he had ridden in a
taxi, but in the backseat, crowded with others, and the traffic had
been nothing like this. Here were fewer trucks, ten thousand times
as many cars, and not a pony cart in sight. And her car was air-
conditioned, as cold as Wong Li's office.

"Look, a Porsche!" she cried. "I want a Porsche so bad I could
die. Look who's driving it! Look at her!"

The sleek silver car, immobile as theirs in the dense traffic, was
driven by a beautiful girl wearing a fur wrap despite the July heat.
Wise Eyes' new friend poked his arm and grinned. "Somehow I
don't believe she earned *that* at her day job."

"Of course," he agreed. "She would have to work two jobs for
such a car."

She looked at him, her disconcerting blue eyes brightening with
laughter and a wilder, stranger light that nothing in his experience
helped him identify. "Of course," she echoed. After exclaiming over
some other cars and pointing out the buildings they were creeping

past on the Gloucester Road, she began gently asking him about himself. Soon he was responding freely, telling her about his career and his brilliant old teacher. She asked about his family and he described the flat—a two-hour bicycle ride from the Forbidden City—that he shared with his mother, father, and grandparents.

"Two *hours*? On a *bicycle*? You wouldn't last two minutes in this traffic."

As the gleaming city flashed and roared about them, he told her about a blissful journey to Sian. He had wandered for days among the terra-cotta statues of Emperor Chin's army. "Third century B.C.! The most remarkable place you've ever imagined. Thousands of clay men real enough to speak."

Her car was creeping around the Causeway Bay approaches to the Cross Harbour Tunnel, where a hundred lanes seemed to funnel into the square tubes. The typhoon shelter seized his gaze. The sheer disorder of the jampacked junks and sampans looked homey after the walls of skyscrapers they had been driving past.

"There's the gweilo yacht club," she pointed out. "The shelter didn't used to be so crowded, but they say people are buying boats to make a run for it. Yacht prices quadrupled last month. One of my clients bought *ten* yachts, cheap, last year—cheap from gweilos who were running? Now he's floating on a gold mine. They say Two-Way Wong's going to fill it in. He's the richest man in Hong Kong. That was his building where we met. Have you heard of him?"

"Yes, I've heard of him," Wise Eyes answered grimly.

She did not appear to notice, for she laughed, like bells. "Well, I took a vacation too. Last summer—the ordinary Pacific trip: San Francisco, Los Angeles, Las Vegas, Tokyo. I gambled a little in Las Vegas. That's in America," she added when he looked blank. "I won. And with the money I bought myself a massage." She laughed gaily. "It was very crude. They didn't really know what they were doing. I think you have to be Chinese to massage. The gweilos confuse pleasure with evil, if you know what I mean."

"Yes, yes," he said, though he hadn't the vaguest idea what she was talking about. Nor was he listening that closely. Her body was in constant motion—little thrusts and inhalations as she manipulated

the brake and clutch and gearshift. Every time the traffic stopped
and she strained to sit higher to see ahead, her white jacket fell
open, revealing her breasts pressing against her snug T-shirt. He
did, on occasion, visit the museum's restricted collection of pillow
books and pornographic pictures, but nothing had prepared him for
this Hong Kong girl, whose short skirt was inching up her bare
thighs.

"So what brings you to Hong Kong?"

"Business."

"Museum business?" she asked, and when he was silent she
laughed, "I bet I know. You're just here to buy a CD player, probably. Or maybe a washing machine for your girlfriend."

"I don't have a girlfriend."

"You're kidding. What, do you play the field?"

"Me?"

"You, silly. What are you doing in Hong Kong?"

"There was a problem I came to see about."

The car had stopped dead in the tunnel again and she turned
her full attention on him in a blaze of blue eyes. "It didn't work
out, did it? You look very troubled."

"It's a terrible thing," he said. Then, after a pause: "Do you
know about the Cultural Revolution?"

"My father swam here when I was a girl," she answered solemnly, the wild light in her eyes bleak and primitive, and frightening. "He lost his leg to the sharks. The British sent him back to us.
So the Red Guards came again. . . . Yes, I know about the Cultural
Revolution."

"China had already been looted of its treasure for a hundred
and fifty years by the Westerners. And then suddenly, what little we
had left was wantonly destroyed. It's the worst crime in our history."

"Of course," she agreed. Lost in his own passion, Wise Eyes
didn't notice the dangerous chill in her voice. She blinked a speck
of dust out of her contact lens.

"So a man who steals now, commits the worst crime of all."

"Is that why you came here? To get something back?"

"Yes. But I failed."

"Perhaps you'll try again." She smiled, hoping he would say yes.

"I most certainly will."

"You sound determined." Wise Eyes would come back to haunt her master, she was sure. That could not be allowed. Which made him hers.

"What time is your flight?"

"Two."

"Oh, you poor thing, you have *hours* to wait."

"Better to be early than miss the plane," he replied stolidly.

"How grim. Listen, this client I have next isn't due until one. I'm going up to his apartment to wait. Come with me. We'll call you a cab right before he arrives."

Wise Eyes was torn by the invitation. She was so pretty, but he had been warned of the pitfalls that awaited the unwary visitor to Hong Kong; it was a city of con men, hucksters, and quick-buck operators. But what did he have that this girl with her own car could possibly want of him?

"A restaurant chef owes me," she said. "He'll send dim sum free if I ask nicely. What do you say? Oh, and we can see a whole other view from this place."

"*Other* view?"

She lost her cheery self-assurance for an instant, stammering, "I mean, from the building you were just in, over in Central. Where we met? This apartment looks south and west over the shiproad and Hong Kong Island. It's beautiful. Would you like that?"

"I don't know if I should. Perhaps I should check in early for my plane."

"You'll have plenty of time. We can telephone if it makes you feel better. I know a chap who works for CAAC."

Typical Hong Kong, he thought bleakly. They all know somebody. She had returned her attention to the road as it flared out of the Cross Harbour Tunnel into a seething metal plain of cars, buses, and trucks. What could she possibly want?

"Maybe"—she smiled—"I'll give you a massage."

So that was it. Business. "I have no money," he said coldly.

Her eyes went wide with hurt. "Not for money. For a friend. And when I visit the Mainland next year you'll show me the clay soldiers at Sian. Fair enough?"

He felt like a fool. "Perhaps I could get permission. . . . Yes, I could. I could take you, I think. I can go where others can't, into the new excavations. You have no idea how vast it is. There are thousands."

"It's a deal!"

She cut across Tsim Sha Tsui, the lower tip of Kowloon peninsula, on a twisting, turning route over the Mody Road, up Nathan, and across Haiphong. The apartment was in an ultramodern block near the Ocean Terminal shopping center. It was not as close to the bridge to Cheklapkok Airport as she had implied, but he was a stranger and thoroughly lost.

She parked under the building. The curator carried her table, and they breezed past the temporarily abandoned security post adjoining the elevator banks. It was a one-bedroom apartment with big windows in both rooms and a miniature kitchen and elaborate bathroom with a Jacuzzi. He helped her unfold the table in the living room. While she telephoned for the dim sum, he wandered about tentatively, marveling at the crisp steel-and-leather furnishings, the Taiwanese cabinetry, and the shiny black electronics and giant-screen TV.

"Your client must be very wealthy."

"No," she dismissed the owner. "Just a working guy. Accountant or something." She shrugged out of her jacket and kicked off her shoes, revealing breathtakingly tiny feet. He flushed when she caught his stare and smiled.

The last time he had been alone with a girl had been on adjoining chairs of Beijing's Fragrant Hills cable lift, ascending over the forest, the summit growing too swiftly ahead. He had kissed her and she had jerked away, terrified that someone descending on a returning chair might recognize her. Gossip could destroy anyone, but it was hardest on a girl. Nonetheless, glimpsing the ground through the trees below, he thought he could see couples sprawled in the shade. She had greeted his hesitant suggestion that they walk back down with stony silence.

His eye skipped to the massage table, draped with towels.

"No," she said, heading to the bedroom and beckoning him to follow. "Let's do it on the bed, so I don't have to stand."

"Do you have a boyfriend?"

"A sniveling coward who ran away to Canada the second he got his passport. I don't want to hear another word about him. And frankly, if the other boys from Beijing are as nice as you, I'm sure we'll all get along fine after '97. Better than the gweilos, right? Go on, lie down. Take your shirt off. And your trousers."

He stared, his hand frozen on his necktie.

"You wear underclothes, don't you?"

"Of course."

"Get undressed then," she ordered briskly. "I can't massage through cloth." Hesitantly, he did as ordered until he stood before her, feeling silly. She grinned. "Your shoes and socks look funny. Take them off. Go on, you silly thing. You're not showing anything you wouldn't at the beach."

He had never been to a beach. The nearest he had come to immersing himself in water in public had been at the baths, and there only with other men. Quickly, humiliated, he tugged his shoes and socks off and climbed awkwardly onto the bed. He lay on his stomach and buried his face in the pillow. He felt the bed creak, heard a swish of cloth, and then she knelt over his back, straddling him. Shooting a look over his shoulder, he saw she had hitched up her skirt. Her fingers settled lightly on his shoulders. Her bare thighs burned his skin.

"You're very tense."

"I've never been massaged."

He closed his eyes to the pleasure. Her hands traveled down his spine, slipped under the frayed elastic of his shorts, and spread across his buttocks. Reversing direction, she skipped over the cloth and down his legs.

"Stop thinking," she whispered. "Empty your mind." She leaned forward, her long hair brushing his back. She touched his temples and walked her fingers around his eyes. "That's better."

Her voice seemed to come from a distance. Thoughts of Wong Li, the forged Chou bell, the corrupt city began to swirl apart, like reflections on a rippled pool. One of her hands slipped under his chest and drifted downward, trailing sensation. He could not believe this was happening. He felt as if he had opened the deepest vault in the Palace of Abstinence and discovered sunlight inside.

When he lay spent and grateful and hopelessly in love, he was alarmed to see that a disappointed little pout had crept into her smile. She kissed him hungrily, caressed him with new determination, but nothing happened. Part of him wanted to do nothing more than roll over and go to sleep. But he wanted to awe her as she had awed him.

Her expression turned sadder and sadder. He knew, suddenly, with a deep and awful jealousy, that she could find someone else—the owner of this apartment, for instance—to please her. Quickly he rolled over on top of her, pumping mightily, to no avail.

She laughed and pushed him off.

"I know a way." Jumping from the bed, and checking the gold watch she had never taken off, she ran for her bag while he gaped, still astonished, at the flickering orbs and shadows of the only naked woman he had ever seen in his life. She returned with a small leather box and opened it to reveal an ancient set of brass-handled acupuncture needles. Early Ching, he thought automatically. Some three hundred years old.

"Where did you get these?"

"Grandfather."

She selected the longest needle, a stiff nine-inch shaft of heat-hardened iron wire, and showed him the tip. "There is a special place, right here." She touched the outer crevice of his eye. "Here. It channels to the Yang essence. I was taught it, but I've never done it with anyone since. Shall we try?"

The curator shied from the point so near his eye.

She laughed. "Silly, you won't feel a thing, except here." She trailed the fingers of her free hand over his belly, and indeed, already he had begun to stir. "Take off your glasses."

His only warning was the sudden bunching of her thighs as she braced her feet against the wall. Even then the rippling beneath her skin was so beautiful that before he realized what she had done to him the long needle was traveling through his brain.

3

AT FIRST GLANCE, Vicky thought, the bar of the Royal Hong Kong Yacht Club *seemed* unchanged, with its scuffed floors, smoke-yellowed ceilings, and memorable scent of air conditioning overwhelmed by spilled beer, cigarettes, and hot summer whiffs from the harbor. More shabby than genteel, it offered refuge from the relentlessly modern city.

Casually dressed members were drifting in from their half-Saturdays at the office—familiar faces, the usual smattering of new ones, and some old faces gone missing, retired to England and Australia, her brother explained. A duffers race was scheduled, and pickup crews were sorting themselves out. Some were settling in for lunch or the long haul at the bar; others were heading down to the boats.

But she had little opportunity to talk business with Hugo, who was looming comfortably beside her with a big hand wrapped around a can of San Miguel beer. The Two-Way Wong rumor kept intruding, prowling like a shark, returning fatter with every friend who stopped to welcome her back. Proof, they muttered, that the PRC wouldn't even wait until July 1, 1997, to screw the Colony.

Hugo raised his beer can in mock salute to an old ship's life preserver hanging in a place of honor on a wall, which was plastered with club burgees brought by yachts from around the world. Back in World War Two, marauding Japanese had occupied the British Colony for four grim years. Gold lettering around the white life preserver spelled out triumphant last words: THIS CLUB RE-OPENED BY HMS *VENGEANCE* SEPTEMBER 8, 1945.

"Who will save us this time?" he asked.

"Not the Royal Navy!" laughed a burly Australian travel agent, who tipped *his* beer toward a yellowed clipping of a cartoon by Fong from the *Hongkong Standard*. A People's Liberation Army soldier presented an election-ballot that offered the post-1997 Hong Kong voter a choice between "I defer to the wisdom of our omnipotent leaders in Beijing to decide what's best for our unworthy Special Administrative Region" or "I am an ungrateful running dog who wishes to be sent for re-education to a commune in Sinkiang Province."

Vicky had only to glance out of the window, north across the harbor, to see the dark hills of China blocking the horizon, and imagine how close they must look to the children of refugees who had already fled China once.

Mass emigration by Hong Kong's educated, ambitious middle class had posed a grave brain-drain threat, even though the Sino-British Joint Declaration of 1984 included PRC promises not to interfere in Hong Kong's capitalist "lifestyle" for fifty years. At first, the fear had been as much economic as political: Would bumbling Communist bureaucrats meddle in Hong Kong's free-wheeling, wildly profitable economy?

The 1989 Peking massacre had shocked economic fear into political terror and the brain drain into a flood. For a while it had seemed as if Hong Kong might simply dry up and vanish as a modern international city. It was because of that crisis seven years ago that Vicky had persuaded her father to let her open the Manhattan Golden.

But Hong Kong's thirty-percent-and-more return on investments, combined with its negligible taxes, continued to be the lure they had always been for foreigners, and the Hong Kong business community had launched enormous private- and government-funded

projects to restore their confidence. Even so, China continued to
lurch between reform and repression, and emigration still siphoned
off the city's skilled workers.

"Plenty are willing to stay," said Hugo. "Of course, your Chinese
are gamblers, every man jack of them."

"Hugo, what century were you born in? Most of them don't
have a choice."

"Anyway, what do you care? It's not your fight, Vicky. You made
your break."

"Break? Do you think that running Dad's hotel in New York is
a break? I'm as tied to him as you are. But if Hong Kong's gotten
so bad, why is he backing away from MacF's diversifying out?"

"Don't ask me. Ask the boss."

"*Before* I ask the boss, could you venture a guess as to why?"

"How about fear of bankruptcy?" Hugo grinned. "It's not every
day one's daughter loses an entire Manhattan hotel."

"I haven't lost it yet," she reminded him sharply. "Does Dad
have the cash to bail me out?"

Hugo sighed. "We've got a lot of new businesses sucking up
money and very little putting it out. I wouldn't be surprised if Dad
cuts our losses in New York and orders you home."

Vicky started to protest. Hugo cut her off, gently.

"*I* could certainly use your help here. I'm up to my eyeballs
trying to finish the new hotels and juggle our property holdings and
keep the air freight business—our one bright spot—from collapsing
under its own success. We just bought another Antropov Two-fifty
jet freighter—smashing plane, makes the Boeing look like the bak-
er's van. Peter's useless, of course, and Dad's a bit distracted running back and forth to Shanghai."

"What's he doing in Shanghai? Hugo, what's going on? He's
up to something, isn't he?"

Hugo hesitated. Industrial Shanghai, the biggest city in the world,
lay eight hundred miles up the coast on the East China Sea. Once
regarded as Hong Kong's flashy big sister, Communist "liberation"
nearly fifty years ago had driven the best of Shanghai's factory own-

ers, bankers, and shipowners to the Crown Colony, where they had flourished.

"Dad *says* he's nailing down a Hong Kong–Shanghai passenger shuttle for Golden Dragon Air, but I don't know if we should put so much time and money in an airline the Reds could ground with a phone call."

Vicky had a sinking feeling that she had been away too long. Too much going on with MacF she hadn't heard about. "But what if Hong Kong simply collapses next year when the Chinese waltz in?"

"The Taipan appears determined to stay," Hugo answered neutrally, and in that empty voice Vicky heard the echoes of a dozen arguments Hugo had lost with their father. There were times she envied Hugo's ability to compromise and simply go along.

"He's playing it close to the vest."

"That's nothing new. Dad's idea of corporate communication is a fax from the Taipan: *Do It! Now!*"

Her brother laughed ruefully. "Any rate, don't be surprised if Dad finds a place for you right here in Hong Kong."

"No way. We've proven we can't work on the same continent, much less the same city."

Hugo downed his beer. "Let's go sailing."

They boarded a low sampan driven by an old Chinese woman half-hidden in the shadows of an egg-shaped canvas awning. The sampan backed into the filthy water of the typhoon shelter and darted into a narrow channel between rows of anchored junks festooned with bedding and laundry.

The quick and hollow beat of its little engine filled Vicky with unexpected emotion. The noise—like the mingled odors of sewage and fried food, the Cantonese blaring from television sets on the junks, and the sight of the dark hills behind the gleaming skyscrapers—was Hong Kong, South China, and, as often as she tried to deny it, home.

Whirlwind lay at the end of a row of smaller yachts—a staysail schooner with a long dark-blue hull, a sleek white trunk cabin, and two thick masts, the taller to the rear. She was Vicky's father's joy, the culmination of a life of working and sailing on the South China coast, and, not incidentally, the last yacht built in the Mackintosh Farquhar shipyard before the loss of British government patrol-boat contracts had forced them to sell out to a Chinese state company.

Vicky scanned the people on deck: her mother, changed into shorts, popping a San Mig in the center cockpit; the boatboys, Ah Chi and Huang, in their black pajamas and scuffed Top-Siders; her younger brother, Peter, scrambling aboard from another sampan with a pretty Chinese who must be his girlfriend, Mary Lee. But the silhouette that riveted her eye was the broad, pugnacious stance of her father.

Duncan Mackintosh spotted Vicky in the second sampan. A big white grin cut his face. "Get aboard, Your Majesty," he roared. "Almost left without you."

Vicky tossed her bag through the lifelines and clambered after it. Her father caught her hand and hauled her onto the teak deck, where he surprised her with a rough, unusually affectionate kiss. He looked very different, she thought—ten years younger and a little wild.

"Stow your gear. We're on our way."

"Better make it quick, Daddy. Everyone at the club says Two-Way Wong's filling in the typhoon shelter."

"He's floating that story to drive up prices in Causeway Bay. Ah Chi! Slip mooring. Chop-chop."

Whirlwind's engines, which were grinding over quietly, shuddered into gear. Ah Chi backed the schooner away from the mooring, while Huang, having released the bow, retrieved the stern anchor. Both men moved calmly and deferentially among the guests who had gathered on deck. The propellers churned the water into a noisome gray soup, and they were under way.

High wooden junk sterns arched over the narrow channel, which twisted and turned as tortuously as the alleys of the Chinese sections of the city. Small sculled boats laced its surface, and a thousand anchor chains entered the water at angles that threatened to hook the propellers of the incompetent and unworthy.

"Take the helm, Your Majesty."

Caught in mid-yawn, Vicky obeyed her father automatically.

Ah Chi surrendered the big chrome wheel with a dubious smile. Vicky throttled back both engines. *Whirlwind* was sixty-seven feet long, and Ah Chi had been motoring several knots faster than she would dare in tight quarters, particularly jet-lagged, with her father waiting for her to prang into something.

Dead ahead, one of the club's sampan drivers chose that moment to tow a yacht across her path. "Bloody hell!"

"I don't know that I would continue on my present course, Your Majesty," Duncan remarked, and she realized he must have seen the tow's masthead moving slowly above the intersecting channel, and had set her up.

Vicky found the air-horn button and loosed an indignant bleat. The old woman at the sampan tiller ignored it.

"Shall I take over?"

Vicky plunged both engines into reverse.

A loud laugh from Hugo drew the attention of everyone on deck. He had changed into a T-shirt with the legend COME SOONER ON A STAYSAIL SCHOONER, and was running the jib sheets back to the cockpit.

"Why don't you tell him to get stuffed?" asked her mother, who was propped cross-legged on the stern deck behind the cockpit. "You're a sailor, not a ruddy docking pilot. That's Ah Chi's job."

Vicky shot a neutral smile over her shoulder. Support from the stern would be more appreciated were Mother not on her third San Mig. Mother was right, of course, technically speaking. As a young woman Sally Farquhar Mackintosh had skippered *Highland Fling*'s all-woman crew to victory in the China Sea Race, and she had the racing sailor's contempt for close-quarters motoring. But Mother missed the point of the competitions Vicky fought with her father: Winning was more important than the rules; changing the game was better yet.

With both propellers churning counter to *Whirlwind*'s forward

motion, Vicky turned her back on the drama ahead and faced the
stern. Casually, she removed her long earrings and shortened the
chain that held her dragon pendant. Still without turning to look,
she bound her hair into a ponytail.

Baring her ears to gauge wind shifts was a helming trick she had
learned from her mother, but her purpose now was to watch her
father's face to judge by his expression whether she had given the
engines enough reverse throttle to stop his beloved schooner before
serious damage was inflicted on its handsome bow.

A cold smile settled on his hard mouth. His dark-blue eyes gazed
back at her, fathomless as stone. He had already guessed the new
game and he would not give her a clue. She either had to turn around
to see for herself, or find the evidence on someone else's face.

"Ah Chi," Duncan Mackintosh warned softly, and his boatboy
obediently discovered interest in the thousands of white and silver
buildings clustered upon Hong Kong's mountainsides in sunlight
and cloud shadows. Her mother was engrossed in fishing a fresh
Mig from the ice chest. The others on the stern deck were two
guests she didn't know. The redheaded, bearded middle-aged American regarding the roiled water queasily was apparently Wally Hearst,
the optimistic China trader her mother had quoted in the car; the
poor guy looked as if he had just discovered that having been seasick
in the past had not rendered him immune.

The other guest on the stern deck was a beautiful Chinese woman
dressed in immaculate white polo shirt and slacks. Part Shanghainese, Vicky guessed by the fineness of her features and the coal-
dark eyes behind her gold-rimmed glasses.

Vicky dismissed her as a sailor's girlfriend, probably with Chip,
the handsome Royal Hong Kong Police inspector who often sailed
with her father. And although the Chinese woman seemed somehow
interested in the father-daughter duel, neither she nor the American
had the vaguest idea whether a collision was likely, so Vicky gave
up on them.

She felt panicked. Only a game, but not one she could afford to
lose, and she had run out of options. A few feet to the side some
Tanka fishermen on a rubber-tire-draped junk had put down the net

they were sewing to watch with interest. But their faces revealed nothing, because what did they care if one gweilo yacht sank another? The sampan itself was surely in the clear. She could hear its engine—the quick, hollow *pock-kk*—speed up slightly.

Vicky was about to give up and look when she remembered the first sailing lesson her mother had drilled into her: Always observe what's going on before you make a move. The sampan had not speeded up frantically—just a little—which meant she had judged her reverse power correctly.

With a triumphant grin at her father, she faced front, smoothly engaging forward gear again as *Whirlwind*'s raked bow cleared the tow by a foot. In the Chesapeake, she knew, the close margin would have provoked howls of protest—threats of lawsuits on Long Island Sound—but not on the China Coast, where the close margin was a thing to be admired.

"Missed!" Hugo cheered from the bow, while Chip the policeman hefted a boathook and called, "Shall I harpoon her instead, Victoria?"

"Daddy wants a bigger one."

She pivoted the big boat on countered engines through a tight turn at the end of the channel, dodged a sampan ferrying yachtsmen to their boats, and forged past a hand-sculled floating fast-food restaurant canvassing the moorings for customers desiring fishballs.

Passing the clubhouse verandah, she glimpsed a vigorous-looking, compactly built man who scrambled her thoughts and set her heart racing. She snatched up the binoculars, which were hanging from the binnacle, and steered with one hand. The wind was ruffling his silky black hair and his broad face was lit by a smile that found pleasure in everything within range of his almond eyes. He was chatting up a pretty redhead.

"Hugo? What is Alfred Ching doing here?"

"Won the Round the Island Race on a windsurfer," Hugo answered. "I sponsored him myself."

Every November, million-dollar yachts raced the twenty-five miles around Hong Kong Island, and every November, in a triumph of technology over tradition, someone with a few hundred dollars to spare, a lot of stamina, and no little courage, won on an eight-foot windsurfer.

"I didn't know he sailed."

"Took lessons from Cynthia Hydes."

"She certainly gets around." At thirty-five, which he must be by now, Alfred Ching was still boyishly handsome. Still charming, too, to judge by the interest on the redhead's face.

"You're about to run into the jetty."

Vicky swung the wheel hard, cast one last look at Alfred Ching, and steered around the massive stone breakwater and into the harbor. A fair swell was rolling in from the east. *Whirlwind* rose to it like a young man leaving home for the evening.

Her father's jaw was tightening pugnaciously.

Vicky thought at first that he was glowering at the huge glass World Expo Center under construction on the former runway of old Kai Tak Airport. Expo was supposed to be a dramatic vote of confidence by the Hong Kong business community: They would host an international fair on Turnover Day, July 1, 1997. Most of the buildings were rising on schedule, nourished by nodding construction cranes and swarms of workmen on bamboo scaffolding. Others, most notably Mackintosh Farquhar's newest Golden Hotel, were not. It stood alone in the middle of the Expo project, its tall skeleton partially sheathed in gold glass, like a half-finished rocket a long way from blast-off.

Hugo had told her that the PRC, which had become expert at manipulating the chronic Hong Kong labor shortage, was making it difficult for Mackintosh Farquhar to get workmen. The Mainlanders apparently wanted something, though they hadn't come around to saying what. All that Hugo and their father knew at the moment was that they were negotiating blindly with Communist Chinese bureaucracy at its most rapacious.

However, it was not the Expo Golden that had roused Duncan Mackintosh's ire, but an elderly, sea-battered passenger-freighter arriving from the east. Vicky recognized her. Her sturdy Clydesbank hull had once been painted white. Now cascades of rust spilled from scuppers and ports. On her stubby funnel, from which rose a black plume of low-grade diesel smoke, she bore the red-and-gold waves and anchors of the PRC's Shanghai Hai Xing Shipping Company.

"Isn't that the *Dundee*?" asked Peter.

"The *Inverness*," their father growled. "As any fool can see. Look at her bloody deckhouse."

Peter's slight frame shriveled with embarrassment. Mary Lee, an intense Fukienese, half-rose from the cockpit bench as if to do battle on his behalf, until she saw Hugo's wife, Fiona, shaking her head and felt Sally Mackintosh's icy glare. Hugo tossed a big-brotherly arm around Peter's shoulder, and Vicky reached automatically to tousle his hair, but her eyes went to her father, for he, too, was suffering.

Years ago, the *Inverness* had been a Mackintosh Farquhar ship, and the *Dundee* as well. The *Stirling*. The *Edinburgh*. The *Fort William*. For every Scottish city and many a town, a Farquhar Line— and later a Mackintosh Farquhar Line—China Sea coaster had plied the ports of Singapore, Hanoi, Taipei, Shanghai, Manila, and Hong Kong. Finally unable to compete with cheap PRC labor, Mackintosh Farquhar had lost it all, forced to sell for a pittance to Two-Way Wong.

Instead of incorporating the MacF line into his enormous World Oceans Red Ship Fleet, the Chinese tycoon had practically given it away to the Hai Xing Company of Mainland China. And now, a presumably grateful People's Republic was earning a fortune in hard currency, ferrying former Hong Kong refugees home for visits to Shanghai, Fuzhou, and Ningbo, bearing VCRs and Japanese washing machines to less fortunate relatives on the wrong side of the border.

Never mind, Vicky thought, that a Scots expatriate shipping line was an anachronism in Asia anyway, or that Golden Dragon Air had rebounded with a modest fleet of jet freighters. Duncan Mackintosh had loved those ships, and their loss still galled him.

"Ah Chi! Let's get some sail up."

"Yes, Taipan."

The Tanka boatboy was probably the last Chinese in Hong Kong to address the head of the last independent Scottish trading company as "Taipan" without irony. He shouted for his assistant, and they started cranking the sails out of *Whirlwind*'s hollow masts.

As Ah Chi and Huang fell to they were joined by a pickup crew who, stashing Bloodies and Migs in safe crannies, unreeled the jib, which was wound like a vertical window shade around the forestay. Vicky steered into the wind to ease the strain on the sail pullers. The boat started bouncing, and Wally Hearst turned a little greener and edged past Vicky as if heading below.

"Are you all right, Mr. Hearst?"

"Wally," he told her, with a grateful smile. "I think I took my seasick pill too late."

"I wouldn't go below if I were you. Just watch something on the horizon. And stay here in the center of the yacht where it bounces less."

"I'll be all right when the pill kicks in, I hope."

"Not too late to go back," said Vicky. "It's four days. You could join us by air."

Hearst shook his head.

"Hey, it's not a test of manhood. Lord Nelson was sick every time he sailed."

"It's not that." Hearst cast a miserable eye back at shore. "There are just certain invitations you don't say no to." He sat gingerly on the cockpit coaming and stared across the water at Kai Tak.

Vicky glanced back. The Chinese woman was alone on the stern deck.

"Who wants to drive?"

Chip, the policeman, took the wheel with a sleepy smile. "I'll give a shout if anything gets in our way again."

"Your turn. I already took my best shot."

She climbed out of the cockpit, past her mother. The Chinese woman was leaning against a backstay, keeping well out of the way. From that vantage she could see the full length of the bouncing boat and everyone on deck.

"I'm Vicky Mackintosh. Welcome aboard."

"Vivian Loh."

She returned a firm handshake, though her fingers looked as delicate as carved ivory. Her nails were done in a pale-pink shade Vicky had never seen before and she thought, not for the first time, how easily Oriental women made Western women feel clumsy.

Vivian seemed about her age or a little younger. She had jet hair, cut shoulder-length, and lightly tanned skin that looked as soft and smooth as butter. She was slight like a Cantonese, no taller than Vicky herself, although decidedly slimmer.

Vicky had guessed correctly that Vivian was no sailor. Her white slacks were too clean, her shoes all wrong, her gold necklace heavy enough to garrote her if it caught on something. Vicky wondered again who she had come with. Chip had certainly not bought that gold necklace on a policeman's salary. Nor were Vivian's exquisite *fei tsu* jade earrings the sort of trinkets found in Cat Street. She spoke with the Oxbridge accent that, often as not, was cultivated locally in the Hong Kong schools, and her voice was low, with a pleasant clear timbre.

"Welcome home."

"Still no secrets in Hong Kong, I see. I only got in this morning."

"I know. I work for the Taipan."

That was a surprise. Though Mackintosh Farquhar employed some two thousand people in Hong Kong, Vicky doubted half a dozen had ever been invited aboard *Whirlwind*, much less on a family cruise. "And what do you do for my father?"

"I'm his China trader," Vivian answered with pride.

Another surprise. Vivian Loh was considerably more than some weekend sailor's girlfriend, for in 1996 in the Orient, the title *China trader* marked a business person above the ordinary. In colonial times, a native "comprador" had been sufficient to act as a middleman between Hong Kong trading houses and the Chinese, but today it was the China trader who scoured the Mainland for opportunity and judged how dangerous such risky ventures might be. They were indispensable go-betweens for running deals inside Communist China. In spite of twenty years of economic reform since Mao had died—

or perhaps because of it—the business climate in the People's Republic, with its corrupt bureaucracy, myriad languages, and ever-
shifting political alliances, was still, as Hugo put it, "unique."

"Have you worked for us long?" Vicky asked.

Vivian Loh regarded her for a quiet moment, as if to let Vicky
know how bluntly proprietary her "us" had sounded. Vicky, who
had intended to sound proprietary, waited her out, noting an envi-
able calm in the woman's dark eyes, which the sunlight burnished
to a deep bronze.

"Four years. Are you re-joining the hong?"

"I never left it," Vicky answered quickly—too quickly, for that
was not entirely accurate. Not knowing that Vivian was a key employee was glaring proof that Vicky's links to her father's company,
like her links to her father himself, while still complex, had stretched
thin.

Vivian had spotted the inconsistency, like a cat savoring motion
from the corner of its eye. She was quick and subtle, and everything
about her suggested secret knowledge of distant places.

"I continue to maintain our New York office," Vicky answered.
That sounded rather grander than it was, which she suspected Vivian knew. For if she lost the hotel, Mackintosh Farquhar's Manhattan headquarters would be reduced to a single suite in the Pan Am
Building, on a low floor that catered to international corporations
with vague names and dubious antecedents.

"How are you faring?" Vivian asked. "I mean, in addition to
your hotel."

Vicky gazed the length of the boat before answering.

Whirlwind was still banging impatiently into the choppy water.
On the foredeck Vicky's father and Ah Chi were battling the jib
roller, which had frozen with the sail half-furled.

Beside her, Vivian lounged against the backstay like an Eastern
sea goddess. For a nonsailor, which she certainly was, this cool-eyed,
elegant beauty seemed awfully comfortable on the pitching deck.
Vicky herself was beginning to recall too many coffees on the plane.

"I'll be presenting my father with new options," she said, turning to look at Hong Kong's vast and densely packed business dis-

trict. Exuberantly modern office towers sprawled along the shore like an endless maze from the districts of Western, to Central, to Wanchai and Causeway Bay, and seemed to scramble up the hills as if, soon, new buildings would mount Victoria Peak itself.

"How does it compare to New York?" Vivian asked. "I've never been."

Vicky, annoyed with the direction their conversation had taken, answered sharply. "Hong Kong looks like the Japanese bought New York, sold the tops of the skyscrapers for scrap and the bottoms to the Chinese, who parked it beside a mountain where they're going to reassemble it one of these days."

Something cold moved through Vivian's eyes. Vicky reminded herself that her problems in New York were not Vivian's fault and that they were going to share four days on a crowded boat. "New York is grand by comparison," she elaborated. "Almost elegant. I'm always struck by all the room between the buildings. Hong Kong is chaos."

"Chinese," said Vivian.

"Definitely Chinese."

You only had to hear their nicknames for the buildings: MacF's gold headquarters tower in Causeway Bay was called The Hakka's Tooth; Two-Way Wong's immense World Oceans House, the second-highest building in Asia, Too-Tall Hong; Jardine House, with round windows, The House of a Thousand Assholes.

"He won't leave Hong Kong, you know."

Vicky looked at the Chinese woman in mild astonishment. "We may not have a choice, next year," she explained patiently. "So we've got to be ready to jump, just in case things get worse across the border and the People's Liberation Army is occupying Central street corners. Or Public Security squads start arresting businesswomen as a negotiating ploy."

Vivian did not smile. "Your father is committed to Hong Kong *after* 1997."

"You don't understand. My family are certainly *not* expats out from England to make a fortune in five years. We're refugees as much as any Chinese family. My mother's father came out of Shanghai in the twenties—criminal Triads like the Green Gang were making it too dangerous to stay honest in the Customs Service."

In old Shanghai, the most corrupt city on the China Coast, the Chinese gangs that controlled the police and kept peace of sorts for foreign businessmen had not looked kindly on attempts to interfere with smuggling.

"My father fled Communist 'liberation' in '49. We have made a life here. Now we're the last independent British trading hong in the territory. But we *are* refugees, so don't think that Mackintosh Farquhar won't move to survive."

Vivian answered placidly yet firmly, as if she had not heard a word Vicky had spoken. "Hong Kong is like the rudder on this boat—your boat," she amended, with a private smile. "Hong Kong can steer China. Your father understands this. As Hong Kong goes, so goes China. Ahead into light, or back to the dark."

"Well, just in case the rudder falls off, my father sent me to New York."

"Hongkongers who have flourished here have a responsibility to stay—to be that rudder."

"But just in case, where's your passport? Canada?"

"I don't have a passport."

Vicky was astonished. She had never met an upper-echelon Hongkonger who hadn't obtained a foreign passport either by working abroad or investing cash in another country or buying or marrying one.

"Why not?"

"I believe that exciting times sharpen the mind."

"Sharpen the *mind*? They'll sharpen your mind in a re-education camp. You could end up slopping pigs in Mongolia for ten years."

"I'm Hong Kong Chinese," Vivian replied with simple conviction. "This is my home."

Quixotic, perhaps, if not downright reckless, but it spoke a sort of bravery that Vicky found humbling. Uncomfortably examining her own rarely called-upon convictions, she wondered whether she would ever put them so irrevocably on the line.

"And it's your father's home too."

That rankled. "You seem very sure of his thinking."

"Not at all," Vivian denied hastily. "Perhaps as his China trader I *hope* your hong remains in China. It is a reasonable hope, from my perspective, is it not?"

"Of course," Vicky agreed. "It's my hope too. Hong Kong is by far the best city in the Orient for doing business."

"Nor," Vivian added with a friendlier smile, "do we want to become refugees again."

Vicky was not appeased by Vivian's gentle retreat. She felt a strange disquiet, a vague uneasiness that had been permeating her thoughts like water seeping through cracks in the hard rock of the impossible. Maybe the Two-Way Wong rumor had set her off, but she thought not. This was the inkling of something real, a threat more basic.

A shout from the bow brought Vivian's head up sharply. Vicky's father and Ah Chi had finally freed the jib, and the Taipan was signaling Chip to steer off the wind. The sails filled. The yacht heeled. The engines ceased their distant pounding, and it was abruptly quiet enough to hear the wake. Vicky had to wrench her gaze from Vivian's shining face. Sick with shock and dismay, she suddenly knew whose girlfriend the Chinese woman was.

VICKY WATCHED HER mother open another beer and touch the cold wet-beaded can to her cheek. It couldn't be.

She held her tongue while they sailed around East Point, tacked near the shabby Kuomintang stilt villages that still flew their defiant flags, and pounded through the choppy Tathong Channel. Her father came back and took the helm, exchanging a quick glance with Vivian. Neither the Taipan's smile nor his China trader's was warmer than was proper, but Vicky imagined that their eyes burned like the embers of a single fire.

Past Shek-O, where Hugo and Fiona lived in a glass house by the golf club, and skirting Waglan Light, *Whirlwind* settled down smoothly on a comfortable reach. Her father dodged the wake of a gigantic Japanese car carrier steaming through the Lamma Channel, and set a course for the open sea.

Seen astern in the murky, humid air, Hong Kong's jagged peaks seemed to drift on the wind. Soon it was impossible to distinguish where the island met the sea, which was growing rough.

It simply couldn't be. In a city where men of means—both gweilos and Chinese—routinely took mistresses, her parents were a legendary couple.

The Mackintosh-Farquhar wedding had been Peak society's most romantic event of the 1950s. As if in a Hong Kong dream, the old

Taipan's daughter, a famous yachtswoman in her own right, had fallen in love with her father's brash young partner. People still talked about the dinners they gave, how they led the dancing at the governor's ball, and the beach parties after the China Sea races.

If over the decades of work and children Sally had begun to drink and Duncan had to fight harder and harder to keep his gains, surely their family had remained—outwardly, at least—one of the more stable on the Peak. No scandal, and none of the tacky love affairs that an army of Hong Kong journalists were paid to exploit.

Vicky stole a glance at Vivian, saw her dark eyes surreptitiously tracking Duncan, and suddenly wanted to cry. Her first instinct had been right. She had noticed the change in him immediately—newly wild, yet oddly at peace.

Her sympathies angled fiercely toward her mother. Yes, she drank. Yes, she could be difficult. Yes, in her airy way, she was needy, if not downright demanding. But so could he be difficult and demanding. And it had worked, somehow, for most of her mother's life. It seemed so cruel to abandon her now.

Vicky pondered for hours, long after the mountain peaks had disappeared astern. She felt sadly adult—older, grimly mature, and terribly alone—grown-up as never before. Even when she was trying to run away from her parents, her hopes for their permanence had given her the strength to drive ahead. She could go anywhere, having convinced herself her back was covered.

At last, Duncan handed the wheel to Sally and went forward. Vicky followed, making her way purposefully forward through the litter of poles, sheets, wire stays, and winches. She braced him on the foredeck, where he and Ah Chi were crouched, again, over the troublesome jib roller.

"May I speak with you?"

"Now? We've got to find out what made this thing freeze." He looked up irritably, but whatever he read in her face prompted him to order Ah Chi below for a toolbox. Vicky waited until the boatboy had lowered himself down the forward hatch.

"All right, Your Majesty. Let me say straight off, I've had a bellyful of the New York hotel business."

"Stuff your bloody hotel."

"Beg pardon?"

"I've left you a sound restructuring plan. If you're willing to spend the money, you'll be in profit in five years. Or, if you'd rather take a loss, I've lined up buyers."

Vicky felt stunned when the words were out. Did the sea wind carry a tang of burning bridge? She had done it, broken free, alone, adrift. Her father shook his massive head in scornful disbelief. She could see in his eyes that he was sure she would come to her senses.

"What the devil's gotten into you, Your Majesty?" he demanded, and under any other conditions she might have kowtowed. But in abandoning her mother he had broken his spell.

"You have one hell of a nerve bringing her on a family cruise."

"Who?"

"Don't insult me any more."

"I don't know what you're talking about."

"Does my mother know?"

Duncan Mackintosh returned a look as dark as the Guangdong mountains, but when his angry daughter did not flinch, he could not hold her eye. Gazing over her head to the cockpit, where Vicky's mother sat and Vivian Loh had resumed her perch on the stern, he answered quietly, "No, she does not. And I'll thank you to keep it that way. There is no point in causing unnecessary hurt."

"What's your cover?"

"My what?"

"Why do people think she's aboard? What does Mother think?"

"The truth. Vivian Loh is a valued member of my staff. I count on her for contacts and damned good advice on how to handle the Chinese."

"Peter knows the Chinese." Peter Mackintosh had actually lived on the Mainland, as a student and a teacher.

"Your brother is white. A gweilo. I don't care how much of a China scholar he is, he will always be a Foreign Devil in their eyes — at best an amusement, like a pet."

"Does Hugo know?"

"He will know when and if he has to know and not before. I don't expect my children to choose between me and their mother. Only you know and only because you're so ruddy clever."

"Women observe, Daddy. They use their eyes."

"Women, hell. *I* taught you to observe. Along with a lot of other things."

"Backfired, didn't it?"

"Apparently so."

"Oh, Daddy, how could you?"

Duncan Mackintosh's sudden, fierce smile said he was done apologizing. "Better ask how I could not—and before you do, Your Majesty, keep in mind you are in no position to judge."

Vicky recoiled as if her father had slapped her. She thought she had managed to shunt the corrosive pain and guilt of both her failed marriage and her recent split with her boyfriend to some far side of her memory, but he had hurled her back into confusion with a few deliberately chosen words.

"Daddy, how can you compare my divorce ten years ago to what you're doing to my mother? Jeff was an unhappy boy you manipulated me into marrying because his father's department stores appealed to you. I was just young enough or dumb enough to let you do it."

"Your mother tells me you broke up with Rod Dwyer. How long did this one last, three years?"

"Screw off!" Vicky flared. "I drove him into the ground trying to save your bloody hotel. But I never had affairs. And he never slept with another woman. He was a warm, gentle man and I loved him very much."

"Jeff did dope. Rod, I had the impression, drank. You must be as much fun to live with as I am."

Duncan Mackintosh grinned—the sudden fiery flash of brilliant teeth and glittering eyes that the Chinese, who eventually found a perfect name for everything, had dubbed Dragon Face—and for a brief second, the overwhelmingly irresistible assault of calculated charm seduced even Vicky into a sad sort of empathy. He had touched the core of her doubts: that she could neither live with a man without destroying him, or choose one strong enough to survive her ambition.

"Oh, Daddy . . . Please, why are you doing this?"

"I'm alive again," he said, with simple conviction.

Her empathy evaporated quicker than his grin. And, as she could not admit to herself that she envied his certainty — and his newfound happiness — she fell back on her wholly legitimate fear of what his love affair would do to her mother. "Could you possibly elaborate upon that naked insight?"

"No."

"I think that destroying my mother's life deserves a fuller explanation."

"There is no fuller explanation. Nor do I expect a girl your age to understand."

"I would imagine you've grown familiar with 'girls my age.' In fact, she looks younger than I am."

"She's your age, exactly. You're both Dragon Children." A Year of the Dragon — as 1964 had been — was an excellent year to be born, by Chinese standards.

"A dragon mistress for Dragon Face?" Vicky smiled sadly.

"She's easier to get along with than Dragon Daughter."

"Oh, she must be. So attractive too. So demure. So 'sharpen-the-mind.' "

"*Don't,*" he cut her off, with real menace in his voice. "Don't judge until you know."

Vicky rounded on him. "Am I supposed to *know* her?"

Ah Chi popped out of the hatch, saw them squaring off like a pair of Thai boxers about to kick. " 'Cuse, Missy."

Vicky stepped out of his way and, by silent mutual agreement, retreated with her father to the bow pulpit, a narrow rail-enclosed platform that jutted six feet ahead of the boat. The bow, rising and falling, cut loudly through the water, affording them privacy. Her father stood facing ahead, confronting her. She gazed past him, aft through a steely forest of masts and stays. Ah Chi waited, twenty feet back, gripping the lifelines with one foot propped up on a spinnaker pole lashed to the deck. He was studying the seas, which had taken on a deeper rhythm, the wave crests rising higher and spreading apart. The sun was growing smaller in a yellow-gray sky. The steely cast overhead had hardened perceptibly, and the mare's-tails had spread wide.

"Where are you taking this?" Vicky asked, nurturing a vague hope of salvaging something for her mother. "Do you have plans?"

Her father's reply was oblique at best. "She's a terrific woman."

"Is that why you hired her?"

"Actually, she was a scholarship child."

Mackintosh Farquhar awarded scholarships to needy Chinese students. Those who excelled were staked through university in Great Britain and invited to join the hong.

"How far back does this go?"

"Don't be daft. She was doing a damned good job for us before it became more. She had a First at Cambridge."

"How nice," Vicky said. "I wanted to go to Cambridge." She fell silent, wishing she hadn't learned his secret. Had he buckled under the pressure of the impending Turnover? Maybe a man, an older man, wanted to be young again when he got frightened. She could almost accept that he had acted out of fear. Or maybe a man just took what he wanted. This man. Maybe Vivian Loh was merely the latest in a lifelong series of acquisitions—Sally, her father's shipping line, the department stores, the airlines, the hotels, and now an exquisite Chinese mistress.

How Hong Kong, she thought bitterly. How bloody Hong Kong. Ship the old wife back to England and start anew. She looked the length of the boat at her mother, whose sun-beaten face was raised in oblivious contemplation of the sails, and thought of herself turning sixty. Twenty-eight years until then suddenly seemed quite short a time. The difference, she supposed, was that maybe, just maybe, when she was sixty she might take a handsome Chinese boy, if she felt like it. Especially if they were still in Hong Kong.

"You're smiling," her father said. "Does this mean I can go back to mending that bloody roller?"

"The guy with the beard—Wally Hearst—who's he?"

"An American."

"I could see that."

"Free-lance China trader. He's got some pretty fair lines into Peking."

"I thought you already had a China trader," Vicky observed acidly.

"Vivian is better connected in Shanghai."

"Peking calls the tune for Hong Kong. What are you doing in Shanghai?"

"Making friends," he replied enigmatically, and Vicky wondered again what he was up to.

"*Look!*" cried Sally. "Duncan! Darling! Look!" She tossed away her beer and grappled clumsily with binoculars. "Off the port side. Haven't seen one in years."

Everyone turned to the east, where a great red junk had appeared on the horizon under full sail.

5

THE SUN MANTLED the junk's sails, which were ribbed like butterfly wings. Stacked in random angles, they cut a ragged silhouette. The towering main swung behind the foresail and covered the tiny mizzen.

"She's turning toward us."

Vicky shivered. The ancient ship was beautiful but strange, materializing from nowhere, out here, all alone. She scanned the horizon. Empty, not even a smudge of freighter smoke. Her mother and Hugo and Peter were enthralled, excitedly passing binoculars back and forth. Vicky looked to her father. He planted his sturdy frame solidly on the deck, braced his legs against the lifelines, and studied the junk's progress. Vivian Loh edged nearer, and Vicky could almost feel her desire to touch him.

Running before the freshening east wind, which was lacing a long roll into the sea, the big junk was moving fast. A good ten knots, Vicky guessed. It cut the distance swiftly, looming larger and larger against the sky.

"Pirates?" Wally Hearst asked Chip with a thin laugh. His seasickness pills seemed to be working; he looked a little less pale. "I've got an automatic in my bag for Manila. Maybe I ought to—"

"I'd leave it below," the policeman told the China trader. "If they're armed, they're better armed than we are."

"But who are they?" Hearst asked.

Chip studied her in the glasses. "PRC, wouldn't you say, Duncan?"

"Looks beat up enough to be."

With her tattered red sails patched haphazardly, and her hull a near ruin devoid of paint and stained black by the water, she was as dilapidated as the grotty PRC fishing boats that occasionally passed through Victoria Harbour. Besides, thought Vicky, no junks flew sails anymore other than for the sea goddess Tin Hau's birthday festival. All but the poorest Mainlanders had switched to the diesel engines that allowed them to trawl year 'round instead of waiting for the winter monsoon.

"I'd reckon a smuggler," said Chip. "No iron to tip the radar."

Vicky passed Hearst her binoculars to put his mind at ease, and showed him how to focus first to one eye, then the other.

"Wow. She's a million crazy angles."

"That's how they disperse load."

"Huh?"

She pointed out the ancient tricks the builders used to strengthen wood, bamboo, and cloth. A framework of straight timbers trussed the half-moon hull, and bamboo ribs divided each sail into trapezial sections that opened to the wind like a giant red fan.

"How the heck you know so much about junks?"

"Mackintosh Farquhar had a boatyard on Apleichau Island. Dad gave me my first job managing it when I got out of school."

"Funny job for a gweipo."

"Daddy thought so."

The smiling Chinese shipwrights had willingly shared the art of junk building with the Taipan's daughter. But all the while they were dazzling her with hand-shaped teak and instinctive measurements, they were also stealing Mackintosh Farquhar materials to construct a high-speed smugglers' sampan in a back shed. That Vicky had stumbled upon them while trying out inventory procedures she had learned in school—and that she had sold the sampan out from under the thieves as an especially swift yacht tender—had never fully outweighed the joke against her, by her father's reckoning. The chagrined sampan builders had been more complimentary, dubbing her Dragon Daughter. But she hadn't stayed long enough for the name to stick.

Bearing down on *Whirlwind*, the junk's sunlit sails were webbed in reef lines, halyards, and boom lifts. An anchor with rusty flukes hung from the bow, and automobile-tire bumpers dangled over the sides. It looked a hundred years old, a survivor, by many miracles, of a dozen wars and revolutions.

"She's coming about."

The junk began to turn parallel to the yacht's course. Timbers creaked and rigging squealed as dark sailors in dark clothing sheeted in the scalloped sails. When they had her lumbering beside the yacht, they hung over the side and stared.

"Ah Chi, ease your helm. They're having the devil's own time sailing this close to the wind."

"*Hai*, Taipan."

"Lowering a boat," Hugo called.

Two men climbed in, started a noisy outboard, and bounced across the intervening water.

"What do they want?" asked Hearst.

"Our blue jeans, VCR, and Sat Nav," Vicky's mother said tartly. Vicky looked at Hugo, who shook his head, not to worry. PRC patrol boats were known to rob Hong Kong Chinese fishermen; there had been one incident back in 1993, when a gweilo yacht had been molested. But it was likely to be the last. The PRC had dispatched the guilty parties at a public beheading in a Canton stadium — an attempt to reassure the international business community. The punishment had had the opposite effect, setting Hong Kong's expatriates to ponder deeply the civil liberties they enjoyed under the Union Jack. Or, as Vicky's mother had written her, "It's the little things I find unsettling, personally."

The sampan chugged alongside, and a plainly garbed sailor rose with a coiled line, which he tossed straight to Duncan Mackintosh.

"Bloody cheek," Vicky's mother snorted, but Duncan took a turn around the nearest winch and hauled in slack as the sampan kissed the schooner's hull.

The Chinese sailor spoke. Vicky glanced at Mary Lee, thinking it was Fukienese dialect, but Mary looked blank. Vivian Loh stepped forward and exchanged a few words, which she translated for Duncan, so softly that Vicky could not hear.

"Hugo!" Duncan called, and Hugo stepped over the safety lines and down into the sampan. Then: "Vivian!"

"I want to come," said Vicky.

"Full boat. I need Vivian to translate."

"I speak Chinese."

"For Chrissake, Your Majesty, do these laddies look like they speak *Mandarin*? That's a Ningbo junk, I'll wager." The East China port of Ningbo, across Hangzhou Bay from Shanghai, was the birthplace of most of Hong Kong's Chinese shipowners. "They'll speak some bollixed-up Wu. Lucky we have Vivian along."

Vicky was helpless to protest. Mandarin, for thousands of years the language of China's elite, was great for doing business across the polyglot sprawling Mainland, but as useless as Latin for conversing with the mass of ordinary Chinese south of the Yangtze.

"Then take Peter!" Mary cried, shoving him fiercely forward by the arm. Duncan ignored her, calling instead to Ah Chi, who was at the helm, his face dark with concern.

"Steady as she goes, Ah Chi." Then, with a big Dragon Grin: "If he changes course, you follow. Quick-quick!"

"Yes, Taipan," the Tanka said, shooting worried looks at the big junk, which could probably outrun them downwind.

"Here we go, Viv. Into the boat." Duncan took the Chinese woman's hand with a gentle grace Vicky had never seen in him, stepped down with her, and flipped the line off the winch barrel, still holding her hand. Didn't the others notice? she cried to herself, grappling with a jealous thought that only dancers or lovers could have effected the transfer with such intimate panache. The noisy outboard clattered, and the sampan struggled away.

Fuming at being left out, Vicky watched them roller-coaster over the waves. "Should have worn Mae Wests," Sally Mackintosh muttered. "Sea's picking up." A gust tore a wave top, wetting their faces.

Vicky raised her binoculars again, bracing her knees against the lifeline, and found the sampan huddled in the lee of the junk as it disgorged its passengers. Behind her she heard Mary upbraiding Peter. "How many times must I tell you to put yourself forward?" she whispered angrily. "You should have gone with him."

Peter mumbled an inaudible reply.

Vicky sympathized, but knew why his girlfriend was so angry. Mary, ambitious for Peter and probably jealous of Hugo's place in the business, had also guessed that this apparent chance meeting at sea was no surprise to the Taipan of Mackintosh Farquhar.

T HE JUNK CREAKED and moaned as it rolled on the gathering
seas, a sound that reminded Hugo of boyhood days on his
grandfather's wooden sloop.

"My son," Duncan Mackintosh introduced him.

The junk captain, a fat, sun-blackened Chinese with a mouthful
of broken teeth, bowed. The People's Liberation Army officer merely
nodded. He wore no uniform, but Hugo had soldiered and knew
another.

A third man, a strapping Northerner, shook hands. Hugo recognized him from news photos—Ma Binyan, a fiery student leader
who had survived the Peking massacre. *Asiaweek* had put Ma's picture on its cover, with blood streaming down his face, a red head-
band, and a T-shirt splattered with the Chinese characters for BLOOD
DEBT. The hardliners had jailed him until his mentor, Party Leader
Tang, had secured his release when the reformers briefly regained
power in '94.

The wire-thin Shanghainese who seemed to be running the show
invited them to sit, which they did around a rough table in the big
aft cabin. The army, the students, and a Shanghai cadre, Hugo marveled—an explosive combination in China's current power struggle.

What Vivian was doing here he had no idea; everyone at the
table spoke English. That mystery was cleared up early. Vivian, it

seemed, had carried a private message from his father to the Shang-hainese—Zheng—which might explain, at last, what she'd been doing to earn her keep.

His father unfolded two sheets of paper from his shirt pocket. They were old, hatched with crease lines. He spread them carefully on the wooden table.

Zheng picked them up carefully, held them to the light seeping through a high, salt-specked window. The others watched, faces impassive. Hugo allowed his own features to settle into a look of mild boredom. Let them figure out whether he knew the contents.

"Would you explain this, please?" Zheng asked.

Duncan Mackintosh said, "Fake billing that shows how Two-Way Wong—Sir John Wong Li—tried to coerce my shipyard, some years ago, into charging fifty percent more to build a yacht than she cost. He demanded the difference kicked back in cash. As the yacht was being charged to his public company, he would have robbed his shareholders of a million dollars."

Zheng, a lean, youthful-looking man with high cheekbones, appeared perplexed. "I have no doubt that Two-Way Wong Li is considered, what is your word—shady?—in Hong Kong. Nor, frankly, is it monumental news that Wong Li goes to extremes to accumulate capital."

Hugo glanced at Vivian Loh, who looked relaxed, and realized that his father had merely opened a subject, politely. The lovely Loh, it seemed, had a certain power to smooth his blunt manners.

Duncan refolded the paper. "This little scam is only a model for a gigantic fraud he's pulling on China's state-run shipyards. Every ship he commissions in China robs the People's Republic of a fortune in diverted currency and materials. Every vessel in World Oceans Red Ship Fleet was stolen from China."

For a long while, creaking wood was the loudest sound in the cabin. Finally, Zheng asked, "Do you have evidence?"

"Oh, yes. I've been keeping files on the bastard for years."

The army officer cleared his throat. Zheng spoke again. "Obviously he would need help from highly placed government officials."

"Very highly placed."

"Who?" asked Ma Binyan.

"Premier Chen," said Duncan, and Hugo sat up straight.

Two powerful men dominated the current struggle to rule China: Premier Chen, hardline head of government; and Communist Party boss Tang, leader of the "New China" reformers. Chen's regime was corrupt, but Chen was firmly in control of the army. Tang was trying to stay alive long enough to convince the elders in the Politburo Committee of Five that reform was China's only hope to end the corruption strangling her economy.

Clearly, Hugo thought, the cadre, the soldier, and the student leader were Tang's reform mob. Hard evidence of a massive state rip-off would sink Chen's hardliners and elevate Tang. Less clear was how Duncan Mackintosh had managed to insert himself in the middle of their fight.

Zheng asked the next question in Hugo's mind.

"Why? Why do you do this?"

"To stop Two-Way Wong's appointment as chief executive of Hong Kong under Peking rule next year," Duncan answered. "If Tang guarantees my choice of governor—Chief Executive Allen Wei, who everyone agrees is already doing a fine job—I will give Tang the evidence to cut Two-Way Wong into a thousand pieces."

"Did not Wong Li steal your shipping line?" Zheng demanded coldly.

"He'll wish he hadn't," Duncan answered, just as coldly.

"And this is all the reward you ask? Revenge on Two-Way Wong?"

Duncan Mackintosh laughed. "Not bloody likely. I'm a businessman. I want my place in Hong Kong to build my hotels, fly my planes, and, God willing, sail my ships. I'm betting Tang is Hong Kong's main chance."

He smiled into the silence. Then he said, "And I'm Tang's main chance to destroy Chen."

"Where did you get this evidence?" Zheng asked, and Hugo

noticed that the Shanghainese was losing his battle to appear casual. His eyes were burning.

"It was given me by a Chinese shipyard manager I'd done business with. A brave man who decided to blow the whistle on Two-Way. I took the original documents for safekeeping. Good thing I did."

"Why?"

"He was crushed by a gantry crane."

"Did Two-Way Wong do that?"

"More likely a PRC official. *Guanshang* is a bullet-in-the-neck crime, isn't it?"

"We must have the originals."

"You must *be* the original, too," Duncan replied. "I'm not handing them over to anyone's assistant. I mean Tang himself."

"Impossible," Zheng snapped, and the faces of his comrades hardened.

Duncan Mackintosh pushed back his stool and rose from the table, Hugo beside him. "I think this has been an excellent first meeting. And I thank you gentlemen for coming out in the storm to meet me and my son."

Vicky raked the junk with her binoculars. Being cut out of the meeting, for whatever excuse, was another harsh reminder of how far she had strayed from the orbit of Mackintosh Farquhar while spearheading the New York effort. In her battle to free herself from her father, she realized now, she had always operated under the assumption that Mackintosh Farquhar was there for her. She could not be the heir like Hugo—there could be only one Taipan—but an integral part of the family company. Now she felt like a mountain climber with no mountain, a sailor on the sand.

Her gaze settled on a man who had joined the helmsman, a tall, handsome Chinese with a proud bearing. He had the height and broad shoulders of a Northerner, and Vicky, imagining him as a Manchu horseman, a wild man of the steppes, wondered how he had found his way to the rolling deck of a China Sea junk. When he swaggered to the gunwales and raised a long telescope, aiming it across the water directly at her, a broad smile lit his face.

"He just winked at you," said Chip.

Vicky dropped the glasses. Beside her, the policeman was braced against a stay, inspecting the junk through his own binoculars.

"Who do you think they are?"

"Ask your father."

And indeed, the Mackintosh men were helping Vivian Loh back into the sampan.

"Move in closer, Ah Chi," Sally ordered. The sampan was having a hard time of it, the seas having built in the interval.

"Yes, Tai-Tai."

Whirlwind halved the distance, and Vicky and Chip stood by to catch their line. Moments later all were safely aboard, soaked by the warm water, and the sampan was retreating to the junk, which retrieved it. The great bamboo yards and battens creaked around, and she returned to her western course, plowing on before the wind.

Vicky burned to know what had happened aboard the junk, but it would be pointless to ask. Her father would relate exactly what he chose to relate when he chose, if ever. Nor would she court abuse by asking Vivian. Hugo, however, might be tricked.

"Well?" demanded Sally.

"Chinese captain says we're in for a blow."

"I could have told him that. What did he want?"

Duncan Mackintosh answered his wife with a wink. "He offered to buy you."

"Me?" Sally laughed. "What Chinaman wants an old woman? He meant Vicky."

"No, you. He likes his women tall."

"Fiona's tall."

"Get on with you, Mother," Fiona cried, shooing her with her hands as if chasing a goat from her kitchen. "Hugo, make your mother behave."

"He demanded you, specifically. Offered taels of gold and a chest of jade. Didn't he, Hugo?"

"Oh, aye," said Hugo. "Dad was ready to take it till I reminded him we need you to navigate."

Vicky had waited patiently through this grotesque parody of the family they had once been. "Did Vivian translate all this?"

Vivian looked up from a private reverie and for a second could not hide the angry fire in her eye. "Didn't have to," blurted Hugo. "They spoke English."

"English?" Vicky echoed, but her older brother was already wincing from their father's black look.

"The captain's wireless was crapped out," Duncan said. "His glass was dropping to thirty and he naturally wanted to know what weather reports we'd heard."

"I thought he told you a blow was coming."

"He feels it in his bones. He wanted to know some specifics. Between his bones, the glass, and the radio I'm willing to believe we've got a gale to contend with. He's not going to risk running for Hong Kong and neither am I. Sally?"

"My father always said the only way to handle getting caught on a lee shore is never get caught on a lee shore."

"Ah Chi?"

"Sea room, Taipan."

"All right, everybody, let's get battened down while we've still got some light. Mum, how about a warm supper while we can still cook?"

"Already on the cooker. Mum's typhoon special: sausage, beans, rice, and shredded duck."

"God help us," said Fiona. "Porker special is more like it."

Duncan Mackintosh gave everyone a job. Vicky's was to issue safety harnesses to all who'd be working on the decks, and lifejackets for those below. The jackets were a worst-case precaution, as well as a psychological pacifier for the nonsailors, but the safety harnesses were vital. Every few years someone was lost at sea; it was almost impossible to turn a big boat around fast enough to find a bobbing head at night. While she rigged the jacklines to which they could tether their harnesses, Vicky pondered what her father was up to.

He had neatly deflected further questions, with the aid of the impending gale, but if it was true that he had expected to meet the junk, then several odd facts emerged: Duncan Mackintosh was conducting business with someone from the PRC; that business was secret; and if he had known whom he was meeting, he must have known they spoke English, which suggested that Vivian Loh had accompanied her father as more than a translator.

The fact that he had brought Hugo with him was also revealing. Her father usually operated as a loner. Asking Sally and Ah Chi's opinion of his storm strategy had been an act to put the nonsailors at ease. There was only one captain aboard *Whirlwind* and only one Taipan at Mackintosh Farquhar. So bringing Hugo, his heir, indicated plans for the future at very long range.

Why meet secretly at sea, and with whom, were questions blazing from her eyes when she bumped into Hugo, who was humping a storm jib up the foredeck hatch. Hugo could do a pretty good imitation of the Dragon Smile, albeit a gentler dragon.

"Forget it," he said.

The yellow sun plunged into the gray sea and darkness fell like a blanket. *Whirlwind* forged southward, her teak, wet from spray, glistening in the work lights as Huang made a final round, stowing loose gear and insuring that blocks and shackles were secure and sheets not chafing.

High in the rigging, the wind began to ring a hollow metallic note, and Vicky, standing watch at the helm while her father, Hugo, and Ah Chi ate and rested below, felt the great yacht come alive in her hands. Heavily built and designed for comfort on the long haul, it took a hard blow to bring out the best in her. Like me, she thought. Best in a scramble.

She glanced at her watch. Midmorning in New York—the lull in the hotel lobby between checking out and checking in, while the bars and restaurants set up for lunch and the chambermaids scrambled to clean the suites. Best out of it, she told herself, but it hurt.

Huang, crouching low, his wet pajamas blowing in the warm wind, returned to the cockpit, and Vicky doused the work lights to see the waves better.

"Snap harness," she said, demonstrating how her own was tethered to the cockpit jackline.

"Yes, Missy." Huang smiled and bobbed his head. He spoke no English and if she had said, "A giant squid is reaching to pluck you off the deck," Huang would have smiled and said, "Yes, Missy."

"Snap harness," she repeated sternly, demonstrating again, and this time Huang attached himself to the line. He was a willing enough worker, but not a natural sailor like Ah Chi.

Vicky's mother came up through a darkened stern hatch, so as not to destroy her night vision, and sent Huang below to eat. The wind-speed indicator, a faint red glow in front of the cockpit, was showing twenty-two knots. When a gust sent the digital numbers racing past thirty, *Whirlwind* buried her lee rail, spraying warm salt water on Vicky's face and tugging the helm as if something large had swum beneath the boat to taste the rudder.

"The main's overpowered," said her mother in the dark.

Vicky reached for the mainsheet, but Sally stopped her. "Feels like someone forgot to tighten the boom vang when you took your reef."

Vicky felt her mother's hand on the wheel, let it go, and worked her way forward, unclipping her harness tether from the cockpit jackline and clipping onto the windward roof line before stepping onto the deck. Mother was right about the vang. Though she couldn't see the sail in the dark, she had felt somehow that it had bellied too full. Vicky found the tail of the vang tackle, took four turns around a winch, and cranked, pulling the boom down and flattening the sail.

"Much better," Sally called, her voice ragged in the wind, and when Vicky returned to the cockpit, the boat was heeling less sharply and the helm felt easy. Clouds had erased the star she had been steering by. "Two hundred and ten," said her mother as she turned on the compass light.

"Yes, I know."

"Isn't this gorgeous?" said Sally. Vicky glanced at her silhouette and saw by the compass glow that she was sipping a martini from a stem glass.

"Have you eaten, Mother?"

"Not hungry."

"What's the weather report?"

"Force six or seven tops. Nothing to this old girl."

"No typhoon?" Vicky asked.

"I certainly hope not. No, we're fine. Though it's going to be a long night. What are you staring at? Oh! Not to worry—it's a plastic glass. My God, you've got the beadiest little stare sometimes—your eyes shine in the dark. . . . So, tell your mum, how's life in New York?"

"Fragmented."

"I guessed that much this morning. I mean, have you started dating again?"

"I told you that's not on my agenda."

"Not to worry. Agendas have a way of rewriting themselves."

"I mean it. I really do want to be alone."

"I have days like that," her mother mused.

Vicky tried to see her face in the dark. Did she have no inkling about Vivian Loh? Was this leading to the topic of grandchildren, or was she talking around the edges of her greatest fear?

"Mother, what do you think Dad did on the junk?"

"Haven't the foggiest."

"Aren't you curious?"

"We never discuss business."

"So it was business?"

"Everything your father does is business."

"But a Chinese boat just pulls alongside and—"

"Why don't you ask him if you're so curious?" her mother interrupted curtly, throwing her head back to drain her glass. "Empty. Like General MacArthur, I shall return." She headed back to the stern hatch.

"Where's your harness?" Vicky called after her, but a breaking sea growled beside the boat and she knew her mother had not heard.

Since her mother's drinking was another subject Vicky did not want to consider at the moment, she put it from her mind and let herself enjoy being the only one on deck. The boat speed was exhilarating and the seas, though rising, were still quite regular, the crests and falls predictable, so that *Whirlwind*'s passage, while neither easy nor smooth, was not chaotic and her rhythm did not vary greatly. In the blackness, white wave crests glowed, and now and then a cluster of stars, astonishingly bright, broke through the clouds. The stars seemed nearer than usual, almost touchable, soft, and buttery through the haze.

"A-Team on deck!"

Hugo's laughing call to action broke her reverie as he clumped up the companionway, leading their father, Ah Chi, Sally, Chip, and Peter. Vicky turned away from the light until they closed the hatch. They settled about the cockpit, laughing and joking as they clipped on to the jackline and the pad eyes, gradually falling silent as their vision adjusted to the dark and the change in the seas became apparent.

"Good Christ," Hugo breathed with mingled awe and excitement.

"How's she doing, Your Majesty?"

"The wind's at twenty-five, gusting to thirty-five. The sea's moving behind us. She's accelerating down the crests. I'd like to slow her down a bit."

"Perhaps you're tired?"

"Not at all."

"Do you need relief?"

"No."

"Just don't let her broach. You let a sea push the stern around and we're really in the shit."

Vicky stiffened angrily. Her mother nudged her in the dark.

"Yes, Daddy," she said automatically, wondering why he had to go out of his way to assume the worst about her. "Do you want to take another reef?"

"She's doing fine," he replied, with deep affection for *Whirlwind*. Just then a wave caught the stern at a new angle and the bow

skittered upwind. Vicky steered out of it long before they were in
danger of broaching sideways to the seas, but the wind spilled from
the forward staysail, causing the sail to luff and crackle loudly.

"Hugo! Take the helm before she jibes."

Hugo reached for the wheel, grinning. "Let a man take over."

"See how long you last." Face burning, Vicky retreated to the
stern deck. As much as she hated failing at anything, she hated it
doubly when her father was the judge. She knew she was not a natural sailor like her mother, had known it since childhood. The boat
never quite spoke to her as it did to her mother. But she could
conquer her deficiency, most times, by concentration and effort.
Straining at the end of her tether, she leaned back against her harness and stared at the white horses raging in the dark.

"Vicky?" Hugo called over his shoulder. "Spot for me, dear?"

At first she thought Hugo was being the kindly big brother,
trying to make her feel better by asking her to alert him to big
waves coming up behind the boat at odd angles. But the rising wind
had begun to shift chaotically, and it was soon apparent that the seas
were growing dangerous and the helmsman needed all the help he
could get.

Vicky snapped on to a more conveniently located pad eye and
turned around, facing aft. It was frightfully dark, and she kept moving her head, cocking her ears for the roar that meant trouble.
Gradually she filtered out the sounds of wind in the rigging, the
heavy slush of the bow waves as *Whirlwind* nearly buried her nose,
the lighter swish of the spray matting the sea, the bang of sudden
gusts in the sails, even the rush of air past her ears: What remained
was a silence, of sorts, pregnant with anticipation. The rollers, which
might have been apparent at a hundred yards in daylight, approached stealthily at night, for they were quiet before they broke.
Until their tops fell ahead of themselves or were shredded by the
wind, the only clue that one was overtaking was a gradual lowering
of the stern as a big wave sucked the sea from under the boat.

"Coming from portside, Hugo."

Hugo steered right, risking the angle of approach to the seas
ahead in order to keep the stern straight on to the sea behind. The

stern rose, the bow tipped, and *Whirlwind* accelerated, Hugo playing the wheel to keep a balance between the forces fore and aft. A slowing as she buried her nose and then a lift indicated he had calculated correctly; a sickening lurch proved him wrong. Once he almost lost control and Vicky knew that had it been she, her father would have been merciless. For Hugo, he offered only mild caution and, moments later, the ultimate compliment of going below. Where, of course, Vicky thought as she peered into the dark for the next sea, Vivian waited. He was gone ten minutes.

"Poor Wally Hearst," Duncan reported when he came back up. "Scared silly but too sick to give a damn."

Hugo lasted an hour. When he was clearly getting tired, their father said, "Give Ah Chi a shot, son."

The Chinese boatboy stepped eagerly to the wheel. Lightning flickered in the distance and muted thunder rumbled.

"Shall I spot for you, Ah Chi?"

"Yes, Missy." But he did his own spotting as well, his head in constant motion as he threaded the yacht through the seas. The lightning got brighter, the thunder louder. A far-off hissing grew until, with a roar, rain dashed across the waves and crashed to the decks. The rain rode a fierce wind that slammed the yacht half-over on its side. Lightning blasted overhead, painting the boat and the sea a deathly white. Vicky saw the rain bursting on the decks, saw the wheel's spokes flicker as it spun through Ah Chi's hands, and saw the seas flattened momentarily by the rain, then tower again in a moving mountain range of twisted crests. *Whirlwind* rammed a huge wave that stopped her almost dead and threw Vicky against her harness.

The lightning blinded her. When it burst again, she saw Ah Chi down on the cockpit floor, tended by her mother, who was inspecting a gash across his brow. Her father had taken the wheel. She looked back. A monster was coming after them, breaking with a roar.

"Starboard!"

But her father was already well into his turn toward safety. Twice more she called big seas angling at the stern and twice he had already anticipated. Vicky was awed. It was as if he could read the storm-blown sea surface through his feet, sensing by *Whirlwind*'s attitude where the sea would attack. If the boat spoke to her mother in the precise language of wind and sail, her father shared with it a private code. The hull was his eyes, the rudder his mind.

"Hugo!" he bellowed suddenly. "Douse that storm jib."

The combined roar of wind, waves, and rain nearly drowned his voice. Vicky lowered herself off the stern deck into the cockpit and huddled beside her mother. Ah Chi was sitting up on the sole, holding his wound shut with his fingers and insisting he was all right.

Chip, however, had a look with his flashlight and said, "Come on, old son. I'll help you below." With an arm around his shoulders, the policeman eased the protesting boatboy to the hatch.

"Now!" Vicky yelled, when the stern was clear of the sea for an instant, and Chip slid the hatch open, helped Ah Chi over the boards, and went down with him to dress the wound, closing the hatch behind him. It was neatly done in a few seconds, and other than rain, little water went below.

Hugo, meanwhile, was trying to douse the storm jib. They had rigged the furling line to the cockpit and he was winching it to roll up the sail.

"She's bloody stuck again, Dad."

"I'll get it," cried Peter, snapping on to the windward jackline and making his way forward along the cabin. Their father turned on the work lights, which blazed down from the spreaders, illuminating the decks and the sea around them.

Vicky had never seen anything quite like it before. The water was patternless, chaotic peaks rising willy-nilly, colliding and racing at the boat from every direction.

"The next time I suggest going around a gale," her mother remarked cheerfully, "perhaps your father will listen." She took a nip from the flask she had exchanged for her martini glass.

Vicky said, "Hugo, shouldn't we help Peter?"

"He's all right."

But Peter was not all right. Having struggled to the foredeck, he was hunched over the stuck roller, puzzling out its mechanism, when a wave suddenly broke over the bow and knocked him flat. He raised his head like a cautious turtle and pulled himself back by his tether.

"Hugo!" their father roared. "Send Peter back and furl that bloody sail. If you can't, cut the damned thing loose before it spins us around like a top."

Hugo snapped on to the jackline and loped forward, timing the rise and fall of the boat to his advantage, covering the deck at twice the speed Peter had. When he got to the foredeck, he unshackled from the jackline so Peter could slide his shackle past him.

"Oh, for Christ's sake," said Sally, "he knows better than to—"

But Hugo was cautious, snapping back behind him on to the top strand of the lifeline that rimmed the outside of the boat, before he knelt over the furler with his rigging knife. Peter struggled back and dropped into the cockpit, exhausted, his eyes downcast. Vicky felt for him. He had wanted to prove himself and had failed miserably. He had changed, she thought; in the past he had avoided such tests. Now he sought them out—thanks, she imagined, to Mary, who either stiffened his resolve or scared him into trying harder.

"Don't trust that lifeline!" Vicky's mother called into the wind. But her voice was lost in the noise. She got up, fumbling to unshackle her own tether.

"Where are you going, Mother?"

"I want him secured to the jackline before another sea hits us. That lifeline won't hold."

"Hugo!" Vicky's father bellowed, projecting mightily from the depth of his barrel chest as he battled the helm. "The *jack*line!" But her brother couldn't hear.

Vicky started forward. "I'll get him."

"Oh, my God!" her mother cried. "Hugo! Look out!"

A rogue wave, triple the height of any they had seen, charged out of the darkness. Duncan Mackintosh spun the helm, steering into it to meet the force head-on. But the wave pulled so much water out from under the yacht that her bow would not rise.

"Hugo!" his mother screamed.

Feeling the deck plummet beneath him, Hugo looked up at the

racing wall of water. He dived for the mast, arms outstretched. Tethered to the lifeline, his harness jerked him up short just as the wave scythed across the foredeck.

Vicky saw it seize her brother. He was thrown the length of the boat, his shackle tearing along the lifeline, snapping off the stanchion tops like tenpins. His body flew past the cockpit in a blur, the last stanchion snapped, and he was gone.

"Watch him!" Duncan yelled.

There were many theories of how to rescue a man overboard, but all agreed the most important thing was to keep him in sight; a bobbing head lost in running seas was lost forever.

God was kind. Lightning struck, and Vicky, leaping onto the stern deck, caught sight far astern of Hugo's blond hair glowing like gold in a frothy white ocean.

"Coming about." Duncan threw the wheel over and *Whirlwind* staggered. Bringing about a big boat in order to backtrack on sudden notice was difficult in the best of conditions; tonight, in a gale wind, driving rain, running seas, and ink-black dark, it was near impossible. A wave broke over Hugo's head and Vicky lost sight of him, even as Chip bounded up beside her with a powerful spotlight. They swept the water with a lonely circle of light. Ah Chi, a stricken Fiona, and even Wally Hearst rushed up from the cabin with more lights and did the same, stopping only to help handle the sails as they beat back the way they had come.

They searched for hours, even as they knew the storm and the wild seas were surely battering them far from where Hugo had gone overboard. Unvoiced, too, were their imaginings of trying to survive in that water, hurled and beaten about. A numbing dread seized them even as they continued to stare into the black and violent sea. All were silent but Sally, who clung to the forestay, keening like the wind.

Heartsick, still praying for a miracle, Vicky went to comfort her.

"Keep looking," Sally screamed back at her.

Vicky retreated and stared again at the white rim of the work lights. She felt a presence, and looking up, she saw her father at the helm, his cold face rigid with grief, his eyes on her. Their gazes locked, and Vicky knew with an awful clarity what her father was thinking. Hugo was gone forever. And she was the only one who could take his place.

BOOK TWO

Two-Way Wong

"**H**ULLO, VICKY. You look lovely."

Alfred Ching offered his hand and, when she took it, leaned in and kissed her lightly on the cheek. Their eyes held and they shared the remembering gaze and "what-if?" smile of former lovers, until Vicky backed briskly away and Alfred sized up her office with an admiring glance that missed nothing. The view was modest by Hong Kong executive suite standards, Mackintosh Farquhar House having been surrounded by the newer, taller buildings invading Causeway Bay, but the woodwork and old furnishings bespoke the trading hong's long and profitable association with the sea.

"Awfully sorry about Hugo. I think about him often."

"I got your card, thanks . . . both of them." Alfred had sent a sweet note about how he admired Hugo's kindness, and another in October when word got around about her parents' divorce.

Suddenly, this morning, he had called out of the blue, and asked to come by to discuss a business proposition. She had been in Hong Kong six months and was a little miffed that he hadn't visited sooner.

But why *should* he come around?

She had used him, disgracefully. There was no other word for it, and though she had been only eighteen, today, at thirty-two, she still felt guilty.

Alfred had asked to marry her. Vicky had had no intention of marrying anyone before she could find some way to break family tradition and make more of a career for herself than organizing charities and breeding the next generation of Taipan's sons and daughters.

But she had strung him along, to manipulate her father—who had no use for educated daughters—into allowing her to attend college in New York. The ploy had worked: Her mother, predictably, protested her marrying a Chinese; while her father, the ambitious son of a clerk in the Colonial Office, had even less use for a penniless bridegroom than an educated daughter. That Alfred did not seem to hold a grudge didn't make it any better.

"Have you been away?" she asked.

"Canada and the States. I'm running a deal to buy Cathay Tower."

"I heard. I'm very impressed." The word was that until recently, Alfred had been earning a modest fortune importing animal parts from North American slaughterhouses for Hong Kong cookpots. Cathay Tower was the biggest new property in Causeway Bay—quite a career jump. "Are you really paying two billion?"

"Close."

Two billion was a colossal price that would rocket property values up all over the Colony. It was the hottest gossip of the moment, and she could not resist plumbing for more information. "Is it true you're raising PRC money?"

Alfred's almond eyes turned a trifle opaque, as if he had heard that rumor, too, and was disappointed that Vicky Mackintosh, of all people, would believe him to be an errand boy for Peking.

"I'm not fronting for China," he answered mildly. "It's a real deal."

Vicky made a mental note to suggest to her father that MacF buy some properties before prices jumped.

"Good luck. . . . You look very well, very prosperous." Indeed, Alfred glowed. He looked splendid in a pearl-gray suit and an easy smile and she was happy that her beautiful Chinese boy of so long ago had come into his own.

Over the years he had haunted her fantasies with a disturbing resilience. Months would pass without a thought of him; then suddenly she'd see a man with a well-proportioned compact build, or notice a bustling walk, or experience some monumental enthusiasm, and Alfred would rush back into memory.

Growing up in Hong Kong, Alfred had grasped at a young age that with "localization" in the Civil Service and schools undermining the teaching of English, a fluent command of the international language would be a doubly valuable tool for an ambitious Chinese on his way up. He had worked hard on pronunciation and had even gleaned an English public school accent from old movies. Later, he picked up some Australian lingo in Sydney, where he had learned the property business with a Chinese company that had emigrated immediately after the 1984 Sino-British Joint Declaration.

He had raced home the instant he got his Australian passport, thoroughly Westernized in dress and manner. In expatriate company he did not indulge the Chinese custom of picking his teeth delicately behind his hand, although, like many others as 1997 loomed, he had added his Chinese given name to the end of his Western name so that his business card now read ALFRED CHING CHU-MING. His fellow Cantonese called him a banana—yellow skin, white inside—which made him laugh: "Make that *top* banana."

Alfred Ching's Chinese friends also claimed that Western women were at best an acquired taste. In that case, he had acquired his taste for Victoria Mackintosh the instant he laid eyes on her—a great-looking woman with pale golden hair, a shapely figure, and incomparable sapphire eyes.

They had met at a charity fete at the Jockey Club—Alfred was there at the invitation of one of the mentors who had given him his start—and had plunged into a friendship unlikely in two people from such different backgrounds. He was the first Chinese boy she had ever found attractive, and she, Vicky would tease him, was the only blonde in the Colony not taller than he.

•   •   •

Back then, straight-arrow Alfred had seemed so exotic to Vicky, so
different from her expat schoolmates. Every conversation revealed
new details of a life below the Peak she had only guessed at before;
every date, different attitudes. His parents were cooks with a little
restaurant in Kowloon. The kitchen, when she finally coaxed him to
take her to meet his mother and father, was a bewildering miracle
of heat, noise, strange smells, and flashing cutlery. What sounded
like violent arguments in Cantonese exploded into laughter, while
Alfred's little sisters and brothers hunched over their schoolwork
under the affectionate collective gaze of an ever-shifting array of
busy adults and serene elders.

To this day, what little Vicky knew about the Chinese — and she
knew just enough to know she knew little, though more than most
gweipos — she had learned from Alfred: their casual cynicism, which
held no bitterness because it was merely a clear eye on things as
they were; that cynicism's dark side, an often paralyzing fatalism;
the practical value of the deferential approach, which was hell on a
forthright woman; their sense of honor toward family, clan, and old
friends, which was tempered by wise expectations; and their total
lack of interest in *what-if*s and *if-only*s.

"That's a smashing desk you've got. Was it Hugo's?"

Vicky nodded. "It's traditionally our Number Two's desk. My
father used it when he worked for my grandfather. It's from an English tea clipper. See how these moldings hinge to secure the drawers in heavy seas?" Alfred seemed happy with every word she said,
which had the effect of making her talk more than she intended to.
"The Farquhar hong bought clippers for a song when steam made
the old square-riggers obsolete."

"Good move." Alfred stroked a polished brass handle. He had
spotted the side door concealed in the room's teak paneling.

"Where does that lead?"

"Taipan's office."

Alfred grinned knowingly. "Old Chinese saying: 'Responsibility without power yield ulcer.' Bet young Peter didn't like it."

"You'd win that bet."

Peter had fought her for Hugo's office with its all-important access to their father—provoked, to be sure, by Mary Lee, to whom he had become officially engaged at the end of the summer. Refusing to kowtow to her brother had earned Vicky the enmity of Peter's fiancée, which was doubly unfortunate during a time when the family had to pull together. But one of the lessons she had learned during her middle-management apprenticeship at MacF was the difference between a turf skirmish and a survival fight. Determined to sway her father at any cost, she had demanded Hugo's office as her price for staying on.

No bluff, she had made it clear, and now it was hers, along with Hugo's desk and door and, sometimes late at night, his sturdy ghost. True, in six months she had yet to push through the paneled door without telephoning first, although during the labor crisis that hit Hong Kong in the early autumn, threatening to shut down every MacF project in the Colony, they had left it open for a week. Nor had poor Peter been her real opponent. Because on the other side of her father's office, with its own private door, was an office formerly held by George Ng, the family's aged comprador, and now occupied by Vivian Loh, who Vicky suspected had accelerated the old man's departure and blocked the promotion of Ng's son.

Vivian Loh prowled a food market in Mong Kok—a dense neighborhood of tenements leaning over narrow lanes, not far from the room where she had lived with Auntie Chen. Vegetables masked the primary commerce, for last spring's riots were not the only instance of the breakdown of British law and order. In some ways more blatant was the illegal sale of various animals for food. Snakes had always been available in season, of course, slow-moving in their wire cages, and overlooked for some reason by the Colonial masters, but until the mid-nineties a Chinese with a palate for exotic tastes had to travel to Canton for bear paw or monkey brains, civet cat and dog. Even then, if he did not consume the delicacies on site, they had to be smuggled across the border with the label *goat*.

Vivian waded through stalls of brilliant radishes and glistening peas and beans and snowy bok choy. Farther along, noodle makers strung their wares like curtains. Then came the fishmongers surrounded by plastic basins of swimming fish, which were sustained by air pumped through a tangle of clear hose. The market smelled rich with hot oil, fresh earth, and dung. The air compressors clattered, cleavers banged, twig brooms rustled, flies buzzed, and sandals shuffled a ceaseless murmur along worn cobblestones.

Attending university abroad, working with gweilos, and sharing her heart with Duncan Mackintosh, Vivian Loh occasionally discovered that a facet of her personality had become less Chinese than Western. It was usually some small perception or inclination—a desire to linger over the dinner table rather than rush off the instant plates were emptied, or a sudden deep craving for silence—but sometimes the changes were more basic. She had learned in England to appreciate privacy and to enjoy anonymity of a sort never found in China. And her eyes had opened to details she had never noticed before, among them the suffering of animals kept alive for fresh or "warm" meat.

Picking her way through an obstacle course of fish basins, she found herself quite suddenly walled in by stacks of cages. Pigs and ducks lay bound in the gutter, but these she was accustomed to. Kittens played behind mesh, blissfully oblivious to their fate. Dogs hung in the shade, already butchered and shorn to show the preferred black skin. Big civet cats struggled to free themselves with bloody paws, and Vivian shuddered at the wounds of the hunters' traps. Presiding over them was a beautiful mountain girl, perhaps fifteen, with eyes as wild as the beasts she ruled.

A hunter with long black hair in a ponytail stood proprietorially close—the girl's father or a hopeful boyfriend; Vivian couldn't tell. She glanced at him inquiringly, and he indicated with a minute movement of his head that she was to follow him into the canvas-draped back of the stall. Vivian brushed past the cages. The girl tracked her with her eyes, as if Vivian and not she were the exotic species.

Inside, in the near-darkness of the shadows, the hunter waited. He spoke a Guangdong mountain dialect Vivian barely understood. His gaze turned murderous. It took her a long moment to realize he expected a password. It was a phrase from the patriotic song "I Am Chinese."

" 'I die a Chinese soul.' "

"You can count on that," the hunter growled, "if Chen's gang catch us."

"Sorry I can't offer tea," Vicky apologized to Alfred, "but I'm rather caught up. Dad's calling from Shanghai and I'll have to excuse myself. What's on your mind?"

"Two things. First, Expat-Emigrants."

"Huh?"

Alfred started grinning as if he had won the lottery. "You're familiar with the labor shortage?"

"Intimately. I can't hire a construction worker for love or money."

"For thirteen years since the Joint Declaration the best and the brightest of Hong Kong's Chinese middle class have emigrated to Canada, the U.S., Australia—forty or fifty thousand people a year, right?"

"Right. People not allowed to vote, vote with their feet."

"All I have to do is look out a window—one with a better view than this—to see some very late jobs, such as your Expo hotel, which looks like you'll be lucky to open the middle of next century. But construction is only part of the problem. You can't hire a top secretary or even a systems analyst. We're running short of doctors, teachers—the whole human infrastructure is disappearing."

Vicky pointed to her watch. "So, what are Expat-Emigrants?"

"What is MacF doing about the problem?" he countered.

"We've been hiring fifty-year-old Chinese middle managers who get forced to retire young by the Western corporations. Beyond that, nothing works."

"Here's my idea. Let's start a business, an agency, to lure Hong Kong emigrants back to work in Hong Kong."

"How?"

"We'll treat them like expats. Bonuses for houses and cars. All the perks the gweilos get."

"That's an expensive idea." But brilliant. Vicky propped her elbows on the desk and her chin on her folded hands. Her eyes locked on Alfred's face.

"The point being to get them to settle, happily, and stay after 1997. They'll be safe with their new passports. They'll see the chance to make it big here. And best of all, I'm betting we'll get their children, many of whom are now attending American and Canadian schools, to settle permanently. A little old-fashioned Chinese nationalism won't hurt, either. And while we're at it, what we really need is a serious university—an Asian Harvard—right here in Hong Kong. Hong Kong can't survive as just another Chinese city. We must remain the English-speaking center of Asia."

"One idea at a time, please."

Alfred whipped a memo from his briefcase. "Here it is on two pages. Why don't you read it when you have time, and we can talk."

"What do you want from MacF?"

"Start-up money and access to your best new housing blocks."

"Warehousing flats will cost money, Alfred."

"I'll fill them with returnees as soon as you get them built. Think it over. Let's talk soon."

Vicky walked him to the door. "You said two things. What was the second?"

"Would you like to go out New Year's Eve?"

Vicky smiled. She felt a little sad. "You've changed, Alfred. When we first met you would have asked me out first, then talked business."

"Would you like or not like?"

He was nervous, she marveled. *Like or not like* was the Cantonese way of asking a question—eliciting either *Like* or *Not like* in reply—and when she first met Alfred, he would retreat unconsciously into Cantonese syntax when he felt insecure.

"Gregorian or lunar calendar?" she asked.

"Both."

"Gweilo New Year's Eve is tonight, Alfred. You're a little late. I'm sorry, I'm booked." She considered and dismissed the thought of inviting him to join her and the family; things were too gloomy at Peak House.

"Of course, of course. I hope you're not too disappointed in my asking so late. I've just got back from Canada. How about Chinese New Year? Big party at my parents' restaurant."

"Sounds great. What's wrong?" He had finally stopped smiling.

"I have to wait six weeks."

"Good Christ, Alfred, I'll take you to dinner midway." She leaned over her calendar. "January twenty-first?"

Alfred consulted his electronic pocket memo. "Smashing."

Their eyes met at the junction of one of their old secrets. Before she could turn away, he asked softly, "To what do I owe my good joss?"

"To finally coming by to say hello. And, I'm hoping you'll fill me in on your Cathay Tower deal."

Alfred's smile swelled. "Don't be surprised if we celebrate that night." He raised a finger to his lips. "Between us?"

"Of course. Good luck." She shook his hand and asked, "How come you waited so long to ask me out? I've been home six months."

Thrown by her directness, Alfred stammered for a second, then recovered with a sly grin. "Old Chinese saying, Vicky. 'Bring gold for taipan's daughter.' "

"You made that up."

"Learned it in my youth."

"Not from me you didn't," she snapped, stung by any suggestion she had turned him down because he was poor.

"From the Taipan," he said, and then, because he laughed, she laughed back at him.

"Now what's funny?" Alfred demanded.

"Mackintosh Farquhar women have a great family tradition of marrying poor men who double our fortunes. My father doubled the Farquhars' and my grandfather doubled the Haigs'—but it doesn't count if you get rich first on your own, Alfred."

"Then while I'm still poor, let me start doubling your fortunes with some good advice."

"What's that?"

"Go back to your roots."

"What do you mean?"

"Forget all this building and running hotels. They're cumbersome. Be what made MacF. Be a British trading company again. The old Anglo hongs understood something that the Communists and the Mafia and the Triads have always understood: Command the junction points. Stand where East meets West with your hand out. Bring the orders to China; carry the goods out. Agent. You know the edges of Asia. Use your access. In other words, be a trader again."

"Do you expect us just to give up the hotels and the land?"

Alfred gave her a tight smile. "Face it, Vicky: Gweilos and gwei-pos are never going to build Asian empires again."

"Alfred, you're daft. Mackintosh Farquhar are more than traders."

"You started out as the friend between two strangers. That's not a bad place to be in interesting times."

"We're much more than traders," she protested again. "We've built our place here."

Before Vicky could say more, her secretary buzzed.

"That'll be my dad. I'll see you in three weeks. Good luck with your project."

"What about Expat-Emigrants?"

"I like it."

Vicky walked slowly to her telephone.

So Alfred Ching had got a little edge on him, shedding a certain excessive deference to his manner. He seemed to be growing into his success. Not that he had been unsure of himself when he was younger. It was just that he had stopped apologizing.

She was glad he had finally shown up. Her private life had not been a thrill a moment, sandwiched between eighteen-hour days at

MacF. Several dinner dates with a fellow she had met at the club revealed an ambitious Londoner looking for a woman to bear the children he felt obliged to provide the world; all the better if she brought an iron rice bowl from Fierce and Mighty Mackintosh Farquhar. Fortune hunters, real and imagined, had always been a problem for a taipan's daughter in Hong Kong, and ironically, it was starting anew as childhood friends, freshly divorced, went on the prowl again.

Inspector Chip was often around the house. He had been a brick since Hugo died, bolstering her father's spirits and even mediating with her mother as the marriage disintegrated under the combined weight of Hugo's death and her father's affair.

Vicky had come in for her own share of the policeman's steady support and occasionally spent the little free time she had with him for a late supper or tea on Sunday afternoons. He seemed interested in her, but Vicky had nudged him toward Fiona instead, thinking that he'd make a decent stepfather for the girls.

Chip reminded Vicky of her beloved Hugo, in fact, with his gentle warmth and quiet humor. But the tall rangy sort, while pleasant to look at, was not exactly her type. A catalogue of the men she had fallen for would show a predominance of short, sturdy builds alarmingly similar to Alfred Ching's and her father's.

She buzzed her secretary. "Run a credit check on Alfred Ching, please." His expat-emigrant idea really did have a solid ring to it.

She took the Shanghai call.

"Hello, Dad. Sorry to keep you waiting."

"Got your fax, Your Majesty. What's up?"

"A Mr. Wu telephoned this morning, just in from Peking. Wally Hearst says he's a real heavy hitter—Comrade Han's boss at Labor. He invited us to a meeting this afternoon."

"I can't leave before evening. And I'm not meeting anyone on Hogmanay."

One of the jobs Vicky had inherited from Hugo was negotiating with the People's Overseas Labor Committee for carpenters, glaziers, and tile layers from the Mainland. During the last six months Vicky had spent the major portion of many a day struggling to assemble work crews at Kai Tak, where MacF's World Expo Golden Hotel was months behind schedule.

The white-collar labor shortage Alfred had referred to was a picnic compared to the shortfall in construction workers. While Hong Kong could easily absorb another 30,000 workers daily for the pre-'97 World Expo building boom, the PRC Labor Committee shuttled fewer than 20,000 across the border and doled them about the Territory by arcane formulas that changed upon mysterious whims.

Three weeks ago MacF had lost their glaziers to a multistory shopping center at Aberdeen on the south side of Hong Kong Island, and the project had stopped dead.

The enormous height of the Expo Golden Hotel exacerbated the mess, as MacF's construction superintendent had explained until Vicky was ready to strangle him. Jobs got in the way of one another, and the resultant backups soared from the half-finished lobby to the missing roof. Material awaiting installation blocked entrances and elevators, and those workmen she had managed to round up often waited for one job to be finished before they could start their own.

As MacF was contracting the job and MacF had financed much of it, they had no one to sue but their own subsidiaries and little opportunity to spread the risk. Typical of the way her father let things go while he negotiated landing rights in Shanghai, Vicky thought. There were too many eggs in one basket.

"Are you sure you can't come back earlier? Wu might be the break I'd given up praying for. His interpreter was very apologetic," Vicky added. "Wu is due back in Peking tonight. You know the bit: hopes he doesn't disrupt our New Year's plans; can't be helped; et cetera, et cetera."

"So they say."

"*I* say it feels like a breakthrough. You know the Chinese, Daddy. When the top dog steps in they're finally ready to talk."

"If he's really top dog. All right, if it's that important I'll lend you Vivian."

"I don't want her."

"Dammit, Your Majesty, you can't meet their number-one man alone. You need a translator and counsel. Vivian's both. She'll sit on your temper for you and keep you on track. I can't leave Shanghai and I can't spare Peter."

Or trust Peter not to screw up, she thought bleakly. Poor Peter was never going to make it as a taipan, no matter how brutally Duncan Mackintosh drove him in a vain hope that he wouldn't have to bequeath the taipan job to Vicky. Peter was a number-two man, and always would be. Fabulously knowledgeable about the Chinese, he still saw both sides of a question long after it was time to choose only one. Nor could he extract advantage from his deep mines of knowledge, because all facts weighed equally with him.

"Then why don't I take Harry Cowes and a translator?"

Her father vetoed Cowes on the grounds that MacF's expatriate construction superintendent did not hold appropriate rank to attend such an important meeting.

"Then I'll take Wally Hearst." She had found the red-bearded China trader informative and eager to help.

"*No!*"

"Why not? What do we keep him on retainer for?"

"I don't want Wally Hearst mixing it up with Wu's crowd."

"What do you mean Wu's crowd? Do you *know* Wu?" Who, she wondered for the thousandth time, had he met on the red junk? And could it be that the Shanghai air shuttle deal was merely an excuse for his many trips to the Mainland?

"Under no circumstances are you to take Wally Hearst to that meeting," Duncan Mackintosh ordered in a stentorian, final-command voice. Mystified, Vicky said all that it was possible to say when her father had made up his mind.

"Yes, Taipan."

"Take Vivian. You won't be sorry."

"I'm sorry already."

He ignored that. "I'm not going to issue instructions that won't fit the moment, but don't give anything away. Remember, the PRC needs to look good on Turnover. The last thing they want is an unfinished hotel sticking out like a sore thumb. You can use that against them, if you're clever."

8

"I CAN'T BELIEVE the People's Overseas Labor Committee hung this picture in their waiting room." Vicky had broken her first rule of conduct with her father's mistress—never speak to Vivian Loh if she did not have to—but she was keyed up about the surprise meeting.

Vivian, who had confessed in the car that she was as baffled as Vicky by the Chinese about-face, had otherwise maintained her own lofty silence, although she had ventured in the elevator that the Mainlanders probably wanted something. Ever polite in Vicky's presence, she rose now and donned her glasses to examine the gilt-framed oil of a three-masted bark beating across a turquoise Asian sea. Sailing ship pictures were as common as copy machines in Hong Kong offices, and she asked, "What's wrong with it?"

Sorry she had opened the subject, Vicky said, "This is the Hong Kong headquarters of the People's Overseas Labor Committee, right? The kindly folk from the North who are supposed to supply us laborers."

"Yes."

"Do you know what the coolie trade was?"

Vivian's expression became complex, a look of guarded anticipation. "Of course."

During the war-wracked nineteenth century, starving Chinese

farmers from Guangdong and Fukien had indentured themselves overseas to plantations and railroad builders. Millions were transported to Cuba, Hawaii, Africa, and America, crammed like slaves into the holds of ships too old to be trusted with valuable opium.

"This ship was a coolie trader."

"Are you sure?"

"We owned a fleet. Everyone did. She's flying a Dent or Butterfield house flag, I think. Somebody here's got a weird sense of humor."

Today, China was still rich in people, if little else, still burdened with hungry mouths, and the PRC had, in effect, reinvented the coolie trade. The Overseas Labor Committee raked in the hard currency, appeased their underemployed masses, and, not incidentally, wielded enormous influence in a Hong Kong desperate for laborers.

"So today the poor devils live in barracks in Shenzhen and get shipped over the border in boxcars. Nothing changes. Coolies become contract workers."

"Perhaps," said Vivian, "this painting was left behind by the previous tenant. I would imagine the Labor Committee moved in recently." Having said her piece, Vivian sat down, still and composed, not a silken hair out of place, her makeup perfect, her eyes remote.

Vicky fell silent. Vivian was right, of course.

PRC officialdom had galloped across Hong Kong like a monsoon fungus. Twelve years after the 1984 Joint Declaration, they were still taking over new offices daily. Entire departments seemed to encamp from Peking, for a Hong Kong posting was eagerly sought by everyone, from the highest administrator to the lowest clerk. The Bank of China had built the tallest building in Asia; it towered over Central district like a silver train stood on end, but Peking had filled it quickly with bureaucrats and had soon gone renting more space.

Cheap space. The early, profligate years of rubbing shoulders with capitalists were over. The Communists had reverted to frugality when inflation had forced them to curtail economic reforms. Today, partitioned offices like these in the aging Jardine House—of "thousand orifices" round-windows fame—were the norm. Vicky could see they had cut the waiting room in half. Behind the airless, dingy chamber would be countless cubbyhole offices crammed with faceless clerks in white polyester shirts and plastic eyeglasses.

She had grown to hate the bureaucrats, which made it hard to prepare mentally to meet this latest official. She reviewed a basic checklist she had learned from her brother Peter and her own experiences of the past six months.

When doing business with Mainland China it paid to remember that every man and woman over the age of thirty still carried scars from the Cultural Revolution; the memory of ten years of chaos did not go away. Also, they belonged, in the deepest sense, to a controlled society where every move was observed by others and any slip could have dire results. Finally, there was the great paradox between the Chinese belief that China was the center of the world, *Zhong guo*, and the economic fact that it was still a much poorer society than the despised *wai guo ren*, or foreigners.

Never underestimate Chinese poverty was the last phrase in her mind when an interpreter appeared, bowing and smiling, to lead them to Mr. Wu. He took them deep into the shabby offices to a windowless conference room, which contained an overstuffed couch flanked by two facing rows of chairs.

Mr. Wu was portly. A brand-new Hong Kong suit draped stiffly on his frame suggested he had probably arrived a couple of days earlier than his translator had said on the phone. He wore a smart red tie flecked with tiny silhouettes of blue junks. He looked, Vicky thought, as if Government Information Services had dressed him for one of their four-color publicity brochures proclaiming Hong Kong's profitable partnership of East and West. He waddled toward her with the self-important bureaucrat's stance Vicky had learned to despise on sight. But he surprised her with an engaging smile and shook hands warmly, clasping Vicky's in both of his, which were smooth and plump. Then, ritualistically, he introduced his staff, who filled the entire row of chairs on his side.

Vicky absorbed a blur of Zhaos, Chins, Hus, and Lis. Several, she reminded them, she had already met at earlier meetings. But Mr. Han, the deputy head of the Labor Committee who had chaired those meetings, was missing. A significant glance from Vivian indicated that she, too, thought that meant some sort of break-through.

When Mr. Wu was done introducing, Vicky presented Vivian, nearly gagging on the title her father had bestowed upon the Chinese woman: "Director of New Projects."

Then they all sat, Vicky on the couch beside Wu, Vivian pointedly taking the second chair from the couch. The first chair was reserved for interpreters, and Vivian was announcing her own importance at MacF—which, Vicky noticed, was not lost on Mr. Wu.

He inquired about the health of Vicky's father. Vicky conveyed Duncan Mackintosh's regret at being unable to return from Shanghai. Wu graciously apologized for the short notice and Vicky insisted he had put her to no trouble.

She had endured Mainland Chinese business-meeting manners for the last half-year on her endless quest for workmen. By now it was second nature to don a dignified smile notable for its reserved cordiality and to lean forward slightly to demonstrate interest in whatever subjects Mr. Wu, who was wreathed in similarly careful smiles, chose to raise. Down the row of chairs on the PRC side, the regular Labor Committee officials wore the same attentive masks, while Vivian's expression suggested that her whole life had been dedicated toward this meeting.

It would take more than six months, however, to shed completely five years of New York habits and her Hong Kong upbringing, and Vicky had to expend serious energy suppressing her impatience. The Peking bureaucrats could expand a simple How's-the-family-fine-what-do-you-got-for-me into an afternoon of creeping banality. Wu, thankfully, was quicker off the mark than his predecessor, and he spoke Mandarin. Vicky interrupted occasionally to ask his interpreter to clarify words and phrases she had missed. When she did she glanced at Vivian, who nodded almost imperceptibly, vetting the explanation.

Wu explained that he was the Overseas Labor Committee's executive director for all China south of the Yangtze River. He controlled the movement of labor from the provinces of Hainan Island,

Guangdong, Fukien, Jiangxi, Zhejiang, the city of Shanghai, and, of course, the Special Administrative Region of Hong Kong. Mr. Han, by contrast, had been responsible only for Hong Kong and the Guangdong border city of Shenzhen.

Vicky professed gratitude, both ritualistic and real, that such a busy official would meet to discuss her small problem. Wu protested he was hardly so important an official to be too busy to meet the only daughter of the Taipan of Fierce and Mighty Mackintosh Farquhar.

Everything stopped while a middle-aged tea lady in a Mainlander's shapeless blouse and trousers poured water from her aluminum thermos into the tea leaves and covered the cups to steep. Finally, the labor czar got down to it.

"We are told you have a problem with the magnificent Golden Dragon Hotel at World Expo."

"Labor," Vicky answered with a bluntness that made Vivian wince. "MacF needs construction workers. We are nearly finished, but there's important interior work to be done, and we have to wait for windows. We pay top wages, of course, but we still can't fill our crews. Not only at Expo, but at our Cheklapkok Airport Hotel, too." Her father was right: Her strongest card was the publicity factor. "Mackintosh Farquhar is embarrassed to have two such visible buildings standing unfinished, as so many foreigners will be visiting Hong Kong for Turnover."

"Did not Mr. Han send you workmen and hotel staff?"

"Occasionally. But we need steady, dependable seven-day-a-week crews. Not a day here and a day there. Nor are hotel staff much use in an incomplete hotel," she added tartly.

"Are there no workmen left in Hong Kong?"

Anger tugged her mask like a cat's paw. Vivian stirred beside her, a warning rustle. Vicky lowered her eyes. "We are a small company, Mr. Wu. We have not been successful in the competition for workers."

"Have you considered hiring Japanese contractors?"

"My father has not forgotten the Japanese occupation of Shanghai."

Mr. Wu acknowledged this sure-fire route to the Chinese heart with a sympathetic smile, although quick calculation would reveal that Duncan Mackintosh had been seven years old when the Japanese seized Shanghai, and the Public Security files would probably show he had been bundled off to school in England.

"It is also true, Mr. Wu, that Mackintosh Farquhar Construction has built all our hotels, and my father preferred that such an important hotel as this World Expo, which is a Hong Kong showplace, should be built to special standards, as it will represent in its small way China's most visible Special Administrative Region."

"We are a poor country," said Wu.

A little alarm beeped in Vicky's brain at this non sequitur. She looked to Vivian, who leaned forward quickly. "Excuse me, Mr. Wu. China is rich in our people's energy. One only has to consider the great harbor improvements at Shanghai and Guangzhou to admire such wealth."

Vicky listened with grudging admiration. In two short sentences Vivian had reminded Wu that China had manpower to spare and that, despite vast labor-intensive efforts to improve two of her major harbors, Hong Kong was still, far and away, the preeminent deepwater port on the China coast, thank you very much.

Wu smiled. "Effort is not always rewarded, is it?"

"Mackintosh Farquhar rewards effort with top wages," Vivian replied. "Those crews Mr. Han was able to procure went home happy."

Vicky liked the reminder that Han was not up to the job, as Wu must be. She added, "MacF has always provided an iron rice bowl. We keep people long and happy. We could do the same for your crews, Mr. Wu."

But Wu went off on yet another tangent.

"In my travels I have noticed that airport buildings are better located to represent cities. So often these days, the important international traveler never leaves the airport, conducting his business there if facilities are good."

"MacF is completing a fine new hotel at Cheklapkok Airport. Of course, there, too, we have labor problems." She glanced at Vivian, who returned a stone-cold stare—an unmistakable *shut up*. What had she said wrong?

Wu knew. His smile got bigger. *"That* is the important hotel to finish. How wonderful it would be if you were open for business on Changeover Day when so many thousands arrive to celebrate."

"The celebration ceremony is taking place at Kai Tak. Our hotel unfinished there would look unfortunate."

"Oh, indeed," said Mr. Wu.

Vicky was painfully aware that she had just played her hole card very badly. "The Golden Dragon Hotel at Kai Tak is the centerpiece of World Expo."

Wu beamed and brought his palms together in a silent clap. "Exactly! And it is *that* which concerns certain powerful officials in Beijing."

The cordial smiles opposite evaporated. Wu's subordinates, even the translator, had turned expressionless. Vivian gave her a look of disbelief. Vicky returned a grim smile. At least now they knew why Mr. Wu had come to Hong Kong. He had come to steal a hotel.

In that light the crazy six months past made sense. The labor shortages had thrown MacF construction behind schedule, but never irrevocably so. If they picked up the pace they could still finish by Turnover Day. Angrily, she realized that the Chinese had been playing her along, wearing her down, softening her up. By cleverly manipulating the labor market, they had kept MacF just behind schedule, probably assuming that MacF could finally be persuaded to give it up. This afternoon of to-ing and fro-ing would culminate in a lowball offer to buy the hotel, couched as a favor to relieve MacF of a troublesome burden.

"Let me see if I understand you. You—"

"It is quite simple." Mr. Wu began to explain, but Vicky barely heard him over the dark wind of memory keening through her mind. Away in New York, she had been astonished when her father had first won the contract to build at World Expo. How on earth had he pulled off the coup? Why had the powerful Chinese-Anglo hongs like Two-Way Wong's and Y. K. Pao's allowed Mackintosh Farquhar to snatch such a prize?

The answer perched beside her on the sofa. The PRC had used its influence with the Expo consortium, the Hong Kong government, and the banks (of which the Bank of China was a major player) to steer the hotel project toward MacF. Why? Because MacF could be trusted to build a better hotel than a Chinese state company, but was not strong enough to defend itself against extortion by a conspiracy of high Chinese officials.

Fleetingly, Vicky remembered her father's rendezvous with the red junk. But whoever he met at sea that day obviously hadn't stopped Mr. Wu and his Beijing cronies from scheming for personal profits behind a wall of Mainland bureaucracy. The thieving swine—as her mother would surely dub them—could teach New York City's Mafia a thing or two.

A second glance at Vivian showed her that her father's mistress appeared to be calculating a compromise. Vicky's face hardened. She would see every official in the room dead before she would accept that.

"I'm sorry, I didn't follow that last. What is quite simple?"

"Some officials—Beijing men, not in my department," Wu repeated with a patient smile, "are questioning whose name is most appropriately found on the centerpiece of the World Expo."

"The owner's name. The name of the 'old friends' who launched the project."

"Ah, but you've cut so clearly to the true question."

"Which is?"

"Some are asking who should own such a singular building."

"A Hong Kong name," said Vicky, "humble as it is"—she was scrambling to inject civility into her argument—"would demonstrate to the world the *fairness* of One Country Two Systems. Wouldn't you agree?"

Wu's wispy eyebrow arched dubiously.

"A gweilo name," Vicky plowed on, "to assure the gweilos in New York, Washington, London, and Zurich that their money and people are safe in Hong Kong. And that it is still safe to invest here. Unmolested."

"It is suggested in Beijing," Wu countered mildly, "that an Asian name would do just as well. Some even say the firm presence of the state would be most assuring of all."

"What do you think, Mr. Wu?"

Wu glanced at his watch, a Cartier knockoff if Vicky could trust her eye. "I, unfortunately, am expecting a call from Beijing. I wonder, could you possibly excuse me, Ms. Mackintosh, for five minutes, perhaps ten, no more? Perhaps you and Ms. Loh would enjoy tea."

Summoning up an icily superior voice that would have done her mother proud, Vicky started to say, "We have had enough tea," but Vivian cut her off. "Thank you, we would like tea. And may we retire to the waiting room?"

Vivian settled quietly into an overstuffed armchair under the painting of the coolie trader and sipped her tea. Vicky paced before the big round window, glaring through their reflections. The PRC, she noted bitterly, had neglected to clean the glass. She breathed deep and tried to ease the kinks out of her neck, but her heart was pounding from a combination of suppressed rage and raw fear. They had her. They had her bad.

Beyond the window the harbor lay blue-green, dotted with a thousand ships. If New York had stolen her soul with its time-spanning elegance and the grandeur of measured space that no Asian city could match, Hong Kong was so much more immediate—a city where everything worth competing for could be seen from one tall building: the glittering towers, the restless ships, and the biggest prize of all, China spreading endlessly north.

Vicky tried to think, but her eye was drawn—as it was so often since Hugo had been lost—to the typhoon shelter, where her mother now lived on the boat. Sally's spirit had crumbled. She had ceased to talk about anything but Hugo, and did little but drink. When Vicky had finally recovered sufficiently from Hugo's death to try to help her, she had mustered the courage to confront her mother with a plea to join Alcoholics Anonymous. "I'll go with you," she concluded.

Sally had laughed. "There are two sorts of people in the world, darling. Those who can afford to drink and those who cannot. I am the former, thanks to your father's beneficence."

When Sally Farquhar Mackintosh had finally tumbled to Vivian, or acknowledged what she had known all along, she had demanded a novel divorce settlement they were still buzzing about on the Peak: Duncan Mackintosh retained control of MacF and kept their houses and their investments. All Sally asked was her husband's beloved *Whirlwind* and enough money to buy gin, pay Ah Chi, and maintain her mooring at the club.

Across the harbor on Kowloon, Vicky could see the Peninsula Hotel's striped awning. She wondered whether her father took Vivian there. He had always liked the showy lobby with the music playing. Not my business, she reminded herself. Her business, her responsibility, jutted into the harbor east of Kowloon, where the glittery Expo buildings clustered around the tall hotel Mr. Wu was maneuvering to steal.

Of theft she had no doubt. Mr. Wu's unspoken offer had hung in the air like a thrown net: China would supply the workmen to finish Golden's airport hotel if MacF would sign over the Expo Golden.

Vicky leaned into the round window's recess, trying to see Lantau Island, but it was too far from Central and hidden behind the bulge of West Point.

Location, location, location—the sorry old refrain she had learned so bitterly on Manhattan's Seventh Avenue, which the luxury clientele had regarded as a hundred miles from Fifth. Lantau was an hour's drive from Central, but it might as well be in Bombay when the traffic was thick.

Her teeth ached from grinding them. Mr. Wu's crocodile smiles would be sheer joy compared to her father's sneering that she had negotiated the trade of a luxury hotel in the hottest project in Hong Kong for an airport motel.

Another angry thought riddled her mind: Her father had sensed this coming and left her to take the blame.

"God, this galls me," she blurted. "It's out-and-out extortion. Wu's got the entire PRC against me." The dirty window reflected a smile on Vivian's face that Vicky—in a state of about-to-explode rage—could only interpret as superior.

"Any bright ideas, China trader?"

"You mustn't let them steal it."

"I don't see much choice."

"You cannot give away that hotel," Vivian said firmly. "Your father's desires are quite clear."

"You are not here to interpret my father's desires," Vicky said coldly. "You're here to translate and counsel."

"I counsel you to obey your father."

"My father's not here. I'm in charge. I see no way to keep that hotel. And you don't either, do you?"

Vivian's silence was all the agreement she needed. "All right, China trader," she said again, "any bright ideas?"

Vivian tilted her pretty face to the ceiling, closed her eyes, and sat silent for ten seconds. "Ask for something else. In return."

"Like what. An exit visa?"

"Something of value," Vivian continued in her maddeningly collected way. "Allow Mr. Wu to give you face."

"Give *me* face?" Vicky exploded. "*Face?* All I ask is fair treatment. They can keep their bloody face."

"You'll both feel better."

"Both?" She whirled from the window, leaning closer and closer to Vivian as her anger grew. "What's his problem? He's getting everything he wants. Did you see that fat bastard gloat? If I were my father I would shut the project down and just sit on it. It would be worth the carrying charges to see how the PRC likes having a derelict tower in the middle of their showplace. Do you know the worst damned thing of all? At the end of the day, after they botch it, they'll hire MacF to manage the bloody thing."

Vivian listened silently, gaze attentive, eyes revealing no reaction. "All right," Vicky finally asked, "what do you mean, allow them to give me face?"

Vivian made to stand up and Vicky realized she was leaning too close. She turned back to the round window, where Vivian joined her. The two women stared straight ahead, speaking to each other's reflection.

"The PRC must not appear to steal your hotel."

"They *are* stealing it."

"But they must not *appear* to steal. Do you understand what I mean?"

"Yes, dammit. I'm not a child. You're saying that the only defense we have is the PRC's desire to appear honest, so the business community thinks it's safe to stay in Hong Kong."

"It is vital," said Vivian, "even though individual officials, and sometimes entire departments, are going to take advantage of their power. The city will be abandoned if they don't seem fair."

It was, Vicky conceded through the haze of outrage that was nearly blinding her, a little like doing business in New York, where powerful international corporations were forced to accommodate unions and contractors controlled by the Mafia in order to build their headquarters. It was an expensive accommodation, immoral, and pernicious to society, though it worked day-to-day. And yet it was one of the reasons corporations left New York.

"Only one of our defenses," Vivian corrected. "Remember that Mr. Wu puts himself personally at risk when his department steals. Someone honest may be listening—"

"Fat chance!"

"Remember, too," Vivian continued patiently, "we can use it against him some day, which is another reason he wants to give you face. Ask for something of value. Something only they can give you. You could come out of this 'old friends.' "

Vicky glared at the city. The highways to the Kowloon tunnels were backing up already, though it was only early afternoon. The Lantau and Tsing Yi bridges would be thick with limos, buses, and taxis, a dragon dance in slow-step. Their hotel guests would need helicopters to get between Cheklapkok Airport and Central.

"I want a high-speed ferry franchise from our airport hotel to our own piers in Central and Causeway Bay." Glancing sidelong at Vivian, she saw a satisfying flush rise to the China trader's cheeks.

It was a terrific idea. Vicky could see the ads: "Central's Best Hotel Is at the Airport." In fact, the ferry service would allow them to go flat-out deluxe. With its own pier, the hotel would be closer in time than the Regent or the Pen. They could even open some five-star restaurants in the hotel as well, because they could transport expense-account travelers from Hong Kong Island.

"They'll want to be partners," Vivian warned.

"Fine. If the PRC wants to go partners, let them crew the ferries. One more labor shortage we won't have to worry about."

"Yes," said Vivian noncommittally. "A good idea."

"Vivian, don't play cat and mouse with me. If you're going to advise, advise."

"It is only that Hong Kong crews have a better attitude."

Vicky almost smiled. But she hated to admit that the Chinese woman was right there on her wavelength.

"And let's ask for a Kowloon pier too. Up at Tsuen Wan, near the factories," she added, thinking of the wealthy American and European garment trade that depended on Hong Kong for their better wares. Up to the factory by luxury shuttle to oversee their operations, then down to Central to swing deals with their bankers and party at night. She offered Vivian a big, bright smile.

"If they must give me face, we must allow them to give me a lot of face. *Shr?*"

"Yes, of course," said Vivian. "*Ju ni hau yun.*" Good luck.

"Do you think we can make it happen?"

"Perhaps you wish to discuss it with your father first?"

Vicky bridled again, resenting Vivian's intrusion in their lives.

"You can tell Mr. Wu you must discuss it with your father," Vivian amplified, "and buy time. Let me propose the barest outline of the swap and the ferry franchise."

Vicky nodded with a grim smile. "Now *he's* under the gun. *He's* got to finish the hotel in time for Changeover."

•   •   •

But Wu had a surprise for them. He had stolen a march. Beaming, he pointed to a videophone attended by a pair of self-important technicians.

"I took the liberty of ringing your father in Shanghai. Perhaps you might bring him up to date on our progress." The technicians fiddled, and a moment later the high-definition Japanese screen lit up with her father's face.

Duncan Mackintosh was not wasting any niceties on Comrade Wu. His broad, high brow was furrowed with annoyance and he looked like a busy man who has been interrupted for a trivial matter. "What's up, Your Majesty?" he growled, as if they were alone on the videophone.

Vicky knew it was partly an act and took his lead, pitching Wu obliquely by answering her father with the proposal she and Vivian had worked up in the waiting room.

Her father turned pink at the idea of surrendering the Expo Golden. His mouth tightened and his eyes narrowed to angry slits. She could only guess how he would yell if they were not under the scrutiny of their Chinese opponents. To her relief, he paid her the compliment of accepting her judgment. And when she launched the ferry proposal, he gave her ammunition in his cool answer.

"I don't like it. And it goes without saying that if I ever did agree, they'd have to match the other offers we've had on the hotel." Those offers were news to Vicky, but they could coerce someone into making a solid-sounding bogus bid. "I'll think about it," he mused. "Of course, we'd require a minimum thirty-year franchise on the ferries."

"Of course, Taipan."

"It'll cost them. We've got land and construction expenses to cover, interest, and quite a few years' lost profits."

Mr. Wu had been listening impassively. At Duncan's last statement his eyes widened slightly, and he leaned closer to the videophone, smiling. "Your daughter much imagination," he said in English.

"Poor imagination," her father demurred, deflecting the compliment in the Chinese fashion.

Wu turned a knowing smile toward Vivian and delivered Duncan an obscene Western wink. "So fortunate, then, she receive wise advice." His voice dripped insinuation, which was a mistake with Duncan Mackintosh.

The Dragon Smile nearly exploded the screen. "You bet, Mr. Wu. I'm a lucky man. . . . Your Majesty, Peter and I will be home for Hogmanay tonight, provided we can get a flight out of this hellhole. Lucky you live in Peking, Mr. Wu. It's absolutely amazing how fast a great city can turn to shit."

The screen went blank, except for the Hong Kong Telecom logo. Vicky glared at Vivian, who was alight with a proud, adoring smile.

Wu, struggling to contain his embarrassment, asked, "What is Hogmanay?"

"A Scottish New Year's party. I'm sorry you have to go back to Peking. I hear it's rather cold this time of year."

Wu shrugged manfully. "Duty calls."

With that, Vicky played the cards that Vivian and her father had dealt her. Wu's answer would tell her how good or bad the odds of agreement were. "Shall we meet again in a few weeks?"

"That could be arranged."

"And we'll see how the building has progressed," Vicky said casually.

Wu nodded to the man beside his translator. "Mr. Hu will see to your labor needs until then."

"You're too kind."

"It is nothing."

"You know MacF owns a little distillery at Glen Affric in Scotland. Could I send a bottle home with you? We can toast the New Year long distance."

"Oh, a *drinking* party."

Vicky's face clouded up. "Not only drinking," she said sadly. "It's really supposed to be a family party. Everyone comes home, who can."

9

"AH CHI!" Tai-Tai shrilled like a Cantonese. "Come down here this instant!"

From *Whirlwind*'s masthead the shape of the boat looked like a gweipo's eye. Ah Chi was swaying high above the typhoon shelter in a bosun's chair, wondering where he could borrow 100,000 Hong Kong dollars for his wedding, now that Dragon Face had bought another boat—the staysail schooner *Mandalay*—which had her own boatboys with their own wedding parties to borrow money for.

Ah Chi had stayed with *Whirlwind*, and this last afternoon of 1996 found him reeving a new halyard through the main mast for want of anything better to do with his time. Other yachts were streaming off on celebrations. The fishing junks were in, and cooking and kerosene smells rose on the cool breeze as a mackerel sky lowered and the city lights began to glow.

"*Ah Chi!*"

He knew she was half-drunk. Less drunk, she was silent. More, she cried.

Whirlwind hadn't left the shelter in six months. Huang had quit, and as they never sailed, Ah Chi had no excuse to hire a replacement, which left him the dirty jobs, while his former, lazy assistant had gone on to prosper, smuggling people to the Philippines. Huang's new boat, an overpowered diesel sampan with long-range tanks, was the envy of the shelter. Ah Chi spent the long days cleaning *Whirlwind* and running the occasional errand for Tai-Tai.

His girlfriend, Hua, liked the arrangement. She lived on a sampan nearby, to which Ah Chi sculled at night, after Tai-Tai passed out. They would lie on pillows in the dark, watching the great lighted wall of the city, planning their wedding. Tonight Hua wanted him to come early. Her clan was gathering on their biggest junk. But Ah Chi was worried poor Tai-Tai would fall overboard if he left her alone before she slept.

"Ah Chi!"

He had rigged the bosun's chair with a hand-held friction brake, which he now released. Plummeting like a stone, he slowed his descent at the last minute and landed lightly beside Sally Farquhar Mackintosh, who had come up on deck in a wrinkled silk robe.

"Take her into the sampan dock, please. It's New Year's. We've got a pickup."

A hundred sampan owners would be delighted with the job of ferrying people and supplies, but Tai-Tai demanded that he drive *Whirlwind* to the dock for even the simplest errand. That was fine with Ah Chi. The six months they had stayed in the shelter was the longest period of time in his life that he had not been at sea, and he felt himself losing his edge. Motoring about the shelter helped a little. He started the diesels, slipped the mooring at the bow, retrieved the stern anchor, and headed for the club.

He wondered who they were picking up. They hadn't bought any of the cheese and pâté oddities the gweilos regarded as party foods, nor had Tai-Tai ordered the guest cabins prepared. She went forward as he negotiated the channels and stood on the bow, steadying herself with one hand on the forestay and staring, as she so often did, at the new jib furler and the broken portside lifelines she refused to replace. Ah Chi had smoothed the jagged tops of the stanchions, which was as much repair as she had allowed.

At the sampan dock, people watched sidelong, the way gweilos did while pretending not to stare. Tai-Tai was aloof in her wrinkled robe and uncombed hair. She tossed the bowline as Ah Chi nursed the boat closer, and someone caught it and took a wrap so Ah Chi could power against the dock.

"Hello," she said in her big, clear voice, and a few mumbled, "Hello, Sally."

Ah Chi was still proud of her. She was a taipan's daughter, and if anyone didn't like it they could piss off. "Not to worry, won't block the dock more than a sec. *There!* Ah Chi. There's a good fellow."

A case of champagne waited on a dolly. Ah Chi went for it, hoisted it easily to his broad shoulder, and stalked back.

"Champers!" Sally explained airily to their audience. "New Year's Eve. Got to have champers! All right, you lot, cast off." Someone threw the line and she coiled it and wandered below with a vacant smile. Ah Chi turned the yacht and drove quickly back to the mooring.

He had to talk to her about borrowing money for his wedding party. He had hoped to ask before tonight, to surprise Hua, but he knew that the holiday hovered darkly in Tai-Tai's heart.

"Ah Chi!" she called up the companionway. "Bring that champers below after you tie up and put a few on ice."

He leaned over the wheel so he could see down into the darkened cabin, where she spent most of her time. "Yes, Tai-Tai."

"Then you take the night off."

"Thank you, Tai-Tai. I stay."

"It's New Year's Eve. You must have a girl waiting. You still go with Hua, don't you?"

"Yes, Tai-Tai."

"Clear off, then."

"Yes, Tai-Tai."

"Take her one of those champers. Happy New Year."

A Hong Kong sunset, Two-Way Wong once read in a glossy picture book his grandchildren gave him, was romantic enough to soften the heart of the most ruthless tycoon. A profoundly ignorant thought, he reflected. Sunset in Hong Kong was like anything beautiful; the greater its beauty, the sharper the goad to own it.

He was overseeing the final preparations for tonight's New Year's Eve party from his favorite perch, an elevated sitting area butted into a sheet-glass corner of the ballroom under the headquarters floor of World Oceans House. The interior corner of his private observation deck was separated from the ballroom by low glass cabinets in which were displayed porcelain objects, including a bowl that had been used by the last dowager empress of China. Two-Way Wong had bought it for eight million U.S. dollars at Christie's, where his agents had standing instructions to bring Chinese art back from the West. Other agents commissioned thieves who stole to order from poorly guarded, impecunious museums.

From his soft leather swivel chair he could observe in one direction his young servants gliding about the reception room and, in the other, Hong Kong, where the setting sun was turning the city and the sky dusky pink and the harbor slate-blue. Some of his Mainland-built Red Ship Fleet rode at anchor, circled by busy lighters, and his gambling liners were boarding passengers at the Ocean Terminal.

Night fell quickly in the subtropical latitudes. Ships, ferries, tugs, and lighters winked across the harbor. The junks traveled dark.

On land Two-Way could see more lights, strings of lights draped from the dark peaks above the office towers, marking the roads that wound up the hills from Central. Streams of taillights showed people heading home from work or out to the many parties scheduled tonight. But even though it was night, and gweilo New Year's Eve, arc welders continued to glint and wink about the city—sharp blue pricks and sudden white flashes that disco-lit the steel skeletons of buildings under construction.

Two-Way turned back to his ballroom, which glowed. He raised a wrinkled hand. A beautiful boy came running.

"Champagne."

"Yes, *Lao Yeh.*"

Few still alive on the China Coast dared call him Two-Way to his face. He was Grandfather or Master to his Chinese help, Sir

John to the Brits, and Wong Li, his common "Old-Hundred-Names" name, to the Mainlanders. Some local gossip columnists had persisted in calling him Two-Way until one of their number lost his typing fingers in a door. International journals like *Asiaweek* occasionally dared, and he looked forward to the day when they, too, found it wise to give him face.

The boy raced back with a brimming glass. Two-Way touched it to his lips, then rested it beside him where he could watch the bubbles.

"Lao Yeh? Do you like or not like?"

An exquisite sixteen-year-old in a silk tuxedo indicated with a trembling hand that the room awaited his approval. The stewards, waiters, bartenders, and kitchen boys had lined up like little soldiers. Two-Way rose painfully, propped his hand on the porcelain cabinets that cordoned his sitting area, and slowly inspected every detail in the room. Tables for ten, set with gold and crystal, surrounded the dance floor. Flowers erupted from ancient vases. Bars in three corners were stacked with champagne glasses, and a fern forest, dense as a hedgerow, concealed the bandstand, except for a runway upon which pop stars of the moment would perform their latest hits.

Suddenly he sensed motion behind him. Turning back to the glass, he saw the bright strings of portholes and the floodlit superstructure of a great ship bearing down on the Ocean Terminal. The Cunard Line's *Queen Elizabeth 2* had arrived in Hong Kong a full day late, her aging machinery having suffered another breakdown in the China Sea. Two-Way knew her well. He had tried to buy the *QE2* for an offshore gambling ship, but the British had balked, apparently committed to nursing along their last symbol of sea might until it finally drifted onto a reef.

He shook his head in mock astonishment. The luxury liner, halfway around a world cruise, was calling in Hong Kong to retrieve a hundred retiring senior British civil servants who had taken advantage of sea-travel allowances issued by the Colonial Office a generation ago. The Brits would never cease to amaze him. Six million abandoned Hong Kong Chinese awaited the New Year in fear and anger, everyone expected new riots in Kowloon, and here the British, who most Chinese believed had sold them out to Beijing, were sailing home in brazen splendor.

At that moment his astonishment soared to new heights. For instead of continuing on to the Ocean Terminal pier, the lighted ship turned her bow to the tide and dropped anchor in the middle of the harbor. The anchor plunged into the water with a roar of dragging chain that Two-Way could hear through the insulated glass. The tide bore her back. Slowly the chain fetched up. And the QE2 came to rest between the tip of Kowloon and Central District, beside the route of the Star Ferry.

The Brits' intent was security; an angry mob might well storm the Ocean Terminal. But, while safer in the middle of the harbor, the luxury liner was doubly visible from both shores, the hundreds of ferries passing daily, the buildings and the promenades. In forty-five minutes every Chinese in the Territory would hear that the gweilos were running.

He couldn't have planned it better himself. He swiveled his chair around to his ballroom and panicked his frightened major domo with a chilly smile. "Excellent. It looks as if we'll have an interesting party—but clear those tables from the windows. Make room for everyone to stand there and watch the show."

The boy caught himself just in time with a mental *aieeyaa*. He had been about to suggest that the harborside window wall presented a poor angle to watch the stage. But fools, no matter how attractive, never remained long in Two-Way Wong's employ. The Taipan had meant that the real show tonight would occur *outside* the windows. One could earn a tidy fortune selling tickets for the roof. If one dared.

10

THE DAUGHTER WAS every bit as bad as the father.

She was as hard and brusque, as much a hostage to her temper as he was to his. She blustered when she wasn't sure and concealed nothing when she was. Her ambition flew for all to see.

Every bit as bad as her father. The question lingered, though: Was she as good? Had Vicky Mackintosh been blessed with Duncan's magnificent stupidity? Could she conjure enormous, brilliant ideas and forge on with them, blind to difficulties? Or was she just the spoiled rich man's daughter she acted like? Time would tell, though there wasn't much time left. But if she was as good, Vicky Mackintosh would be a dangerous enemy.

Vivian Loh had her driver drop her at the Lung Kee restaurant above Central, where she shopped for dinner for her mother. She bought roast goose with plum sauce at Lung Kee as a treat, then picked up some kale and some fresh noodles, and wended her way up into the steep and narrow lanes of the ancient neighborhood where they had moved from Auntie Chen's Kowloon flat. She could still remember her bitter tears when Mother had persuaded Father that they would get ahead faster living on Hong Kong Island.

Chinese squatting in their stalls looked up curiously at the well-dressed young woman, took in her high heels and European skirt and jacket. Some spat in the gutter; others broke into broad smiles when they recognized the daughter of Old Man Loh, the chop-maker.

Her father had failed at his attempt to start a blue-jeans factory and, in grim succession, her mother's various other ideas for "making it." Vivian remembered each doomed business for the corner of a desk or a counter top or a worktable where Father expected her to come straight from school to do her homework—a radio shop, a toy factory, a jewelry shop, a candy store, and an electronics assembly plant. Finally, his health failing—and Mother gone so long they thought she would never come back—Father had found the courage somewhere to assert himself and had begun to carve chops—the stone and ivory personal stamps used to sign documents and letters and contracts—discovering, at last, a way to employ his education and his artistic talents.

"Lay ho ma?" they greeted her. "How are you?" And Vivian waved back: "Still good."

Unlike the temptress she was certain Vicky Mackintosh thought she was, she had always lived alone and regularly went home for dinner with her mother, who lived in a little flat above what had been her father's shop. Her mother rented the long-leased space to a 7-Eleven store, shoehorned into the space, and never saw the irony of finally making some money off Vivian's father. The income made her proud. She wanted to go out to a restaurant, as always, but Vivian placated her with the goose. She felt battered from too long a day in bland public places and wanted nothing more than to be inside the cozy four walls of the cramped apartment that had been her home.

From the street below came a ceaseless noise of footsteps, conversation, shouts, and radios. Through the walls TV sets blatted. Vivian put water on to boil and rinsed the kale.

"We could eat at your place," her mother said, hefting the noodles. She hated to cook, but like any Shanghainese she admired good food, and the noodles were lovely.

"It's a mess," Vivian said. "My amah's off visiting her village and I've got work strewn all over."

"At least you've got a view."

"Had a view," Vivian corrected. "Jardine Property just planted a new high-rise in the way."

"Ah." Her mother smiled, and Vivian could see her thinking that if one must lose one's view, best to lose it to a mighty hong like Jardine, Matheson. "Well, with your friends, you can always get another view."

"Frankly, I've hardly noticed."

"You work too hard."

"You're telling me."

"Where does it take you?"

"Through the day, Mother."

"Nothing more?"

"I enjoy my work. And I'm making headway."

A sly gleam shone from the depths of her mother's Shanghainese eyes, like someone clever watching from a dark cave. "You have something big cooking, don't you?" she asked, still the schemer in a world she imagined was conquered by tricks and secret codes. Figure the trick and you won. "I can tell," she whispered. "Something big."

"Just work."

Her mother wasn't fooled. "You have patience," she marveled. "I never had patience. You're going to make it big. All you need is a plan. And you have a plan. I know. I know you."

"And how was your day, Mother?"

"Look at my hair, if you must ask."

"It looks fine."

"That horrible hairdresser. The good ones have all emigrated and I'm left with the dregs that couldn't get a job in a Communist hotel."

Vivian felt her hackles rise. As long as she could remember, through their poorest days, when her father worked himself to death, her mother had tootled down to the tram, hopped off at the corner of Chater Street and the Pedder Road, and strolled to the Mandarin Hotel, where she had her hair combed out. She had grown up comfortably in Shanghai, before the Cultural Revolution, and couldn't be bothered to learn to comb it herself.

"I'm sure you'll find wonderful hairdressers in Toronto."

"It came today," her mother said casually.

"What came?"

"My Canadian visa."

"Why didn't you tell me?"

"It's not New York."

"We knew it wouldn't be. Still, you must be so relieved."

"You, too, getting me out of your way."

Vivian let her eyes settle on her mother's smooth face. Fifty-five years old, in the rose light she preferred in the flat she looked forty. She had been a devotee of the wrinkle remover Retin-A since the late '80s when it had arrived in Hong Kong, even though dermatologists questioned the efficacy of the drug on Asian skin. Her dream was to have her face done by a high-priced plastic surgeon—preferably the flamboyant sort she watched on *Dallas* reruns—a dream Vivian had no intention of paying for, because it would seem like condoning a hundred betrayals of her father.

"It's your choice, Mother. We've agreed. But change your mind if you want."

"You'll do better without me. Free to run around."

"What do you mean, Mother?" Vivian had long ago discovered that the only way to deal with her was to call her instantly on her insinuations and vague implications. Not that her mother disapproved of Duncan. If anything, she was jealous.

"I mean, you're busy traveling and working."

"I'm working when I'm traveling."

"Well, you certainly don't need an old woman dragging you down."

Vivian shrugged and spoke the truth. "I'd just as soon you stayed, Mother. I'm going to be utterly alone when you're gone. Father's gone; Auntie Chen's gone—who's left but a few old aunts and uncles I hardly know?"

Up until five or six years ago she would not have believed she would miss her mother. But they had become acquainted since Father had died, like two strangers meeting for the first time. Mother had slowed down. The demons that had driven her from dream to dream and man to man were less energetic now. She had a companion of sorts in Mr. Tam next door, who drove a cab, a steady, hardworking guy like Father. Occasionally she might talk nonsense about starting a radio taxi fleet, and now and then she would still disappear for a while, almost like a cat, returning with another mystery in her smile. All of which mattered little to Vivian now that Father was free of her.

"Well, you won't be all alone," said her mother.

Suddenly, without warning, the old hurt burned as raw as a new wound, as harsh as when she was a child. Her mother was making excuses to leave her again. She hadn't slowed down at all. Emigration was merely her latest adventure—off to something new, and screw everyone left behind.

"What do you mean?"

"You've got your friend."

"I don't ask him to be everything to me. Certainly not my mother."

"Ah."

"So stop being coy. . . . Have a good time."

"And you make the best of *your* time."

"What?"

"You're not getting any younger."

"Mother, I'm only thirty-two years old."

"Thirty-three this year, and before you know it you're thirty-five and who will marry you?"

It was too silly, and Vivian said, "I'll find someone desperate. Maybe some poor guy who's lost his business to the PRC. We'll raise pigs in Mongolia." She smiled to herself, hearing the Mackintosh expression on her own lips.

"You don't know what desperate is, young woman. You don't know."

"Maybe that's what I'm trying to remember," Vivian murmured.

"What did you say?"

She shook her head in silence. Her childhood memories of fleeing China and of China itself were vague. She found it impossible to

separate her earliest recollections from the stories she heard from
her elders. Father's uncles used to talk of warlord chaos. One claimed
to have been on the Long March with Mao. Mother constantly
mourned her family's lost comfort in Shanghai and cried for the
servants she had probably never had, but had heard about from *her*
mother.

The China Vivian knew best, however, was the China of her
father's dreams, for he had been political—fiercely and optimisti-
cally democratic, an intellectual heir to the old May Fourth Movement of 1919, which had proclaimed that democracy and science
would restore Chinese greatness.

Chiang Kai-shek's Nationalists had crushed the men and women
of the May Fourth Movement; Mao Zedong's Communists had attacked their descendants. In the Cultural Revolution the Red Guards
had tortured the last generation who dared to hope.

Vivian's own memory of China was of cold sand under her feet
before Father picked her up and waded into the dark. Her recall
ceased at the surge of water that had lifted them as the shark approached. Her first vivid image of childhood had her sitting at the
head of the class in a Hong Kong school, spouting the English Father had taught her.

Yet China filled her with wonder.

Some years ago, shortly before the Beijing massacre, she had
persuaded her father to accompany her on one of her early business
trips to Canton, the Guangdong Province capital where he had been
born. Fearful—though it was fifteen years since he had escaped the
Cultural Revolution, and Hong Kong refugees had been traveling
to the Mainland for some time—he longed to visit his mother's grave.

They had traveled up the Pearl River on a cheap overnight
steamer. The city had changed dramatically since Mao's death—whole
neighborhoods pulled down for lavish business hotels, commercial
exposition halls, and new factories. Father's house was gone, and
after much confusion tramping about cleared sections in the steaming heat, they had finally discovered a new warehouse built on the
family's grave site. Their burial ground had been looted and burned

because the Red Guards had marked it a bourgeois-class cemetery. Her father had wept. "They wouldn't even leave the dead alone."

"Where is your friend tonight?" Mother asked.

"With his family."

Her mother nodded wisely. "Holidays are always the worst."

Vivian said, "It's not like that." But of course it was, and the words in her head were: *I'm not like you.*

After 150 years merchanting in Asia, the Mackintosh and Farquhar families were still Scots at heart. So while Christmas was a simple celebration, with toys for the children and a roast in the afternoon, Hogmanay at New Year's was the biggest night of the holiday season, and all who could trekked home to Peak House for the party. Vicky remembered the upstairs and the guest house crowded with visiting cousins and the special excitement of dressing up for a party at home. The men wore kilts, the women long white dresses with tartan sashes. And Hugo would play the pipes.

There were no overnight guests this year. Gloom penetrated every room of the big old house, like a cold fog. Hugo's death was too fresh in their minds, and Sally and Duncan's separation still a live wound. Vicky had stopped by *Whirlwind* earlier, of course, and had found her mother drinking, saying little, and preferring to be left alone. Vicky had come home feeling strangely rejected.

The servants were hiding in the kitchen. And if Vicky had any doubts that it would be a grim evening, they were dispelled when she noticed her father's dinner jacket laid out instead of his Highland rig. She thought hard upon what to wear and decided that Hugo's children, at least, needed a party.

Fiona, who had struggled bravely through Christmas, was on the verge of tears. Peter was drinking, a recent failing that seemed to be beyond even Mary Lee's ability to curb. Vicky felt sorriest for Melissa and Millicent, Hugo's redheaded daughters. Ten and twelve, they seemed afraid to appear to enjoy themselves. The six months since their father had died was a long time in their short lives, yet they clung close to Fiona. Vicky couldn't figure whether they were worried their mother would cry, or afraid they would lose her next. The girls brightened visibly when Vicky came down the curved staircase in a red silk halter-top gown, and crossed the polished wooden floors on clicking heels.

"Auntie Vicky!"

"Look at you!"

"You must be freezing." This last came from Melissa, the ten-year-old, who inquisitively stroked her aunt's bare shoulders, and it struck Vicky that by the strange events of the past half-year she, of all women, had somehow become Melissa and Millicent's racy Auntie Victoria.

Millicent circled behind her. "I love your hair."

She had gathered it in a French roll with a diamond clip her mother had given her the day she moved out, proclaiming she had no need for jewels on a boat.

"Thank you, Millicent. You look lovely too. Both of you. What's everyone drinking?"

"Uncle Peter's drinking whisky," Melissa reported.

"I think I'll have champagne."

"Mum says we have to wait till midnight."

"I'll ask if it's okay now." She crossed the drawing room to where the Englishwoman sat in a window seat, gazing down at the city. "Darling. Join me in a little champers?"

Fiona raised brimming eyes. "Come on, girls," said Vicky, casting her arm around their shoulders and steering them away toward the bar, set in a mirrored alcove. "You lot help me with the bottle. Granddad's not down yet?"

"He went to telephone."

"Oh? Well, then we'll just have to open it ourselves, which is to say, you'll have to help me not break a nail. Okay?"

"Auntie Vicky?"

"What, Millicent?"

"Where will we all be next Hogmanay?"

Vicky pulled a vintage Piper-Heidsieck from the silver ice bucket. "Hey, look. It's older than you two." Probably too old. She struggled distractedly with the foil and the wire cap, wondering where, indeed, they would all be next year.

"Well, you'll be home on holiday from Gordonstoun." Hugo's old school admitted girls now. "And you, Madame Melissa, will still be in school in Hong Kong, where you will remain for the next eighty years if your grades don't improve."

"What about the Chinese?" asked the ten-year-old.

"They'll be here too."

"Won't they kick us out?"

"No way."

"What if they arrest us?"

"For what?"

"For being us."

Melissa had the steady Mackintosh eyes, and they were wide now, pretty and intense, as she waited for an answer.

The only answer Vicky knew was that, thanks to her father's committing them so exclusively to Hong Kong and refusing to diversify out, MacF had no place to go if the situation turned bad. Not even the Manhattan Golden, which had been sold at a loss.

She spotted rescue in the form of the Taipan wandering down the stairs, wrapped in thought. Let him explain. "There you are, Dad. Are the Chinese going to arrest us for being us?"

Duncan Mackintosh focused morosely on Vicky. But when he noticed his granddaughters, he smiled. "Who wants to know?"

"Melissa."

"The Chinese are going to arrest all small ladies who don't do well in school and send them to slop pigs in Mongolia. I'll have a glass of that." He took the bottle from Vicky and filled a third glass. "And you lot carry this to your mother. Tell her the Taipan orders it drunk— Walk, ladies! Don't run with a glass." He winked at Vicky.

"Cheers, Dad."

"Happy New Year, Your Majesty. Cute stunt you pulled on that Wu son of a bitch."

"I appreciate your backing my decision."

"Wouldn't do not to in front of the bastards. . . . Vivian any help?"

"Actually, she kept me from pouring my tea in Comrade Wu's lap."

Her father chuckled. "She's good at that. Pulled my chestnuts out of the fire more than once when I've lost my temper. That's why I sent her to help you."

"I'll keep her in mind, next time we have to give away a hotel."

"She told me you made the best of a bad deal. I don't love it, but Wu holds all the cards."

It was as close to a compliment as he had given her in six months, and Vicky was at a loss how to answer. "I sent him a bottle of Glen Affric."

"Hope he chokes on it." His eye slid to the view down the Peak. By some perverse geomantic coincidence that a Chinese *feng shui* expert might explain by the principles of wind, water, and dragon bones, the Causeway Bay Typhoon Shelter could be seen through a gap in the Mid-level's housing blocks, several miles and a thousand feet below. Vicky was tempted to set up a telescope so they could pick out *Whirlwind* in the carpet of boats.

"Where's Vivian tonight?"

"Get stuffed."

"Sorry," she said, not meaning it but not wanting to fight either.

He glanced around the room, seeing nothing. "God, it's a bloody morgue in here." A look passed between them and suddenly, unexpectedly, they were conspirators. "Let's clear out," Vicky whispered.

"How?"

"Let's go first-footing."

Her father brightened at once. "Get your coats, everyone. We're going first-footing. Ah Ping, get the car. Ping! Where is that scoundrel?" He pressed a nearby intercom. "*Ping*. Car. Chop-chop!"

"What," asked Mary Lee, "is first-footing?"

"We go calling," explained Peter. "For drinks. Right, Dad?"

"First we shoot off guns. Then we bring whisky and oatcakes. The darkest one goes in first. For good luck."

"Me," said Mary.

"Women are bad luck. So are redheads, small ladies. So, for that matter, are blond women. By God, we're going to bring disaster down on some poor house. But we'll try me first, then Peter, then the dark Mary, then Vicky and Fiona." His voice trailed off. They all heard the two missing names ring in the room and avoided one another's eyes. There were times Vicky could see her father's shoulders actually shrink, for in some ways, it was he who had been diminished most by the loss of his son.

"Actually we're a little early," said Peter. "Hours from midnight."

"So we'll first-foot the Chinese first. What do they know?"

He hurried to the tray in the front hall where were heaped the New Year's Eve invitations they never accepted. "We'll wander the Territory like gypsies." His voice echoed, and Vicky wondered what had suddenly gotten into him. He returned, sifting a stack of engraved stationery.

"Here we go."

He waved a sheet of thick red vellum printed with gold. "The pleasure of our company is requested by none other than Sir John Wong Li, CBE. Let's first-foot old Two-Way."

"You're kidding."

"We'll hold off firing guns and we'll leave the whisky in the car. Don't want to bring him too much good joss."

"Dad, we can't."

"We certainly will."

"We can't bring the children."

"We're fine here," said Fiona, ignoring the disappointed howls from Millicent and Melissa. "You go ahead."

"Well, let's wait a while, till Chip gets here."

"Right," said her father. "Champers for the small ladies."

Vicky put down her champagne and accepted a cut-crystal Stuart glass of malt whisky from Peter. They clinked glasses and she took a long sip of the hot, smoky liquor. Peter downed his fast. "I suspect we're all going to embarrass ourselves mightily."

Mary descended and plucked the bottle from his hand. "It's early to drink so much."

"It's been a hell of a week," said Peter, snatching it back. "Hasn't it, Vicky?"

"Leave me out of this," she answered lightly, reminded forcefully of the last year with Rod Dwyer and recent evenings with her mother.

An hour passed, and a battered old Toyota swung under the porte-cochere. "Chip's here!" The girls went tearing out to greet him.

Tall and spare in ancient evening clothes, Chief Inspector John Chypwood-Chipworth (Chip-Chip to his fellow police officers and simply Chip to his sailing friends) unfolded out of the little car like a portable easel.

Vicky's father joined her at the window. "We better give him a drink before we push on. The children love him, don't they?"

"Why is Chip only a chief inspector?" It was a rank vaguely comparable to a New York City police sergeant, rather low on the ladder, Vicky thought, for an expatriate officer in his mid-forties.

Her father shrugged. "Probably devoted too much effort to sailing. Not your hardest-working bloke, but a hell of a foredeckman." Duncan thought a moment more and added, "Localization too. Chinese ten years younger are passing him by. At any rate, he seems happy enough."

Vicky nodded. Hong Kong saw many like him—policemen, civil servants, teachers, and mid-level corporate men and women who came out for a two-year stint, fell in love with the East, and stayed a lifetime. God knew what '97 held for them.

Chip sauntered in, greeted Vicky and Fiona, pronounced every gown "super," and with Melissa and Millicent scampering around him like a pair of spaniels, accepted a whisky from Peter. He had brought little corsages for the girls, and sat with Fiona while she pinned them on.

"You won't leave Hong Kong, will you?" asked Millicent.

"I'd miss the sailing and I'd miss the girls," Chip answered with a reassuring wink at the twelve-year-old who had fallen head over heels in love with him.

Finally Duncan said, "Let's go. I can't hang about the house anymore. Wraps, ladies. Cold fog predicted tonight."

Vicky went for a shawl, inspected her face, and headed out to the car, where Peter and Mary and Chip were waiting. "Dad's on the phone again. Where's Fiona?"

"Said she'd rather not," Chip said.

"I'll stay with her."

"She'd just as soon be with the children. She means it, Vicky. Do come."

"I'll just talk to her a moment." Vicky hurried into the house. Her father was still in the side hall, his voice an indistinct rumble, his whole body hunched over the phone.

"It's him again," Vivian's mother whispered. "His Shanghainese is excellent."

"All ten words of it . . . Hello, Duncan. Happy New Year."

"Sorry to interrupt your dinner. Why don't you show up at Two-Way Wong's?"

"Tonight?"

"I'd love to see your face."

She knew by his voice the times he really needed her. He had called earlier, just to talk. Now he had a plan. "Me too. Can you give me an hour?"

"Thanks. See you soon."

"Wonderful . . . Mother," she said, hanging up, "I'm sorry I'll have to leave early. Why don't you invite Mr. Tam in for the goose?"

"More hard work?" Her mother smiled.

"I wonder if I could borrow a cheongsam?"

"Mine would be too long on you," said her mother, clearly reluctant to lend a favorite gown.

"Since you wear yours so short it will be just right on me."

"But your shoes are all wrong."

"I thought perhaps I could borrow shoes as well. Mother, I'm a little pressed. I don't want to go all the way home to change."

"Where are you going?"

"Two-Way Wong's."

"*Aiyeee.* Of course you can borrow my dress. Why didn't you say?" She dived into her wardrobe. "Here, here. This with sequins. No! No! Here, this silver lamé."

Vivian hesitated. "It's a bit much, Mother."

"Don't be such a stick-in-the-mud. It's beautiful. You'll stand out."

Vivian held it to her. "It is quite something."

"A friend . . . a gift. Take care. I've only worn it once." She shook it on its hanger, and the gown shimmered. "Shoes. Aren't they lovely? Same source."

"I hope they're not too large."

"What? How dare you? My feet are as tiny as yours. Just because I'm tall doesn't mean I have big feet."

"You're right. They'll fit."

Her mother was steaming. There was no greater insult to a vain Chinese woman than to imply her feet weren't dainty, so Vivian said, "They're a little tight."

"Don't stretch them."

"Promise."

"But you have no jewelry. That gold necklace won't go."

"I'll get by."

"You can't go to Two-Way Wong's without jewels." She flung her hands in despair. "I have nothing."

"Mother. Look." She unbuttoned her blouse, revealing hidden beneath it a large diamond suspended from a platinum necklace.

"*What?* Where did you get that?"

She was, in fact, embarrassed, but it made her mother so happy that she covered her feelings and said, "Christmas."

"By God and heaven, he's rich."

"Not really. In fact, he's hanging on by his fingernails." She realized instantly she shouldn't have said that, but then, her mother was not likely to repeat bad news about her daughter's lover. Still, she hated it when she forgot to be careful. A blunder could destroy everything.

●   ●   ●

"I'm happier here with the girls," Fiona told Vicky. "I don't want to go out."

"I'll stay with you."

"Go," she said, smiling. "You look lovely. Have a good time. First-footing the Chinese. What will you think of next?"

Vicky hesitated, reluctant to appear anxious to run out while the girls were watching every move from a careful distance. "Do I look fat in this dress?"

"Not at all. Go on now, leave. The others are waiting."

"My friend Susan in New York always says there's nothing uglier than a fat blonde in a red dress."

"You're not one bit fat. You look wonderful. Did you see your mother today?"

"I stopped after my last meeting. . . . She was well into the champers."

"It's a terrible time," Fiona said. "Just terrible."

"Peter's drinking."

"At least he's got Mary to stop him."

"Dad's pushing him too hard."

"He's pushing all of you. Hugo was like a lightning rod, you know. He absorbed so much of your father's force. He was strong and placid. It rarely bothered him. Now he's gone, and with your mother away, who's to absorb it but you and Peter?"

"Vivian."

"I'm sure she makes him quite happy," Fiona said neutrally.

Vicky paused in the doorway. "You know, this house would be unbearable if you and the girls hadn't moved in."

"I wanted them to have a family."

"Some family."

"It's *their* family. Run along, Vicky. I'll come next year."

Vicky kissed the girls good night on the way out and ran to the car. They started down the Peak, descending the switchback road like a leaf drifting into a fire.

11

THE MACKINTOSH DAIMLER crept along in the line of scarlet, silver, and gold limousines on the final approach to World Oceans House. Like an aging raven, Vicky thought, in a row of parrots. Two-Way's liveried servants were helping guests from their cars.

"They're *children.*"

"I believe he owns an orphanage," said Chip.

"Who allows that?"

"There've been inquiries. All receive the best education. Many go on to university. And there's a job waiting when they graduate."

"Like MacF's scholarship girls?" Vicky could not resist asking, but her father did not rise to the bait.

The jade-green Rolls-Royce ahead of the Mackintoshes decanted an elderly Chinese gentleman and a young lady wrapped in a floor-length fur, dyed to match the color of the car. She was handed out by a bowing boy in scarlet tails. When the Daimler moved forward and it was Vicky's turn, she dodged the little hand. The child wasn't a day older than Millicent.

"You ought to be in bed."

"Yes, Missy," came a wary but smiling response.

Mary Lee accepted the hand as her due. She and Peter and Vicky and Chip followed Duncan into the lobby of World Oceans House, where a double row of smiling adolescents, all in scarlet tails, formed a human corridor to the elevators.

"Can't help but wonder," Duncan Mackintosh boomed in a voice that echoed off the three-story marble ceiling, "which century Old Two-Way thinks is coming up."

"You mean which dynasty, sir," laughed Peter. Duncan laughed, too, muffling Mary Lee's whisper: "You're the guest of an important man. Respect your host."

"Right," Peter mumbled, and Chip looked down at Vicky with a sympathetic grin. "And what century do *you* think is coming up?"

"I'm concentrating on the next six hours."

They filled an elevator, which appeared to be paneled in pale marble. As it headed skyward Vicky stroked the yellow-green stone. "This isn't marble. It's *jade.*"

"Apparently Two-Way's had a good year," said Duncan. "I say, Chip, got your marlinespike? Pry some bits off for the ladies."

"Left it in the car, Taipan."

Vicky glanced at her brother. They hadn't heard Duncan this light-hearted since Hugo died.

"Things went well in Shanghai?" she asked quietly.

Peter shook his head emphatically. "No."

The elevators opened on a broad foyer that emptied down a grand staircase into a chandeliered ballroom, which thundered with loud music and a cacophony of Cantonese conversation. Some three thousand Hong Kong elite had answered Two-Way's call. The dance floor was a sea of gesticulating humanity, of whom few were dancing. It looked, Vicky thought, like an old-fashioned stock exchange, a bourse before computers, where thousands stood toe to toe shouting bids. A wall of glass overlooked the dark harbor, which was surrounded by millions of unblinking neon advertisements. The *QE2* lay midway between Hong Kong Island and Kowloon, like a bar of diamonds on black velvet.

What at first glance appeared to be shiny life-size statues scattered about the foyer, down the steps, and on pedestals in the ballroom were, on closer inspection, mimes in sequined tights. At a

secret signal the young men and women shifted poses in strict uni-
son and froze again. Even their faces were covered in sequins, so it
was impossible to distinguish their eyes.

A flurry of adolescents took Vicky's and Mary's wraps and guided
the Mackintoshes to the head of the stairs, where a six-foot eight-
inch Englishman was announcing arrivals in a thunderous baritone.
The lady ahead surrendered her jade-green mink, revealing a tight
beaded dress of the same hue, which Vicky noted to Chip looked as
if it had been applied by a chemical process.

"Mademoiselle Anita Fang and Henry Wong," the Englishman
roared, and Miss Fang descended to appreciative murmurs directed
at her dress, her emeralds, and the elderly restaurateur and race-
horse owner gripping her elbow.

The servants were herding the Mackintosh party toward the giant
announcer, who had the ferocious mustache and ramrod stance of a
sergeant major mistakenly left behind in a British retreat. But when
his eye fell on the Mackintoshes, it was clear that he had been imported to Hong Kong for the evening.

"The name, sir?"

Duncan Mackintosh reddened. "Same name it's been for one
hundred and fifty-seven years."

The Englishman wet his lips and lowered the volume to a conspiratorial murmur. "Sorry, guv. I'm new here. One Brit to another,
what shall I say?"

"Fierce and Mighty," Duncan growled.

Vicky went to the panicked Englishman's rescue: "Back in colonial days, the Scots hongs took Chinese names to impress the
natives. Dent's, for example, was 'Precious and Compliant,' which
explains their early bankruptcy. Jardine is 'Happy Harmony.' We
are a feistier lot. I strongly suggest you announce us properly before
my father is provoked."

The announcer drew himself up to his fullest height and, displaying the timing of a trained actor, located a sound blank between
two phrases of the music. His voice rolled over the ballroom like a
tidal wave.

"FIERCE AND MIGHTY!"

All eyes swiveled toward the stairs.

Vicky dropped Chip's arm and stood beside her father.

"Where the devil are you going?"

"With you, Taipan."

"Bring Peter."

"I'm not carrying him tonight. Bring him yourself." She expected Mary Lee to thrust Peter into the limelight; instead, Mary kept him tightly by her side, as if she had decided it was better for the Lee family that her intended not share in the Mackintoshes' flamboyant entrance.

They began their descent, Vicky ignoring the angry glint in her father's eye. There might be a gleam of admiration mixed in with it, or there might not. She didn't care. Duncan's testy claim to 157 years had stirred her own spirit. Her father was actually a relative newcomer to Hong Kong. But she was her mother's daughter, too, which made hers an older blood connection, one that few in the city—expats *or* Chinese—could claim.

Up from the cauldron of watching faces, she sensed the heat of one set of eyes tracking their entrance. The long fine features, the unusually high brow, and the piercing eyes were a staple of countless newspaper and television reports. The crowd around him, who were watching his every move, maintained a respectful distance. He was standing, tall and braced firmly on a cane in a circle of light in the center of the ballroom.

"Our host notices, Daddy."

Duncan replied with such relish that Vicky wished her mother were along, either to restrain him or to enjoy the mayhem if she couldn't.

They plunged into the gaping crowd at the bottom of the stairs. Vicky felt them closing in behind her like a following sea. Sir John Wong's depredations were chronicled avidly, so everyone had heard a hundred times the story of how Duncan Mackintosh had lost the Farquhar line; now here they all were, about to meet in the flesh, Hong Kong gossip at its inception:

The girl on his arm must be the Taipan's daughter, the one who lost all that money in New York. Certainly not the mistress. The mistress is

Chinese. A China trader. And what does she trade? Besides, the family resemblance is unmistakable. Soften the old brigand's jaw, add the mother's famous blond hair and down-turned nose, and you have the daughter. The mother? Back to England, one supposes. Where do old gweilo wives go when their husbands drop them? No, haven't you heard? Drunk on a boat in Causeway Bay.

Faces flamed with curiosity. What would the Taipan of the struggling MacF hong say to the richest man in Hong Kong? Or put less charitably, Vicky thought grimly, what would the last independent Scot say to the Chinese who symbolized, as much as any man alive, the shift of commercial power in the East?

"It seems the dumb children grow up to be his bodyguards," she murmured to her father. Several dangerously large teenagers in black dinner jackets were lurking near Two-Way Wong. A youthful aide stood at his elbow, while servants waited with gold trays bearing champagne.

The Taipan and his daughter entered the sacred space around their host. Duncan spoke first, pointedly not extending his hand.

"Two-Way, how are you? Got your invitation. Glad we could make it this year."

The aide started to translate Duncan's greeting, but an angry tightening of the World Oceans chairman's lips indicated he understood enough English not to like his nickname. He answered in a rough Wu dialect too fast for Vicky's ear.

"Sir John welcomes you back, Duncan Mackintosh," the translator said. "Too many parties have been diminished by your absence."

"I would have come sooner, but it took a while to get the knife out of my back."

Vicky, braced for some inflammatory remark, was still barely able to stifle a laugh. Two-Way spoke again, and the translator said, "Sir John inquires about the young lady on your arm. Is this the concubine we have heard so much about?"

Vicky jerked her head up angrily. The World Oceans Taipan returned an icily indifferent gaze. She might as well have been one of the mimes scattered about the room like furniture.

"Two-Way," her father said with quiet menace, "you owe my daughter an apology."

The Chinese seemed to reflect on Duncan's demand; his piercing black eyes probed her face. Finally he spoke. Vicky smiled even before the translator repeated the familiar Chinese proverb.

"Tigers do not breed dogs."

"I take that as a compliment, Sir John. Happy New Year."

Two-Way assessed her again, probing deeper, until Vicky felt herself stripped to her soul. She suppressed a shiver and had to fight to hold his eye. When he finally spoke, the translator chose his words carefully. "Tigers are dangerous. Sir John accepts your warning, Taipan's Daughter."

"Two compliments. Sir John is a kind host." If she was hoping for a friendly reaction, she was disappointed. The tycoon planted his stick and pivoted back toward her father and spoke again through his translator.

"Sir John inquires whether you have plans. Will you retire to England when Hong Kong is China?"

"Apparently Sir John hasn't seen the Peking newspapers," Duncan replied mildly. "I'll be right here in Hong Kong. Premier Chen announced to the People's Congress that he intends to appoint me governor."

Vicky was startled to see a flicker of alarm in Two-Way's eyes. Duncan Mackintosh laughed and led her away.

"You really had him going, Dad."

"If you think witty repartee is the way to his heart, Your Majesty, you're badly mistaken."

"Your approach didn't exactly gain points."

"I'd see him in hell before I'd try to 'gain points.' He's my enemy. That makes him your enemy too. And don't you forget it."

"Dad, it's been ten years since we lost the Farquhar Line. Two-Way is a major player in Hong Kong. He's a very expensive enemy. Unless there are things I don't know. Are there?"

Her father turned on her, his face like stone. "Your enemy too," he repeated. "Be warned. If anything happens to me, he'll come after you next."

"I'll remember. But you're keeping information from me. Are you putting me in danger?"

"I'm trying to protect you, you ninny. Chip!" he called over his shoulder. "Do you see Allen Wei?"

"Dad? Did you know Two-Way in Shanghai?"

"I was eighteen when I left Shanghai."

"So was he," she said, but her father merely repeated to Chip: "See him?"

The tall policeman scanned the ballroom for Allen Wei, Hong Kong's chief executive. "There, Taipan. Standing by the windows. Vivian Loh's with him."

Behind her, Vicky heard Mary murmur to Peter: "Looks like she borrowed her cheongsam from a Club Volvo hostess."

"Dad, who'd you meet on the red junk?"

Duncan ignored her. "Peter, Your Majesty, we'll pay our respects to Allen and then blow this hellhole." Vicky took his arm again as they moved through the crowd, exchanging greetings with those they knew.

Wally Hearst waved from the side. The bearded American China trader had a very young Chinese girl on his arm, a bright-eyed, voluptuous creature with a pouty mouth and extravagant hair heaped high.

"Who's the cutie with Wally?"

"Wife," Duncan growled, with a curt nod to the China trader, who returned an obsequious smile.

"She looks young enough to be his daughter."

Her father did not rise to the bait. "Her name's Ling-Ling. She's twenty-two, with the brains of a twelve-year-old. She's got Wally Hearst wrapped around her pinky."

"Remarkable."

"Vivian!"

A soft, familiar voice floated above the roar of the party. Not believing her ears, she backed out of Allen Wei's circle and turned in delight to see the last man she expected to see here tonight.

"Steven." She flung an arm around his neck and buried her face. "What are you doing here?"

"Father unbanished me."

Steven Wong, Two-Way's eldest son, was by general agreement the single most beautiful-looking human being, male or female, Hong Kong had ever spawned. He had his father's lean, handsome build, while his English mother had bequeathed him aristocratic cheekbones, fair skin, and startling gray-green eyes. He was the classic Eurasian — the best of both, a synergy that doubled the sum of his parents. In appearance, at least.

Steven's mother was said to have been a charmer and a great tennis player. Steven had inherited both qualities, which was fortunate, because other than good looks he had inherited nothing discernible from his father. A sportsman, a drinker, and a gambler, he was neither as quick-witted nor as ruthless, and not at all ambitious, though he was a legendary spender of money and quite happy to live off Two-Way. Occasionally the dupe of those trying to influence his father, he was too sweet-natured to be really devious, much less treacherous — with the notable exception of his bedroom manners, which, while impeccable in the moment, suffered from his short attention span. Inevitably, the Cantonese had nicknamed the playboy son of the richest man in Hong Kong "No-Way" Wong.

"Hot threads," he complimented her gown. "Borrowed from Mummy?"

"Of course."

"How is she?"

"She got a Canadian visa."

"Lucky you."

Vivian considered herself fortunate to have known him the summer she had, and probably just as lucky that her return to Cambridge had ended things before she got hurt. He was the only wild man she had ever taken a chance with, before Duncan, and she had spent a lovely English autumn afterward, mooning over him on long walks between her studies, and writing him romantic letters about the tang of leaf smoke in the air, which he had finally answered with an amiable postcard from the Canidrome, Macau's dog track. They had stayed friends, and would share the occasional dinner, until his father had banished him to New York for unspecified crimes.

Steven had been vague about his offense, hinting at irregularities at World Oceans' casino subsidiary. She had also heard rumors of Triad connections, which was not particularly shocking because people were always whispering about Hong Kong Triads. She had known them primarily as street gangsters her father had routinely paid for protection. Steven, of course, was the sort of aimless wastrel who attracted gangsters hoping to worm themselves into his father's confidence. Whatever his crimes, Vivian had to assume they had cost his father dear—to send him away three years, because if Two-Way Wong had a single soft spot in his crippled body, it was for the handsome son by his first wife.

Vivian found herself appraising him with unexpected detachment. He must have turned forty by now, but if drinking, drugs, cigarettes, and bedding too many women had had any effect, it was only to make him handsomer. She kissed him warmly.

Steven broke into one of his effortless smiles. "What was that for?"

Vivian's own smile was private. "Thank you," she said.

"For coming home? Thank Dad."

"Just thank you."

The sight of Duncan Mackintosh plowing toward her through the crowds, broad and blocky, had lifted her heart. She had carried Steven's memory for too many years, and tonight was proof that Duncan had put it to rest.

"Ah," said Steven, following her gaze toward the parting crowds. "I'm beginning to understand. Say, who's the cute blonde?"

"The boss's daughter."

"*His* daughter?"

"Victoria."

"Nice. What's she like?"

Vivian thought, *Why not?* A distracted Vicky Mackintosh could be very much to Vivian's advantage, and if any force on earth could distract the Taipan's arrogant daughter, which was doubtful, Steven Wong was that force.

"She's like a hungry tiger. You'd find her quite a challenge. Would you like to meet her?"

Steven shrugged. "If I do," he said nonchalantly, "I'll make my own approach. Ta-ta." He slipped into the party and was gone while Duncan and his family were still some distance away. Vivian felt pleased. Steven had not fooled her at all. He would be all over Vicky Mackintosh by midnight. A sudden image of two tigers tumbling among tall trees flashed into her mind. She stifled a little stab of jealousy and turned smiling toward the approaching Duncan.

"Here comes your Taipan," Allen Wei whispered over her shoulder. She and the chief executive of Hong Kong were old friends. Vivian had managed his first political campaign for a Legislative Council seat and then worked for his electronics firm as a China trader until Duncan stole her away.

Allen, the Colony's first Chinese governor, was a youthful fifty-five, a wealthy engineer who had parlayed an American engineering degree and a flair for business into a string of electronics factories on both sides of the border. He was holding informal court in front of the great windows that overlooked the harbor, joking with Vivian and half a dozen others—including his stunning Eurasian secretary, Debby, who was never far from his side—while issuing enthusiastic off-the-cuff assessments of the New Year for a reporter from the *South China Morning Post*.

"The Joint Declaration has to work! In China, rule comes from education, no longer out of a gun. The Party *must* improve people's lives. And we in Hong Kong are the steering engine of that improvement. So, Happy New Year."

"Where do you see us a year from now, Governor?" In everyday usage, people clung to the title *governor*.

Allen responded with the big laugh he was famous for. "I, for one, plan to be right here at Sir John's party, if he'll have me, and I see no reason why he shouldn't."

"What if Sir John—or should I say Comrade Wong Li?—were to replace you as chief executive?"

But Wei refused to be provoked. He laughed again, waving to Duncan Mackintosh as the Scots clan broke from the crowd. "I would take the opportunity to doff this damned monkey suit, roll up my sleeves again like an honest man, and go back to work in my factories. I'd be richer than ever, so Chief Executive Sir John Wong Li would have to invite me anyway. You don't expect the governor of Hong Kong to give a party without capitalists, do you? Hullo, Duncan. Heck of an entrance. You fellows ought to go to Hollywood."

"Happy New Year, Allen." The two men clasped hands warmly. Duncan had worked tirelessly to rally the British and American expat communities to lobby Peking on Allen's behalf. As far as MacF was concerned, Allen Wei was the one bright spot in the otherwise grim Turnover picture.

"Taipan," the *South China Morning Post* reporter interrupted, "the chief executive just told me he's not worried about the emigration explosion. How is MacF coping with the resultant labor shortages?"

"Hong Kong will be a magnet drawing the best and the brightest out of China," Duncan answered quickly, and when the reporter's expression said he had heard that line before, Duncan derailed his next question with introductions.

"Allen, you know my son Peter, of course. And you've met Victoria."

"Indeed. Understand you had an interesting meeting with Wu Deming this afternoon, Victoria."

"That's fast," said Vicky, a little surprised, despite her dislike of her father's mistress, that Vivian would discuss business indiscreetly. "Do you mind my asking how you found out?"

"Mr. Wu told me just ten minutes ago."

"I thought he went back to Peking." She exchanged glances with her father, who seemed as startled as she by Wu's connection to Two-Way Wong.

"Stayed for the party. You know how persuasive Two-Way can be. Now, let's see, you know everyone here . . . my administrator, Debby."

"Hello, Debby."

"This scamp with the pencil is from the *South China Morning Post.*"

"Hello, scamp."

"And, um, well, of course you know Vivian Loh." Allen grinned.

Vicky stared past her, out the glass wall. Her angry eyes traced the shoreline eastward from Central to Wanchai to her mother's sad lair in Causeway Bay: The typhoon shelter sprawled in the dim light of the junks where the Tanka clans had gathered for family parties; somewhere in their shadows *Whirlwind* rode her mooring.

It was a tossup whether she was angrier at her father for clumsily setting up this so-called surprise encounter, or at Vivian for having the nerve to be seen so openly with him. Vivian won, if only for the high slit in her tight gown. Something was different about her tonight, something cool and sexy. No glasses; she was wearing contact lenses instead.

"Allen"—her father broke the heavy silence—"I'd like you to meet Chief Inspector John Chypwood-Chipworth."

Chip and the chief executive shook hands. "Staying on, Chief Inspector?"

"If they'll have me, sir."

"Good," he said, jerking a derisive thumb over his shoulder at the floodlit *QE2*. "I wish more Brits felt the same."

"Do you feel abandoned by your friends?" the reporter asked.

Allen's big, broad face brightened with another laugh and the sober moment flashed away. "Listen to me, young fellow. My mother spent her last dollar to buy me an exit certificate out of Mao's China when I was fourteen. Hong Kong took me in, gave me work, gave me school. I was *shocked* by the beauty of capitalism. The food, the homes, the cars, the stores. That is still Hong Kong's job. . . ."

Nodding agreement with the chief executive, Duncan leaned closer to Vicky and muttered in her ear, "Don't ever snub Vivian again."

"Don't give me reason to," she shot back.

"I will not forgive you."

Their eyes locked, blue fire to blue fire.

"What will you do? Give her *another* of my mother's diamonds?"

". . . While the Communists struggle to make their people's lives better, we will *shock* them with the beauty of capitalism," Allen concluded, pounding a fist into a plump hand.

The reporter, pretending to scribble notes as if his life depended on it, delivered his next question like an underhand knife thrust. "How shocking will Beijing find more street riots?"

"We've had no riots since last summer."

"But the Legco Commission predicted riots could break out at any moment, sir. Every poll finds people angry and frightened."

Allen Wei's broad, flat face set like steel. "People should know better than to resort to violence in Hong Kong. I warn them, there will be no violence that the Hong Kong Police cannot control."

"Hear, hear," said Duncan Mackintosh.

"Beijing has nothing to fear from Hong Kong criminals," the governor said grimly. "Isn't that so, Chief Inspector?"

"Absolutely, sir," Chip shot back, as if they had rehearsed.

Vivian Loh turned away before she said something she would regret. Greed and ignorance still marched hand in hand.

She remembered a Cambridge dinner party back in 1984, the weekend after the Joint Declaration. The guest of honor, a British Foreign Office China hand, just back from Beijing, had been quite pleased with himself. "We've settled the Hong Kong problem and won ourselves a billion-customer Chinese market."

"At the cost," an angry Vivian had called bravely up the table, "of the freedom of six million British subjects." For which, she recalled tonight, the precocious Chinese student had not been invited back.

Suddenly, a flash of orange light dancing beside the liner drew her eye to the anchored QE2. Across the harbor she saw the source.

"There's a fire in Tsim Sha Tsui."

As they all turned to the window, gasping at the jagged flames, Vivian was startled to see the fleshless face of Zheng, the Shanghainese cadre leader, reflected in the glass. She felt a stab of raw terror, a nightmare that they had been betrayed and Beijing's Public

Security agents would emerge from the party and arrest them all. Zheng was dressed in a dinner jacket, risking contact under his own name. He spoke to her, low and swift, and slipped away.

Vivian waited for Vicky to leave; then she translated for Duncan with a whisper in his ear.

12

THE FIRST MOB had formed in the Nathan Road, a neon bou-
levard of nightclubs, shops, and restaurants fed by a hundred
alleys. A rumor had spread that the Mainlanders were going to
ban trade unions—a rumor, the subsequent police report concluded
drily, that seemed tailor-made to provoke the tens of thousands of
factory and construction workers, truckers, and stevedores celebrating the start of a frightening new year. The younger, hotter-
tempered started breaking shop windows.

Alarms shrieked; gold and diamonds flickered into the dark. Wives
and children dived into the MTR stations and home to the new
towns, while their men waded into the street to overturn cars. The
notable exception was taxicabs, whose drivers swiftly vacated the area,
returning on foot, in many cases, to join the battle. A double-decker
bus tipped over with a crash on the Mody Road and burst into flames
in full sight of the terrified guests of the Hyatt Regency and the
Holiday Inn.

The Royal Hong Kong Police had written the book on urban
riot control, developing tactics more reminiscent of the nineteenth-
century British Army square formation than the casual training and
disorganized response practiced in older cities like London, New
York, or Paris. They had proved as long ago as the Star Ferry fare
riots, and the Mainland-inspired Cultural Revolution riots of the

late 1960s (for which they were dubbed "Royal" by the Queen of England), that a small, disciplined force could stop a riot by dispersing a mob quickly. The drill was to open with a show of force and escalate to tear gas, wooden bullets, and, very rarely, rifles and shotguns. No constable was permitted to break ranks, and no rioter was ever allowed within striking distance of the police.

The first of two Kowloon-based anti-riot platoons left their vehicles at the Carnarvon Road and swept south down Nathan on foot, dispersing the mob and covering the fire brigade that extinguished the burning bus. Forced out of the congested commercial strip, the mob broke up quickly down the alleys and side streets, and nothing more lethal than a few canisters of tear gas were fired by the advancing platoon. There were so many people, however, that a great number were forced across the Salisbury Road, onto the already crowded harbor walk that rimmed the tip of Kowloon. On the promenade, the report concluded later, all hell broke loose.

In the middle of the harbor lay the floodlit *QE2*. A great lighted barn door was open in her side, receiving launches, and a damp south wind wafted music over the water as several hundred retiring British civil servants danced in the New Year before upping anchor and steaming home to England in unspeakable luxury. The ship lay far beyond rock-throwing range, although more than a few paving stones were pried up and hurled in her direction.

Suddenly a man in white shirt sleeves jumped on the railing. "*Sell*out!" he began to chant. "*Sell*out! *Sell*out! *Sell*out!"

The crowds took up the angry beat, the oft-repeated charge that Great Britain had bartered Hong Kong's freedom to enhance its own trading stance with the PRC.

Up and down the promenade, more men jumped on the rail to lead the invective. Fists rose, beating the rhythm against the night sky. "*Sell*out! *Sell*out! *Sell*out!"

The million lights of Hong Kong Island, blazing from Western, Central, Wanchai, and Causeway Bay, fueled their anger, mocked their frustration. As the ship lay beyond their reach, so did the wealth of the island itself, and in every heart on the promenade beat the angry truth that the rich could escape and they could not.

There stood the Bank of China building, packed with the Mainland bureaucrats and rule-makers they had already learned to hate. There, beside it, World Oceans House glittered, the top floors bright as a diamond stickpin. Above the buildings the Peak mansions had all their lights burning for the lavish parties that the magazines and newspapers would report so breathlessly. The rich and the mighty had already made their peace with the bosses from the North. And if it didn't work out, so what? They could leave. But the ordinary man in the street could not. Old Hundred Names would face another catastrophe, alone.

The city, however, was too big to focus their anger. The ocean liner, so much nearer, yet so far, dared them to attack.

A double line of police had been drawn up behind barriers to protect the five-star Regent Hotel at a point where the soaring glass walls of its lobby were vulnerable to stones. One Chinese constable broke discipline to mutter to another, "Think they'll swim out to it?"

"That bastard on the rail will swim if I get my hands on him."

A constable down the line asked, "What if this union ban applies to our union too?"

"Silence!" their sergeant barked.

The nearest chant leader glanced down the rail and seemed to take a signal from the next man. Suddenly a new cry galvanized the mob, and the constables' blood ran cold.

"*Ferrrrrryyyy!*"

Ten thousand people turned as one. A short distance along the promenade, the Star Ferry terminal piers thrust into the harbor. At the moment, two diesel-powered double-enders were shuttling between Kowloon and Hong Kong Island, and three more were tied at the pier.

"*Ferry! Ferry! Ferry!*"

The mob burst the thin police line, stormed around the Emperor Hotel and the space museum, through the bus terminal, and rampaged onto the ferry pier. They tore apart the metal gates the crews tried to close and poured aboard the nearest boat, the *Celestial*. Hawsers were flung off bollards, while truckers and heavy-equipment operators made quick sense of the simple controls in the engine room.

Celestial lurched from the pier without warning, tumbling a dozen last-minute boarders into the water, carving a twisted wake as the gang in the wheelhouse fought one another for the helm.

Finally a Hakka backhoe operator sank a fire axe into the shoulders of the truck driver who was trying to steer, and set a steady course for the wide-open barn door spilling light from the side of the luxury liner. A collective howl bayed through the ferry as the rioters crowded into the bow to be the first to board, dragging lengths of pipe and wooden slats they had torn from the benches for weapons.

A tiny Marine Police launch buzzed across the black water, blue lights flashing, siren howling. Three hundred yards from the immense wall of the *QE2*—gaily speckled with lighted portholes—the little boat bounced to a stop in the path of the charging ferry.

"Run him down!" howled the mob on the bow. "Sink the *sui laun ging.*" The Hakka steering had suffered many a boarding and search of his family's sampan by the zealous water snakes of the Marine Police. He tightened his grip on the helm, rejoicing in this gods-sent opportunity to slam the water-cop pricks to the bottom of the harbor.

*C*hip wedged himself in the stern of the tossing police launch, one weather eye on the Chinese sergeant commanding the half-dozen Marine Patrol PCs, and the other on the stolen ferry, which was closing rapidly. Knowing the harbor tunnel would be blocked, he had loped the quarter mile from World Oceans House to the police dock at the Old Queens Pier, produced his warrant card, and jumped aboard the launch as they roared off to intercept.

The lad in charge looked twenty-five at most and had never expected to confront a riot in the harbor. Hesitating while his driver revved the engines and the launch pitched on the nasty chop, watching as the ferry grew rapidly larger in the night, the sergeant fiddled with his radio. All he could raise was static of an odd tone Chip associated with electronic jamming, though it probably just needed a charge. He banged the radio against the gunwale, to no effect, and shot a murderous glance astern, cursing the fornicating-foreign-devil fools on the *QE2* who hadn't the brains to close the barn door in her side. Did the Cunard Line expect the mob to beg permission to board?

Chip was deliberately keeping out of the way. While all Hong Kong police rotated into riot units, he was not up until June. He had no business being here and did not want to muck up the chain of command. But he realized, suddenly, that he had probably been put on this earth to issue a single command in crisp, sure English.

"Sergeant. Stop that ferry!"

"Sir."

Possessing neither an army nor a navy, Hong Kong required its police to defend its borders as well as uphold the law. Thus, like every officer in the department, the Marine Police sergeant was, by dint of training, tradition, and leadership, half soldier. Commands from above begat orders below, and he immediately took command of his boat.

"Light the wheelhouse," the sergeant ordered.

Their halogen spotlight soared skyward, locked on the ferry windows. A dozen faces pressed to the glass. A burly fellow at the helm raised a hand to shield his eyes and steered for the light.

"Load the Armalite."

A PC unlocked a hatch and flanked the sergeant with an automatic rifle.

"Engage engines, quarter ahead."

The boat moved against the chop, steadying the wet decks.

"Shoot that man!"

The rifle cracked. Glass flew, heads ducked, and the Hakka at the wheel pitched backward out of sight. The ferry heeled into a sudden steep turn, hurling rioters into the rails and spilling some overboard.

"Bear away, helmsman. Take me alongside."

The launch ran parallel to the careening ferry, which was running full speed in a wide circle. The sergeant ordered them closer.

"Remingtons!"

Pump shotguns were unlimbered.

Closer still, until they were only a few yards from the open-sided engine room.

"Fire away!"

Three grinning PCs blasted the machinery. A hail of buckshot shredded pipes, lines, and cables until, engines spewing electric sparks, diesel fuel, and hydraulic oil, the commandeered ferry wallowed to a stop a few hundred yards off Tsim Sha Tsui.

"Cease firing. *Cease* firing." But the PCs had really gotten into the swing of it and it took a third order and a rap on the shoulder to get their attention.

As the smoke cleared and the volley echoed in his ears, the sergeant turned to Chip, who said, "Well done, Sergeant."

At that moment the radio crackled to life, demanding the sergeant's report, and Chip observed that despite the rigorous program of "localization," the Royal Hong Kong Police had retained the British penchant for understatement. The sergeant radioed, "Could you spare a tug, sir?"

But his superintendent sounded a little less than crisp. In fact, thought Chip, the superintendent sounded scared. "Nip over to Causeway Bay. There's a new lot attacking the typhoon shelter. Looks like they're after the yachts."

Rounding the bulk of the *QE2*, they saw a huge pyre of burning cars where the Eastern Corridor cut the corner of the typhoon shelter. The flames stood a hundred feet tall, and, reflected in the glass buildings behind them, they made it seem as if the buildings were burning too.

"*Say la,*" breathed the sergeant.

Death indeed. Back on the Kowloon side the ferry terminal was still afire, and the first flush of victory was fading fast.

13

CHIP HAD WARNED Vicky to stay off the streets because the Kowloon riot could jump the harbor like wildfire. But she slipped away from Two-Way Wong's party shortly after he did. Everyone was crowding into the windows watching the battle for the Star Ferry terminal, and the dance floor was deserted except for the mimes, frozen like abandoned machinery, and a Filipina duo belting "We Did It Our Way" from the fern-covered stage.

She had promised to drive home with her father. On reflection, though, she worried that if a disturbance broke out in Causeway Bay, her mother would wake alone and frightened on the boat.

"Hold the elevator, please." A man running after her bounded up the staircase. He looked vaguely familiar, as had many at the party, and stunningly attractive—a Eurasian with silken jet hair and gray-green eyes.

"Thanks." He smiled.

"It's not here yet," said Vicky, turning away with simultaneous thoughts—*gorgeous*, and *trouble-beyond-calculation, which I don't need in my life*—but not before a near-tidal wave of desire had flooded her body. She forced herself not to look again and concentrated on the long view across the empty dance floor.

Two-Way Wong had settled into a raised niche in a corner of windows with a party of elderly Chinese. They were attended by young girls in figure-hugging cheongsams—so tight and slit so high as to make Vivian's look modest—who were refilling their brandy snifters and lighting their cigarettes. She recognized several of Two-Way Wong's fellow Shanghainese shipowners who had fled in '49. They seemed to be the only people in the ballroom not intent upon the riots, which seemed odd for a group of men who had already lost one city in their lifetime.

The handsome Eurasian was watching them, too, she discovered, when she shot a quick glance his way. If Alfred Ching's enthusiastic grin had its engaging qualities, this guy would make her crazy with his eyes. They crinkled in a smile and she found herself opening a conversation against her better judgment.

"The old pirate's a cool one, isn't he, drinking mai tais while the city burns?"

"Maybe he figures to buy the rubble cheap."

Two-Way's gaze flickered beyond his group, and Vicky tracked it. For reasons she could not entirely explain, she was not surprised that the subjects of his interest appeared to be her father and Allen Wei. The Scots taipan and the Chinese governor were standing belligerently at a window, hands on hips, heads thrust toward the flames across the harbor. The glass reflected their faces. Allen looked utterly bewildered, as if he could not believe that the good and sensible capitalists of Hong Kong had run amok.

Vicky's father, however, was tight-lipped grim. He knew a disaster when he saw one. Even if the police stopped the riot in the next five minutes, which wasn't likely, satellite TV news was already beaming coverage around the world: Hong Kong afire against the dramatic backdrop of Britain's luxury liner. Thank God the markets were closed for New Year's, but come their opening bells, every stock connected to Hong Kong was going to sink like lead ballast. Which raised in Vicky's mind a strange question: What did Two-Way Wong have to smile about? Didn't World Oceans have even more to lose in Hong Kong than MacF?

A jade-paneled elevator *ding*ed open.

"Please," the Eurasian said politely, stepping aside to let her enter first.

The uniformed Chinese operator grinned her aboard with a cheery, "Down, Missy."

But when he saw the Eurasian, he bowed low.

"Relax, kid. I don't bite."

The door slid shut, and Vicky realized belatedly who this man was—and that she had just badmouthed his father.

"Ohmigod, you're—" In her confusion, she had almost blurted his nickname.

"No-Way." He smiled. "The prodigal returned from banishment."

"I'm, uh, sorry?"

"Nice to meet you, Sorry. Wha' do your friends call you?"

"I'm Victoria Mackintosh." She extended her hand. "It's very nice to meet you . . . Steven, is it?"

"To my frien's." His voice seemed to flow like a warm liquid that submerged his final D's and T's. "No-Way, to my father's detractors an' the media." Vicky sensed something very open about him and guessed that while he could joke about his nickname, it hurt.

"I met your father, this evening."

"What did you think of 'the old pirate'?"

"Listen, I'm really sorry. I mean, about calling him a pirate."

"I forgive you. I mean that. There is something bent in my makeup which prevents me from holding grudges against women."

"He surprised me. . . . I don't know. I mean, he was rather witty, in a way. . . ."

"Known up an' down the China Coast for his comedic appeal." Steven Wong grinned. "Or so the old legends would have you believe."

Exiting into the lobby, they made their way through a corridor of sleepy children in livery. "Somebody should tell these kids to go to bed."

"You're right." Steven spread his arms and addressed them in Cantonese. They laughed nervously, but stayed in line. "They only respond to their master's voice," he apologized. "Sorry, but I tried."

"I can't tell you how strange it seems to me. They're so young."

"Not so strange. My father has re-created an old-fashioned extended Chinese family. They're all orphans. Here they have the best of everything. Most of his company staff have been with him since they were babies."

"Does he worry how the PRC will look upon his private orphanage and capitalist training school?"

Steven Wong grinned. "My father don't worry about nothin'. Keep in mind the PRC is Chinese. Are you waiting for your car?"

"Um, no. I came with my father. I'll get a taxi."

"I'll drop you," he offered, indicating the scarlet Bentley that had raced to the door as they appeared.

"Just ask them to call me a taxi, please."

"Taxis are going to be scarce with a riot going on. Where are you headed?"

He was right, of course, about the taxis. She started to say the Causeway Bay Typhoon Shelter, but amended it to: "The Yacht Club."

"I'll drop you. Hop in."

He had a courtly manner Vicky was not used to in a man his age, holding the door and asking whether she was comfortable before starting out. His response to the threat of Hong Kong collapsing in civil disorder seemed one of wry detachment. On the way out of Central, on the Harcourt Road, they caught a glimpse, between buildings, of a Star Ferry racing in circles.

"Rioting ferries?" Steven asked. "What will they think of next?"

But Vicky was getting tense, worrying about her mother, and just as they passed from Central into Wanchai, the heavy traffic came to a dead halt. As far ahead as she could see were stopped taxis, trucks, and buses. "What is this?"

"Look. Another fire."

In the distance, high above the road, a red glow lit the building tops.

"What's burning, I wonder?" Steven asked with mild curiosity. "Maybe your Yacht Club. Hey! Where you going?"

She was already tearing at the seat belt, jumping from the Bentley, running through the stopped traffic toward the lights of an MTR station entrance. She slid under a turnstile and raced down the steep escalator, two moving steps at a time. A silver train was boarding passengers as she neared the platform. She put on a burst of speed. Her heel caught in the escalator treads, and she nearly fell on her face. Stuck fast, she abandoned both shoes and ran barefoot between the closing doors. Two stops on the swift and silent train seemed to take forever. Her imagination rampaged—her mother alone on the boat, rioters swarming over the closely moored junks.

Causeway Bay. Dead run up the escalator, up a flight of stairs, out onto the Lockhart Road. The air stank of burned rubber and gasoline. Gangs of teenagers were running toward the water. She ran with them, her hose in ribbons, her soles stinging on the pavement, down Percival Street, into the crowds thronged deep beside the harbor. Pressing through them, she rounded the corner onto the Gloucester Road and found the way blocked by thousands more gawping at the cars burning on the elevated Eastern Corridor.

The flames on the highway lit the typhoon shelter, and in the garish light the junk dwellers looked as if they were dancing on their boats. Vicky—unable to move ahead or back—could only stare at the distant figures, knowing their dance was a desperate scramble to extinguish the sparks raining from the sky.

The crowd that had trapped her swarmed ten deep on the pavement, squeezed between the buildings and a hastily formed police line along the Gloucester Road. It was a miracle there were any police at all; every vehicular route was blocked. Stopped cars jammed the Gloucester Road and the mare's nest of the Eastern Corridor and Harbour Tunnel approaches between her and the Yacht Club.

Farther east along the typhoon shelter an unruly crowd pushed across the roads and stampeded the public shore. Junks and sampans backed away, opening a water moat between them and the mob. Vicky's only chance to hire a sampan was at the club's own dock.

But first she had to cross the roads. There were pedestrian stairs over, or a long tunnel under. She was nearest an overwalk, but people had mobbed it for the view it offered of the crowd storming the shelter, and the police had barricaded the stairs on the harbor side and were clearing it, pushing people back even as she watched.

The Police Officers Club shared the little peninsula that formed the western boundary of the shelter with the Yacht Club, and Vicky could see expat officers in dinner jackets manning the barricades.

She fought her way toward the tunnel. The entrance was beside a cinema next to the Excelsior Hotel. She could see the neon theater marquee advertising the latest Raymond Chow ghost-and-sword thriller. It took an exhausting five minutes to get half a block, and by that time the crowd had grown denser and its mood was turning. People's faces, curious just minutes before, seemed to redden in the flame light: Eyes flashed, lips stretched over teeth, and numbing moans began to rise from a thousand throats. Intent, until now, upon reaching her mother, she was suddenly aware she was white-skinned and half-naked in a red evening gown. Someone grabbed at the diamond clip in her hair. Angrily, she tore it loose and shoved it into her evening bag.

Suddenly a gas tank exploded with a hollow *boom* that lofted burning debris hissing into the shelter. Everyone ducked and retreated for the cover of the buildings. Vicky sprinted a hundred feet before they surged out again. She was still too far away to distinguish *Whirlwind* in the muddle of yachts and junks, much less her mother among the distant figures stamping out fires on their decks. A second car explosion sent people fleeing again, and Vicky gained another block.

Police in riot gear were guarding the tunnel door.

She struggled out of the crowd, up to a Chinese constable wearing a plastic face shield.

"Let me pass."

The man did not budge.

"I said, let me through."

"What's all this?" came the welcome sound of an English voice. An expat inspector marched over with tense eyes and a mouth disdainful, Vicky realized, for what must appear to be a New Year's drunk.

"I'm Victoria Mackintosh, Inspector. My mother is sleeping aboard her yacht. I'm going in to see that she's all right."

This was still British Hong Kong, and her name captured his interest, if not his attention, which seemed riveted on her feet.

"Mackintosh, you say."

"Victoria Mackintosh. Duncan Mackintosh is my father. . . . I'll ask my mother to lend me shoes."

"All right, miss. Let her through, Sergeant."

"Thank you, Inspector."

She bounded down the stairs and raced through the long, empty tunnel, her breath echoing in her ears. Emerging near the tarpaulin-draped Noon Day Gun, and startling some constables guarding the tunnel, she hurried along the water's edge. The Tanka were all out on their junks, standing on deck armed with boat hooks and fishing gaffs, and eyeing the crowds behind the police lines with a mixture of fear and disdain. Twice she noticed guns in their wheelhouses, an unusual sight in Hong Kong, where firearms were strictly controlled.

Skirting the Police Officers Club and the Yacht Club, she hobbled across a gravel-strewn launch yard, dodged a mechanical sling and some cradled yachts, and ran onto the wooden sampan dock. An old woman was holding her boat a cautious ten feet off shore. She eyed Vicky with deep suspicion from the depths of her canvas cabin.

"Whirlwind!" Vicky cried.

The old woman stared across the water, then glanced fearfully at the mob and the fire as if Vicky were the rioters' emissary.

"Tai-Tai's boat!" Vicky screamed, and that, or the fact that the woman had seen more than her share of shoeless gweipos stagger out of the club bar over the years, caused her to nose her boat to the dock. Vicky jumped aboard, and the old woman motored into the shelter.

"Hurry, please."

The leaping flames on the Eastern Corridor threw orange lights and black shadows among the high-sterned junks. Low on the water, the sampan offered only glimpses of the shore. Police sirens wailed, but the dominant noise was human, a collective howl of anger and discontent. As they progressed along the channel Vicky could see the Tanka standing high atop their wheelhouses, silhouetted against the red canopy of the sky.

Megaphones boomed, *"Saan hoi! Saan hoi!* Disperse! Disperse peacefully! Disperse! *Saan hoi!"*

"Come from park," said the old woman driving the sampan.

"Who?"

"Riot." A big park bordered part of the shelter to the east, a trysting spot at night. The megaphones boomed again. Then, a different voice, cold in command.

"Fire."

She heard a hollow popping sound and felt, for the first time, really frightened. If the police were shooting guns the mob must have the upper hand. She strained to see, expecting a human wave to come leaping over the moorings. But a glimpse of the shore between two fishing junks revealed a rolling cloud of white smoke, driven at the mob by the northeast wind.

"Aiyaaaaa," cheered the old woman at the tiller. "Tear gas. That'll teach 'em."

And, indeed, their next glimpse was of a crowd melting before the advance of a solid mass of armed police.

"Fire!"

Tear gas in another direction, and this time the retreat caused the fishermen standing overhead on their wheelhouses to cheer their ancient enemy, the police. Then another gasoline tank exploded on the flyway and bits of fire spiraled down from the sky.

"Aiyaaah!" the old woman cried. Flames were licking the canvas shelter. Vicky grabbed a bailer and splashed filthy water on them. *"More,"* the old woman shrilled, and they splashed water until both were satisfied that no sparks remained in the cloth or the dry wood around it.

New sirens heralded the fire brigade weaving through the traffic. Firemen poured water on the burning cars, and the flames dropped, casting sudden darkness over the typhoon shelter. The sampan engine slowed and Vicky heard the clank of a yacht's fire pump and then saw the familiar rake of *Whirlwind*'s bow and, above it, the sturdy silhouette of Ah Chi hosing down the teak.

She fished money from her evening bag and pressed it in the old woman's hand. Ah Chi reached down and pulled Vicky aboard. "Yes, Missy. Everything okay."

"Mother?"

"Okay, below. I come back. She fine."

She jumped down the companionway as the police opened fire again with a loud volley of tear gas. Megaphones blared, sirens screeched, and a helicopter thundered over from Kowloon.

"Mother? Where are you?"

She felt her way across the darkened salon and down the aft passageway, heading for the stern stateroom where Sally was probably hiding. "Mother," Vicky called. "I'm here. It's all right."

She found a light switch and knocked on her mother's door. "It's me." Hearing nothing, she knocked again and opened it fearfully. "Mother. It's Vicky."

The light was low and by it she saw her mother curled up in her robe on top of the bed with an empty champagne glass on the night table and an upended bottle in the cooler.

"Mother?"

Sally Farquhar Mackintosh opened her eyes with a smile. "Hello, darling," she murmured sleepily. "Happy New Year."

"Are you all right?"

"A little drowsy. One just doesn't stay up the way one used to. Is it midnight yet?"

"Almost."

"You're sweet to come. You left your friends?"

"I was worried for you."

"Whatever for?"

"The riot."

"What riot?" Sally yawned, stretched, closed her eyes, and passed back into sleep.

Vicky slumped in a chair. Gradually, the noise from the shore began to die down. She went up on deck and saw that the fires were out and the police in control.

"Ah Chi, thank you. I'll stay tonight. You go home."

"Thank you, Missy." He gave a sharp whistle and a sampan motor started.

"Is your family all right?" she asked.

"All family okay. One rioter try to board junk. Stick 'em gaff."

"Good for you. Do your family need help with the police?" Lord knew how the cops had assessed the Tanka defending their boats in the heat of battle, and it was incumbent upon her family to protect Ah Chi's.

Ah Chi grinned. "No' yet."

"Tell me quick, quick. I'll tell the Taipan."

A low sampan came alongside, driven by a pretty girl. A gold tooth gleamed in a shy smile. Ah Chi swung over the lifelines and was gone. Vicky wandered below, found a beer in the fridge, and went back to her mother, who was snoring lightly. She loosened her robe and pulled a sheet over her. Then she sat, sipping the beer and growing sad.

What a horrible year it had been. Poor Hugo. Poor Mother. Her boyfriend crumbling under the pressure. The hotel lost in New York. Another about to be lost at Kai Tak, the Chinese closing in. She began to cry, thinking of her husband, Jeff, whom she hadn't seen in years. Why cry for him? she wondered, and realized she was crying for herself, for the girl she had been when she had allowed her father to bully her into marriage. The stupid girl who still raised her head so he could chop it down. Her life would have been so different if she hadn't married, if she had stayed in New York after college and followed her own career. She would have succeeded. She could come home as an equal now, instead of sweeping up the pieces of Duncan Mackintosh's crumbling empire.

Hugo would never know what he had missed, she thought bitterly. Poor Fiona. Poor children. It was hard to imagine 1997 being worse than 1996 had been, but she knew it would be. With that thought, her control slipped again, a little more, and she let a deep sob build inside and shake her whole body.

She tried to tell herself it was just a letdown from racing frantically to save her mother, only to find her safe. A perfectly normal reaction, she told herself, a delayed response. The trouble was, she was getting overwhelmed by a wave of delayed responses to all the terrible things that had happened this year. She tried to resist it with a slug of beer. But she had let herself go too far and the bottle rapped her teeth as a louder sob shook her to the core.

Her mother stirred.

Vicky was lonely, but not that lonely. Softly she rose, turned out the light, and backed through the door and down the corridor to the main salon. She found her mother's foul-weather jacket hanging by the companionway and shrugged it on over her gown, then headed up on deck, thinking the night air might clear her head of stupid things.

The tears were still thick in her throat, so she went forward to the bow, far from her mother's stateroom, where if she must cry she could cry in peace. She sat on the deck with her back to the mast, stared at the dark silhouettes of the junks around her, and, still clutching her half-finished beer—like a baby, she thought—waited for something to fill the emptiness.

She didn't know how long she sat, but she must have dozed off, because she was suddenly awake, stiff and cold. She tried to see the time but she couldn't read her dress watch in the dark.

She heard the ocean roar of traffic in the distance. They had cleared the Eastern Corridor and the cars were moving again. There was near silence otherwise, as if the city had simply absorbed the riots. Whatever had started them was over for the night. Somewhere from within the maze of junks and sampans and yachts, she heard a big marine engine start up with quiet authority.

A second engine murmured to life and they ran a while, warming, growing smoother in their sound, then abruptly dropping a note as they were simultaneously put into gear. Looking down the channel, she saw a pair of masts moving against the red canopy of the neon-lit sky.

A dumb time to go sailing, she thought, with everyone on board sure to be drunk, boatboys included. But as the masts neared, she heard no music, no party shouts, no laughter, only the quiet engines barely ticking over as the big yacht slipped stealthily from the moorings.

Curious, Vicky went forward onto *Whirlwind*'s bow pulpit and saw to her surprise the distinctive schooner masts of *Mandalay*, the sailing yacht her father had purchased after losing *Whirlwind* to her mother. The old MacF yard had constructed *Mandalay*, a near twin of his beloved *Whirlwind*, for a couple who had sold her back to him when they bought an even bigger boat, having made a vast fortune importing Irish whisky to a Hong Kong suddenly sentimental for things Celtic.

Mandalay was running without lights, and Vicky was about to dash below and radio the Marine Police that someone was stealing her when she saw, silhouetted against the light from a fishing junk's wheelhouse, the unmistakable figure of her father at the helm. Mystified, Vicky watched him draw near. This was no night for a spontaneous cruise. It was cold and damp and a fog was blowing in, which made a tryst with Vivian highly unlikely. A second figure materialized from behind the mizzenmast, but by the rail-thin shape and the easy stride aft to the cockpit, she knew it wasn't Vivian; more likely it was her father's new boatboy, Back Door Ping, a notorious smuggler no one else would hire.

Vicky started to lean out on the pulpit to call to her father, but the memory of being left behind when he boarded the red junk was still strong. He would lie when she asked where he was going in the middle of the night.

For a wild moment she thought about following him. But it would take too long to find Ah Chi and get *Whirlwind* under way. Besides, the radar was circling purposefully at *Mandalay*'s masthead. Even if she could catch up in the fog, her father would surely stop to investigate the source of the fiery blossom on his scope.

She retreated to the cockpit and crouched in the shadows, watching him nurse the big yacht through the tight turn around *Whirlwind*, the last boat in the row. Both boats were so long, and the channel so narrow, that he had to back and fill, quietly reversing the engines to swing her stern around. For a second the boats were next to each other, the bow of *Mandalay* two feet from *Whirlwind*'s hull. She heard her father growl at Back Door Ping to watch the stern, and in the instant that both men looked behind the boat, Vicky hitched up her gown and stepped lightly over the lifelines and onto *Mandalay*'s bow.

BOOK THREE

Dragon Face

14

January 1997

VIVIAN LOH FEARED she had made a terrible mistake, letting Duncan meet their "old friends" without her. But Duncan, who always felt time looming behind him like a breaking sea, had insisted. Frantically she paced her apartment. If her mother was right that she possessed the magic power of patience, then it would be tested tonight.

She could not recall ever really losing an argument with Duncan before. They thought so much alike that they rarely argued at all. One of the miracles between the bombastic son of a transplanted Scot and the self-contained daughter of a Chinese teacher was a confluence of minds and ambition. They were like two rivers descending opposite mountain ranges into the same ocean.

She had lied to her mother. There was never work strewn about her apartment. The bed-sit where she had lived her first year at Cambridge had been the first room she had not shared in her entire life, and the habits of neatness and privacy cultivated in close quarters would stay with her always. Her work was contained on a glass desk behind a silk screen that depicted a pastoral view of the nineteenth-century fishing harbor known as Hong Kong, or "Fragrant Harbor." A Total Integrated Computer terminal-videophone hooked to MacF House, a compact printer, a fax machine, Chinese stationery, her chop, her brushes and inkstone, and her checkbook were all in their assigned places, and she would not dream of leaving the three-room flat otherwise.

That Jardine Property had blocked her view with another high-rise bothered her not at all. She usually drew the drapes at night anyway. The pleasure of her home was inside, where she had transformed an ordinary modern apartment of low ceilings, wafer-thin parquet floors, and windowless kitchen and bath into a traditional Chinese home with its defenses against worldly chaos and evil spirits.

Immediately inside her front door she had erected a *ying bik*, or shadow wall, designed to deflect invading spirits, which, legend had it, were unable to turn corners. Such a spirit stopper was supposed to stand outside the front door, of course, which wasn't practical in an apartment block. She made up for the deficiency with hexagonal spirit-deflecting *pat kwa* mirrors on the door frame, and paintings of the same door gods, Chiu Shu-Pao and Hu Ching-Tai, who guarded Tin Hau's temple in Public Square Street where, as a child, she had worshiped with her father. To enter, she passed along the corridor this wall created and stepped over the high raised sill of an interior painted door and turned at last into a living room that felt deep and safe.

"What is all this?" Duncan had smiled the first time she had invited him home.

"To keep out ghosts."

He raised trembling fingers to her cheek. They were both still surprised by where things were going, still balancing on the edge between friendship and sex. As soon as his finger touched her skin, it stopped shaking, and his touch turned sure, trailing an electric wake to her lips, tracing their outline, rimming the edges of sensation while their eyes joined in a liquid embrace.

"I'm one gweilo who's glad it didn't work."

Nor did it work tonight. His ghost, her gweilo's ghost, haunted the flat: the couch, where he would sprawl while they talked; the kitchen, where he would watch her cook, loath to separate for even five minutes when they had their rare times together; her bedroom, where they had quickly shared what they remembered from a suddenly diminished past, and rushed on to invent better things of their own. When she was dead in heaven she would still remember how he felt that first time he entered her. He had discovered nerves she never knew she had. Such novelty. And he was so sure. Steven Wong had been a sure lover, but Steven's ease and comfort came from his love and knowledge of women. Duncan's surety came from his love and knowledge of her, alone.

She turned for solace to a porcelain statue of the goddess of mercy that Auntie Chen had left her. But Kuan Yin was little comfort. She needed more than mercy; she needed protection. Kneeling before her elaborate red-and-gold shrine to Tin Hau, she lit candles and joss sticks. The sea goddess who had saved her from the shark was better situated to help Duncan tonight. But Tin Hau's expression was frightfully remote.

She rose from the altar and telephoned for her company car, rousing her driver from God knew what revels, and ordered him to drive her to North Point in hopes of a glimpse of Duncan putting out to sea. The man glowered at the wheel, glared in the mirror, and she wondered where he had been during the riots. Thousands had rampaged over the ferry terminal and thousands more at Causeway Bay. They could not all have been faceless demons. By logic, she had to assume that most of the mob had erupted from the skins of ordinary men. "Ah Wong? Did you see the riot?"

"No, miss. I drank soup with the other drivers while you were at Two-Way Wong's party. When you left with the Taipan I went home to my wife."

Vivian dismissed him from her mind. He had no reason to tell her the truth and she had no means to test if he was lying. She leaned to the window to see why traffic was slowing and saw an enormous police wrecker towing a burned-out car off the highway. As they crossed the east end of the Typhoon Shelter she looked for Duncan's boat, but he had already gone.

At North Point she got out of the car and walked to the end of the ferry pier and scanned the dark water. The fog was rolling down from China, just as Duncan had said it would, and already it was difficult to distinguish the towers directly across on Kai Tak. She thought she heard boat engines, but she saw no lights moving. Bowing her head with worry and frustration, she gave up and walked back to the car.

"Home, miss?" Ah Wong asked hopefully.

"Shek-O." Maybe she could see him from the eastern headlands. Even a glimpse was better than nothing. She had begged him not to go, and when he insisted, she had begged him to take her with him.

"No."

"Duncan, please."

"I won't risk it."

"And what am I to do if something terrible happens?"

"Nothing's going to happen."

"Then what's to risk? Let me come with you."

"No. And no debate." He gave her a melting smile and put his big hands around her waist. "You're too valuable."

"You sent me to Shanghai without a thought."

"That was before. And I did think. And I did worry. And I also had people watching out for you, as you know. This is now and this is different and you are too valuable and too precious."

"I will die," she said quite simply, "if something happens to you."

His hands tightened until they hurt. "No, you won't. You have a job and a responsibility, Vivian." He let go and took an envelope from his dinner jacket. "My new will," he said. "Allen Wei's got a copy. He witnessed it."

She pulled away, but he pressed the envelope into her hand and gently closed her fingers around it. The paper was warm from his chest.

"I don't want your will."

"I'm just keeping things orderly. Nothing's going to happen tonight. But if my joss turns bad, you're covered legally."

"What about Victoria?"

Though he was still holding her, he spoke in the level tone he used at the office. "If you have to read it, you'll see that I don't intend to run this hong from the grave. But if you want my advice, you'll need Vicky the way I need her. And if you don't want my advice, there'll be damn-all I can do about it."

Vivian looked away, not sure what he would see in her eyes.

"Now what's wrong?" he asked with a quizzical smile. There were times he could read her mind, but maybe not this time.

"Why meet at sea?"

"If you'd been through what Tang's been through, you'd be careful too."

"I *have* been through what Tang's been through. And I am very careful."

"You were a kid. This bloke sat in a cell for five years. And he knows damn well Premier Chen's gang are watching him like hawks."

"Duncan," she pleaded, "don't go tonight. I have a terrible feeling."

He hesitated then, and she saw his doubts, that even he was concerned by the sudden unscheduled request for a meeting. But Duncan Mackintosh was not a cautious man. "I gave my word," he said. "They're waiting for me." And that was it. He had kissed her goodbye, and left.

Vivian huddled in the backseat of her car, wrapped herself in her own arms, and tried to force her mind from the terror beating in her heart. Wherever the road skirted the water she lowered the window and stared at the dark. One glimpse, just one glimpse. Nothing at Quarry Bay. Nothing at Shau Kei Wan. Nothing at Chai Wan, Cape Collinson, Big Wave Beach. Not a light, not a sound.

Shek-O, at last.

A cool wet wind was blowing off the Tathong Channel when she got out of the car on the cliffs above Shek-O beach. She borrowed Ah Wong's jacket and left him smoking and listening to the radio while she wandered into the night. Hers was the only car parked at the end of the road. In the summer, people might drive out from a party for a midnight swim, but the winter monsoon guaranteed privacy, and the cliffs were primitive in their emptiness. The fog was blowing in patches. She looked back and saw the glow of Ah Wong's cigarette light the car, and when she looked again it vanished. To the south, every half-minute a bright double flashing light made a periodic soft appearance over the sea. Otherwise, she might have been watching from these cliffs a hundred years ago, or two hundred, or a thousand.

She heard the waves beating the rocks below and the wind passing her ears and her own heart thudding inside. Then a mutter from the darkness to her left. A boat engine. She strained to see, but there were no lights, and she had no idea if it was a junk or a patrol launch or Duncan's yacht. She tracked its approach, straining for a glimpse of moving light. She saw nothing. The sound stopped abruptly, almost directly below her.

She stared where it had been, baffled. Behind her, she heard the car horn. Ah Wong, probably afraid she was lost in the fog. She started to turn away, back to the car, when suddenly she caught a glimpse of sails in the double flashing light. They stood ghostly for a half-second, disappeared, and stood again, before the fog swallowed them up forever. In that flash she knew for certain it was Duncan.

She put her palms together, raised her eyes to the dark heavens, and prayed to Tin Hau, prayed that the goddess of the sea would watch over her man, and prayed that if she could not protect him, then Tin Hau would give her the patience to wait for their second meeting.

15

VICKY HAD FOUND the forehatch screwed down tight, which demolished her plan to hide in the sail locker. When *Mandalay* left the typhoon shelter and turned east into the wind she knew she was in for a miserable night on the bow. The northeast monsoon had kicked up a fierce chop, and the air was thick with a cold, clammy mist. As soon as her father had speeded up the engines, when they were out of earshot of the shelter, the schooner started taking spray over her bow.

Her mother's foul-weather jacket was enormous. While it almost covered her knees, it kept filling with cold air. She pulled the hood over her head, tightened the drawstrings as far as they would close, adjusted the Velcro cuffs, and lay in the rolling, bouncing wet. She gripped the heavy anchor chain with one hand, wrapped her other arm around a spinnaker pole that was lashed to the deck, and rested her head on the locked hatch, reckoning she would have to endure several hours of this before they were well at sea and she could make her presence known. Any earlier, and her father would stop the boat and put her off.

At least he wasn't wasting any time. The engines were shuddering, running full throttle. Even through the heavy chop Vicky guessed they were making eight knots. At this rate they'd pass Waglan Light in an hour and a half. She felt a course change to the right, which meant they were skirting North Point. She still couldn't see her watch, but she had sailed these waters since childhood, and the next slight turn, signaled by the waves hitting from a new angle, suggested they were passing the junk-building yards at Shau Kei Wan. The night was dark, the fog thicker. Her teeth started chattering. *Mandalay* ran long and straight, seemingly forever.

The water got rougher, the wind-driven chop roiled by a sea swell, which told Vicky they were entering the Tathong Channel. They must have passed Cape Collinson or at least, she prayed, Chai Wan. Then a curious thing happened. They had been running without lights, a dangerous practice in a shipping channel, when suddenly she heard the distinctive thunder of a high-powered police launch. Immediately, her father switched on the running lights and the white light at the main masthead, complying with the navigational rules, then extinguished them again as soon as the police engine faded astern. Vicky sensed movement close behind her. Turning carefully, she saw his boatboy loosen a halyard and lower the radar reflector. They forged on, invisible.

After another interminable period of cold spray and colder wind, the sky ahead began to flash softly at intervals. Waglan Light. Which put Shek-O somewhere in the dark and fog to their right. A line on the foredeck began to move under her leg, startling her; it sprang taut and pulled the jib squealing off the forestay. The sail filled, steadying the boat. Vicky looked up and back and saw the other staysails unfurling, one by one, and finally the main, which bellied hard. *Mandalay* heeled to the new power and her father shut down the engines. They were flying under full sail on a broad reach, southeast in silence toward Waglan Light and the China Sea beyond.

Vicky shifted crosswise on the steeply slanting deck, her feet down near the gunwale, her head propped on the hatch, her legs draped over the thick spinnaker pole. She waited until Waglan Light was blooming smaller and smaller behind them. At last she rose, aching and shivering, climbed the angled deck to the windward side, and worked her way carefully aft, gripping the safety lines and then the firmer cabin roof handholds. With the lighthouse astern, she could see her father and Back Door Ping silhouetted against the double flashes. The Taipan was still at the helm, braced against the heel, his eyes shifting between the dark sails and the compass, whose pale, dim glow underlit his face in red. His hand lay easily on the helm, but his shoulders were rigid with tension, as if he thought he could drive the boat faster by sheer will. A growled command sent Ping from winch to winch, cranking in one sail, easing another. Adjustments made, the smuggler rocked back on his heels, locked his eyes on the Taipan's face, and waited.

"Hi, Dad."

Vicky stepped into the cockpit.

Back Door Ping leaped up with an astonished "*Aieeyaaa!*" and snatched a shiny cleaver from the folds of his shirt. Duncan Mackintosh restrained him with a whipcrack shout. He grinned at his daughter, the compass light glowing red in his eyes and gleaming on his teeth.

"Ping. Nip below and brew up some tea. I imagine Missy caught a chill."

"You saw me?"

"You looked like a Gilbert and Sullivan boarding party. All you lacked was a dirk in your teeth."

"You knew I was on the bow? You let me freeze there for two hours?"

"I should have dropped you into the typhoon shelter, let you swim in shit." But he hadn't, she thought. He had chosen to take her with him.

"Why didn't you?" she asked, hoping he would acknowledge aloud his decision to accept her.

"Because you'd have wakened the dead with your howling. Dammit, Victoria, you've got a hell of a nerve."

"I have a nerve?" Vicky exploded. "I'm working twenty-hour days to keep MacF afloat and the Taipan's sailing off for secret meetings."

"You sound like a jilted wife."

"A familiar sound, I'm sure."

"Ping. We'll have that tea now."

The boatboy sidled cautiously past Vicky, as if unconvinced she was not a ghost, and scurried down the companionway. Vicky shut the hatch after him. "Where are you going?"

"To meet an old friend."

"Blacked out and with no radar reflector? Who are you afraid of?"

Her father's eyes flicked to the compass and he moved the helm a degree.

"The red junk again?" Vicky asked.

Eyes still on the compass, her father asked, "What were you doing on Mother's boat?"

"Looking after her. It's New Year's."

"Happy New Year," he said bleakly. But she sensed he was hiding or damping down a volcano of excitement.

"There was a riot, remember. I was worried about her."

"Good girl."

"Who are we meeting on the junk?"

"*We* are meeting no one. You will remain aboard *Mandalay*."

"I will not."

"You will, if I have to have Ping chain you in the sail locker."

"Who are you meeting on the junk?"

"None of your business."

"It was Hugo's business. And Vivian's business. Why not mine? Dad, you know what I'm doing for MacF. Are you going to deny my role?"

"The reason I didn't want you along tonight was that it could be dangerous. It's why I didn't bring Vivian, either."

"Vivian? Screw Vivian. I'm your blood."

"You're my daughter."

"But you would have brought Hugo?"

"Absolutely not. If something happens tonight and you and I are both, shall we say, incapacitated, who's going to run MacF? Peter? Fiona?"

"Well, in that case you should have thrown me over in the shelter."

"I'll do the next best thing. Leave you on the boat with Ping. If I come back, fine. If not, you can run for it."

"In a sailboat?"

"They're on a junk. They can't sail close to the wind. Sail into the wind and radio for help."

"Slim chance."

"I tried to minimize the risk to MacF. You've gone and doubled it. Fortunately, if we both end up slopping pigs in Mongolia, Vivian can carry on for us."

"That's not even vaguely funny."

"She's capable."

"What about Peter?"

"He's not."

"But Vivian's not a Mackintosh or a Farquhar."

Her father's shadow moved slightly in the dark. A shrug. "Our family has always thrived by taking in outsiders."

"What are you saying?"

"Your mother's father was an outsider. Even old Amos Farquhar—old Iron Ships—was an outsider to the Haigs. And God knows I'm an outsider. Your mother often said that when the women of this hong get in trouble, they at least know enough to marry bright young men."

"Mother's phrase," Vicky corrected him icily, "was 'when the women were in need.' "

"Same thing."

"It is not. And besides, she meant the days when women were not allowed to run the business themselves."

"Perhaps they knew something about themselves the present generations have forgotten."

"Dad, Chinese women have run their own hongs in Hong Kong for a hundred years. It's only we gweilos who deny their women. I know five women shipowners in the Colony, all Chinese, and all prospering."

"Maybe they know something about ships I don't."

"They know something the women in our family have always known."

"What's that?"

"The difference between wives and concubines."

"I won't have that talk. Apologize or go below."

"I will not apologize," she said hotly. "You don't trust me. You treat me like I'm worthless. You won't accept that I'm your heir. And now you say you'll leave our hong to *Vivian* if something happens to you and me."

"I didn't invite you tonight. I left you behind, in charge. Instead you sneak aboard and attack Vivian. I won't have it."

"Dad, please let me come to the meeting."

"Go below."

"All right. I'm sorry I said what I did."

He was silent.

"Dad."

She listened to the sea race past, and the hiss of the bow spray. "You're not welcome here," he said. "Leave me alone."

"Yes, Taipan," she said bitterly. "Forgive me for having an opinion."

"Damn your opinion."

"And forgive me for having feelings, too."

"You're not the only one with feelings, you silly bitch."

"What?"

"When I told you last year that she makes me feel alive, all I got from you was some smart remark."

Vicky jumped from the cockpit bench and shoved the hatch open with a bang. The light from below flew in their faces. Her father flung his hand up to block it. "Douse that damned light. You're blinding me."

Vicky whirled on him, spewing rage. "What did you expect from me? Approval?"

"I don't need your damned approval. I just tried to make you understand. Close that hatch."

"Understand what?"

"How it happened— *why* it happened."

"You betrayed my mother. Now you've deserted her."

"Grow up, Your Majesty. These things go two ways. She left me. I didn't desert her. She left. You can't keep blaming me alone."

"*What* did she leave, Dad? Hugo was dead. She needed your help. And you were fucking Vivian."

"I didn't kill Hugo," he shouted, his hand fluttering as if to erase the memory.

"No one said you did."

"We sailed in worse weather, your mother and I."

"Before you started fucking Vivian." As she said it, she listened, for the first time, to a quieter, more rational voice that suggested she was really intruding on lives she had no right to, and delivering judgments that were not hers to make. She started to apologize, but her father was already lashing back, "I'm warning you, Your Majesty," and they were—as Hugo used to say, wincing—off to the races.

"*Stop calling me that!*"

"Calling you what?"

"I hate it. Can't you call me Vicky?"

"What?"

"Can't you just once call me your daughter?"

"What are you talking about? It's your nickname."

"It's *your* nickname."

"It's been your nickname since you were a wee lass."

"It's filled with hate."

"You're daft."

"I'm not daft. I don't know why it is, but you hate me, Dad. I'm finally beginning to see that you hate me."

"Bloody nonsense."

"You treat me as if you blame me for something. As if I did something to you. You don't trust me. You—"

"Don't start that again."

"Dad, if there's one person in Hong Kong, other than you, who can lead MacF, it's me."

"You're a thirty-two-year-old woman."

"I think like you. I'm bold like you. I'm your blood in a way Hugo never was. I'm your true heir."

"I'm not through yet."

"It should be my turn when you are. Take me to the meeting. You took Hugo."

"You're not Hugo."

"I'm better."

"That's not for you to say."

"I don't have to say it. You already said it for me."

"The hell I—"

"The night he died you looked at me—you remember, you know you did—you looked at me. You didn't have to say a word. It was in your eyes. For one second you admitted it."

"Admitted what?"

"Say it out loud."

"What?"

"Say it."

"I'll say nothing."

"Say it!" she screamed. "Say it."

"Say what?"

"Say I'm your worthy daughter. . . . Please."

Duncan Mackintosh glanced at the compass and corrected with the helm. "You've a bloody high opinion of yourself."

Vicky started to cry.

"I don't think very highly of myself at all," she whispered, struggling to contain her tears. "I'm an awful mess. I have no friends, except Fiona. I have no man. I can't do anything especially well. I can't sail like Mother or speak Chinese like Peter. I could never raise the girls like Fiona and Hugo, and I know I'm not as clever a negotiator as Vivian. But I can lead MacF and you know it. . . . Please, say I'm your worthy daughter."

Her father looked away. "Close that hatch. I can't see a bloody thing."

Vicky plunged down the companionway.

Back Door Ping, maintaining a careful distance in the galley, indicated a mug of tea on the gimbaled stove, and retreated quickly up to the cockpit with one for her father. She heard the hatch slide shut. The noise of the wind and waves faded and it was quiet except for the water rushing under the boat.

Her head storming, her body shaking with anger, she sagged against the thick foot of the mainmast, reached into the dim galley, and stood there for a while with her hands trembling around the hot tea mug. Gradually, she grew aware that she was exhausted. Her feet ached, her skin prickled with dried salt. Her gown was ruined, and when she checked the time, she discovered that her watch had stopped at 2:30, thanks to the soaking on the bow.

The digital clock on the nav station read 3:30. Shivering in spite of the tea, she went aft to her father's stateroom and took a long hot shower. She shampooed the salt out of her hair, which she then blew dry. It struck her when she had finished that she had never seen one of the battery-draining electrical appliances on any of her parents' boats. Her mother and father were much more of the roughing-it school. This must be Vivian's. It hung from an antique brass hook in the shape of a dragon, screwed into the bulkhead beside the mirror.

Calmly and methodically, Vicky opened the narrow window above the sink, then unscrewed the steel port cover that protected the glass, and pushed the hair dryer out the hole and into the sea.

She felt infinitely better as she dog-latched the window and the port cover, and her only regret as she rummaged through her father's clothes locker to borrow a warm sweat suit and socks came when she discovered a pretty beige cotton sweater and a neatly hung pair of slacks, and had to accept that she didn't have the energy to open the port again and throw them out too. Instead, she crawled onto the leeward bunk, let the heel of the boat wedge her against the bulkhead, and closed her eyes.

She came out of sleep with a violent start. *Mandalay* had stopped. Gray light flooded through the Lexan skylight. She fumbled for her watch: 2:30. She got up carefully, holding on, because the boat was rolling on the swell. A clock by her father's desk said 7:00. Overhead, she heard her father and Ping in urgent conversation.

She stumbled out to the salon, smelled coffee there, and worked her way forward to the galley, poured coffee from the pot in its rack, and tasted it black; then she climbed the companionway, balanced the cup on a tread, and slid open the hatch.

"Don't come up," her father said. "Stay where you are."

She started to protest, but there was high tension in his voice. He and Ping had their binoculars out and were scanning the cloud bank that lay close to the water a quarter mile aft. A gray circle of sea extended around them. Ping had his ear cocked astern to a distant thunder.

"What do you hear, Your Majesty?"

"It sounds like a police boat. Where are we?"

"Miles out of their territory. Dammit, Ping, what do you think?"

"Two big engine, Taipan. Maybe three. Maybe fishingmens."

"Goddammed Thai pirate, maybe. Coming fast." He stooped to the cockpit instruments.

The engine-on warning whistles shrilled. He ground the starters hard, and *Mandalay*'s engines rumbled to life, drowning out the noise of the approaching boat. He put them in gear without waiting to warm them, and set the boat moving at half-speed. "Go below, Vicky."

"Dad—"

"And stay there."

"I want to come to that meeting."

"Ping, take the helm. Make like we're cruising. I'll give them a wave. Vicky, for the last time, get below. I don't know who's out there and I don't want to tempt them with a yellow-haired gweipo. I'm on a sailboat. I can't outrun them. Hide."

"If it's who you're meeting, can I come along?"

"*Taipan!*" called Ping.

A high, broad bow broke the cloud line and sent a massive wave surging to either side. Before the stern had cleared the cloud, the boat changed course to angle straight at *Mandalay*. The song "The Ship the Black Freighter" ran through Vicky's head.

"Get down!" her father shouted at her. He spun in a full, frantic circle and Vicky realized with a jolt that she had never seen him confused before. "Where the hell's that junk?" But the half-mile circle of sea was empty, except for *Mandalay* and the dark ship bearing down on her.

Vicky retreated down the companionway to the salon and pressed her nose to a port. The fishing boat was big, considerably longer than *Mandalay*, easily triple her tonnage, and huge in the bows, which swelled to accommodate its fish hold. It could be exactly what it looked like, one of the many fishing boats out of Hong Kong or Mainland China that worked these waters. It had the lines of a modern shrimper or a stern trawler.

From on deck she heard Ping say, "No pirate. Chinese boat. Maybe Fuzhou. Maybe Ningbo."

"Ningbo?" Her father relaxed. "Maybe that old junk sank. Too bad. She was a beauty."

Twenty seconds later the fishing boat was close enough for Vicky to see that its hull was made of steel and that Back Door Ping was right. The bow was cross-hatched with sloppy welds — shoddy Mainland work.

"Victoria, grab a Mae West," her father shouted down the companionway. "Get out the forehatch. They're going to run us down."

16

DUNCAN MACKINTOSH THREW the helm hard over, swinging *Mandalay* violently to starboard. His attempt to save Vicky, who was scrambling out the forehatch and into her life jacket, was Back Door Ping's death sentence. The boatboy was on the stern deck when the fishing boat slammed into the schooner, and the impact pitched him into the water, where he was crushed between the steel and aluminum hulls.

Duncan, clinging to the wheel so hard he bent it in his effort to keep his feet, saw Vicky flung headfirst against the foremast. Her legs crumpled under her. And when the fishing boat pushed *Mandalay* on its side, Vicky sprawled over the lifelines like a towel hung out to dry and tumbled into the water.

Instinctively, Duncan twirled the helm as if to turn the schooner upwind to right her. The rudder took hold, causing the fishing boat to slide sternward along her hull, and *Mandalay* righted herself, dragged erect by the weight of her lead keel. But the victory was short-lived, because the fishing boat had shattered her hull.

The sea rushed in. Duncan felt the deck plummet beneath him like an express elevator, she went down so fast. And now the fishing boat, which had ground past, swung back around in a wide circle and crashed into *Mandalay*'s sinking stern, driving it under the water and breaking the back stays. Duncan, flung to the cockpit sole, looked up to see the mainmast falling from the sky.

Hip deep in water, he couldn't move. It slammed across his back and shoulders, driving the breath from his lungs and pinning him to the gunwale of the sinking boat. He felt cut in half. He was numb below the waist.

The engines roared again. He flinched from the next attack. But the noise faded. He twisted his face out of the rising water. The fishing boat was speeding toward the horizon. Seconds later, he was alone, the waves breaking over his head, his legs gone God knew where, his boat sinking, and his daughter lost.

"Of all the stupid bloody ways to die," he growled aloud, damning himself for a fool and then screaming his rage to God for letting Two-Way Wong beat him. "Should have listened to Viv," he lamented. "Should have listened to Viv. God damn it."

He gathered his courage, waiting for the sea to wash over him. But first came the pain, sudden, unexpected, and compelling. The legs and waist that had lost all feeling were in that instant afire with feeling—burning, ripping feeling that made him scream out before he caught himself by sheer will. He had no intention of dying screaming. He had lost everything, but he would not lose his courage. He clung to silence, the last thing he owned, the one thing Two-Way Wong could not take away from him.

The pain coursed through him like electric charges. This is what it feels like to be tortured, he thought. Waiting for the worst to come. But he vowed he wouldn't give in. Vaguely, he wondered why he was still alive. He was still pinned to the gunwale, but he hadn't drowned. It dawned on him that the shattered boat had stopped sinking. He nodded his understanding. There'd be air trapped in the after cabins, and combined with the flotation foam in the bilges, that air would let her drift a while until the air seeped out and let her rest. Let him rest. For if he didn't die of drowning, he would die of pain.

"Daddy!"

He opened his eyes, unaware he had closed them.

"Daddy?"

He gathered the air into his lungs. "In the cockpit." She swam into his view. Her forehead was red and swollen, with a huge lump where she had hit the mast. Pinned half in, half out of the cockpit, Duncan looked down blearily at her. "We're in the shit for sure, old girl."

Awkward in the bulky life vest, Vicky dog-paddled to the side of the boat and closed her hands over the nearly submerged toe rail. She looked as if the blow had knocked her silly. There was blood in her hair. "Are you hurt?" she asked.

"Of course I'm hurt. The bloody mast is on me."

"Just stay there. I'll get it off."

He almost laughed at his calm Victoria. Where the devil did she think he would go under half a ton of aluminum? The pain rampaged through his lower body again, suddenly, with no warning, and he gasped. "Off?" he choked. "How do you intend to lift it?"

She hadn't the strength to climb onto the boat. The decks were awash, but the lifelines blocked her like a fence. "Take off your vest," he said.

Vicky did so, clumsily shoving the life jacket aboard before she tackled the lines. It seemed to take forever, but she finally mastered the rising, falling sea swell, using it to her advantage. At last she was lying on her back on the partly submerged deck, her body heaving with the effort.

"Good girl."

She stood over him, weaving, studying the fallen mast. "Daddy, can I raise this with the foremast halyard?"

"You'll get a better angle with the boom lift."

He watched her calculate the angles with a cool eye.

"No," she said. "It's better with the halyard."

"Just don't drag it over—" He gasped as the pain struck again.

Vicky knelt beside him and hesitantly brushed the wet hair from his brow. "Is there morphine in the first aid?"

"Just get the bloody mast off me."

Moving slowly and deliberately, as if she were sleepwalking, she went forward, out of sight, and returned dragging a halyard, which she wrapped around the upper end of the mast. "Make bloody sure it can't slip."

"I have. Can you move when I raise it?"

"I'll move."

"Are you sure about the morphine?"

"No bloody morphine. I want to feel what you're doing to me."

"Right. Try to slide backward." She disappeared again. He heard the halyard winch buzz as she hauled in the slack. "All right," she called, when the line grew taut. "Here we go."

He heard the winch click-click-click, saw the line hum tauter, felt the vibrations through the mast. The winch-clicking slowed, the vibrations took on a deeper tone, then faded, as the weight on his back diminished.

"Carry on," he shouted, the effort wracking him with new pain. "Carry on."

The weight was less now, markedly less. He tested his position, bracing his hands on the gunwale and pushing his dead legs into the submerged cockpit. The pain in his chest forced tears from his eyes. He groaned and growled past the pain, pushing as if to birth himself again.

Vicky was beside him, pulling, tucking his head under the mast, and he was free. "Stay there," she said. "Let me lower it before it falls." The mast was swaying at the end of the line.

"I'm not going anywhere." That was an understatement. He had no feeling now in his legs, a spreading numbness in his gut, and a pain in his chest that threatened to rip him apart. Vaguely, he noticed Vicky winching the mast down to the deck, where it seated itself and stopped swaying.

She came back slowly, sloshing along the submerged deck, steadying herself against *Mandalay*'s heavy, drunken roll by holding the lifeline.

"Shall I sit you up?" There was something a little blank in her eyes that frightened him. Her voice was a little blank, too, and un-

naturally bright. Either she knew he was dying and was resolved to
jolly him to the end like a professional nurse, or she was hurt badly
herself. "Shall I sit you up?" she asked again.

"You can try."

The boat was down at the head, her bow under the waves, the
decks angling toward it. Victoria put her hands under his arms and
tried to drag him toward the stern. He felt her strain with all her
might. Hopeless.

"Just prop me against the line. Get my head out of the water."
Slowly, she worked him around, flinching when the pain made his
body jerk, and heaved him into a sitting position with his back against
the lifelines and his feet dangling in the submerged cockpit.

She collapsed beside him, pale and breathing hard.

"You all right, Your— old girl?"

She glanced at him sidelong. "Topping, thanks."

"Head hurt?"

"Like a champagne hangover without the memories."

"Concussion?"

"I'm afraid so. I was out cold for a minute or so." She looked
out at the sea, covered one eye and then the other. "Everything
looks a little red."

"Mackintoshes have hard heads."

"So do Farquhars. . . . It feels as if the worst is yet to come.
My neck is stiff as cement. Who did us, Daddy?"

"Two-Way," he said grimly. "I was such a fool."

"Two-Way Wong? Why?"

He turned to her, the breath fierce in his chest. "Get him," he
said. "Get him."

"Why?"

"Why? He got me."

"Why would he do this?"

"Vicky," he said, enjoying the bright taste of her name on his
tongue, "Vicky, I've made a deal with Tang's New China reformers.
I've got the goods on Two-Way for bribing Premier Chen's mob
and ripping off the PRC shipyards. Billions in diverted materials.
Money stashed in Switzerland."

"How?" Vicky interrupted.

"Been keeping files on the bastard for years. Since he tried to pull that kickback scam at the Apleichau yard."

"What files?"

"Evidence. Swiss bank numbers. Phony billing. Cargo manifests. Recordings. I'll sink Two-Way and I'll sink Chen. Tang takes control and pays us back with guarantees in Hong Kong. . . ."

Vicky was silent for a while. "I'm awed," she said at last. "I feel like a child. I said I think like you, but I don't know if I would have thought that up."

"Sure you would have. Or something better. Better than this, at least. Two-Way got wind of it, apparently."

Her head lolled toward him. "How?"

"Somebody fucked us. Told Two-Way I was meeting the junk."

"Who?"

He had thought of little else. "If the junk doesn't show, it was someone in Shanghai."

"And if it does come? You were betrayed in Hong Kong?"

"If the junk does come, I was betrayed in Hong Kong."

She tried to imagine Two-Way ordering her father's death. It was easier to believe the PRC doing such a thing, easier to imagine a huge, faceless bureaucracy labeling Duncan Mackintosh its enemy and letting a death sentence seep down through its many layers, until finally a fishing captain motored out of a Mainland port to smash the gweilo yacht. Two-Way, for all the stories and all the rumors, was a businessman, not a gangster. A powerful businessman had ample means to destroy a weaker rival, short of murder.

"How'd you make contact with Tang?"

"Vivian."

"Oh . . . How?"

"Plugging away in Shanghai. She's got a fine sense for where the power lies."

"I've noticed."

"She's served me well, dear. I'd not have gotten this far without her."

Vicky surveyed the nearly submerged yacht. "I think," she said, "that might not have been such a bad thing."

"Don't muck about. Get Two-Way."

"Revenge?" she asked dubiously.

"It's still the only way to save MacF. Tang is China's main chance. China's main chance is Hong Kong's main chance. Hong Kong's main chance is MacF's main chance."

Her eyes drifted to the horizon, still a cloud ring a half-mile wide, then down at her father sprawled against the lifeline. "How do you propose I 'get' him? Where's your proof that Two-Way corrupted Chen's people?"

"Below in my cabin."

"Forget it, unless they've got divers on the junk."

Duncan nodded. He could feel that *Mandalay* was sinking fast. He couldn't move and Vicky hadn't a hope of locating the papers underwater.

"There's more . . . much more."

"Where? Safety deposit box?"

"Daren't trust a bank vault these days. Too many 'old friends' involved."

"Where'd you hide it?"

"The one place no one would think to look for it."

"On Mother's boat," she guessed.

Duncan stared at her. "Maybe you do think like me. It's in the mainmast. Perfect hidey-hole. Mum's not going anywhere."

"What am I supposed to do with it?"

"Get it to Tang without getting killed. Make a deal to protect MacF."

"And how am I supposed to get to Tang?"

"Vivian."

"Vivian," she repeated slowly, spacing the syllables of her name like a doubtful taste on the tongue. ". . . Daddy, what's Wally Hearst about?"

"Wally Hearst is 'old friends' with some of Premier Chen's people—ones who might shift over to Tang, if Tang deposes Chen."

Vicky started to protest. Her father cut her off with an ironic smile for her naïveté. "Nobody wants a civil war. If Tang's to win and hold power he has to accommodate his enemies. Wally's job is to make friends on Chen's side."

"Then why didn't you want Wally to meet Mr. Wu?"

"I didn't want Wally wasting influence for the hotels. MacF needs bigger favors down the road."

Duncan watched her turn it over in her mind. Her next question — as far off-track as it was — did not surprise him.

"How did you get involved with Vivian?"

"I fell in love with her," he said.

"Setting up this Tang scam?"

"I didn't bring Vivian into it until after."

"After what?"

"After we became lovers."

"How could you fall in love with . . ."

"With a Chinese girl half my age?"

"It's the oldest story in the book. It's not like you."

"That's true."

"Was it sex?"

"That turned out to be an unexpected bonus."

"What, then?"

"She made me feel strong."

"Strong? You're the strongest person I know. You're a born taipan."

"I wasn't born to it. I had to fight for it, then fight again to keep it."

"You didn't have to fight for Mother."

"I had to fight for your mother every day," he said bleakly.

"What do you mean?"

"Your mother is a demanding woman."

"She was demanding of all of us, in her way. Even before the drinking."

"I had to fight to keep up. I wasn't born to her life, so every day was a test. Try to understand."

"I've never heard you talk like this," said Vicky, thinking he had never tried to understand her.

"You've never talked to me dying," he whispered, and she hated the selfishness of her thoughts.

"You're not dying," Vicky said too quickly.

Her father did not reply.

The stump of the main and the tall foremast swayed against the searing sky. Occasionally, as the hulk that was left of *Mandalay* drifted in circles, the foremast would pass across the sun, casting a moment's merciful shade. She whispered again, "You're not dying," but he was staring blankly at the sky.

"Daddy?"

She moved closer, propped against the lifelines, her legs nearly submerged, her face wet with tears and burning in the sun. Her head felt as if it would explode, and yet she felt oddly detached from her body, only vaguely curious how badly she was injured. Her vision had faded to a small circle of burning haze and flashes of memory.

"Are you all right?" Duncan whispered.

"Like a knife in my brain. And a rope around my neck."

"Too bad Viv's not here. She gives a mean massage." He chuckled. "Magic fingers."

"Do you remember the matador, Daddy?"

"Spain? Say, that was a trip, wasn't it, Your Majesty? Oh, sorry, old girl. I'm not supposed to call you that."

Vicky had not noticed. All she had heard was the voice warm with affectionate memories. "Madrid. Remember the matador?"

He dodged her again. "I remember that poor bull. You'd think it was enough for one dumb animal to fight one man. Beast faced a bloody mob—all those blokes on horseback, picadors. Ruddy bull didn't stand a chance. Rather like our lot battling it out with China. What?"

The family had done a sort of Grand Tour the summer before Vicky went off to school in New York. She'd been eighteen, Peter fifteen. Hugo was stationed in Northern Ireland and had come down to meet them in London, a tense, hollow-eyed Hugo unlike the brother she knew. Then it was off to Spain, leaving Peter with Scottish friends. They had gone to Madrid and the bullfights and she had lost her heart, at some distance, to a young matador she saw tossed and trampled, only to spring miraculously back to the fight. That night her father had a friend introduce her to the bullfighter, so it was unlikely he would have forgotten.

"Don't you remember?"   ·

But Duncan's mind had wandered to a later day, a day in 1985, some twelve years ago, when the Joint Declaration first had been ratified and the enormity of the British sellout to Peking was starkly apparent. His giant rival Jardine was packing it in, moving head-quarters to bloody Bermuda, and property prices had dropped into the cellar. Vicky was coming home, finally, from NYU's School of Business, and he had gone to meet her at the old Kai Tak Airport. Scanning the arrivals streaming out of Customs, he had heard a small voice at his elbow.

"Excuse me, Taipan."

The voice belonged to a pretty little Chinese girl wheeling a baggage cart heaped with cheap suitcases and cardboard boxes wrapped in twine and tagged from the just-landed London flight. She looked about fourteen and her eyeglasses made her seem very serious.

"Yes?" he had asked, glancing impatiently at the doors where Vicky was due to appear.

"Please excuse me, sir. I believe you are Mr. Duncan Mackin-tosh."

"Who are you?"

"My name is Vivian Loh."

"Yes?"

She spoke in long measured sentences divided by parenthetical phrases, and he could almost hear the commas. "There is, of course, no reason for you to remember me, sir, but I am a Mackintosh-Farquhar scholarship student."

One of scores of shining faces over white shirts and middy blouses to which he must have pinned a ribbon for hard study. Sally had overseen the scholarships. They were a way of getting the Chinese involved, and certainly over the years MacF had picked up some decent employees.

"What are you studying?"

"I read economics at Cambridge. Selwyn College."

"Jolly good."

"With a minor in Chinese literature."

"How is it going?"

"I was most fortunate to receive First Class Honors in both."

Duncan was surprised. He thought she was just starting, but she must be older than she looked. He could never reckon Chinese ages. At any rate, she was a bright one.

"Firsts?" he said. "Well, good on us. We backed a winner."

She looked embarrassed. "Thank you, sir. I'm so sorry to disturb you. I just wanted to tell you how grateful I am for the opportunity."

"Sounds like you earned it. Economics, eh? Nip 'round to MacF in the morning. Ask my hiring chap to find you something suitable."

"Thank you, Taipan. But I fear I have little to offer a Hong Kong trading house, yet. I have been nothing but a student my entire life. I must gain practical experience before I ask more of your kindness."

Duncan had been listening with half an ear while he watched for Victoria. Now he looked at the Chinese girl. Vivian Loh's words rang familiarly. Thirty-five years ago he had declined his first job offer from Old Man Farquhar, Sally's father, with almost precisely the same phrase. Gain practical experience. Vivian returned a level gaze, and his finely honed instinct for what people of either race wanted told him that her motive was very likely the same as his had been. He had sensed correctly that he would have a long, slow climb if he entered the Farquhar hong at the first level the old boy offered.

She was a very pretty girl, he realized at last. Her eyes were unusually dark and seemed to sparkle with intelligence. Cheeky bit of crumpet, marching up to him and introducing herself without a by-your-leave. Precisely how he had gotten to Sally's father. Escaping the 1949 revolution in a sinking yawl, he had known enough even at eighteen to make his Hong Kong landfall at the Yacht Club. He had seen Farquhar on the sampan dock, spotted him for a taipan, chatted him up, got invited into the club for a drink, then home to his Peak mansion for dinner. He must have talked a hell of a line, because he had been as penniless as this little student with her heap of string-tied bundles.

"Where do you intend to gain your practical experience?"

"China," she said, completing in one word the picture that Duncan Mackintosh had formed of her—bright, ambitious, determined, and hungry. "I will work in China."

"Daddy!"

Victoria came running at him, pushing a cart piled high with matched luggage and shopping bags of the gifts she was always dragging home. She had a knapsack over her shoulder, her hair in a ponytail, and looked, he thought, about sixteen in her blue jeans. She hugged him hard. "Let's buy a hotel in New York."

"Victoria, this is Viv—" But the Chinese girl had disappeared.

"Dad, with this so-called Joint Declaration, we've got to start diversifying out of Hong Kong. The New York hotel market is about to take off. I've been checking out older hotels we can renovate into luxury—"

"This all your bags?"

"Listen to me."

"In the car. Your mother's waiting a dinner party. We've asked your friend Jeff Grey to join us."

"Whatever for?"

"His father's retiring. Jeff's going to take over Partridge and Grey."

"Jeff's an idiot."

"Which is why they could use MacF's help. It's the biggest department store chain in Asia."

"And the worst run. What about my hotel idea, Daddy? I'm done with school. I want to work in New York."

"Think you could manage the shipyard at Apleichau Island?"

"You want me to build *junks*?"

"If you can handle it, Your Majesty." Those were the days when he could still control her with a few well-chosen words.

"Of course I can handle it," she had shot back, hotels forgotten for the moment, and blind to the role he expected her to play in his plan to annex Partridge and Grey.

.   .   .

Vicky could feel *Mandalay* disintegrating under her.

"Dad," she whispered into the silence, "is Vivian your first affair?"

The yacht lurched on the swell, jetting new pain through Duncan's broken chest. He fought to recover his senses, and when he
had, Vicky saw a new reflective light in his eyes and thought he
might speak the truth.

"Once before," he whispered. "Long time ago. Before you were
born."

Vicky was a little surprised. She had supposed that if Vivian was
not his first affair, then he had had many. A smile tugged at her
mouth. "Twice in forty years? Makes them both sound serious."

"Both," he agreed.

"What was she like?"

Her father smiled. The hard lines of pain and his fight to master
it vanished from his face. He looked in that second like a young
man. "Just a simple English girl. Easier to keep up with than your
mother. We were alike."

"What happened?"

He took a slow and careful breath, and the pain the effort cost
him drove the smile away. "I had to choose between it — her — and
your mother and Hugo. . . . No one ever loved like us. . . ."

"Long before I was born?"

"You were the mending job, Your Majesty. Your mother and I
had you to seal our renewed 'vows.' "

Vicky felt numb with discovery, stunned by her sudden perspective on the central struggle in her own life. She finally understood
"Your Majesty, Victoria." He did hate her. Hated what she symbolized. Seething with resentment, he had blamed her for his having to
give up the love of his life.

"Mother knew?"

"I didn't think so, at the time."

"But?"

"God . . . I can draw a line," he said, "looking back, between the way she used to drink before and how she drank after. Maybe she knew. Maybe she did. . . . We were in similar straits, my beautiful mistress and I, both boxed in by our lives. I was impatient—just like you—trapped by Old Man Farquhar. She was trapped too. Sex was a magnificent way out. She was so lovely . . . and so very much in need. Like Jeff, Vicky. Like your husband. Like your mother. Look out for the broken-winged birds, Vicky. They'll get you every time."

"Is Vivian a broken wing?"

The Dragon Smile drove the pain from his face.

"Not so I could notice. She's a real high flyer. . . . Look out for her, dear."

"Sorry, Dad. I'll have my hands full taking care of Mother."

"I didn't mean it that way," he whispered, closing his eyes.

"What do you mean? A warning?"

The air rattled in his chest and for a second he tried to rise from the deck. She took his hand and held it until it turned heavy in hers.

"Daddy?" He had turned to face her.

But it was only his head rolling with the ponderous movement of the sea, and she began to cry with a depth of loneliness she had never known. All the answers, all the mysteries solved, too late. The man she had chosen to test her standards, fire her ambition, and give her courage, was gone. She wished to lay his body flat, to put him in a position of rest. But the seas were running over the deck as *Mandalay* sank. Mustering her last strength to stand and stumble about the yacht, she gathered stray lengths of line and sail cord to tie her father's body to a boat built in his own yard, so he would not drift alone on the China Sea.

17

IT BEGAN TO dawn on Vicky that she was seriously injured, because it was not her way to lie down and die. There was danger all around. She had to act. She had to get up, find the life raft, launch it, and climb aboard. Raise the canopy and drink cold water. She was thirsty. But she hadn't the strength or the will.

When she opened her eyes again the sun was high overhead and the sea grabbing her chest. The boat was entirely submerged. Even the cabin roof was awash. Only the top lifeline still showed, like a wire fence around the two trees of the masts. She saw something orange bobbing away and recognized, with a stab of fear, her life jacket.

A shadow crossed her face.

She thought it was *Mandalay*'s mast again, but the sun didn't burn back around it, and the air in the shadow felt almost cool. Wearily she turned toward the dark.

Her father slipped from her, down, under the water, tied to the yacht. The stump of the mast dropped from view. She felt an insistent tug of air and water that pulled her down. A sea broke over her aching head, the water warm, and her mouth filled with salt.

Vivian Loh sat up in bed, her heart beating hard and fast. She was dreaming of Duncan and she closed her eyes again, squeezing them shut to try to bring his image back. He was sailing alone on his schooner, standing at the helm, his eyes on the sails instead of the sea, which ended abruptly a short distance in front of the boat.

She was watching from the side, close enough to see his face, the squint lines arrowing into his eyes, the gray riddling his mustache. But he couldn't hear her warning. Where the sea ended was nothing, a void, broader than heaven and forever deep. The rim was cut square, the water held by the same dark magic that allowed her to see what could not be stopped.

She called to him in Chinese, which he didn't understand. Crying out to Duncan, she switched the languages she was speaking, from Shanghainese Wu to Cantonese to Mandarin, to the Ningbo dialect, to Fukienese; but he knew none of those tongues and she could not remember a word of English. She screamed and screamed, every language she knew, but he sailed on, as oblivious as any gweilo to the insults flung by the peddlers when he wandered down a Chinese street.

She opened her eyes and he was gone.

Vivian got up, hurried to the shower, and stood under the hot stream. The dream clung to her mind. The image of the boat on the rim kept flashing into her thoughts. Still groggy even as she toweled dry, she continued to avoid the clock. It had been nearly four in the morning when she got back from the Shek-O headlands. Even then she had lain awake. Thank God the office was closed. Though it might have been easier to go in and work than stay home wondering if Duncan was all right. She thought of going down to the Yacht Club to wait for him, but her reception there was always frosty. His wife had too many friends.

Alone, without his fierce presence, they would feel freer to attack her.

Several hotels overlooked the typhoon shelter. As much as she hated to go out, she decided to breakfast in the dining room that offered the best view. The Excelsior, it turned out, was perfect, with a New Year's Day brunch. Judging by the ashen faces at the neighboring tables, she was one of the few this afternoon not nursing a hangover.

She sat alone, drinking endless cups of green tea, staring at the speck of open water in the typhoon shelter where *Mandalay* moored, and calculating and recalculating the time Duncan should return to Causeway Bay. She vowed not to worry until four o'clock. But at three she felt the terror build. Four passed without a sign of his yacht. Four-thirty. Five. The dark crept in from the east and north where the Mainland mountains melted into the sea and sky.

Just before total darkness, when it was still light enough to read the Marine Police rescue markings on its side, a huge helicopter passed over the typhoon shelter. She leaned into the window and saw it continue up the shore to the landing pad at the old naval dockyard at the edge of Central. Moments later the dark completed its descent.

She called for her check and went home.

There was one last thing to do and she dreaded it. Her TIC computer, which was tied into MacF's mainframe, carried — in addition to the various market wires — Reuters and AP. It was a simple matter to query the automatically stored news reports of the past twelve hours. She typed DUNCAN MACKINTOSH, ignoring the blinking message light. The story jumped to the screen.

> HONG KONG (1701, 1/1/97)
> HONG KONG YACHT *MANDALAY* SUNK IN SOUTH
> CHINA SEA COLLISION SIXTY MILES SOUTH-
> EAST OF HONG KONG. DUNCAN MACKINTOSH,
> "TAIPAN" OF MACKINTOSH FARQUHAR TRAD-
> ING COMPANY, LOST AND REPORTED DEAD
> BY VICTORIA MACKINTOSH, HIS DAUGHTER,
> PICKED UP BY PRC FISHING JUNK, HELICOP-
> TERED HONG KONG, ADMITTED SERIOUS
> CONDITION, MATILDA HOSPITAL.

Vivian Loh turned off the monitor. She closed a crack in the drapes that had admitted the garish red glare of the rooftop neon sign, double-locked her god-guarded front door, and shut the painted door to her living room. She felt as helpless as when she was a child and she wanted her mother to stay home with her father. Nothing she could do would change the moment.

BOOK FOUR

Dragon Daughter

18

February 1997

BEFORE FIONA HAD married Hugo to serve in Northern Ireland as a British Army captain's wife, she'd studied psychology in London. Love had derailed her dreams of being a doctor, to the great relief of her family. They were country people, complacent Hampshire gentry. And while marriage to a clan of money-grubbing Hong Kong China traders was hardly their first choice for their odd-duck daughter, the amiable Hugo—Gordonstoun and a good Scottish regiment, after all—surely beat hollow Lord-knew-who the girl might tie up with in a London hospital.

When they went home to his Hong Kong to live like latter-day colonials, Fiona had kept her bargain scrupulously. As Tai-Tai-in-waiting (her own description to her old school friends) she was a wife, a social leader, and a mother, with no time to resume her education. For a while she had subscribed to the professional journals, until they began to pile up unopened, and she still hoped to do volunteer therapy at a clinic once Melissa and Millicent were both off to school. But she had remembered the basics and believed fervently in the healing powers of release and articulation. She had let herself weep for Hugo. Nor had she hidden her grief from the girls. So she had a fair idea what was troubling the chief of psychiatry at Matilda Hospital.

An elderly Chinese with a scholar's wispy beard, he hid his exasperation behind thick eyeglasses and a lukewarm smile. Fiona sympathized. He would find it easier to open an oyster with his fingernails than to peel the mask off Victoria Mackintosh.

The girls rushed her bed before Fiona could stop them.

"*Kung Hay Fat Choi*, Auntie Vicky!"

"Happy Chinese New Year to you, too, Melissa. *Kung Hay Fat Choi*, Millicent." From among the computer, telephone, and fax machine cluttering her night tables, she fished out a couple of red *lai see*—lucky money—envelopes and tossed them to the girls. "Wishing you to prosper, Number-One and Two Nieces. Double New Year's? Do you know how lucky you are? Back in England they're giving up treats for Lent."

Fiona exchanged a private glance with the psychiatrist. A month after the death of her father and just two weeks since the physical effects of a hairline skull fracture and two concussions had begun to recede, Vicky was acting as if *Mandalay* had sunk a decade ago.

Fiona was convinced it was an act, and had told the doctor that she thought Vicky was frightened, though of what they could not suss out. Fiona had bounced another theory off Alfred Ching: With the towering figure of her father gone, the girl who had fought so fiercely for his love her whole life was utterly alone in an empty arena.

Alfred had laughed. "She's tiptop, Fiona. She's just thinking."

"Thinking what?"

"Sorting out her next move."

"She's not that cold."

"She hurts," Alfred had agreed. "But she's got more on her mind. What, God knows. She plays it close to the vest. Like the Taipan."

"Sorry to interrupt, Doctor," said Fiona. "Didn't realize you were still here."

"He was just leaving," Vicky said. "I've got a secretary in the hall waiting for letters."

"Actually, we have five more minutes, Victoria," the doctor said. "We started late. You took an urgent call from Kai Tak."

"Don't remind me."

"We'll be outside. . . . Melissa. Millicent." Fiona gathered up her daughters.

"Stay, Fiona, please. The doctor's not looking for secrets, are you, Doctor?"

Fiona glanced at the girls, who had gone still as chairs in hopes their presence would not be noticed. "You can stay too," Vicky assured them. "No X-rated revelations this morning."

The doctor shook his head in resignation. "Yes, why don't you all stay? Now, Vicky, let's be serious a moment."

"Right. You were saying it's commonly agreed that too many traumas at once will precipitate a breakdown, and I was saying the failure of common knowledge is that it doesn't fit the individual."

The doctor sighed. They had circled this contention before and the woman wouldn't budge. "Look here, Victoria. You—"

She cast him a sharp smile. "You're going to be stern."

The doctor did not smile back.

Fiona worried about the rigidity of Vicky's expression. She was clever and monumentally self-contained—more so than ever since the accident—but her rigid smile, her arms knotted under her breasts, her head held high and wary as a cobra's, her narrowed eyes, formed an image of an animal at bay, or a frail container about to explode. She wore an excessively modest high-necked nightgown more appropriate for a nun than for a pretty unmarried woman in her thirties, and she had knotted her beautiful blond hair into a tight bun. At the rate she was going, Fiona thought, she would bob it soon. Her eyes flickered toward Fiona, and Fiona would not have been surprised if Vicky burst suddenly into tears, or simply stepped out the window.

"I *am* going to be stern," said the doctor. "Obviously, you're not about to open up in front of your present audience, so I'll list what's happened to you in the last year and then I'll ask you to think later why you display less emotion about these events than that bowl of roses."

"You know I don't have to sit here for this. It's one thing to CAT-scan my skull weekly, quite another to badger me with questions I don't care to answer."

"No, you don't," the doctor agreed mildly. "But I'd rather have this conversation today than a month from now while you're foaming in a straitjacket."

"You're really exaggerating," Vicky protested. "I'm not displaying any less emotion than I ever display. This is how I am, always. Ask Fiona. Ask the girls. You can't make me fit some textbook mold."

"Then humor me."

Vicky laughed. "You're supposed to humor me."

"So let's humor each other for five more minutes and then I'll leave you to your work."

"Five minutes." She looked at her watch. Fiona waited for her to say "Go," and when she didn't, the realization that Vicky was actually timing the doctor scared her again.

The doctor glanced at the children, then held up a long thin hand and ticked off her troubles on luminescent yellow fingers. "The Year of the Rat has been brutal. Your long relationship with your boyfriend dissolved. You suffered a business failure in New York. You came home to see your brother killed before your eyes. Your parents divorced. And now your father's been killed and you yourself suffered serious injuries."

Vicky stared through him.

"Have I left anything out?" the doctor asked coolly, obviously trying to provoke her into a reaction.

"Yes. Turnover. Five months from now we could be having this conversation in Mongolia."

"Do you believe that?"

"Whose passport do *you* hold?"

"I'm looking forward to a happy retirement right here, on Lamma Island."

"But whose passport do you hold, just in case some PRC bureaucrat declares Lamma a guano-mining commune?"

"Canada," he admitted. "Only because I have a brother there, and it seemed prudent—"

"Then you agree that I—who am responsible for the fortunes of my family's trading hong—would be crazy *not* to be worried about Turnover."

"You're changing the subject and begging the question. The question is, why, with everything that's happened, have I seen you shed no tears?"

"I'm not a crier," Vicky said airily. "My father did not encourage crying and neither did my mother. As it wasn't encouraged, it did not accomplish anything, so I never learned to use it. What do you want me to do? Fall apart? I can't fall apart. Every misery you listed is another reason why I have to keep going. Who in hell is going to manage my family's affairs if I don't? My dead brother? My dead father? My drunk mother? You left out her drinking, by the way. Who? Me, that's who."

"Your brother Peter."

"Peter can't cut it—this is a not-to-be-repeated conversation, by the way, small ladies," she added with a stern glance at Fiona's wide-eyed daughters.

"Yes, Auntie Vicky."

"Yes, Auntie Vicky."

"That goes for you, too, Doc."

"Of course," he said stiffly. "I'm your doctor."

"Not for long." She grinned. "My *medical* doctor assures me that I'm out of here any day."

"All the more reason to press you, Victoria. You mustn't walk out of here encased in ice."

"That's my Scottish blood," she fended him off, with a look to Fiona for support. Fiona averted her eyes.

"I've treated many Scots, thank you," the doctor said. "You can't fool me with that ethnic nonsense."

"I'm not trying to fool you, but your five minutes is up, my post-concussion headache is back, and I really must get back to work before some PRC bureaucrat steals my hong."

The old man stood, reluctantly. "Shall we talk next week?"

Vicky hesitated. The throbbing behind her eyes was deep and intense. Two weeks ago she had thought the pain would kill her. It still visited daily, and at times she paced the hospital halls, as if to walk away from it.

"I won't be here next week."

"I could stop by your office if you're busy."

"What about Chinese New Year?"

"I could use the break from the festivities. I'm too old to eat so much."

"You would come to my office?"

Fiona suddenly ached for Vicky. A poignantly vulnerable note had crept into her voice. It was almost a plea.

"Perhaps I will write a paper on your case when I retire to Lamma."

Vicky smiled back. "Thanks. I'll see you next week, wherever. *Kung Hay Fat Choi!*"

"Happiness and wealth to you, too, Taipan's Daughter."

"Stop looking so worried. I'm fine."

"When is the reading of your father's will?"

"Monday week."

"Call me if you need me." He stopped at the door and sniffed a rose. Every day, three dozen red roses arrived with a card chopped with a Chinese ideogram for love. "Who's your secret admirer?"

"I don't know. Probably Alfred Ching. Take the flower with you, Doctor. Goodbye."

"Alfred Ching? Hong Kong's newest tycoon?"

"We're old friends."

Alfred had come by daily as soon as the hospital allowed her visitors, pacing her room like a busy lion while he regaled her with the progress of his property deal and made her laugh with imitations of the various international bankers he was courting. She had cherished his visits, because his excitement was contagious, he was great fun—even if laughing made her head ache worse—and his concern for her was, she had to admit, quite touching. One night, during a relapse that clearly had the doctors worried, she had awakened from a long sleep to find Alfred holding her hand, his face an ocean of fear.

"I'm all right," she assured him, slurring with a dry mouth.

"You better be," he whispered back. He wet his fingers and moistened her lips, then helped her drink from the glass.

"How long have you been here?"

"Not long."

"Sixteen hours," interrupted the nurse, who had come running when the monitors showed her awake. "You ought to get some sleep, Mr. Ching, before we have to put you down beside her."

"I'm ready." Alfred grinned, winking at Vicky. But even then he was watching anxiously for some light of recovery in her eyes. She had recovered and they had had their scheduled dinner date on hospital trays, celebrating, as Alfred had promised, his closing the deal on the Cathay Tower—which he renamed in Hong Kong style Ching-Cathay Tower.

Then, suddenly, Alfred had vanished.

An apologetic fax from Toronto explained he had gone out to Canada on their Expat-Emigrant scheme. It seemed a very curious time to leave Hong Kong and she suspected he had a second motive, probably seeking additional Canadian-Chinese investments for a fol-low-up deal now that he was hot. Soon after, the first roses had arrived, which was pleasant, though she would have much preferred his cheerful voice on the telephone, or waking to his smile.

"Do you really think it's Alfred sending the roses, Auntie Vicky?"

"Who else? Mao?"

"Who?"

"Mao Zedong. Don't they teach history anymore?"

"I'll bet it's Chip," said Millicent.

"Chip?" Melissa retorted scornfully. "Chip couldn't afford so many roses. He's only a policeman."

"Melissa!" Fiona cried. "What sort of talk is that?"

"Roses are expensive, Mother," explained the ten-year-old. "Chip doesn't earn a lot of money. Look at the silly car he drives."

Millicent puffed up, red-faced and speechless at this attack on her crush.

Vicky laughed. "Hong Kong heart and soul, Fiona. Time to ship her off to Scotland to learn some values."

"Can I?" Melissa cried. "Can I, Mum?" And Millicent, whom

Fiona had enrolled in a Hong Kong school rather than send her alone to Gordonstoun so soon after her grandfather's death, brightened at the sudden possibility.

"Not yet. You're too young."

Fiona's youngest favored her with a steady glare. "Then I'll go to Gordonstoun when the Chinese kick us out."

"No one's kicking us out!" Vicky snapped in a voice much sharper than her no-nonsense warning not to repeat her remark about Peter. Mother and daughters exchanged glances and fell silent.

Finally, Fiona asked, "Is your doctor actually releasing you?"

Vicky recovered her equilibrium with a joke and a grin. "I told him I'd rappel down the side of the building if he didn't. All right, you lot. Glad you came by, thank you. But I've got work to do."

"Girls, run ahead. I want a moment with your aunt."

"Come back tomorrow night, small ladies. Bring your homework."

They kissed Vicky goodbye and trooped out. Fiona closed the door after them and returned to the bed. She straightened the sheet and plumped the pillow.

"Look here, Vicky. The old doctor's right. You've got to let some of this go. Otherwise you'll explode."

"Don't start. My head is splitting."

"If I don't, who will?"

"No one," Vicky replied curtly. "Which is fine by me. I've had it with doctors and therapy and the lot. I'm all better and I have work to do."

"You sound like your father."

"Two-Way Wong told me that. I accepted it as a compliment."

"I didn't mean it as a compliment," Fiona said evenly.

"Fiona, I'll work this out in my own way in my own time. That's all I care to say. Thanks for stopping. I hope you can come tomorrow with the girls."

"I'll drop them and whiz down to visit your mother."

"Thank you for that. I hope it's not too hard."

Fiona said, "Actually, she's agreed to have dinner with me at the club."

"Not on the boat? How'd you get her ashore?"

"Just asked."

"Maybe you can ask her to visit me?"

"It's very hard for your mother to come up the Peak. She came every day you were in danger. But once she knew that you would recover, she reckoned it was all right. Her whole life was up here. The house, friends."

"Sure."

"She grieves for your father, too, you know. She still loved him. Give her a break, Vicky."

"Sorry. I'm really sorry. I'm so uptight."

Fiona leaned over the bed so they could kiss cheeks. "Hope something good comes along to pry you loose."

"I'll be all right," Vicky whispered. "I promise."

"Secrets?" piped a voice at the door. It was Peter's Mary Lee, dark and round and pretty.

"Oh, Mary. I'm so glad you're here. My head is like a cement mixer."

"Mary'll fix you. Hello, Fiona."

"Mary. Well, I must dash." She backed out of the room as Vicky turned over on her stomach and Mary began massaging the back of her neck. Fiona marveled at the transformation in Peter's fiancée and Vicky's attitude toward her. Turned out the Chinese woman had an astonishing ability to massage, learned, she said, from a grandfather.

Ten minutes with Mary Lee and Vicky's headaches disappeared. The doctors were mildly nonplussed. Unable to treat post-concussion symptoms with drugs, they were helpless to ease Vicky's pain. But Mary could, stopping by once or twice a day. The same grandfather had taught her acupuncture, but at that the doctors balked. Not that they discounted the value of the ancient treatments, but Mary was not licensed and had no formal training, and so was firmly instructed to leave her needles at home.

Vicky groaned with pleasure. "You ought to bottle this, Mary."

She closed her eyes and drifted. Peter had chosen well. Mary Lee was a treasure, rising to the occasion when the devastated

Mackintosh family needed her most. The Chinese values of filial piety and family feeling—*hsiao*—were more than words to her, for she perceived herself as part of the whole, not merely an individual. The Lee clan had Mary's first loyalty. In return, Mary had an uncle, cousin, sister, or aunt prepared to serve *her* in every Chinatown from Southeast Asia to San Francisco.

From what Peter had learned, a great clan of Lees sprawled across the *Nan-yang*—the coasts and towns and cities of Southeast Asia—where overseas Chinese controlled every form of commerce from banks to shops. No one knew how rich they were, but their combined wealth and power vastly exceeded Mackintosh Farquhar, with its frail connections to the Philippines, New York, Vietnam, some Edinburgh banks, and a hardscrabble Highland estate. And despite her kindnesses, Vicky sometimes wondered whether Mary hoped to marry Peter as the opening move in a takeover of Mackintosh Farquhar, intending to march home one day with the hong in tow.

"Chinese New Year shuts us down next week," Peter Mackintosh concluded MacF's weekly construction report. "Otherwise, we're full steam ahead at Lantau, Kowloon, and, thanks to your 'old friends' in the PRC, Kai Tak."

Wally Hearst had come with him. The China trader could never figure whether to stand or sit in Vicky's hospital room. The sight of her propped up in bed made him nervous. Prim as her embroidered nightgown was, his eyes kept darting to her breasts, then guiltily at the floor, the fax machine, the video phone, or the vases of red roses. Vicky hid a small smile. It was almost flattering, considering his sexy little wife.

"Full steam, except for the water problem at Kai Tak," she corrected him.

Mr. Wu of the People's Overseas Labor Committee had kept his word. MacF's Expo Golden Dragon Hotel was forging toward completion under 'round-the-clock crews imported from the PRC. State projects in Canton had ground to a halt as a result, but at Kai

Tak the roof was on—a startling gold-glass peak that reflected the sun like a polished dagger. Tiling was down, the windows installed, and finish work was progressing on schedule. Peter reported that even the wood cabinetry was first-rate, which indicated Wu had shanghaied joiners from every first-class project in South China.

The one hitch was the hotel's water supply.

The Hong Kong Waterworks Office operated two systems: salt for toilets and fresh for drinking and bathing. The hotel's freshwater main, which had been laid a year and a half ago with the foundation, had failed a government inspection. The bribes routinely offered had been spurned, and uncharacteristically honest inspectors had ordered the pipe dug up and replaced. That was in early January, while Vicky was still sleeping twenty-hour nights. Now, a month later, permits to lay a new pipe were still shuttling between government departments.

"At least we've got our salt water," said Peter.

"Great. Our guests can flush but can't bathe. Any ideas, Wally?"

The American looked away from her chest and tugged his beard. "Not off the bat. The Taipan told me to keep my nose out of your labor problems."

"I'm aware of that. I'm acting Taipan now. I want you to help straighten this out."

Wally nodded dubiously.

"Thanks for coming by," Vicky told him. "Please drop me a memo about ways around Comrade Wu."

Wally bolted for the door. "Hope you're feeling better."

"Much. I'm going to rappel down the side of the hospital if they don't let me out soon."

Wally gave her the dutiful laugh accorded the boss's joke. Vicky signaled Peter to stay.

"Is Wally worth his retainer?"

"He's been in Hong Kong since the end of the Vietnam War. He knows the Peking crowd here and he knows their bosses back in China."

"He's bloody independent," Vicky said.

Peter answered more shrewdly than she had expected of him

and showed he, too, had been wondering about Hearst. "Maybe it's because he's free-lance. Dad thought he was all right. Why not hire him exclusively? Put him on salary."

"Do we know anyone better?"

"No one for hire."

"Let's do it. . . . And how are *you* doing?"

"Staying on top of things, more or less."

"So I see. You're a changed man, Peter."

Her brother ducked his head guiltily. "I know. I feel wonderful. Like I'm free. Isn't that terrible? Dad's dead and I'm alive, at last. Weird."

"Weird," she agreed.

Their eyes brushed, locked for a second. A question hung in the air. Who would run MacF? She was reasonably certain that her father's will would leave her in charge, but Peter would have certain legitimate claims, depending on how the will was worded and which way their mother would swing her equity in the company if it came to a fight. Vicky grinned. "One day at a time. Right?"

"Right." He smiled back. "I'm learning, one day at a time. Bloody waste, all those years. I've got a lot of catching up to do."

When he left, she dictated her notes of the meeting, keyed the terminal to bring them up next time, and swung her feet off the bed and onto the floor. Rising slowly and moving carefully, she walked to the window where, to her annoyance, she had to place her fingers on the sill to steady herself.

"Hello, Victoria."

She turned, her back stiffening.

Vivian Loh stood framed in the doorway, her face dark with grief, her jet hair draping her shoulders. She wore white, and Vicky remembered vaguely that the Chinese wore white or undyed cloth for mourning. Undyed hemp. Rough hemp. Leave it to Vivian to maintain the tradition, stylishly.

"Hello, Vivian. Where've you been?"

"Forgive me. I needed a little recovery time. Then I was called to Shanghai."

"On MacF business?"

Vivian hesitated. "On your father's business. May I come in?"

"Oh, you mean Golden Air?" she asked sarcastically.

"No."

"Golden Air Freight?"

Vivian stepped into the room and closed the door behind her. "I'm sorry, but I must talk with you alone."

19

VICKY WANTED TO stay by the window, where the glare of back-light gave her an advantage, but she was so shaky that she had to put a distracting amount of energy into standing. She walked to the bed and climbed in and sat back against the pillows.

"Sit down."

Vivian took the armchair offered, crossed her legs, and made an unusually visible effort to compose herself.

Vicky asked, "Who did you see in Shanghai? Ma Binyan?"

Vivian's eyes flew wide open when Vicky spoke the student leader's name. "So you remember?"

Vicky just stared. She still wondered whether Vivian had been her father's acolyte, as he had claimed, or his inspiration.

Vivian said, "Ma Binyan didn't know whether you would re-member your conversation. You were apparently quite seriously in-jured."

"I remember everything."

She remembered the shadow of the great red junk creaking alongside as *Mandalay* broke up under her. Sailors in black had lowered a boat. Strong hands had plucked her from the water. She remembered coming to in a cabin alive with the sounds of wood pressing wood. The pain in her head seemed to cut her mind in half and stood like a barrier between the memory of the fishing hull smashing into *Mandalay* and the eerie aftermath when she and her father finally came to an understanding as the wreck sank beneath them.

The sun had finally burned off the haze. She saw with alarm that the pattern it played on the cabin floor indicated the junk was sailing southwest, a course far south of Hong Kong. She tried to sit up, setting off barrages of pain in her head. *Mandalay*'s thick mast flew at her again and again and again. She had smashed her head a second time, she realized, on the hull as she tumbled over the life-lines.

A huge figure loomed over her, a Northern Chinese so tall that he had to duck as he passed under the ceiling beams, and she flinched when he held her down with a massive hand. "Take it easy," he said in English. "We don't know how bad you're hurt."

"Who are you?"

"Old friend of your father. How you feel?"

He laid a cool, damp cloth on her brow and, when she complained of thirst, brought her the covered teacup he had been drinking from.

"Where are you taking me?"

By the sun's low angle she guessed she had been unconscious for several hours. Her head hurt so much she felt sick. Yet she remembered everything that had happened up until her father died. And she recalled with equal certainty that she had seen this man before, sauntering the decks of the red junk last summer, catching her watching him in a long spyglass. But up close, his face was familiar for more than that encounter, a face from the news of years ago. Ma Binyan, the Peking student leader, Tang's protégé. Vicky had guessed right the first time she had seen him on the junk. He *was* a wild horseman of the steppes, a part-Manchu whose followers had nicknamed him Genghis Khan for his reckless bravery. Her father had chosen a dangerous man to conspire with.

Propped on one elbow, she tried to drink the warm tea; it nauseated her. "Where are you taking me?" she asked again. Ma Binyan hesitated.

"You don't trust me?" she asked.

"Let us say we don't know who to trust."

"I don't know who to trust either."

A cagey look crossed the big man's broad, flat face. "What do you mean?"

"One minute I was sailing with my father, and the next we were run down by a PRC trawler. Who would you trust?"

"I would trust the man who rescued me."

"I would trust the man who brought me straight to hospital in Hong Kong. I'm hurt badly. I need help."

He stared, silent. Behind him, through a window, she could see the legs of the black-clad sailors working the deck.

"Unless you have a surgeon on board." It struck her that everything she said was spoken in a low whisper and very slowly. That would explain his worried expression. If she looked half as bad as her head felt, she must look ready to die.

"Did your father tell you why we were going to meet today?" he asked.

"Meet?"

He stared some more, and Vicky knew she was home free. Ma Binyan had no way of knowing what her father had confided.

"Miss Mackintosh, your father had the best interests of Hong Kong and China at heart. Of that I am convinced. You must honor your father by carrying on what he can't finish."

"I intend to," she whispered innocently. "Mackintosh Farquhar will be as much a part of the new Hong Kong as the old Hong Kong, no matter whose flag flies."

"You dishonor Duncan Mackintosh by pretending ignorance."

"My father agreed twice to meet with you, Ma Binyan. The second time he lost his life. What am I to conclude?"

Ma Binyan grinned proudly at the mention of his name.

"Conclude that your father gave his life for a new China — a China that works."

Despite her injuries, Vicky sensed that something didn't add up. She took a guess at why the junk had been late to rendezvous. "Tang didn't show, did he?"

"So you do know."

"I know nothing. But if you're conspiring for a 'New China' you'd better have Party Leader Tang in your camp or you'll be slopping hogs in Mongolia. Is he aboard?"

Ma Binyan glared, and Vicky knew she had guessed right. The party leader had not come and Ma Binyan was winging it.

"It is obvious your father told you," he blurted.

"I'm not about to repeat my father's mistakes," Vicky whispered, vowing that Duncan Mackintosh's remaining evidence of Chen's and Two-Way Wong's corruption would remain hidden in the mast of her mother's yacht until it rotted, before she would risk MacF's future on the dreams of a firebrand.

"Your father trusted me," Ma Binyan pleaded.

"My father is dead, and your party leader didn't show."

"Your father would never have brought all the evidence at once. Where's the rest of it?"

"I can't help you."

"I will do whatever I can to make you trust me."

"You can start by radioing for a police helicopter to take me to hospital. . . ."

Five weeks later, in Matilda Hospital on the Peak, Vivian Loh had finally surfaced to remind her: "Ma Binyan saved your life."

"Actually," Vicky replied coolly, "the CAT scan showed no bleeding in the brain. There isn't a whole lot the doctors can do for concussions but wait. I could have waited on the junk. Same headache, more fresh air. Might have picked up a few sailing tips from the captain. Of course, everyone at home would have worried, wouldn't you?"

Vivian ignored her sarcasm. "Vicky, please. We have a chance— thanks to your father's evidence of Two-Way Wong's corruption— to change the leadership of China."

"Ma Binyan is dangerously out of control."

"Ma Binyan is a brave patriot. Victoria, listen: We can replace the corrupt with our friends."

"One set of 'old friends' for another?" Vicky asked, but Vivian was too immersed in her scheme to get the irony.

"Tang will let Hong Kong survive. Tang knows China must leave us be. . . . He's Cantonese; he understands Hong Kong. He doesn't envy us the way the Northerners do. Listen, if you're afraid, give me the evidence and I'll take care of it. . . . After all, if what you seem to suspect is correct, then you're in danger holding it."

"What evidence?"

"Don't play with me. He must have told you."

"The only thing I can't suss out is why my father didn't tell *you* where he stashed this evidence—if there is any."

Judging by the frustration on Vivian's face, Vicky saw that the Chinese woman did not know whether there was more evidence than had sunk with the yacht. Vicky had wracked her brain repeatedly, but could not come to any satisfying answer to the question of why her father hadn't told her. He had trusted Vivian with everything, including his life. Why not with that? Other than the highly un-likely existence of a player Vicky didn't know about, it seemed that she was the only person alive who knew both that the evidence did exist and where it was hidden.

"May I ask something?" said Vivian.

"What?"

"What were your father's last words?"

" 'Look out for Vivian.' "

"I can look out for myself, thank you, Vicky."

"It was a warning, not a request . . . Which leads me to a rather unpleasant subject. I frankly cannot see a future for you at MacF, now that my father is gone."

Vivian looked astonished. "But you need me more than ever now that your father is gone. You can't manage it yourself."

"I bloody well can."

"But Shanghai. Who will represent you in Shanghai?"

"I have a number of employees in Golden Dragon Air to choose from."

"They don't have the contacts," Vivian protested.

"Are you seriously saying you want to work for me?"

"I want to work for MacF."

"Well, I'm afraid that's not possible. Nor will I lie and say I'm sorry. You ruined my parents' marriage and—"

"It was not that simple," Vivian retorted firmly. "And, forgive me, Victoria, I think you know that, growing up in the home you did."

Vicky glared, truth and anger warring on her face. Then she lowered her head. "All right," she said. "Maybe you didn't break them up. Maybe you were just the catalyst for what would happen anyway."

"I was *not* the catalyst. Let me tell you, please, a man like your father is not seducible. A man like your father takes. He is not taken."

"You don't strike me as a woman easily 'taken.' "

"I'm not. It was different with him."

"I'll bet."

Vivian Loh recalled her mother smiling that same cynical smile, and she knew she could talk all day and yet never convince Vicky that Duncan had not been a conquest. She had not gone hunting for a taipan. Nor had she coveted a no-strings affair with a married man. As for her attraction to an older man, she considered it quite natural in light of her strong attachment to her father and the rewards she had enjoyed for pleasing her teachers.

"We knew each other very well," she tried to explain. "There was respect, as well as . . . interest." When they had become lovers, she had been reminded of nothing so much as her first pair of eyeglasses—the sudden, shocking clarity. She was half-blind again, without him. "And there was love. Great love. You must understand that."

"I don't want to understand him that way. I never got any understanding from him."

"You still hate him," Vivian marveled.

"I never hated him. All I wanted was for him to show me he

loved me, and sometimes he did. Which is why I cannot forget—
and I will never forgive—that your schemes in Shanghai led directly
to his death."

"That's not true!"

"And now you're trying to manipulate me into your plan. . . .
Listen, Vivian. I went along with Ma Binyan's story that we were
accidentally run down in the fog because I don't know whom I could
tell the truth to anyhow. It wouldn't change a thing, and I don't
want any part of it. But don't tell me my father wasn't killed. He
was murdered for trying to blackmail Two-Way Wong. He was betrayed. You two got into water so deep over your heads that he
drowned."

"You would just let his death go? Your own father? You would
let his murderer live as if nothing had happened?"

The Taipan's daughter returned his mistress a look of deep contempt. "Do you think you're the first to raise that question? Do you
think I don't hate Two-Way Wong? Dying, my father said, 'Get
him! Get Two-Way.' "

"You would deny him?"

"My father's death leaves me custodian of a seven-generation
family hong. We have two thousand employees in Hong Kong alone,
and all hell's about to break loose. Simple revenge is a luxury I can't
afford just now."

"That sounds like a convenient excuse to do nothing," Vivian goaded
her. But all the while her doctor and Fiona had been worrying about
Vicky's apparent lack of feeling, Vicky had been dwelling long and
hard on her hatred of Two-Way Wong, on the blinding aspects of
bitterness, and on the limits of revenge. No one—and least of all
Vivian Loh—could stampede her into her father's fate.

"*Survival* is my revenge. Two-Way Wong will not drive MacF
from Hong Kong. He will waken every day to the fact that Duncan
Mackintosh's daughter is still in business."

"Business as usual?" Vivian sneered.

Vicky picked up a paperback from her night table. *The Art of War*. "Ever read Sun-tzu, Vivian?"

"Yes. And I can't say I'm surprised you have too."

"I read it first when I was twelve. Hoping to impress Daddy. Sun-tzu says, 'She who knows when she can fight and *when she cannot* will be victorious.' I'm a businesswoman, Vivian, acting taipan of a struggling hong. I'm not a policeman. I'm not a detective, and I'm definitely not a politician. I'm not a revolutionary either. I don't know how you convinced that old man he was, but he paid the price."

The accusations washed over Vivian like scalding water. She would never give Duncan's daughter the satisfaction of arguing who convinced whom and who paid the price of failure. But there was one lie she would not let pass.

"He was not old," she said with quiet dignity. "He was my beautiful lover."

"Get out!" Vicky screamed. Her hands flew to her head, her face contorted by pain. "Get out!" she screamed again. The pain took her breath away. When she could speak again, she whispered, "Get out. Please go."

"You're jealous of me?"

"Does that surprise you? How would you feel?"

"That's crazy, Victoria. Your father never gave me anything you would want from him."

"Love?"

"Not a father's love, I can assure you."

"Don't make fun of me."

"I'm not. Victoria, if my father were alive and your being his lover made him happy, I would be happy. Why can't you do that for your father?"

"Because my father risked everything that is mine, my mother's, and my brother's, for you."

"Not for me. Don't you see, Vicky? Not for me. For the future. For Hong Kong. For all of us."

"You're very passionate in your belief. I can see how you persuaded him. But you won't do it to me. I'm still going to fire you."

Vivian opened the door. Anxious nurses had descended on the noise. "I'm afraid you can't fire me."

"What? You quit? Please yourself. Just vacate your office by tonight."

"It's not so simple as that."

"Oh, it isn't? Watch me." She spun her TIC monitor in Vivian's direction, knowing she was out of control and hurting too much to care. "Watch the screen, Vivian. Watch me type a press release." She lashed out at the nurses: "Go away!" and banged at the keyboard with tears streaming down her face:

> VICTORIA MACKINTOSH, ACTING TAIPAN OF MACKINTOSH FARQUHAR COMPANY, LIMITED, HONG KONG, ANNOUNCES THAT MS. VIVIAN LOH HAS RESIGNED AS DIRECTOR OF NEW PROJECTS AND IS LEAVING THE COMPANY TODAY. MR. PETER MACKINTOSH HAS BEEN APPOINTED DIRECTOR OF NEW PROJECTS IN ADDITION TO HIS CURRENT DUTIES AS A COMPANY DIRECTOR.
>
> MS. LOH SAID, "WHEN MS. MACKINTOSH AND I MET THIS EVENING WE AGREED THAT IN VIEW OF ALL THAT HAD TAKEN PLACE SINCE THE NEW YEAR IT WAS NOT PRACTICAL FOR US TO WORK CLOSELY TOGETHER WITHIN MACKINTOSH FARQUHAR. IN THESE CIRCUMSTANCES I BELIEVED THAT THE ONLY PROPER COURSE OF ACTION WAS TO ACCEPT HER INVITATION TO RESIGN."
>
> MS. MACKINTOSH SAID, "MS. LOH PERFORMED AVIDLY UNDER MY LATE FATHER, DUNCAN MACKINTOSH" — MAKE THAT "SERVED ARDENTLY" — "AND I WISH HER WELL IN SIMILAR POSITIONS IN THE FUTURE.

"IT IS OUR FIRM INTENTION TO DEVELOP
THE MACKINTOSH FARQUHAR BUSINESS IN
BOTH HONG KONG AND CHINA AND CON-
TINUE OUR 157-YEAR TRADITION AS A BUSI-
NESS PARTNER OF THE CHINESE PEOPLE
AFTER TURNOVER."

"It's not so simple as that," Vivian repeated and hurried away.
Vicky wiped her cheeks with the bed sheet, then, still weeping, stabbed
the SEND button. But hours after the release had gone to the wire
services and the Hong Kong and London newsrooms, she could not
shake a disquieting sensation that Vivian had information she did
not.

The MacF House security officer stationed outside while Vivian Loh
cleared her things had not asked whether Duncan had given her the
key to their shared side door. Moving quietly, feeling part patriot,
part petty thief, Vivian slipped into Duncan's office. It was gloomy,
lighted only by the windows. Crouching in the shadows was his grotesquely carved English Gothic desk. He had been so proud that it
had arrived in Hong Kong in 1900 aboard a P & O steamer.

It was a warren of cubbies, slots, and drawers, although fortunately as uncluttered as his mind had been. And a trifle better organized, Vivian discovered, as she removed the drawers to see if he
had cellotaped an optical-storage computer disk, or a safe-deposit
key, to their backs.

She doubted she would find anything, but this was her only chance
to search. While her banishment from MacF House was not destined to be as permanent as Vicky Mackintosh presumed, Duncan's
daughter was certain to move into the Taipan's office as soon as she
was released from the hospital.

It was ironic, Vivian thought, and therefore fitting, that this one
secret that Duncan had kept from her was related to the only secret
she had kept from him. As they grew close, she had told him all
about her mother's habits, her father's fear, their escape from the

Red Guards, their poverty, and even her love life, such as it was—even about Steven Wong, whom Duncan had dismissed with a laugh: "If it hadn't have been for No-Way turning your head, you'd probably have gotten married to a proper Chinese boy, and now I'd have to contend with a jealous husband."

But Duncan would be monumentally jealous of any affair of the mind or soul. Which was why she had never told him about Ma Binyan. Lying did not come easily to her. She abhorred it, for it reminded her of her mother's infidelities. But in the case of Ma Binyan, instinct had warned her to keep it from Duncan. It had been only an affair of the mind. They shook hands like comrades on greeting, and exchanged fierce hugs goodbye. For they had fought evil together, lost the battle, and dug in for the war.

Ma Binyan was a man who could say, "We believed that it would be worth sacrificing our lives for the sake of progress and democracy in China."

Vivian Loh had thrilled to those same words at home, her father passing from his the spirit of the May Fourth 1919 student movement. Progress and Democracy, the two advances that would march hand in hand to finally change China and banish the chaos.

She had met Ma Binyan during the Tiananmen massacre eight years ago, when she was twenty-four. She had been traveling constantly on the Mainland, to establish herself as a free-lance China trader. Representing four small Hong Kong clients, and angling for a fifth, she trekked between Hong Kong, Shanghai, Canton, and Beijing, cultivating ministry officials and factory bosses, crisscrossing China on hard-seat trains and PRC motor vessels, and sleeping in student hostels to save on expenses.

So recently a student herself, she had fallen easily into the young intellectuals' discussion groups at night. Thus the flowering of the 1989 Student Democracy movement had come as no surprise. For over a year she had felt their disappointment at the stalled economic reforms, the misery of inflation, which was impoverishing the already-poor students and workers, and the anger over the corruption rampant among the children of high party officials.

As the demonstrations grew and spread, she had had to return to Hong Kong to romance her clients, but had followed the events, like everyone else in the colony, on the television news. One morning early, she awoke to find her father switching frantically from channel to channel. His expression was grave. Li Peng was waving his fist as he condemned the hunger strike and declared martial law. Vivian thought the army would never support him. Her father feared the worst, because Li Peng was wearing his Mao suit instead of Western business clothes. More than his words and more than martial law, Li Peng's costume promised a return to repression. "Don't go back to Beijing," her father warned.

Like many Hongkongers, lulled by years of free and easy travel and commerce between Hong Kong and the Mainland, she had believed that the totalitarian Chinese Communist Party would somehow magically dissolve when faced by the will of the people.

Hong Kong had exploded with a joyous Chinese unity never seen before in the supposedly money-mad colony. One-sixth of the entire population—a million people—had marched to Happy Valley Racecourse in support of the Beijing students. An unbroken chain of demonstrators stretched from Central all the way to North Point and doubled back to Happy Valley.

When the speeches were over, Vivian had defied her father and, sacrificing the money she had been saving to buy a portable fax machine, paid for a fast airline flight to Beijing. There she had wandered, wide-eyed, through Tiananmen Square. To see inexperienced students actually organizing a working city out of nothing, arranging transport through the crowds, food, medical facilities, and astonishing communications systems that webbed the Square to the rest of China and the world beyond, was a brilliant affirmation of everything her father—and his father before him—had dreamed and had taught her to dream.

The deep humanity of the protesters, even in the passionate climate of their revolution, meant that China at last would spring from the dark. Time and again, students protected hapless soldiers or policemen cut off from their units. Vivian herself held a bloodied soldier's arm and helped escort the frightened man to safety.

But Tiananmen Square was no place for the fastidious. The stench and squalor of so many bodies living with no facilities had been overpowering. Epidemics of dysentery and conjunctivitis had raged through the tent city, and Vivian had been grateful to retreat each night to her modest, relatively clean hotel room. She was in that room on the night the army attacked, and hated herself for being so protected.

But the next day, when people were cut down on either side of her by wild machine-gun fire, she gave thanks to Tin Hau that her own body had somehow been spared.

Then began the Terror. The government hunted the surviving student leaders. Vivian had her Hong Kong papers and she was not a student. She was free to set out for home, like any foreign business person. But she felt deeply responsible. She had seen pain, but not felt it; experienced fear, but only in anticipation. She had escaped the worst—which meant, she knew, that she did not have her father's excuse to stop fighting.

She kept her appointment at an obscure office of the Railway Ministry. The electricity was back on, but the two officials actually at their desks had locked the door. They stared at her as if she were insane. Her client in Hong Kong, she reminded them, had acquired Asian distribution rights for a revolutionary new lubricant that would reduce friction wear in their new generation of diesel locomotives— which, she had on good authority from an old friend, were about to come on line at the Datong Locomotive Works.

When a higher-up paid a visit to make sure their office was open, as the government had decreed, she had scattered her brochures and sample containers of the stuff on their shabby desks. After he had delivered the customary political statement, Vivian had drawn him into the commercial discussion, and had actually closed a deal. That night, she sheltered two students in her hotel room. One, a philosopher from Guilin, was arrested in the street the next day. The other was Ma Binyan.

Together, they devised an underground railway to smuggle the hunted leaders to safety. Sympathetic PRC officials had turned a blind eye, and she would never forget the bravery of ordinary people.

Vivian flew home to Hong Kong. The city was in shock. No one could believe, at first, what the PRC government had done. China had gone back thirty years. And 1997, which had loomed for years like storm clouds piling almost unnoticed on the horizon, was suddenly thundering overhead. She had conferred with a student group Ma Binyan had told her about at the Chinese University of Hong Kong. She already knew a few from her vote-organizing efforts. She bore messages back and smuggled passports they had forged, a simple item in a city where anything could be counterfeited for a price. On her third trip, she had smuggled Ma Binyan out, disguising him as a Singapore Chinese tractor salesman. But Ma Binyan had grown restless, and had returned to spread the word in remote Chinese villages of what the Communist government had done in Tiananmen Square.

After they caught him, Vivian did not dare go back to China for fear he had implicated her under torture. She threw herself into organizing Allen Wei's Legco campaign, then worked for Allen managing his China sales group. Two years later word came. A student, whose father's high position had gotten him paroled, reported that Ma Binyan was alive and well and had convinced his interrogators that the few "criminals" he had "conspired with" were all dead.

Heart in her throat, Vivian had traveled to Shanghai to test her position. They hadn't looked at her twice. She was once again free to travel in and out of Mainland China. There were, she decided, other ways to change things, and she took Duncan Mackintosh's offer of a job as his China trader. The goddess of heaven had done the rest, in the guise of a former student in Chengdu, who had mentioned after too many mai tais that agents of Vivian's gweilo Taipan had displayed a powerful interest in the Hong Kong devil Two-Way Wong Li.

20

MILLICENT MACKINTOSH SAT cross-legged on one corner of Vicky's hospital bed, dreamily flipping the pages of the latest *Elle de Chine*. Melissa perched opposite, zapping television stations with the remote control, while they filled Vicky in on the day's happenings and continued to speculate about the anonymous sender of red roses. Millicent was still a steadfast Chip supporter; Melissa suspected a married admirer.

The business day was over. The markets had closed. The last of Vicky's managers had trooped up the Peak to report. Vicky's daily postconcussion headache was throbbing in earnest, exacerbated by the TV blizzard of Chinese soap operas, pop singers, news reporters, game shows, American reruns and Mainland drivel. She was about to order the set turned off, when a live interview caught her eye.

"Stop!"

"What?"

"Melissa, back up a channel . . . another. There!"

"It's just some Chinese people."

"They're Alfred Ching's parents. Turn up the sound."

Alfred Ching—the suddenly rich and famous Alfred Ching, hero of the city's latest rags-to-riches saga (and the rat who pretended that roses were a decent substitute for a friendly telephone call to an old friend stuck in the hospital)—was the toast of Hong Kong. His picture was in every newspaper and magazine; now that he was abroad, the media had apparently discovered his parents.

"Turn up the sound."

A breathless Chinese reporter was interviewing the middle-aged couple in front of their little Kowloon restaurant. Red neon framed the doorway like burning vines, and the stairs to the second-floor dining room were flanked by a pair of pretty girls in slit cheongsams whom Vicky recognized as Alfred's fifteen-year-old nieces who were studying to be computer programmers. His mother wore a working woman's shapeless black pajamas; his father, a cook's dark pants and clean white T-shirt. Their broad smiles revealed a gold tooth each.

"What are they saying, Melissa?"

Melissa excelled at Cantonese, which Hugo had encouraged her to study since she was five. Millicent, like Vicky, had gone for Mandarin.

"They're saying, 'We still cook . . . run our restaurant.' The reporter asked, 'Won't you retire now that your son is such a big . . . um, property man?' "

Alfred's parents exploded in embarrassed laughter. Then his mother dispensed some of the homey advice the Chinese of a certain age loved. Melissa translated her comment as: "The old man living at the frontier lost his horse."

"Beg pardon?" asked Millicent. "New translator, please."

"It's a proverb, stupid."

Alfred's father nodded sagely, and even the pushy reporter allowed a moment of respectful silence for the traditional reminder that for every good fortune, calamity lurked.

"They're going to keep on cooking, no matter how rich Alfred gets," said Melissa. "They're saying, 'What goes up can fall down. Who knows what will happen next?' "

"They're nuts," said Millicent. "They could retire."

"They probably like their restaurant," Vicky explained. "It's been good to them. They came from Canton with nothing."

"But Auntie Vicky, Alfred's rich as Two-Way Wong."

"Hardly. He's just starting out. He's a director of a consortium that owns the most expensive building in Hong Kong. But old Two-Way could buy him in a second."

"Is he as rich as us?"

"We're not rich," said Melissa. "Mum says we're going to hell in a handcart."

Vicky flushed. Fiona had a maddening fetish about openness with her children. "What did the reporter just ask?"

"Are you surprised by your son's making it big?" supplied Melissa.

"If you plant melons," answered Alfred's father, "you gain melons."

And then came the question that concluded every interview: "Are you afraid of changing the flag?"

"People have to eat," said Alfred's father. "That's why we keep restaurant."

"So you're optimistic about the Mainlanders."

"Of course we're optimistic," snapped Alfred's mother, as both smiles fixed like sugar glaze.

"We all are," the reporter gushed at the camera, "thanks to your son's big deal." And he had the numbers ready. "Property prices in Central, Causeway Bay, North Point, and Kowloon have jumped twenty-three percent in two weeks."

The New Year's riots had been forgotten the instant Alfred's consortium had made their down payment, and Hong Kong had gone predictably mad. Speculators were buying and selling properties at prices so inflated that torrents of money from Australia, Tokyo, California, and London started pouring into the Colony. Incredibly—with only five months until the PRC took control—MacF's choicer holdings had risen a full fifty percent, on paper.

Vicky, whose father had always had a superb sense of market peaks, was wondering what to sell before the bubble burst.

The PRC ought to award Alfred the Order of Mao, she thought. Peking's bureaucrats couldn't have dreamed up a better fantasy themselves than a property boom just before Turnover. Stock markets were following the upswing as new millionaires borrowed against their new properties to speculate, and the volatile futures markets were rocketing off the indexes.

As the final close-up on Alfred's parents faded from the screen, Vicky was struck by the complexity of their expressions. Like millions of "Old Hundred Names" Chinese their age, they had lived much of their lives just ahead of chaos, like riding the crest of a wave hurtling toward a dark shore. Escape from chaos was the driving force behind their sixteen-hour workdays and the firm bastion of family life. Behind the fixed smiles, they knew that the reporter had missed the entire point of the interview.

Vicky picked up her telephone. "Turn the sound down, Melissa." Each of MacF's managers' numbers was keyed in the speed dial. Three connected her to James Wade, who directed MacF Land. "Sorry to interrupt your dinner, Jim. We'll need a list in the morning of every property offer we've received this week at forty percent over last month's value. . . . Yes, we just might sell a few as soon as the will is read. . . . Yes, I recall what we agreed yesterday, but I've changed my mind. . . . Because, as my father often said, what goes up can fall down. . . . No!" she snapped. "I am *not* betting against Hong Kong. . . . I *am* aware how long it has taken to amass our holdings. When these prices collapse, I want to be liquid. With a little joss, maybe we'll end up owning *more* Hong Kong."

She banged the telephone down, imagining Wade freshening his wife's martini with some world-weary comment about the Old Man's impetuous daughter: "Perhaps we really ought to buy that cottage in Vence, m'dear. But wouldn't it be nice if old Dragon Face cut her out of his will? Leave her her share, of course, but put MacF in charge of its professional managers—Brit and Chinese—who know a thing or two about Hong Kong."

"What's *liquid*, Auntie Vicky?"

"*Liquid* means having cash on hand to buy bargains while everyone else is going to hell in a handcart. And keep what comes in those big ears under your hats, small ladies. We wouldn't want your school chums' mums and dads setting off a panic. Would we?"

•   •   •

"Good morning, Victoria. Ready to face the world?"

Her doctor was a young Englishman about her age, as smooth and charming as if he'd stepped out of a nostalgic British film like *The Shooting Party*. She half-expected him to stroll into her room in plus-fours with a Purdeys draped over his arm. He was quite handsome and on some of her better days she had fantasized a weekend in the country, at some country house half a world from China, with a canopied bed.

"I still can't smell the roses."

"That's what comes of butting yacht masts with our head."

"It's been more than a month, Gordon."

Gordon shone a light in her eye and studied her reactions. "Could be years, old girl. How did your breakfast taste?"

"Weird, but I'm getting used to it. I hate this."

He tested the other eye. "Thank your gods, Christian and heathen, you can see, you can hear, you can talk—at some length—and you remember your name. And, best of all, you're getting out of here this morning. That's what you've been railing about, isn't it?"

"About bloody time, thank you. And thanks for everything. You've been a great host."

"Dr. Cha's rather put out with you, you know. Wants you to loosen up." He grinned and took her pulse. "I told Cha your recovery might accelerate if your rose-sender ever showed up in person."

"Dr. Cha's taking advantage of the fact that I hit my head rather than my arm. I'll loosen up with a double whisky."

"Not just yet, please," Gordon said hastily. "No whisky until I prescribe it."

"Frankly, the idea of a whisky makes me sick."

"Well, get dressed and send a removals van to clear out this office of yours. I'll see you next week." They shook hands, and he kissed her cheek. Vicky handed him a red envelope.

"Kung Hay Fat Choi!"

"What's this?"

"Lai see. Lucky money."

"That's for children." He opened the red packet and stared at the check. "This is a lot of money, Victoria."

"Sister tells me you owe on your old-folks clinic in Western. Bad joss to end the year in debt."

"Actually, we were doing all right before the riot. Blighters burned us out. Thank you, Victoria. Happy Year of the Ox. We'll need all the good joss we can get, eh?"

Vicky dressed slowly in a skirt and a red silk blouse Fiona had brought her. Despite a blunted appetite, she had put on weight lying around the hospital, but wise Fiona had chosen a pleated skirt. She wore flat shoes because she still felt too shaky for heels. She was combing her hair for the third time and debating whether to put it back up in a bun when it occurred to her that she was a little afraid of leaving the hospital. She felt safe here. Her last memory of the outdoors was *Mandalay* sinking under her.

"Come in." She answered a soft knock at the door.

Steven Wong entered with an armload of peach blossoms. "Good morning."

"You?" Two-Way Wong's son was the last person she had expected to encounter.

He extended the peach blossoms. "Good joss in boy-girl relations."

Her head was spinning. "Are you the one who sent the roses?"

Steven Wong's face melted in a perfect smile. "Even if I wasn't, I would say I was."

"Why didn't you visit, yourself?"

"Hate hospitals. I got word they were springing you today. Like a ride?"

"How'd you know I was getting out?"

"Hey. Two-Way Wong's Number-One Son knows *everything*. How do you think I win money betting horses— Hey, you okay?"

Vicky backed to the bed, where she sat heavily, her mind spiraling around the question: Did Two-Way Wong's son know his father had killed her father?

"You want the doctor?"

"No. No. I'm all right, I think." She studied his face, which was dark with concern. He looked afraid she would keel over in front of him. "I just get a little wobbly."

"I heard you were fine. . . . Listen, I'm sorry about your father."

"Thank you."

"I think maybe we have lots in common with fathers. You know?"

Vicky stared hard at him, not believing he was serious. "They were competitors," she protested, waving off the comparison.

"No. I mean what it's like for you and me to be their kids. You know? Yeah? Well, they're both hard-to-avoid guys. From what I hear you did a better job with yours than me with mine."

"I don't know about that," Vicky said.

"They don't call *you* No-Way, sweetheart. They call you Dragon Daughter."

"Not in years."

"Yeah? I just heard it on the street. Dragon Daughter. Big compliment . . . Hey, listen. You wanna picnic? Come on—beautiful day. We'll put the hood down and drive out to Shek-O."

"I've got to get to my office."

"You sure?"

"Yes, I'm sure."

"So I'll drive you, okay?" He stood there, shifting anxiously on his feet and combing his fingers through his silky black hair.

Vicky just stared at his handsome, open face, wondering whether Two-Way Wong had included his playboy son in whatever conspiracy he was planning next. There was one way to find out whether he had sent Steven to find her father's kickback evidence.

"Okay," she said. "Thanks."

"Just please don't jump out this time."

"No promises."

He had the red Bentley convertible he had driven New Year's Eve. That night, five weeks past, seemed like years ago. Steven remarked that her blouse matched the car perfectly, and for a second she felt so paranoid that she suspected he had asked Fiona to bring it. He lowered the canvas top, and the sky suddenly loomed frighteningly large. But the midwinter sun felt delicious on her face.

She cradled the peach blossoms in her arms. The wind plucked the petals from the stems. He drove fast down the winding Peak roads, skillfully weaving the big car like a slalom skier. He slowed down abruptly when he noticed the speed was making her tense.

"Strange being out-of-doors," she said. "I've been cooped up so long."

"Good thing you were. Hong Kong's gone nuts. Never saw so much partying in my life. People act like the PRC's gonna ban drinking, eating, and screwing. Five old guys had heart attacks last week, chugging brandy."

"Sounds like you've been keeping busy."

"Always." He grinned. "No rest for the wicked." He rattled off a list of divorces and love affairs and scenes of public drunkenness enacted by the famous and near-famous. No one, from the lowliest office worker to the highest civil servants, seemed immune from the end-of-the-world climate gripping the Colony.

"Was the newspaper story true?" he asked as the car squeezed into the traffic entering the Causeway Bay district.

"Which story?"

" 'Bout the fishing boat running you down and not stopping?"

"It was a pretty big trawler and the fog was thick enough to cut. We couldn't see our own bow. I don't think they even knew they hit us."

"Experience to tell grandchildren, *hai*?"

In the distance, above the crowded street, which was dense with overhanging signs, she caught a glimpse of the gold walls of Mackintosh Farquhar House. "There was something not in the papers."

"What?"

"My father did not die immediately. I climbed back on the boat. We talked, finally talked."

"What did he say?"

Wouldn't you love to know, she thought. That's what you're pumping me for. More evidence. "I think we finally figured each other out."

"Like how?"

"Like the things we've fought about all these years."

"What did he say?"

"The details aren't important."

"That's true," Steven said seriously. "It's the talking, right?"

"Right," she said, waiting for him to press her for details anyway.

"Then he died?"

"Yes."

"That's a bitch," said Steven. Vicky caught his eye. He looked genuinely sympathetic. "That's really a bitch."

"Better than if we'd never talked at all."

"You're telling me I should talk to my dad?"

Vicky shrugged. "What do you have to lose?"

"Thing is, I got nothin' to tell him. I'm no Dragon Daughter. I'm just a guy with a rich father. It's too late to talk. I'm nearly forty."

"That's not old."

"It is in Hong Kong. Forty-year-old guys who made a killing in this town, made it in their twenties."

"I can't tell if you feel sorry for yourself," Vicky said, wondering how to steer him back to asking questions.

"Hell, no," Steven laughed. He threw his head back and the sun blazed gray-green in his eyes. "I'm having a ball."

"Are you working for your father?"

"He brought me back to run his gambling ships. He's got a couple of old liners laying offshore. He's trying to buy the *QE2*. Big floating casino. I'm stuck twelve miles out every night."

"Does he ever confide in you?"

"Me? You kidding?"

"Does he ever ask you to do special services for him?"

Steven turned and looked at her straight on. "Like what?"

"Like checking me out."

"Whoa, baby. What are you saying?"

"I'll get out of the car here, Steven. I'll take a taxi."

"Hey, wait."

"What for?"

"Okay. He told me to check you out."

"And you said you would."

"Made no difference to me. I was going to check you out anyhow."

"Please stop the car."

He pulled to the curb, ignoring the angry horns. "Listen, I don't care what he wants to know about you."

"What *does* he want to know about me?"

"He wouldn't say. He'll wait till I get alongside of you. Then he'll ask."

"Sounds like he's done it before."

"Once or twice," Steven said with a self-deprecating grin. "I'm pretty good at getting inside info from lady executives."

"I appreciate your frankness. Thanks for the ride."

"Hey. Please don't go."

"What, do you think I'm daft? The most powerful businessman in Hong Kong sets his son to spy on me? Am I supposed to stay around for him to rip me off?"

"I'm not going to ask you any questions."

"What are you going to tell him?"

"Nothing."

"What about *hsiao*?"

"Fuck filial piety. He's using me."

"Won't he be disappointed?"

"He's used to it," said Steven. "He don't expect much."

"Of MacF?"

"Of me. So your secrets are safe."

Vicky shook her head. "This is crazy. I don't know why I believe you, but I do."

Steven reached toward her and touched her face. His soft fingers felt like four little suns on her cheek. "You believe me because you know what I really want from you."

"What's that?"

"It ain't information." He swung the car back into traffic, where he blithely cut off a PRC timber truck heaped high with logs from the Mainland. A half-dozen exhausted peasants sitting on the logs stared down at the Bentley.

"Listen, Vicky, you want to do Chinese New Year's with me?"

"I have a date with Alfred Ching."

"I hear he's stuck in Vancouver with money troubles."

"I doubt that."

"Maybe just a rumor. Anyway, if he don't come back, let me put my bid in."

She had to admit that a blitzed-out night with Steven Wong would probably resonate for a lifetime. And, odd as it seemed, she was probably as safe with Steven Wong as anyone in the Colony. Whoever had betrayed her father to Two-Way Wong had likely been someone in the Mackintosh Farquhar circle who had known when Duncan left the party. By the strictest accounting, she could afford to trust only herself, her mother, Fiona, and Peter.

"Okay," she said. "If Alfred doesn't come home in time, I'll go out with you."

"Great. Now what about our picnic? I already got lunch in the boot. Perrier, 'cause I know you can't drink yet."

"How do you know that?"

"I checked it out. Hey, I know everybody. People tell me stuff. They say you can't taste too good. But you like cold poached salmon and dill. Yes?"

"Did you chat up the hospital cook?"

"And strawberries, right? You can taste strawberries."

Vicky smiled. "Right."

He stopped the car half a block from the entrance to MacF House. "So?"

"I might fall asleep. I was still having afternoon kips in hospital."

"So we'll kip together. I work late on the ships. Picnic?"

All of her objections aside, her first take on Steven Wong had been trouble, and that hadn't changed. What was changing was her inclination to avoid the sort of complications he promised.

"You know what else I got in the boot?"

"In addition to the salmon, the strawberries, and the Perrier? I shudder to guess."

"Portable fax-phone."

"What?"

"Battery-powered, so the Lady Taipan send memos from her picnic. What do you say, Lady Taipan?"

Vicky laughed. "Let's do it."

The capacious trunk of the Bentley also contained a fine wool Scots blanket in the subtle greens of a Mackintosh tartan, a silver champagne bucket worked with Victorian hunting scenes, a wicker basket fitted with Royal Doulton china and Stuart crystal, a Ching vase of roses, and a CD collection for the car stereo.

"How did you know I like country music?"

"Two-Way Wong's son knows everything."

"You scare me a little when you say that."

Steven looked up soberly from the blanket he was spreading on the grass. "Then let me say that Two-Way Wong's son knows everything that's not important. Just the fun stuff. Okay?"

"Sorry. Yes. Okay."

He had given her sunglasses in the car. Now he offered her a hat, which she refused because the sun felt so wonderful on her skin. The sea breeze was almost warm, coming up from the south and displacing the cooler northeast monsoon, which was beginning to weaken early this year.

My father died trying to destroy his father, she thought. What am I doing here? *Testing Steven* was the only answer she could accept. But hadn't he passed the test already?

"Hungry?" Steven asked, and her breath caught in her throat when he stretched out on the blanket and smiled at her to join him. She knelt to accept a crystal glass of sparkling water.

"Cheers," he said.

"Don't let me stop you from drinking."

"That's okay. Maybe some champagne later."

"Maybe me too."

"You not supposed to," he cautioned.

"I've been obeying doctors for a month. I'm sick of obedience."

"Then you are picnicking with the right fella."

Gently, as he did everything, he removed the water glass from her hand and fished a pair of champagne flutes from the wicker basket. A bottle of vintage Moët appeared next, beaded with cold. Throughout the operation of tearing the foil, opening the wire, and quietly popping the cork, Steven's eyes never left her face.

Vicky grinned back at him. "I've never seen anyone so seductive in the morning. It's not even noon yet. What do you do when it gets dark?"

"It's just my reputation." Steven smiled. "You're seducing yourself on expectation. I'm just lying here letting it happen."

"Nothing's happening, Steven. I'm just observing your style."

He set the glasses on a tray and filled them to the brim. Vicky turned away, pretending interest in the spread of blue-green sea below the Shek-O headlands. The water was peaceful, checkered with sunbeams and dark ships. Here and there, plumes of smoke rose from their stacks, and sails glinted like tiny white mirrors.

Steven's reputation troubled her. She felt powerfully attracted to him, but had no desire for a place on a dreary list of conquests. Nor did she want to see her photograph splashed about the tabloids, which was the price of running around the Colony with its favorite playboy.

"May I interrupt that obviously important thought with a toast?" Steven asked, extending a glass.

"That depends on the toast."

"You expressed appreciation of my A.M. seductiveness?"

"Yes?"

"If I may quote poet?"

"Which poet?"

"Lao-tzu?"

"Oh, do."

"For a whirlwind does not last a whole morning, nor does a sudden shower last a whole day. Cheers."

"I bet you say that to all your girls."

"I'm not known for my talking, Vicky."

"Why do I rate?"

"That's another Lao-tzu says better than me: *She who is open-eyed . . . is immortal.*"

Steven was still holding both glasses. Vicky took one from him. "Thanks. Cheers."

"Cheers."

"Oh, my God, that's delicious." One sip drifted lazily into her brain. Colors grew brighter and the breeze felt liquid on her face. "Oh, heaven." She felt happy, bold, and monumentally free.

"Was that 'sudden shower' quote as in 'clouds and rain'?"

Steven laughed. "Who's seducing who? Of course 'clouds and rain' should start slower and last longer than a sudden shower. Don't you think?"

"Ideally."

"Hey, if it isn't ideal, you shouldn't do it."

"You believe in perfect sex?"

"Sure do."

"What's it like?"

"Haven't the foggiest, yet." He grinned. "What do you think it's like?"

"Both wanting the same thing at the same time, maybe."

Steven shook his head. "You're an odd duck, Vicky. Everything's very serious with you, isn't it?"

She took a second taste from the glass. "Very."

"Why?"

"I don't know."

"Yes, you do."

"Just guesses." She lay back on the blanket and stared at the sky. Far below their blanket the breakers tumbled against the cliffs. "This is so wonderful."

"Like some music?"

"No. Just keep talking to me."

"Careful, you get a Chinese boy talking, he's only gonna talk about one thing."

She turned lazily and smiled at his beautiful face. "What's that?"

"His mother."

"His *mother*?"

"She was blond, like you."

"Tell me more another time."

"And she played tennis. And she was very, very beautiful, like you."

"Are you close?"

"She died when I was five."

"Of what?"

"Of a broken heart, according to my amah."

"Did your father leave her?"

"No."

Vicky turned to look at him. Steven shrugged. "That's all I know. That's what my old amah said, and she died soon after. Who knows. Romantic story, eh?"

"Sad story to tell a little boy."

"She died in England. I guess that means she left my father. But he never speaks of her. Except that he left their old bedroom the same until he moved house to the office tower. Can you believe the fearsome Two-Way Wong has mourned a woman thirty-five years? I still wonder what the hell happened."

"I get the feeling you're in the middle of a big change."

Steven laughed. "Even playboys get mid-life crisis."

"You're not nearly the jerk you pretend to be."

"Hey, Vicky. In my experience, the worst thing women do to themselves is mine rubies where there are no rubies. Chinese or gweipo, you're all the same: The better the woman, the worse the guy she tries to straighten out. Save yourself some grief. Take him like he is."

"What if he's better than he thinks he is?"

"Not your job."

"I won't echo your putdowns of yourself."

"Ever been married?"

"Yes."

"I bet he wasn't the jerk he pretended to be."

Vicky turned her face away, more hurt than angry. A huge red bulk carrier was emerging from the Lamma Channel, flying the house flag of the World Oceans fleet. She watched it put to sea, its blunt, ugly lines dissolving through tears that she blinked away. "He wasn't a jerk."

"What went wrong?"

"He was just . . . overwhelmed. I overwhelmed him, I think. God, I don't know. My last boyfriend too. Neither of them was strong, that's for sure."

"Sorry to get so heavy. I'm going too fast. It's just that we're easy together. Aren't we?"

"We are."

"Hey, you want salmon?"

Vicky turned back to him, propped herself on an elbow. She felt she was slipping into his eyes, out of control and glad of it. "You know something very strange has happened to my little brother, Peter. He's grown by leaps and bounds since my father died. And now I think it's happening to me too. I feel so emotional, all torn up. But I'm so happy to be here with you, right now. So free."

Steven cupped her chin in his soft fingers. She thought he would kiss her lips, but he didn't, just explored her face a moment, then let her go.

"What do you want, Steven?"

"She's becoming a moving target," he answered.

"Me? I'm a moving target? What do you mean?"

"I started chasing a pretty girl. You're changing before my eyes, like a . . . like a beautiful dragonfly—all hungry, and free, and full of hope. Maybe I fly too."

His eyes found hers. They were beautiful and filled with hope, and at that moment Vicky believed she could trust him with her life.

21

GEORGE NG, Mackintosh Farquhar's comprador before Vivian Loh edged the Ngs out, was Chinese-born and British-educated. He spoke precise Oxford English, wore Jermyn Street suits, served as a deacon in the Anglican Church, and cloaked the discretion of a Queen's Counsel in a cloud of Eastern enigma. Insulated by triple-glazed windows, his Central District office was so quiet that Vicky wanted to part the heavy draperies to confirm that Hong Kong was still outside.

Ng watched with a benignly disinterested expression on his smooth yellow face as the family took seats—Vicky, her mother, Peter and Mary Lee, Fiona accompanied by her girls. If the old man resented losing his position at the hong, or was angry his son had not been allowed to continue the traditional relationship between the Ngs and Fierce and Mighty, or if he grieved for his former employer, he revealed nothing. But when he began to speak, Vicky, who had known him as Uncle Ng her entire life, thought she detected a certain sly pleasure in this final power that Duncan Mackintosh had bequeathed him.

"Good morning. It was the Taipan's wish that I remain his personal lawyer and that I read his last will and testament. You will be relieved to know that, his untimely death notwithstanding, his affairs are in good order, and the future of the Mackintosh Farquhar hong rests in capable hands. The Taipan was aware that we live in interesting times and took pains to prepare for them."

Vicky, who was not expecting any surprises, found her mind wandering, as it had for days, toward Steven Wong. Between the incandescent memory of the picnic at Shek-O and Mary's massages, her headaches had all but disappeared. Steven's face floated before her eyes, glowing with his ready smile. She had never known a man so comfortable in her presence. He anticipated her moods and totally disarmed her natural inclination to defend her personal territory. He was like a Trojan horse, she thought with a private smile, encamped by invitation well inside her walls.

George Ng rustled the papers he held. "Permit me to read the last will of Duncan Mackintosh, Taipan of Mackintosh Farquhar:

" 'To my grandchildren, Millicent and Melissa, and their mother, Fiona Mackintosh, I leave my firstborn son Hugo's share of profits, but not equity, the control of which will reside in the hands of my executor.' "

Vicky glanced at her mother, who looked like a heavily made-up ghost, with too much rouge on her cheeks and dark circles under her eyes. Sally returned her thin, bored-with-business smile. No surprises there. Fiona and the girls were taken care of, while the power would reside in the new taipan's hands.

" 'To my former wife's son, Peter Mackintosh—' "

"What?"

Peter, Mary, and Vicky rose as one. *"What* did he say?"

"Wait, Uncle Ng. What is he talking about?"

"I'm sorry, Peter," the lawyer answered. "He was not your father."

"Who is?" Peter turned in shocked anguish to his mother. Mary's mouth ballooned open in a startled O.

"That vindictive bastard," said Sally Farquhar Mackintosh. Anger firmed her face with a stony beauty. Her chin rose, and she suddenly looked ten years younger.

"Who is, Mother?"

"Not to worry, Peter. A fair portion of MacF is still mine, his will be damned. I'll write my own will and you'll not want."

"But, Mother, who—"

"Never mind," she said, and it was clear to Vicky, at least, that her mother had spoken her last words on the subject.

"Don't worry," Vicky assured Peter. "Nothing changes for us."

She was appalled by her father's cruelty. It seemed that every time she thought she finally knew him, he turned up a new and terrible secret. She stole a look at Mary Lee and flinched from the rage on the Chinese woman's face.

"We'll fight it," promised Mary. "We'll fight."

That was all they needed—one of Hong Kong's infamous legacy suits. Many a Chinese hong had died a slow death while the heirs battled it out in the courts. And then, suddenly, Vicky understood what her father had done. The price was Peter's to pay forever, but Duncan Mackintosh had completely eliminated the threat that the Lee clan would move in on MacF. A business decision, after all. And a gift to her. She would not have to fight her brother for control.

The lawyer cleared his throat. "If I may continue, please . . . 'To Peter Mackintosh I leave a yearly stipend, equal to his present salary with the hong, to be increased yearly taking in account inflation and his efforts.'"

The so-called repair child hadn't worked at all. Her mother had had an affair, had given birth to Peter, and finally, in despair, had turned to drink. It amazed her how her parents had hidden all their unhappiness. Or had they? How much of it did she and Peter carry? Only Hugo away at school had survived unscathed and normal.

She swore a solemn vow to herself, that moment, that she would raise happy children. Immediately analyzing the promise as if it were a business proposition, she plotted a course of action for treating the children she did not yet have. She would think before she acted; she would stop each day and force herself to notice how the way she lived her life was affecting theirs. If there was a fantasy element to her vow, she would ground it in reality. If she never had her own children, she would adopt. But either way, she swore she would accept the responsibility for helpless lives.

George Ng waited until the many emotions swirling across Vicky's face had fused into an expression of stern resolve. Then he continued reading:

" 'Control of the Mackintosh Farquhar hong and all its equity— less certain specified gifts to loyal servants and my former wife— passes to my remaining children.' "

Vicky looked up sharply, but Peter and her mother were still reeling from the first shocker and hadn't noticed the second.

"The gifts," Ng explained blandly, "are generous, but not consequential. I'll list them later. Finally, Duncan Mackintosh concludes, 'My executor, with full discretion to carry out my wishes, will be my oldest surviving child, Victoria.'

"Your father attached a note, Victoria, which says, 'For one hundred and fifty-seven years, the brains of Fierce and Mighty, and maybe the guts, seem to pass through the women. Your turn, Your Majesty.' "

Ng stood up, carried the will to Vicky, and placed it ceremoniously in her hands. It was handwritten on MacF stationery. "Congratulations. If I can be of any help, Taipan, merely ask."

"When did he write this?" she asked in a stony voice.

"New Year's Eve." Ng indicated the scrawled date and signature.

"Will it stand up?"

"You'll notice it was witnessed by the chief executive of Hong Kong and his personal secretary," George answered drily. "It ought to hold up quite firmly in British, Hong Kong, and Chinese courts."

Vicky looked into the lawyer's pale-brown eyes. He really was enjoying himself. "I have to talk to you."

"I've already booked us a lunch table at Shit and Feathers." He smiled back, using the Brit name for the Eagle's Nest restaurant.

Behind her, she heard her mother's voice rising. "I'll be late," Vicky told him. "I've got to help my brother first."

"I refuse to discuss another word in a solicitor's office," said Sally Mackintosh. "I'm inviting you all to lunch and Bloodies on the boat."

"Excellent idea," said Vicky. "Fiona, why don't you and Mary and the girls take Mum to the boat. Peter and I will catch up."

"I'll ride with you and Peter," said Mary as everyone rose and milled toward the door. Vicky drew her aside.

"I've really got to talk to Peter. I'm very upset and I think he is too."

"Don't think you can talk him into accepting this."

"Frankly, that is the furthest thing from my mind. I've got bigger problems. But I just want to be his sister for a moment. I think he needs me."

Mary tossed her head. "I take care of his needs."

"Listen, he's a new man since Dad died. I don't want this awful thing to derail him. Give me a half hour, please. He's not going to give anything away. You talk to him first, then let me. I'll give him back in half an hour."

"No," said Mary.

Vicky turned on her coldly. "You heard the will. You haven't a hope in hell of cracking it. All I'm trying to do is minimize the damage to Peter."

Mary stared back as coldly.

Vicky said, "I want you and Peter to work for my hong. But my father's will gives me the power to fire you both. Don't make me."

To her surprise, Peter's girlfriend capitulated gracefully.

"Forgive me, Vicky. I'm upset too. But I haven't the right to stand between a brother and sister. I'm sorry."

They found a marble nook in a window of the lobby of George Ng's office building. Peter curled into it, his back to the glass. Vicky stood, facing him. Through the window she could see hundreds of people hurrying along the sidewalk.

"Peter. First off, I need you to work with me. And I need Mary too. So let's just start off realizing nothing changes. All right?"

"Sure."

"You know, frankly, I don't believe Dad. I think he was lying."

"Mum didn't say he was lying."

"I think Mum was hurt."

"Vicky, don't lie to me to make me feel better. I don't give a fuck. Do you understand that?"

She nodded and held his arm. Peter shook off her hand. "I always thought he was kind of dumb. I wondered how I got so smart." He looked up and met Vicky's eyes. "Relax," he said. "That's a feeble joke."

"What can I do for you?"

"Hey, it's not your responsibility. Just because he made you Taipan doesn't make you the villain. He's the villain."

"He is that. I can't believe he would do such a thing."

"Do you think Mum will ever tell me who my father was?"

"No . . . but if she ever tells me, I'll tell you."

Peter smiled. "That's the best news I've heard all day. . . . Oh, God, I can't believe this."

"You know, I was telling someone the other day that Dad freed us by dying."

"Well, now I'm doubly free." Peter laughed bitterly.

"Can I count on you?"

"For what?"

"I'm really counting on you and Mary to establish us in Taiwan and Fukien Province. We have got to reconnect in China. Are you going to be all right, or do you want to take a little time off? Though frankly, I need you now."

Peter expelled the air from his lungs. He turned his face and looked out the window at the busy sidewalk. When he answered, Vicky discovered that Peter had more troubles on his mind than his father's awful will.

"You're counting on Mary?"

"You and she together. You're virtually partners at the office — What's the matter?"

"How can I put this?"

"Try directly."

"Well, Mary is very Chinese. She'll exaggerate, thinking to please. And she'll promise to deliver things she can't."

"Like what?" Vicky asked. Peter hesitated. "Go on," she coaxed.

"Well . . . you see, there are many Lees in Hong Kong and many more across the Nan-yang."

Vicky nodded. Southeast Asia was strewn with the family name, one of the more common in South China, particularly with its variety of spellings: Lee, Lie, Li.

"They're not all rich and powerful. Just as every Kuomintang veteran was not necessarily a general."

"So Mary's branch of the family isn't quite as powerful as she led you to believe."

"Ever been up to Mong Kok?"

Vicky shook her head. The Mong Kok slum, in northern Kowloon, was the most crowded urban area on the face of the earth, Chinese density in the extreme.

"They still fly Chiang Kai-shek's flag up there at half mast. A real right-wing proletarian stronghold. Tough, hardworking, dirt-poor refugees."

"Is that where Mary is from?"

"Maybe. I don't really know where she's from. She's . . . I know you're not going to believe this, but she lives sometimes in a sort of fantasy world. That tough veneer—and I don't mean it's just a veneer—covers a lot of . . . make-believe."

"But she speaks so well. She's so articulate. She's one of the few women I know who can hold her own with Vivian Loh."

"It's not all fantasy. She got herself through Hong Kong University and did really well. But . . ."

"So, I'm not sure I follow."

"I'm saying I frankly don't know where my fiancée was born, or who her parents really are. There's a slew of uncles and aunts and grandfathers, but I've never actually met her parents."

"Didn't you wonder?"

"Not really. The Chinese scatter so. It's very common. She said her father and mother lived in Los Angeles. Then one day, I heard they lived in Seattle, then Sydney. I suppose it doesn't really matter. She is what she says, in that she's a savvy businesswoman."

"She certainly is."

"And very ambitious."

". . . Does she love you, Peter?"

Peter faltered. "She's there for me whenever I need her."

Vicky took his hand. He was trembling, but at her touch he calmed. "Sounds pretty good. Doesn't it?"

"You think so?"

"It sounds good," she said.

"Of course when we get to Taiwan and Fukien Province, we discover a little less clout on the ground than I had assumed we'd find."

"Well, we'll build our own clout. She doesn't have enemies there, does she?"

"Oh, no. It's just that they don't really know her as an 'old friend.'"

"Listen, I'm glad you told me this. I won't make certain assumptions about what to expect. But I don't think you should worry so much. Even if you look at it coldly. So she's engaged to the son of a British taipan. But it's not as if she's lounging about buffing her fingernails. I get memos that make sense, and concise, clear telephone calls. She has a very good mind. . . . Are you thinking of having children, if you marry?"

"She says she can't."

"When did you learn this?"

"Early on."

"Oh, Peter, I'm sorry."

"It's just that . . . I found a diaphragm."

"Oh."

"Right. Oh."

Vicky put her arms around him. He was trembling again. "Oh, you poor thing. How deep in this fantasy world is Mary?"

"I don't know. I really don't know."

Vicky hesitated. There was another question. She hated to upset Peter still more, but she felt she should test the extent of the deception. Mary, after all, occupied a place with Peter quite near the core of MacF. There were few secrets on the executive floor, other than those Vicky kept in her own heart.

"Where'd you find the diaphragm, Peter?"

He gave her a bleak smile and shook his head. "Her handbag."

"Oh, Peter. I'm so sorry."

"I love her so. But I don't think I can stand this."

"Have you confronted her?"

"Not yet," he admitted.

"May I offer you some sisterly advice?"

"God, yes."

"Don't, until you have a plan to deal with her answer."

The Eagle's Nest was a superb Chinese restaurant atop the American-owned Hilton Hotel. Uncle Ng was waiting at a window table when Vicky arrived, peering down at the thousand ships in the harbor. The bright light made her wince and she headed for the chair with its back to the glass.

He rose smiling, clearly enjoying his role as stage manager for the drama her father had left behind. "I'd rather not hold this conversation at my club, if you don't mind."

"I doubt they'd blackball you at your age, Uncle. . . . What the devil was my father up to?"

"A drink?" Ng stalled.

"Pellegrino."

"And green tea," he said to the waiter.

"What was he up to?" Vicky asked again.

"Excuse me while I arrange for starters."

The lawyer made her wait while he engaged the dining room captain in a Cantonese discussion of hors d'oeuvres. Finally he turned to Vicky. "Which part of the will are you referring to?"

"You know damned well which part. Unless you're agreeable to telling the court that my father's will contains a typo."

"Sadly, it does not."

"Children?"

"Children."

Vicky's heart was pounding.

Somewhere in Hong Kong was the offspring of her father's first affair: the affair he had ended to be with her mother and Hugo; the decision that led to her own birth as the repair job that failed. A person she knew? Or a stranger? A bastard, with whom his will forced her to share MacF. It could be anyone. It could be someone she had gone to school with, a friend, or a total stranger.

"Who is it? Do we know him?"

"She's not born yet."

"What? *Vivian's?*"

"Preggers." Uncle Ng smiled. "Three or four months. The little bastard just might be born on Turnover Day."

"Oh, *fuck*! . . . Wait. How do we know it's a she?"

"The amniocentesis."

Vicky sagged in her chair. The elegant restaurant swam before her eyes. "Do tests prove it's his?" she asked with bleak expectation.

George Ng smiled indulgently. "Of course it's his."

Vicky snorted and took a deep swallow of her sparkling water.

Ng said, "I've got less reason to like Vivian Loh than you do, m'dear, but she's an old-fashioned girl. There wasn't a hope in hell it wasn't his."

"Are you sure about the tests?"

"Absolutely. We can demand more, of course, but that would be a graceless way to start your relationship."

"Our relationship?" Vicky echoed. It was still sinking in. "She's going to demand to be my partner, right? She's the so-called guardian of my father's child?"

"Regent, as it were, until your little sister attains her majority."

"My sister? Oh, my God, of course."

"Guardian of your sister. Vivian is, or will be, the mother and legal guardian of your half-sister and co-Taipan of Mackintosh Farquhar. Thanks to your father, you're going to be a very close family, like it or not."

"Regent? I'll have to deal with her for twenty-one years. Why'd he do it?"

George shrugged. "I could guess that he cared for Vivian and felt a responsibility for the child."

"He didn't have to give them half the fucking hong. Excuse my language, Uncle, but I am very upset."

"Do you remember how your mother used to say that your father never did anything that wasn't business?"

"Until he started going 'round the bend."

"He never went 'round the bend. He fell in love, but he didn't go 'round the bend."

"Look what he's done to me with this will."

"Whether you like it or not, Victoria, it's a business decision."

"Right. He didn't trust me to handle MacF alone. He's forcing me to take a goddam Chinese partner."

George Ng's smile fixed, tight and hard. He laughed to hide his anger. Then he lectured her gently. "For one hundred and fifty-seven years you had a Chinese comprador. We didn't do so badly together, did we?"

"I'm sorry, Uncle. I didn't mean it the way it sounded."

"Yes, you did. You don't understand that, but you did mean it precisely the way it sounded. . . . It's all right. You're not a bad person, Victoria. You're a little young and a little impulsive. You know, ironically, it was your father, of all people, who saw it was time to change if MacF were to survive in our"—he paused to select the right word, and found it with a wry smile—"in our new environment."

Vicky barely heard him. "I can't stand the woman and she hates me."

Only then did she realize how deeply she had insulted the old comprador. "Your father's will does not require you and her to pillow together," he replied sharply, not disguising his glee. "Merely to share Mackintosh Farquhar."

"Not before the child is born," Vicky shot back.

"You would be well advised to make your peace before."

"She doesn't want peace."

"Don't project." Ng smiled. "Ah, here's some food."

"Permit me, Uncle," Vicky said silkily, reaching with her chopsticks and placing the most succulent of the shrimp dumplings on his plate. Uncle Ng gave the translucent morsel an ironic smile.

Chinese New Year tradition said that to treat an employee like family by offering the best meant that he would not work for the hong in the coming year.

"You're shooting the messenger."

"It's a business decision, Uncle," Vicky explained with deliberate formality. "How can I trust a lawyer who takes such pleasure in my misfortune?"

At the end of their silent meal he asked, "Would you like me to arrange a meeting with Vivian Loh? Perhaps I can make amends for my behavior by helping you."

Despite the disasters, her mind had fixed firmly again on Steven Wong. Her answer surprised her. Instead of distracting her, thoughts of Steven seemed to clear away the nonessentials and helped her focus on reality.

"Go right ahead, Uncle Ng."

"Excellent." He beamed. "You ought to find now whether you can talk."

"There's only one problem. I already fired her and I hear she's gone to Canada with her mother."

"Not permanently, I wouldn't think."

"No such luck. She doesn't have a Canadian visa. Does she know about the will?"

"I imagine your father gave her a copy."

Vicky recalled Vivian's remark: "It's not so simple." Doubtless she knew. "Maybe I can get Alfred Ching to talk to her. He's over there someplace."

"A personal approach would be an excellent beginning. Start off on the right foot by giving her face."

"Of course." Vicky picked up her bag. "Thanks for lunch, Uncle George. I know *you* enjoyed it."

"Wait, please."

Vicky lowered herself back into her chair. Ng looked very serious. "Now what? Are you going to tell me my mother is really my aunt or something?"

Ng didn't smile. "You know that McGlynn and Kerry were on the auction block?"

"Have been for donkey's years. Did someone finally buy them?" McGlynn & Kerry, a publicly held old-line trading hong, had concentrated on the slim Australian trade—since the Joint Declaration, to their detriment. "Who bought them?"

"Sir John."

"So? If it isn't nailed down, and Two-Way Wong can't steal it, he buys it."

"He's putting a lot of cash into broadening their trading base back into China. He's bought up some smaller Chinese hongs with excellent Peking and Shanghai and Canton connections to merge with them. He's obviously committed to turning M and K around."

"What does this have to do with Mackintosh Farquhar, other than the fact that we're expanding our China trade too?"

"Sir John is looking to hire a managing director."

"So?"

"McGlynn and Kerry are destined to become a major Anglo-Chinese hong."

"A major *Chinese*-Anglo hong," Vicky corrected. "Provided they find the right manager to pull it together."

"Precisely."

"I still don't understand why you're telling me this."

"Sir John is curious whether you would be interested in the job."

"What? Two-Way Wong wants to hire *me* to run McGlynn and Kerry?"

George Ng nodded.

"What about MacF?"

"He's prepared to make you an extremely generous merger offer."

Vicky sat back, nonplussed. "Wait a minute. What does he want, Uncle Ng? Does he want me to make McGlynn and Kerry viable, or does he want to destroy Mackintosh Farquhar?" But it was neither, she knew. Two-Way feared that her father had more kickback evidence than had sunk with *Mandalay*, and had left it to her.

"He's not a man to waste good money destroying a rival company. Conglomerated, the hongs would be a force to contend with."

"Is that your advice?" Vicky asked, wondering what Two-Way had paid her father's former comprador to pitch the takeover.

"No advice," Ng demurred hastily. "I'm merely bearing the message."

"It's a bribe," she murmured half-aloud.

"I beg your pardon."

"I said, he's trying to erase us." But in her mind she knew Two-Way's true motive. Yes, he would be pleased to see the name Mackintosh Farquhar vanish with the Union Jack, but there was much more to his offer. It was really a bribe to keep her quiet.

First, Two-Way had set his son on her. Now he was trying to seduce her with a managing director's job. She had no intention of waiting passively for his next move. Her father's evidence could stay where it was; she didn't even want to touch it. The very thought—like holding a gun that had killed him—made her sick.

"I want you to rent me a safe-deposit box."

Uncle Ng looked bewildered at the sudden change of subject. "Victoria, your secretary can do that."

"I want you to rent me a safe-deposit box in the safest bank you know. I want you to bill me both by computer and mail. And I want a letter of confirmation that you've done it. And I want you to both mail and fax me the confirming letters from the bank."

"Victoria, you can't trust faxes, and secretaries talk. This will be the best-known secret safe-deposit box in Asia."

"Then I want you to draft a letter in my name giving your firm permission to open the box if I die. Mail and fax copies; messenger the original."

"Shall we hire Raymond Chow to make a movie of it? Just in case someone in the Colony doesn't learn you've rented a box?"

"Do it quickly and when you're ready, send one of the armored car services to pick up some packets."

"What's in the packets?"

"A secret."

"Hidden in the most famous safe-deposit box in the Colony?"

"You've got the message, Counselor Ng— In fact, rent several boxes. In different banks."

Ng scratched his head. "Whatever you say, Taipan . . ."

Let Two-Way ponder what was in the packets, plumped full of newspaper.

"As to this other matter, what shall I tell Sir John?"

"Are you supposed to bring him an answer?" Vicky asked.

"If you like, I can pass the word."

"Tell him tigers don't breed dogs."

22

ALFRED CHING FLEW in from Vancouver for the second night of the Chinese New Year, *Hoi Nien*, "The Opening of the Year," to take Vicky as promised to a family banquet at his parents' restaurant. They met at MacF House first so Alfred could report his progress on Expat-Emigrants. In Canada he had approached Chinese executive headhunters and made speeches to business groups in Vancouver and Toronto. Vicky had inventoried new apartments becoming available, provided MacF Construction got them finished. They shook hands on a partnership and headed for the party.

The Orchid Garden was packed with customers, but on the main floor several enormous round tables had been reserved for the Chings themselves. Vicky had dined with the cousins, siblings, uncles, and venerable elders years ago and noticed that the seating arrangements had changed little, despite the fact that Alfred had come home the conquering hero. She and he sat as they had before, among their own generation, and while the curious looks cast their way had less to do with her blond hair than they had in the past, no one seemed unduly awed by Alfred's success.

As his father—popping in and out of the kitchen—and his mother—jumping to the cash register—had expressed on TV, life went on, perhaps better, perhaps more secure, but nothing changed forever, and family and clan were still more important than one star of the moment. Alfred didn't seem to mind, though he did act a little distracted or jet-lagged.

Occasionally, when she felt one of his family staring, Vicky would meet fathomless eyes and wonder whether they blamed her for Britain's abandoning them to the PRC, from which they had fled. How frightened they must be, and yet, as they feasted Vicky found herself envying the Chings.

Last night she had taken Fiona and the girls for their traditional New Year's banquet at the Mandarin Hotel. Chip was away in the Philippines to buy an old sloop he had found cheap and was hoping to live aboard, and Peter was celebrating with Mary Lee's clan. Somehow not having any man at the table had turned a family gathering lonely. When Melissa had asked where they would all be next Chinese New Year's, neither Vicky nor Fiona had an answer.

The worst part of the dismal evening, though, for Vicky, had been that her mother had demanded they come first to *Whirlwind* for drinks, then got too teary to go on to the restaurant. Vicky had sat with her a while, and went back after the meal, too, but nothing helped, and poor Sally had finally drifted to sleep murmuring that everything was lost.

The Chings, by contrast, were vast and lively.

Their restaurant was hung with bright-red festive New Year's lanterns. Hordes of children rampaged under the smiling gaze of adults who tempted them back to the table with morsels from each new dish. Through the windows Vicky heard illegal firecrackers crackling in the street, and the hot, smoky room was loud with laughter and cries of *Kung Hay Fat Choi.*

"You like or not like?" Alfred shouted over the noise.

"Like," she shouted back, meaning it, though her thoughts kept drifting to Steven. "Great food. Tell your mother she put my tastebuds back on track." The feast had been presented in the elaborate nomenclature reserved for celebration. Chicken was dubbed "phoenix"; oysters, "splendor"; and mushrooms, "opportunity."

"*Kung Hay Fat Choi!* Hope you get rich, Vicky."

"Hope you get rich too, Alfred. Actually, I have a feeling we both will on Expat-Emigrants."

"I'm afraid I have to take you home early. I'm leaving for New York."

"You just got here," she said, disappointed. Steven aside, she had been enjoying Alfred's company. "I was just about to forgive you for abandoning me in hospital."

"I'm real sorry, but I have a meeting scheduled with some bankers."

It suddenly struck her what he had done. "Alfred?"

"What?"

"You got in this afternoon from Vancouver and now you're flying to New York?"

"Right. Via London."

"Why didn't you just fly from Vancouver to New York?"

Alfred looked astonished that she would ask. "We had a date."

"You're flying around the world in thirty hours for a date?"

Alfred grinned. "Not just any date."

Vicky was awed. It was a truly romantic thing he had done. "Alfred, you're daft, but I feel deeply flattered." She also felt hideously guilty because she had almost canceled their date so she could go out with Steven instead. "Well . . . you must be tired. Shall we go?"

They made their goodbyes to Alfred's parents and the Ching family elders, and walked through the gaily crowded streets to the Star Ferry. The noise from exploding firecrackers was deafening, and sometimes they had to run to escape it. Whole families were wandering about in the neon lights, the children kicking and laughing through mounds of spent firecracker paper. Alfred bought her a bright concoction of miniature pennants and artificial flowers, which she tossed into a fire as an offering for good luck in the New Year.

"Happy Year of the Ox."

"I rather wish 1997 were a snappier-sounding year than Ox. Like a Dragon year."

"Dragon years usually end disastrously. Earthquakes, hailstorms, locusts."

"Revolutions."

"Civil wars."

On the ferry, as they watched the magnificent lighted walls of the city sparkling on the water, Alfred looped a friendly arm around her shoulders.

The wind was cool, and Vicky snuggled against him, glad of his warmth. He had always had a gift for knowing how and where and when to hold her. She was half-inclined to lift her face and brush her lips on the soft skin of his neck, or throw both arms around him and hug him as she used to years ago. She stopped herself, quite consciously, thinking it wouldn't be fair to lead him on. But by then Alfred seemed to guess her thoughts. His arm tightened gently, and his fingertips began to play on her skin, as sure as kittens nursing. Vicky pulled away, suppressing a shiver.

"Have you run into Vivian Loh in Canada?" she asked lightly.

Alfred took a slow breath. "I hear she's in Toronto."

"Are you going there?"

"Might. Depends on New York. Also, I've got some of our Expat-Emigrant business I've been putting off there."

"Would you look her up for me?"

Alfred's teeth flashed in a big grin. "What do you take me for, Vicky? A hit man?"

"Very funny. Tell her I'd like to talk as soon as she gets back."

"About what?"

"She'll know. But I want to keep it friendly. Alfred, you can do that for me, can't you? One friend to another. Tell her . . ."

"Tell her what?"

"Tell her . . . tell her we have to talk."

"That sounds terribly friendly. Why don't I just kick her shin."

"Please, Alfred. Put it in words she'll understand."

"Then she'll kick *my* shin."

"Alfred, goddammit."

"Okay, okay. I'll see if I can tart it up in Cantonese."

"Thank you. Thanks a lot."

They found a cab at the ferry terminal and held hands on the ride up the Peak. He kept the cab, walked her to the door, declined regretfully her offer of a nightcap.

"I had a lovely time, thank you. Next time you fly around the world I'm your girl."

She kissed his cheek with affection, and he nuzzled her back, doing little teasing things to her ear and neck that tempted her to demand he come in for a drink and take the next plane. Before she could, Alfred stopped the game with a friendly kiss on her nose and a worried glance at his watch. "One of these days, Vicky. One of these days."

"When?"

Alfred returned an enigmatic smile. "When I get the guts? Or you do . . . Good night. It was great seeing you."

"When are you coming home?"

"Soon as I can."

"Alfred?"

"What?"

"Can I tell you something?" Speaking of getting the guts. How was she going to say this?

"Shoot."

She was so afraid, still, that she pressed her face to his chest so she would not have to look him in the eye. "I'm really sorry for what I did to you."

"What you did to me?"

"You know, letting you think I'd marry you . . . you know, back then."

Alfred turned very Chinese, laughing to cover his embarrassment. "No problem, Vicky."

"No, I mean it."

He laughed some more, obviously flustered, then finally met her eye with as serious a look as she had ever seen from him. "No problem, really. It's over."

"A month's never gone by when I haven't felt guilty about stringing you along. You must have thought I was such a bigot."

"Not a bigot. You just used the bigotry around you, back then.

Things have changed. Look at Peter and Mary. Look at your dad and Vivian. I knew what you were doing. Hurt like hell, but I knew. . . . It wasn't so much it hurt as I felt we had lost something we could have had. That's always been the hard part for me." He took her shoulders in his hands and kissed her mouth. "Hey. We're still alive. It's not like we're eighty. We'll work something out."

Vicky quailed inside. She hadn't meant to start over. "I just wanted you to know how I felt back then."

Alfred gave her a shrewd look. "Back then. Right."

Fiona and the girls were not downstairs, and she was just heading up herself when she heard a knock at the front door. She flung it open, glad that Alfred had changed his mind about a drink, but discovered to her surprise and heart-pounding confusion that Steven Wong was standing there with peach blossoms and a smile.

"Steven, I just got in."

"I know. I've been waiting down the road in your bushes."

"How'd you know I would come home early?"

"Two-Way Wong's son knows everything."

"Oh, really? You're rather sure of yourself. How'd you know Alfred wouldn't stay?"

Steven Wong laughed. "I know a girl at Cathay Air. I called her to see if Alfred was coming back in time for your date. Bad joss, he was. Good joss, the girl said Alfred's booked out again tonight, London, New York. I put one and one together and waited in your bushes. Shall we go out?"

Vicky hesitated. She wanted to go with Steven, but she felt bad about Alfred. "Where?"

"I'll take you to the Canton Club."

"Isn't that a Triad hangout?"

"I'm going to blow those gangsters' socks off with a gorgeous blonde on my arm."

Vicky laughed, a little uneasily. "I'm not so sure I want to consort with Triad gangsters."

"Hey, you're already consorting with No-Way Wong."

"Is it safe?"

"Is what safe? Me or the Triads?"

"The Triads."

"Don't worry about 'em. You're safe with me. You might want to wear some sort of flashy fur. You'll fit in better."

"I think I'd prefer a shawl. Be right back." She returned with a red silk shawl, muttering, "My father would kill me. He hated the Triads. Said they were bullies and scum."

"Your father was a smart guy." They walked down the driveway and out the gate. Steven whistled, and an elderly Chinese chauffeur backed a red Rolls-Royce out of the bushes. "Dad's," Steven said, grinning. It carried Two-Way Wong's famous "1997" vanity license plate, for which, the tabloids claimed, he had paid $5 million at the government's "lucky car number" auction. As soon as it was rolling, Steven offered champagne.

"Why aren't you with your family for the *Hoi Nien* banquet?"

"I have eighty-seven little brothers and sisters who are all big deals in World Oceans Company." He meant, Vicky knew, his many half-siblings by Two-Way's various wives and concubines. "I'm the only bum. It's more fun for them when I'm not there. And it's for sure more fun for me."

"Does your father mind?"

"He'll get over it."

"He offered me a job," she said casually, watching his reaction.

"Don't take it."

"Why not?"

"No future. You can't go up in the hong with all his kids ahead of you."

Vicky waited in vain for him to comment beyond that warning. "Don't you think it's odd that he offered me a job?"

"Not at all. I figured he had some reason asking me to check you out. He buys people all the time. Probably figures to suck up MacF, keep whatever you have he likes, and throw the rest out— you included."

"Surely he didn't think I would allow that."

"He doesn't like loose ends. The Brits are leaving—he figures to pick up the pieces."

"*We are not leaving.*"

Steven looked up from the champagne bottle with mild disapproval. "Make you a deal, Vicky. You don't talk about your business and I won't talk about gambling boats. Unless it's really important to you. Then, for sure, we talk about anything you like."

"What happens to my hong is important to me, Steven. It's my family and all we have."

"Yeah, I know. But I wasn't brought up with no work ethic, you know?" He dazzled her with a smile. "I would rather not discuss my old man—unless it's really important to you."

He poured the champagne, which had a pretty blush, handed her a glass, and touched the rim with his. "Our picnic won't leave my head. I wanted to call you all weekend, but I was stuck on the boats and I figured you needed your sleep anyhow."

Marveling at the sheer comfort she felt with him, Vicky said, "I wanted to call you too. I was . . . longing to talk to you. I felt like a kid. Feel like a kid."

"Do you?" He reached for her hand and bent his head to kiss it, sending a shiver down her spine. "Me too. Hey, you make me so happy." They sat smiling at each other in the dim light as the silent car moved through crowded streets toward the harbor tunnel. Vicky was vaguely aware of firecrackers in the night, parades of families with sleepy children, and leaping fires where people were burning offerings like the ones she had made earlier with Alfred.

The neon galaxy of the Golden Mile of the Nathan Road smeared brilliant colors over the hood of the Rolls-Royce and splashed the windows with waves of red and green and yellow. A long line of customized BMWs and Mercedes dripping chrome, and another line of people on the sidewalk, pointed the way to the Canton Club. The Wong driver, an old hand at the cruder symbols of the city's pecking order, pulled ahead of the cars and decanted Steven and Vicky

directly in front of a red velvet rope, which the burly doorman hastily pulled out of their way. Nor, Vicky noticed, did anyone ask
Steven for the $50 cover charge the other patrons were paying. Mu-
sic was pounding through the walls, and when the door opened, it
thundered.

Steven took her hand and led her through the crowds, past a
long black bar draped with beautiful girls, the consorts, apparently,
of the wiry young men displaying their muscles in tight shirts and
crisp white pants. Steven kissed her ear to whisper, "Kung-fu fighters. Very tough."

"What do they do?"

"Make cripples. These kids get so good with the chopper they
can cut all the muscles in your back without killing you."

Vicky shuddered, and wondered what she would say to Chip if
he saw her here. Most of the people in the bar were watching her
and Steven, while pretending not to. If half she had heard about the
Triads was true, then some of these boys collected protection money
from Alfred's mother and father.

Steven bent to her ear again. "They got much more powerful
the last couple of years because the police are so corrupt, with the
Brits leaving. Trouble is, when the PRC comes in they're in trouble.
Come on, dance floor's upstairs."

The music was even louder upstairs. Steven, not surprisingly,
was quite a good dancer and Vicky felt inspired by his grace. Somehow, he managed to slow her down enough to feel music she had
only heard before. He grinned as the discovery dawned on her
face.

"Hey, it's just sex with clothes on."

They found a bar in a quieter corner that served icy champagne.

"Steven!" called a muscular, heavyset Chinese in his thirties,
with slicked-back jet hair and a silk suit and gold chains. "Hey, man.
Have a drink." He snapped his fingers and the bartender immediately filled three tall glasses to the brim with cognac. "Hey, *Kung
Hay Fat Choi!*" Steven's friend drained the cognac like water and
turned crazy black eyes on Vicky, who had taken a small sip. "You
no give me face?"

"Just out of the hospital," Steven explained. "Doctor says no drink."

The Chinese scowled. "You no introduce me girlfriend. You no give me face, Steven?"

"Next time," Steven replied, with a chilly smile that sent the man away.

"More gangsters?" Vicky asked.

"A lotta bad guys." He laughed.

"Colleagues?" It troubled her that he could move among them. But what had she expected of a man who had run Macau gambling casinos and now the notorious offshore operation?

"I'm not a bad guy."

"But you're friends."

"Back when I played tennis and got seeded at Wimbledon, you know what they did? Asked me to throw a match. Take a dive. Everybody in Hong Kong was betting real heavy on me. The Triads figured they'd make a killing. They were kind of upset when I said no."

"Did they threaten you?"

"Threaten the son of Two-Way Wong?" Steven smiled to himself. "That brave they are not."

"It turns you on to hang around with them, doesn't it?"

"Used to, when I was younger," he admitted. "You get a little older and you see the guy in the silk suit for what he is."

"Which is?"

"A street fighter whose dream is to survive long enough to buy a BMW."

"Did you throw the match?"

"What do you think?"

"No," she said, though she wasn't sure.

"Didn't have to. Lost fair and square." He laughed. "My sports career went down the tubes, but I'm these guys' hero. The older ones. Most of these kids weren't even born yet."

Vicky cast her eye over the room. A near-black darkness was punctuated by strobe flashes from the dance floor. They *were* very young, she realized, mostly teenagers, though here and there a table was occupied by a chain-smoking, silk-suited veteran in his twenties. Suddenly she rose from the bar stool.

"What is it?" asked Steven.

She was staring at a stocky figure in a white silk suit. The lights flashed as he turned toward her and for a split second their eyes met. It was Huang, Ah Chi's assistant boatboy on *Whirlwind*. He whipped around and plunged into the crowd. Vicky started after him, caught another glimpse of his face as he hurried down the crowded stairs.

Pushing through the people coming up, Vicky struggled down to the bar; the kung-fu crowd stared. She kept pushing toward the door, through the dark foyer, and suddenly into the brilliant street. A chromium-encrusted car screeched from the curb and disappeared into the gleaming traffic.

"Who was that?" Steven asked, catching up with her.

"I saw one of our boatboys. A Tanka kid named Huang. I thought the Tanka kept to themselves."

"Used to, but they getting rich smuggling people. He's probably hit the big time."

"He was such a sweet kid. A little dumb and lazy. I can't imagine him a kung-fu fighter."

"He's not. If he's got his own boat, he hires his own tough guys."

"What for?" she asked, not sure she wanted to know the answer.

"You think he brings that boat home empty? But he better make it while he can. Come July one, he better sail for Australia. PRC and Triads don't mix. The Reds drove 'em outa Shanghai and they'll drive 'em outa Hong Kong. Unless, of course, somebody makes a hell of a deal with Beijing."

"I can't get over Huang. Maybe I was wrong. I'll ask Ah Chi, my mother's boatboy. He'll know."

"But will he tell you?" Steven smiled. "Okay, what about us? More dancing?"

"I'm a little tired again. Sorry."

Steven put an arm around her and raised a lazy hand in the air, which produced, immediately, his father's Rolls-Royce. As they stepped into the car a photographer's flash exploded in Vicky's face. She ducked, too late.

"Oh, God, Steven, I don't need newspaper pictures of me at the Canton Club."

"Get in the car. I'll be right back."

He advanced quickly on the photographer and returned in a minute. "Move out," he ordered his driver, and tossed Vicky a roll of exposed film.

"How'd you do that?"

Steven grinned. "I promised her exclusive shots of me and whatever starlet in a position of her choice."

"Thank you. I appreciate that. I just don't think a British taipan's supposed to be running around with gangsters."

"At least not in the papers." He kissed her lips, very softly. Then he poured fresh glasses from the champagne in the ice bucket. "Are you going to invite me home?"

"Can't. My sister-in-law and my nieces and the servants are there. . . . Why don't you invite me home?"

"Can't. Old Man's there."

"The car?"

"Not the first time," he grinned back. "How about a nightcap at the Regent?"

"I don't know that I want to hang about the lobby of the Regent Hotel with a playboy who's a hero to gangsters."

"Upstairs," he said, kissing her again.

"It's Chinese New Year," she whispered into his mouth. "There isn't a hotel room in the Colony."

"We have a reservation."

"I didn't know playboys planned ahead."

"I've had a room booked all week—hoping I'd get lucky."

Vicky pressed against him, her mouth dry with anticipation. Alfred flickered through her mind and then, oddly, an image of her father with a disapproving scowl on his face. She banished them both. Steven was new and fresh and hers to do with as she wanted.

23

TRAVELING IN CHINA, Vivian could always spot another Hong-konger by his walk. Here came one now, bustling up the Nan-jing Road, weaving and jinking around the slower-moving Shanghainese, dodging the black-market money-changers, shoulders forward for speed, legs pumping, wrist bent for a glimpse of his watch. The poor Mainlanders, by contrast, ambled along like brows-ing sheep, as if they had long ago given up hope that something, anything, exciting might be waiting around the next corner. And this was Shanghai! Elsewhere, the citizens of the PRC moved like prisoners of a glacier.

"Vivian! Hey, Vivian Loh!"

Vivian ducked into a coffeehouse, but the Hongkonger, whose face she still hadn't seen clearly, charged right in after her. "Vivian!"

"Alfred Ching! What are you doing here?"

"Thought that was you. You looked too bright for a local."

They shook hands. That small action, Alfred's snappy suit, and the fact they were speaking Cantonese, drew an audience. In sec-onds, two dozen people were standing around, new arrivals asking what was going on.

"You believe these people?" said Alfred. "Do anything in this town and you've got a hundred fans. Poor buggers. No work, no spending money. What a life. What are you doing here?"

Vivian could hardly tell Alfred that he had just frightened off a woman who had promised to take her to Party Leader Tang's private secretary, so she improvised. "I'm trying to spin something off my old Golden Air contacts. And you?"

Alfred's face closed slightly, as if he had realized, belatedly, that he, too, had secrets to hide. But he just wasn't built that way and after a moment's internal debate, he spewed out what sounded to Vivian like the truth, and faintly ominous-sounding truth at that.

"Don't laugh," he said, smiling, "but I'm talking to investors." He gave their surroundings an ironical nod. A man squatting on the pavement outside was selling glass-cutters, demonstrating his flimsy tools by cutting up stacks of scrap glass. A crowd had gathered to see if anyone would buy. On its fringes, an old woman hawked sweet potatoes she had roasted in a crude coal grate fashioned from a ruined bucket.

"Here?"

"Told you not to laugh. Seriously, I've got some state companies interested in kicking in. Sold them on the idea of preferential office space if they invest in the tower. A lot of them are hoping to open branches in Hong Kong."

Vivian nodded politely. She found it hard to imagine he'd get much cash out of the Shanghainese. On the other hand, Alfred Ching had proven himself to be a high-flying operator.

"Can't hurt to make new 'old friends,'" she said. "But didn't you already close on the Cathay Tower?"

"Just fattening the kitty."

She wondered, fleetingly, whether Alfred had run into trouble, and hoped he hadn't. Hong Kong property values would tumble disastrously if he went belly-up. Alfred consulted his gold Rolex. "Have you time for coffee?"

Her contact had fled, so she said she did and they took a table. Shanghai was still sprinkled with relics of International Settlement days. Here, the coffee was excellent, the pastries divine. Aside from the fact that the customers ate with chopsticks, they could easily have been in Vienna. Alfred ordered the lemon meringue pie and Vivian indulged a sudden craving for chocolate cake.

"This is a perfect coincidence. I tried to find you in Toronto. But all your mother could tell me was she thought you'd gone to Hong Kong."

"You were looking for me?"

"I bear a message."

Vivian's face closed up. "Oh. I can guess."

"Hey, she's not as bad as you think."

"I know you're old friends."

"She takes some getting used to, sometimes," Alfred agreed amiably.

"That's putting it mildly."

"She's really a remarkable woman, though she's been through hell this last year."

"I know the feeling."

"Sorry. I didn't mean to say you didn't. So you do know the feeling. So you can imagine."

His face underwent a remarkable change as he talked about Vicky, revealing emotional depths she had never noticed. There was a solid man in there, someplace deep down under all that self-promotion. And it seemed that breezy, bright, ambitious Alfred Ching, who could have his pick of women in Hong Kong, was besotted by Vicky Mackintosh.

"What's the message?" she asked, hiding a smile. If she had learned anything in the last four years, it was that love was strange.

"She's trying to make up. She wants to talk. I think she wants you back in the hong."

"Why?"

"She's smart enough to know it's more than she can handle alone."

"You're dreaming, Alfred."

"Maybe I'm exaggerating, a little," he admitted. "Let's just say Vicky senses she needs your help."

"Victoria Mackintosh needs no one. Or so she thinks."

"You don't understand her. Vicky is—"

Vivian cut him off. "Alfred. I think you're in love with her. Either that or you're the worst judge of character in the world. I hardly know you, so I have no way of knowing which, though your reputation suggests you're usually pretty savvy."

She glanced significantly at her watch, quite willing to let him off the hook. She didn't really care what he thought of Vicky Mackintosh, though if he was in love with her, God help him.

Alfred put down the chopsticks he'd been poking nervously into the meringue. "She's a lonely woman. And she's a generous woman. But she can't really connect with people, so she covers her loneliness by taking over."

"She is as imperious and high-handed as—"

"Her father," Alfred finished her sentence.

"He was not," Vivian said quickly. "No, he wasn't. You don't know. Duncan was . . ." Vivian looked away. She felt tears coming.

Alfred Ching smiled. "I guess we have something in common."

By the end of March, with less than four months to Turnover, a melancholy air had gripped the Crown Colony, and American country-and-western music, which had always appealed in Hong Kong, suddenly rocketed to new popularity. Rooted in Scots tradition, the bittersweet music beguiled the nervous expats and charmed the Chinese, who took the simple songs to their sentimental hearts.

Old recordings were suddenly new favorites, and the city's high-tech film studios turned Patsy Cline and Hank Williams into unlikely pop stars. They were seen as if still alive in Plastimation music videos rummaged from forty-year-old film clips, which were colorized, computer-enhanced, and integrated with laser pyrotechnics. Willie Nelson tapes were hot bootleg items, and every Filipino band in the Colony was clumping around in cowboy boots and ten-gallon hats and dusting off their grandfathers' steel guitars.

"Crazy" was a big hit; "Sunday Morning Sidewalks" blared from the radios of taxi drivers who had never been to church nor wandered a quiet street in their lives; "I'm So Lonesome I Could Cry" wailed in the crowded markets. But the greatest hit heard on expat radio and a dozen Cantonese stations was the poignant "Sweet

Dreams." Even the Mandarin Hotel's sedate swing orchestra was sawing through it as Vicky Mackintosh climbed the stairs to the Clipper Lounge for afternoon tea with Vivian Loh.

Vivian had mailed a polite note from Shanghai saying she had bumped into Alfred Ching and suggesting they talk when she got back to Hong Kong. Vicky had responded with her own polite note and now, after two broken dates, they were finally going to get together.

She found Vivian waiting patiently in line behind some tourists. She looked prim and proper in a raw-silk suit and her gold-framed eyeglasses. The long suit jacket hid any evidence of her pregnancy.

"I'll get us a table."

"That's all right. It will just be a minute."

Vicky raised an eyebrow in the direction of the Clipper Lounge's hostess, who rushed up with an effusive "Please come this way, Miss Mackintosh. How nice to see you again."

"Good afternoon. This is Vivian Loh, who is an old friend of Mackintosh Farquhar."

"Very pleased to meet you, Ms. Loh. Sorry to keep you waiting."

Vivian ordered Chinese green tea. Vicky asked for Darjeeling. "Look at us," she said, noting that Vivian looked very well, with glossy hair and a healthy glow in her cheeks. "Two ladies taking tea without a care."

"I sometimes wonder what it must be like to have always been treated so kindly," said Vivian, with a nod at the accommodating hostess. "As if to belong so thoroughly."

"I beg your pardon?"

"It's nothing. Just a passing thought."

"Do you mean what's it like to grow up a taipan's daughter?" Vicky asked. "Marvelous, in the outside world. But at home it's what your parents are like that counts, not who they are. Whatever relationship you had with your mother and father would have been the same if they were taipans instead of whatever they were."

"Refugees."

"What were they before refugees? You know, it's funny but I know nothing about you, except my father said you had been a scholarship child." She had been about to say that Vivian had been "one of our scholarship children," but caught herself in time.

"My father was a teacher in China."

"An aristocrat."

"Teaching lost its cachet during the Cultural Revolution," Vivian replied drily.

"So what did he do in Hong Kong?"

Vicky saw cold anger in the Chinese woman's eyes, like a light shining through a diamond, and realized she had better temper her patronizing tone if she wanted to make peace.

"My father had several careers in Hong Kong. He operated a metal press during the day and cooked in a restaurant at night. Then my mother helped him start a series of businesses, all of which failed. Eventually he became a chop carver with a little shop of his own in Western, so his story ended happily."

"And your mother?"

"Mother emigrated last month to Toronto, as you know. She couldn't get into the States. I fear for her. Toronto seemed a cold and lonely place."

"Alfred Ching says it has a big Chinatown."

"It's not a Hong Kong Chinatown. The buildings are too low and too far apart. There's too much sky, if you know what I mean. At any rate, I got her settled in a nice apartment. I felt bad for her. The people with money live in the suburbs. She can't afford that, and when I offered to help she said the suburbs were even drearier than the city. She said to me, 'Shanghai, Canton, Hong Kong, and now Toronto. My whole life,' she said, 'has been downhill.' She loved her Shanghai, you see."

"Did you ever take your mother back to Shanghai?"

"Shanghai is a slum. Beijing destroyed it."

Vivian watched the Taipan's daughter listening with a polite expression fixed like lacquer on her face. She knew Victoria hadn't the slightest idea what she was talking about, even though she had exposed only the surface of her family. The important things she would never tell; her mother's loose habits and her father's fear were too central to her own life to discuss with even the closest friend, much less an enemy. Only a lover could hear such things.

Victoria needed her. Duncan's will made it so. What Victoria probably did not understand was how desperately Vivian needed her help to finish Duncan's work. Duncan had been overly protective. Out of love and old-fashioned Western chivalry he had never told her where he had hidden the evidence against Two-Way Wong and Premier Chen's ministers. He had given her a key to a safe-deposit box in the Hong Kong and Shanghai Bank, which held a cache of names of Mainland bureaucrats and their Swiss bank accounts, but it was small stuff, something to give up if the worst happened and Two-Way Wong was desperate enough to have her tortured.

The bulk of the evidence was hidden elsewhere, and if the location hadn't died with Duncan, then Victoria, the last person to see him alive, probably knew where it was.

She had to persuade Victoria to let her use it, which was why she was willing to meet for tea at the Mandarin. Her only weapon was inside of her—Duncan's baby, who had begun to stir. She had never wanted a baby before, and had never felt any particular maternal instinct. Now it was the joy of her life, central to everything whirling about her—her magnificent connection to her beloved Taipan.

Victoria's eyes were upon her, inspecting her body for signs. She inhaled deeply, touched her teacup to her lips, and said, "It took me quite some time to adjust to the fact that you're carrying my half-sister."

"It is a curious circumstance," Vivian agreed carefully. "We are bound, are we not?"

"Well, we can be," Vicky replied, equally careful. "At least if we can agree that we share the same goal."

Vivian sat back, a little awed by how cleverly Victoria had seized the initiative. She nodded. "Our well-being depends upon the hong."

Anger flickered in Victoria's eyes. "The hong" was a proprietary way of referring to Mackintosh Farquhar, which was exactly what Vivian had intended.

Vivian softened the reminder now by saying, "The future of Mackintosh Farquhar in Hong Kong will affect all of your family, including your sister."

"All of us," Victoria agreed with a grim smile.

"As will the future of Hong Kong itself."

It was Vicky's turn to sit back and contemplate Vivian's move. Across the open pit of the lobby stairs, the Filipinos had set lush violins upon "I Fall to Pieces." Waiters glided by, bearing an elaborate tea service to a nearby table, where five well-dressed members of an informal women shipowners' club were pretending interest in tonnage and shaft horsepower while shooting glances at Vicky.

A dozen rumors about Duncan Mackintosh's will were flying around the Colony, so Vicky had chosen this public meeting place carefully. On the one hand she wanted to present a picture of unity within MacF, and on the other, she had purposefully put herself in a place where she could not, under any circumstances, allow herself to lose her temper. She pretended a carefree smile for the benefit of her friend Linda, a striking Philippine Chinese who was staring openly. But Vivian had just confirmed her worst fear, which was that Vivian intended to use her new power at Mackintosh Farquhar to support her political goals.

"The future of Hong Kong is out of our hands," Vicky countered firmly. "The future of MacF is our very real problem. We can change MacF to meet the challenge."

"Forgive me, Victoria, but the future of Hong Kong is the future of MacF."

"Please call me Vicky. I really don't like being called Victoria."

"Of course. That was your father's name for you."

"One of them. Listen, we're businesswomen. We have a business to operate. It requires all of our attention." *We*, she thought angrily. I actually said *we*. She heard blood storm in her brain, and her headache started grinding like a junk's diesel. Forcing herself back on course, she said, "Let me tell you my plans. I had scads of time to think in hospital and I've launched all sorts of new projects while you were away."

Steven Wong invaded her thoughts. She had never felt so loved by a man, so naked beside him. Steven emptied her mind when they were together. Hong Kong, the Mainland, Turnover, Mr. Wu, the Golden Expo, Lantau, the misery of Vivian and her father's will, and MacF's roller-coaster ride on the daily shifting terrain, simply vanished when they met in their room at the Regent. And to her amazement, she would return to work from their fierce and total lovemaking a million times better. Sharper, bolder, swifter. Her boast that she was as good as her father was no longer bravado. She had come alive with Steven. Instead of fighting the chaos engulfing Hong Kong, she had joined it, had hurled herself into the whirlpool and discovered she could swim.

"Yes?" prompted Vivian.

"I'm taking MacF back to our roots. We started out a trading company and we will become one again."

"I'm not sure I follow," Vivian said, but Vicky knew she did. The ancient Hong Kong hongs had started as traders, as Alfred Ching had reminded her. In opium days, her predecessors had been go-betweens for East and West. Negotiators between the distant Europe, England, and the United States and the vast, mysterious China— as well as daring experimenters with shipping technology—they had exchanged goods for profit by searching out markets and producers to supply them. Or, as Alfred put it, they stood where East met West with their hand out.

"The Mainland is still vast and mysterious and needs the West more than ever. The PRC needs Hong Kong, and if MacF can serve that need, MacF will survive. I've instructed Wally Hearst to expand our Peking and Canton offices and hire Chinese to open agencies in Tianjin, Shenyang, Wuhan, and Chongqing."

Vicky noticed Vivian's curiosity at the mention of Wally Hearst. She wondered if her father had told Vivian about Wally's contacts among the Chen followers—people he and Duncan hoped would switch to Tang's reform movement if Chen was deposed.

"I would like you to expand in Shanghai and move into Ningbo and Hangzhou. I want Peter and Mary Lee to take charge in Fuzhou and use her contacts in Taiwan. But the big thing is Shanghai—there's a huge industrial base we can serve."

"How?"

"Air freight will be our wedge into trade."

"We haven't the capacity."

"I'm going to buy twenty more Antropov Two-fifties."

"Twenty?" Vivian echoed.

Hugo's research had convinced her that the Russian jet freighter planes were not only the biggest but also the best in the world. "Cheap to run," said Vicky, "and simple to fix."

"Your father liked them too. But twenty—"

"Meantime, we'll buy more freight gates in Europe and California. Golden Air Freight will be China's premier carrier."

"With what money? Twenty planes and all those gates will cost a fortune."

"We're rich—on paper, at least—thanks to Alfred's land boom. I've sold some properties and remortgaged most of the others. We have the cash to change."

"May I say, you're taking a terrible risk assuming debts based on a land boom?"

"It's worth it. What do you think, Vivian? Can you get behind that?"

"You could lose everything in one night. . . . What is happening with Mr. Wu and the Golden Expo?"

"Still no water permit. Mr. Wu is making damn sure the PRC gets the Golden Expo for a rock-bottom, pre-land-boom price. I doubt we'll break even on our construction costs—not to mention losing the profits we'd been counting on. I mean, that hotel was supposed to generate a lot of money." She shook her head in disgust. "And we can't even open the ruddy airport hotel until the PRC allows the Director of Marine to approve our ferries—which they won't do until we hand over Golden Expo."

"So things aren't exactly ideal."

"Far from it. That's why we're changing. I need your answer, Vivian."

"Forgive me, Vicky. My answers are the same. What you're doing is dangerous. But more important—far more important—MacF cannot operate in a vacuum. In three months Britain will return Hong

Kong to China. Hong Kong's role in China will be our role. We must affect that role. That was your father's purpose."

"That was *your* purpose, and it got him killed. His plan was clumsy and dangerous. I am not going to repeat his mistake."

"Your father saw it as MacF's only hope."

"I told you in hospital and I'll tell you again. I want no part of Ma Binyan or any other Chinese politician—including 'Reformer Tang.' MacF should never get caught up in factions."

Vivian shook her head.

Vicky seized on an image the Chinese woman would appreciate. "We're like a reed in the wind. *We are not the wind.*"

"Your father was bolder. We can be the wind."

"I will not permit MacF to take sides. Warlords come and go. Traders return."

"You must forgive me, but it is not entirely your decision."

"It is until that baby is born, and don't you forget it."

Vivian stood up. "I won't forget it, Victoria."

"Where the devil are you going?"

"Shanghai. I must see an old friend."

"What for?"

"You are a British citizen. You have a British passport. You and your brother and your nieces. I'm Hong Kong Chinese. And I have a Hong Kong Chinese baby in my body."

"A baby with a British father. Don't give me that sharpen-the-mind nonsense."

"I'm Hong Kong Chinese. This is our home."

"You can still take the baby to Britain, if you have to."

"Would you?"

Vivian spun on her heel. The lady shipowners were staring. She forced herself to turn back to Vicky and lean over the table and brush her cheek with hers. "For the face of MacF," she whispered.

"It doesn't change anything," said Vicky. "I'll run MacF without you until that baby is born."

"You'll come around," Vivian said. "You will see the light. Oh, and my best to Steven. I'm happy for you both."

So much for privacy. "Why?"

"Because he will help you understand your father."

"Did you sleep with Steven too?" Vicky shot back angrily.

"It was so long ago I don't remember and I'm sure he doesn't either. I saw him jogging the other day. He looks dazzled by love."

Vicky was not appeased. "You're like Mao's army, Vivian. Everywhere."

"Everywhere in China," Vivian corrected. "Chinese armies don't invade."

"Oh, yeah? What about Korea and Vietnam?"

"They are vassal states of the Chinese Middle Kingdom," Vivian replied, with a smile so enigmatic that Vicky could not tell whether she was joking. "And that reminds me, Victoria. If you are intent on buying so many Russian Antropov air freighters, may I be permitted to suggest that you purchase them through a Beijing government agency? The Chinese-Russian Friendship Trade Agency, perhaps. If you cut the PRC in on your deal, they may look more kindly on your landing rights."

"Excellent idea. Thank you. I ask you one last time: Work with me now for MacF. Help me make it. Do it for your baby. We've got a long life ahead of us. I don't want to be your enemy."

"And I ask you, again, to follow your father's course. He knew what was right."

Vicky glanced about the tea lounge and whispered, "Then why didn't he share the evidence against Chen and Two-Way with you? Why didn't he tell you where he hid it?"

"To protect me. He was a fool sometimes. A Victorian fool."

"Was your baby an accident?" Vicky asked bluntly.

"No. He wanted it after your brother Hugo died."

"And you just went ahead and gave him one."

"I was ambivalent," Vivian admitted. It was the first time she had said it aloud. She had, in truth, been terribly ambivalent, because getting pregnant threatened the independence she needed to pursue both her career and her dream of a better China. The time had seemed all wrong. She was still quite young and had so much to learn and 1997 loomed so close. But time, of course, was the enemy of any man Duncan's age, and she could not deny him.

"I'll bet his will cleared up the last of those doubts."

"His *death* 'cleared up' my doubts," Vivian shot back. "He is in my body, more than a memory." Tears filled her eyes and she looked down at the carpet.

"I'm sorry I said that," Vicky apologized. "I really am. That was a terrible thing to say."

Vivian looked up to see Vicky shaking her head with an expression less bitter than sad, as if suddenly she had had a revelation that she wished she had not.

"I don't think you understand my father as well as you think. You don't get it, do you? In protecting you, he was protecting his baby. Which is to say, MacF's future—in case I didn't come up with a satisfactory heir."

"You make him harder than he was."

That wasn't possible, Vicky thought, realizing at last that her battle with Vivian was a continuation of her war with her father. Dead in the South China Sea, he was still in command. Which meant that fighting with Vivian was a waste of a good China trader, when MacF needed all the talent Vicky could muster.

"Sit down," she said. "Please. I really am sorry I said that. I'd appreciate it if you'd move back into your office. There's no point waiting until you're 'guardian' of the new heiress's inheritance. I need you now."

Vivian settled into the chair and reached solemnly across the table to shake Vicky's hand on it.

"But forget my father's fight with Two-Way Wong. I don't want any part of it. Understand?"

"I understand you," said Vivian. "Perfectly."

The two women stared at each other for a long moment. Much had been left unsaid. Vicky felt some relief at the realization that Vivian Loh was somewhat of an innocent in assessing her father's actions. Vivian congratulated herself on finally regaining the clarity of purpose to accept her reinstatement at MacF, where she would have more opportunity to influence Vicky Mackintosh to take up Duncan's mission.

24

ARLY IN MAY the red junk furled its sails at the mouth of
Shanghai's Huangpu River. It was dawn, low tide, the spring
current swift, the mud flats broad. The marshes of the Yangtze
delta stretched gray and endless under a shroud of coal smoke, and
the air was thick with the noise of pounding engines and horns and
whistles signaling. A low motor sampan slipped from the double
procession of ships and barges and naval patrols and came alongside.

While their captains entered into a loud and acrimonious ne-
gotiation of the price for a tow upstream, sailors dressed in ragged
black cotton clambered between the two boats.

A bargain was struck, a towline bent.

The sampan's diesel — a clapped-out London bus engine — began
the thirty-mile voyage with a ragged, unmuffled bark, and Vivian
Loh, who had effected the transfer from sampan to junk dressed in
sailor's pajamas, wiped the grime from her glasses while she waited
to be admitted to the aft cabin.

She hated Shanghai. Forty years of corrupt PRC rule had reduced the city of her mother's dreams to a slum. She hated it because what had happened to Shanghai would happen to Hong Kong
if Premier Chen remained master of China. The Communist government in Beijing had systematically siphoned off Shanghai's profits for so long that outside a splashy international business core built

around a few modern hotels, it was impossible to find a building with a fresh coat of paint.

Passing through last night on the way to the sampan, she had been revolted by the stench, the crowding, the rutted streets, the burned-out lights, the aimless throngs of underemployed young. Whatever life remained in the city was a testament to the Shanghainese assumption that they were more clever, smarter, and wittier than the oppressors from the North. A memory that would stay with her always was of an exhausted pedi-truck coolie, pedaling a massive concrete beam through the streets of the Old Town with the English word JOGGING emblazoned on his sweat-stained T-shirt.

Pregnancy had begun to erode her courage. It grew harder each week to ignore fear, while physically the constant traveling was taking a toll of her strength. She suddenly missed her mother. Though when, she demanded angrily of the smoky sky, had her mother ever been a help? She promised, then and there on the junk, that she would never make her child wonder if she was ever coming home.

The smoke burned her eyes and stung her throat. She wiped her glasses again, praying that this time, after all the clandestine, often dangerous meetings, Tang was finally aboard.

They passed other towboats—pulling strings of sampan barges heaped with coal—and seagoing ships at anchor, surrounded by sampans like nursing pups. The flat, empty land began to sprout low factories with belching stacks. Ferry points appeared at the ends of roads swarming with people pushing bicycles. Three years from the twenty-first century she saw trucks and animal carts, but not a private car.

The baby stirred within her. Provoked to action, she did the unthinkable: raised her fist and knocked loudly. The door was opened immediately by a startled, pimply-faced secretary. "I was just coming for you, Comrade."

It was dark in the cabin and it took Vivian a moment for her eyes to adjust. Party Leader Tang Shande was here, seated with his inner circle around a rough wooden table lit by a hanging oil lamp and the gray glow of a high, small window. They were smoking cigarettes, and a covered tea mug sat before each.

Of the six men and a woman, she recognized three with whom she had negotiated in Shanghai for over a year: the woman; Tang's pimply secretary; and, of course, the rambunctious Ma Binyan. Zheng was not present. The others she knew by reputation; they came from Tang's most trusted cadres. One was the stern People's Liberation Army general who had met with Duncan and Hugo last year.

Tang Shande himself—a short, broad-faced, oft-smiling, and startlingly young man from Canton—was familiar from television and newspaper photos. In person he looked bigger and cruder. His hands were enormous and work-hardened, the left missing a finger lost in a fishnet winch when he was a boy. He was wearing his trademark sport jacket and open shirt, an image to show China that he bridged the formal world of the international businessman, the simple needs of workers, and the high-minded concerns of students. Two of his circle were genuine workers, a coal miner from Wuhan and a textile miller from Shanghai, while Ma Binyan was the ultimate student rebel, aging a little but still flashing the requisite fire in his eye and smirk on his lips.

She was neither invited to sit nor offered tea, for they knew by now that she didn't have Duncan's evidence, only excuses. Ma Binyan gave her a rude wink and an irreverent grin, which she acknowledged with a grave nod, but the others looked fed up.

Tang started off with the bluntness he was known for, reminding Vivian of Vicky Mackintosh. Ironically, the fisherman's son and the Taipan's daughter would get on rather well. "I'm told that after you boarded this morning you admitted you didn't bring any evidence. Why the hell did I risk a secret trip from Beijing?"

Vivian hesitated. She had one small advantage and didn't want to play it too soon.

Tang misinterpreted, perhaps deliberately. Though a Cantonese, he spoke Mandarin, as befitted a national leader.

"We're meeting on this old wooden junk because there are no telephones to tap or any other twentieth-century electronic conveniences that might give us away. You may speak freely."

Vivian was struck again that Vicky would handle Tang better

than she. The first thing she had to do was slow him down. He was very "un-Chinese," bulling ahead like an expat. She would be more Chinese.

"Forgive me, Comrade Party Leader. My hesitation to speak freely stems from personal embarrassment. I have failed to bring what I promised."

"The kickback evidence."

"Yes, Comrade Party Leader."

"*Comrade*'s fine," he snapped. "Or just Tang, if you want. Let's just move it along."

"Yes, Comrade."

"Is there any more evidence? Or did it all sink on the Taipan's yacht?"

"I believe there is more. But I cannot swear it."

Tang turned on his secretary. "By your father's hairless balls, what am I doing here?"

"I was misled, Comrade."

"She lied?" he asked, with a sly glance in Vivian's direction to see her reaction.

"Well, not exactly."

"I did not lie," Vivian interrupted.

"No, she didn't lie," Ma Binyan chimed in. "She admitted difficulties. It is possible that I and your comrade secretary put our faith in hope."

There was more to it than that, Vivian knew. Ma Binyan had committed fully to Duncan's plot to discredit Chen. Without the evidence, Ma had nothing. Tang, however, was almost certainly working other options. His face darkened.

"To govern with the aid of fools is lamentable. To conspire with fools is deadly. Will you be surprised to find agents of the Public Security Committee waiting when our junk docks at the Bund?"

"No, no, no, Comrade Party Leader," a frightened Ma protested. "It's not like that. It's just—"

The others ventured opinions all at once, and the din of recriminations grew louder until Tang, sitting like an ugly jade Buddha in the midst of flickering candles, finally sought Vivian's eye with an angry glare.

"I did bring one small thing," she said.

"Let's see it."

The others fell silent. She pulled from the folds of her sailor's clothes a plastic envelope. She walked to Tang's end of the table and placed it before him. "The Taipan left me this one packet."

Tang tore it open himself and riffled suspiciously through the several sheets. The paper was of a thick, coated sort used in old-fashioned copy machines found on the Mainland. He donned plastic-framed eyeglasses and read, line by line. "God and heaven," he breathed, when he had done. "Chen's brother-in-law? Look at this. Bank numbers. And here, steel for a shipyard diverted to Wong Li's Canton hotel. Is the other evidence like this?"

"Better, I would imagine."

"Sit down. Sit down," he said, jerking his thumb at his secretary, who leaped from his stool. Vivian sat next to Tang. "Where is it?"

"Only his daughter knows."

"Get it."

"I will try."

"I don't want you to *try*. I want you to *get* it. Understand, the next two months are crucial, because Chen must show restraint while the world is watching Hong Kong. Turnover is my last opportunity. My deadline. Chen knows this, of course. He has already started his campaign against me." He snapped his fingers. "Show her!"

The secretary pulled some large character posters from his case. The first accused Tang of passing state secrets to the Japanese. Others painted the Party chief as a counterrevolutionary, an official profiteer, and a Western decadent. Vivian was frightened. This was the PRC language that presaged a fall from power.

"Last week," Tang said quietly, "Chen warned me that he has the army behind him."

"Does he?"

"Some of it," Tang answered, with a glance at the silent general. Vivian shuddered. A divided army meant civil war.

Ma Binyan interrupted. "But you have the hearts of the people. That means Chen is finished."

Tang gave the student leader a condescending smile. "If he has the army, Chen has the power to parade those hearts through Tiananmen Square on sharpened sticks." He turned back to Vivian. "You see, I have a considerable 'stake' in finding a way to retire him."

"But how much do you need Hong Kong?" she asked bluntly, reminded that Hong Kong was a small part of Tang's problems.

"Very much."

"Then you must do *very much* to save her."

"And you must get me that evidence. Because if I'm stripped of my Party role before I can expose Chen, I'm through and Hong Kong is fucked. Can I make it any clearer?"

"No." ·

"What is this woman's hesitation?"

"She thinks it's too dangerous."

"Remind her we live in dangerous times."

"She believes that her hong will prosper if she avoids taking sides in China."

Tang shook his head in disgust. "The whole point of dangerous times is that one *must* choose sides."

"She *is* a foreigner."

"I understand you've inherited a part of her hong?"

It had taken all of three hours for fantastical rumors about Duncan's will to cross Hong Kong. The subsequent two months had been more than enough time for the gossip to reach Beijing.

"I'm not empowered until the Taipan's baby is born."

Tang eyed her speculatively and for a frightening second she thought he was calculating the possibilities of inducing an early birth. "Why don't you convince her that she ought to turn the evidence against Two-Way Wong Li over to me before Two-Way Wong Li *takes* it by force?"

"I've raised the possibility and I know it worries her. She takes

comfort in the fact that no one knows whether she even has the
evidence. At the same time, she's made a point of rehiring old George
Ng, the former MacF comprador—with the clear implication that
she could have given him copies which he would reveal in the event
something happened to her. She's no fool."

"Two-Way Wong might surprise her. Why didn't the old Taipan take precautions?"

"It wasn't his way."

"A fool?"

"In some ways," Vivian agreed reluctantly, explaining: "He was
not a natural conspirator."

"Ng is the MacF comprador you unseated?"

"Yes, Comrade."

"Why not get Chief Executive Wei to do a little persuading?
Surely Allen Wei understands the advantage of destroying Chen."

Vivian answered carefully. "The Taipan did not confide his plan
in Allen Wei. Perhaps he's too . . . scrupulous."

Tang sneered. "I've always suspected Allen Wei lacked belly."

As they continued their discussion, while the others listened
nervously, Vivian began to see Tang in a disturbing new light. How
long would it be, she worried, before his earthy, brusque manner
hardened into arrogance?

When, for the third time, she protested, "The business community trusts Allen Wei to lead them," the Party chief exploded.

"Hong Kong needs a *tiger* to grapple with Beijing—a *tiger*, no
matter which faction wins—someone who knows what the world's
about. Who else can convince this gweipo to help? What's this I
hear about a lover?"

"Steven Wong. Wong Li's son."

"Two-Way's wastrel? I heard that, but I didn't believe it. Is this
coincidence or did Two-Way set him on her?"

"It's not coincidence. *I* set him on her before the Taipan was
killed."

"To occupy your rival?" Tang asked with another sly smile.

"In essence, yes," Vivian admitted.

"My admiration grows. I thought at first you were an idealist.

I'm beginning to suspect you have the makings of a Shanghai Woman."

Vivian laughed with embarrassment. In all China there was no higher compliment for a strong woman.

"I would rather be known as a Hong Kong Woman."

"What is a Hong Kong Woman?"

"Clear-eyed."

"Surely you're not that dangerous," Tang laughed. But his smile was remote. "I suspect you will find a way to persuade the Taipan's daughter to help us."

Vivian was not so sure. "Even if I can," she cautioned, "Victoria Mackintosh will make the same stipulations as her father. She'll demand to turn it over to you in person."

Reverently, Tang held the copies Vivian had given him to the light. "If she has more like this, I will agree to meet her in whatever sewer she chooses. After all, I came to this pesthole to meet you, Hong Kong Woman."

His compliment gave her courage to voice the concerns his harsh manner had provoked. "May I ask how your New China will be different from the old China?"

Tang chuckled. "You wouldn't believe me if I promised."

"Forgive me, but I fear—"

"Let me tell you how 'my' New China will be different. There will be no corruption. *Guanshang* will be nipped in the bud—a few shootings at the top should turn the trick. Will it be democratic? More than now. Will I take advantage of my new power to accumulate more power? If I didn't I'd be the first leader in the history of China not to. Will I use my new power wisely? Wiser than most would. Will China be a better place when I am gone? I hope so. Will idealists like yourself become my enemy? I hope not. . . . Now what would you say if I were to tell you that there are indications that Wong Li had a hand in Hong Kong's New Year riots?"

"Nothing could surprise me about Two-Way Wong. But to what purpose would he foment riots?"

"To give the hard-liners an excuse to deny the rights the Joint Declaration called for and to crush opposition."

"That makes no sense. The international community would abandon the city."

"Perhaps Two-Way has some other motive."

"Perhaps your indications are wrong."

"We'll know soon enough. Changeover's less than two months. Time soon for Wong Li to make his move."

Vivian said nothing. Party Leader Tang had just made his own move, and she did not know whom to trust. But she had an awful feeling that Victoria Mackintosh might be right, that MacF, and by extension Hong Kong herself, should not choose sides in another Chinese civil war. In which case Duncan had been wrong, leaving her, like Hong Kong, drifting on a sea of doubt.

25

"WE FIT SO WELL," Steven marveled.

For three months they had met regularly at the Regent. This afternoon had flown as fast as the first. It was dark now, and they were reflected softly in the sheet-glass wall. A pale image of their bodies seemed to float against the lights across the harbor like a flimsy cloud in a starry sky.

Vicky was curled on top of him, one languid leg bent, the other entwining lazily with his. Her cheek lay on his smooth chest. She listened to his heartbeat return slowly to normal.

She kissed his chest, lifted her lips to his mouth. His fingers traced a light path down her back while with his other hand he gently lifted her hair off the nape of her neck. "It's either love," he whispered, "or cardiac arrest."

"I'll call the doctor. Guys like you don't fall in love."

This was a regular game they played when she needed reassurance. It wasn't that she doubted he loved her, but she did wonder how long it would last. Steven, for his part, professed endless love and boundless passion. Vicky had transformed him, he claimed. Sometimes she believed him, but often she was frightened because she had never put her heart so at risk.

"You're not in love. You're in eros."

"Eros too," he agreed, his hands moving. "But I fell in love New Year's. Gweilo New Year's."

"First sight? Go on."

"No," he answered seriously, his sleepy butterscotch voice and his hands making her shiver. "When you ran from the car."

"A lot of guys have a thing for blondes running in tight red dresses."

"Your face," he whispered. "I loved how committed you were. Nothing would stop you."

"My mother was in the middle of a riot."

"You were so fierce. So beautiful. Like a tiger. Then, one day I snuck into the hospital. You were sleeping."

"When?" Vicky propped up on an elbow to look in his face.

"Right after you got out of intensive care. You looked like a child but I could still see the determination."

Across the room, in a heap of clothing, her beeper went off. Vicky rolled off him.

"Hey."

"I told them nothing less than an earthquake or a Peking coup." She bounced from the bed, fished the beeper out of her blouse, and touched the message switch. The eight-line mini-screen lit up, black-and-white.

"Oh, God and heaven."

"Earthquake or coup?" Steven called from the bed.

"Worse," she breathed. "Alfred Ching's consortium missed their April payment on the Cathay Tower."

"I told you Alfred was in trouble. You wouldn't listen."

"He's defaulted. The deal's fallen through."

Steven laughed.

"*What* is so funny about that?"

"Well, a little while ago when I thought the world moved? It was just property prices crashing."

•   •   •

"And the stock market," Vicky shot back. "And the futures index. It's not funny, Steven." She ran to the telephone. "People are going to be wiped out. The entire Hong Kong economy could collapse."

"I know, I know. It's just . . . it's just so Hong Kong. One guy blows it and a million nickel-millionaires go belly-up. Hey, who you calling?"

"Alfred Ching." She punched his office and got a busy. Then she called his home number and let it ring ten times. Steven leaned out from the bed and licked the back of her leg. She reached down absently and stroked his hair. Alfred's answering machine finally cut in. "Ching here," came his clipped British accent. "Tell me who you are and I'll get back to you."

"Alfred, it's Vicky. Are you there? Pick up, Alfred." She thought she heard a click as if he were monitoring the call. "Alfred, dammit, are you there? Is this rumor true?" She listened until the end-of-tape signal and banged down the telephone. "Dammit."

"Hey, what are you doing?"

Vicky was turning a sleeve of her blouse right-side out, while she searched for her panties. "Every property my family owns is mortgaged to the new market limit. The banks are going to call in loans."

"So pay 'em back."

"It doesn't work that way." She had already committed the money she had borrowed to buy the Russian air freighters. Besides, where would MacF Golden Air Freight be without the planes?

"Why not?" Steven asked.

But she never discussed details of MacF business with him, and answered only: "Steven, you don't understand. The entire property boom is based on the inflated price Alfred paid for Cathay Tower."

"What I don't understand is why you business types think you're different from mah-jongg players and horse bettors."

"From the mouths of babes." She found her panties under the bed and stepped into them, kissed Steven's mouth, and dodged his hands. "Bye, babe."

"Where you going?"

Her mind was galloping in circles. She was as guilty as anyone in the Colony of exploiting the property boom. Would the banks restrain themselves? But how could they, when they were badly overextended into property loans? How many of them could survive a run if a crash rampaged through the rest of the economy? Would the PRC influence the markets to close? Closing the markets in the crash of '87 had been disastrous.

"Where you going?"

"To deal with this."

"It's night. You can't change anything tonight. Tell you what— come back to bed. Take those clothes off. We'll make love, order up a great meal, get a good night's sleep. Rarin' to go in the morning."

She tucked in her blouse, went back to the bed, and kissed him again. "Can't. Gotta get to the office."

"To do what?"

"Get on the telephone and be reassuring. . . . Will you stay here tonight?"

"Want me to?"

"You know I do. More than anything. But I just can't promise when I'll be back. Please understand."

Steven found his watch on the night table, sighed, and ran his fingers through his silky hair. "I guess maybe I ought to run out to the ships—gonna be a hot night at the tables when this news gets around."

"It's around already. Count on it. All over the city."

"I'll try to get back after midnight."

"Don't leave your work just for me, but—"

Steven stopped her with his laziest smile. "Well, who do you think I would come back for?"

"I didn't mean—" She hugged him fiercely. "Steven, I have to go. My mind's a million miles from here."

"Every time you gotta go I think there ought to be a way to send your mind to work and keep your body here."

·   ·   ·

She was right about the bad news getting around. The elevator was packed with grim-faced Japanese.

Pandemonium reigned in the lobby: Half the people shouting at the desk clerks were trying to check out early; half were demanding to get into the hotel without reservations. Lines snaked out of the wire and fax rooms, and the telephones were surrounded like bars at the race track. Doormen and taxi drivers looked stricken; as in every Hong Kong boom, working people had withdrawn their life savings to speculate.

The tunnel to Causeway Bay was a mess as the news spread and tens of thousands abandoned dinner to rush back to the jobs they had gone home from a few hours earlier. It was nearly 9:30 by the time she got to MacF House, where many of her key managers, traders, and analysts were already on the telephone. She gave them brief instructions they hardly needed. It was the middle of the day in Europe, and the American markets were about to open. Then she got on the phone, too, calling everyone she knew. The gist of the early overseas reaction boiled down to three questions: Now what had gone wrong in Hong Kong? What would happen next? And what would China do?

MacF's answers were: Nothing had gone wrong. Only one deal had fallen through, and after some initial panic selling, those who hung tough would fare all right. Nor would the PRC allow a financial collapse this close to Turnover.

"How are they going to stop it?" asked the hard-nosed president of the New Woman's Bank of New York, with whom Vicky had gone to NYU.

"China will bolster the market by buying through fronts," Vicky assured her, knowing in her heart it was at best a hopeful guess.

"Maybe China will lend money to overextended borrowers," the banker said sarcastically.

"*That* is not a bad idea. Thank you. Also, you can count on the big money to start buying bargains."

Indeed, by eleven o'clock that night, with the business day supposedly still nine hours off, low-ball bids on choice properties began drifting into MacF House. Exploratory calls revealed similar offers being received by other Hong Kong companies. Meanwhile, known PRC fronts were bidding up the initial offers.

At eleven-thirty, Allen Wei issued a statement from Government House that the Hong Kong economy was sound and had survived many an up and down in the past. These swings, he asserted, were typical of a free and open society.

Wally Hearst wandered into Vicky's office, tugging his beard bemusedly. "Here's the latest," said the American China trader. "Guy I know turns down an insulting offer on his hotel in Repulse Bay. Ten minutes later, a PRC company doubles it, making it half as insulting."

"They're trying to cushion. Good."

"The first offer was PRC, too," said Wally.

"Competing bureaucracies?"

"The greedy bastards are bidding against each other."

"They're certainly moving quicker than usual. Almost as if they were ready," Vicky said.

"Maybe they were."

"Where's Vivian Loh?"

"God knows," Hearst replied, definitely uninterested in the whereabouts of his rival China trader. "You want me to try to rustle up some Peking buyers for anything?"

"No. Rustle me up a Peking bank loan for my airplanes."

"In this climate?"

"Tell them it's their chance to stabilize the situation. Tell them a strong MacF means a strong Hong Kong."

"You want to listen in on the giggling?"

"Do it now."

"All right. Sorry, Taipan."

"And Wally, if any of your Mainland friends need a front to spend PRC money on Hong Kong real estate, we're their man."

"You're kidding."

"Somebody's going to make a fortune out of this."

"Two-Way Wong, that's who."

"Why do you say that?"

"With his kind of money, he can just snap up the best as it falls."

Vicky turned to the window. The surrounding buildings were also burning lights late. "Right. Thanks, Wally. Make those calls. We'll talk later."

"Did I say something?"

"No one I've talked with tonight has mentioned World Oceans' buying a thing. It's as if they're out of town. You'd think with all their cash they'd be low-balling every property in the Colony."

"Maybe Two-Way's waiting for it to fall further."

"Maybe. Talk to you later." She got up, opened her side door, and walked into her former office, which Peter now occupied. He was on the phone speaking robust Cantonese. His shirt sleeves were rolled up his thin arms. He covered the mouthpiece. "What's up?"

"Do you know anyone at World Oceans?"

"Sure."

"Have any of them called you tonight?"

"No, now that you mention it."

"Wouldn't you think they'd have floated a few nasty offers, knowing the trouble we're in?"

"I didn't think about it, but now that you mention it, maybe they're holding back."

"I want you to stop what you're doing and chat up your Mainland friends. Anyone in any kind of a bank."

"What for?"

"I want MacF to be first in line to borrow money from the PRC."

She went back to her office, closed the door, and telephoned George Ng at home. She had, upon reflection, kept the old comprador on retainer; he was wise and he knew secrets. "I hope I didn't wake you, Uncle Ng."

"I've heard the news, Taipan," Ng said gravely. "An old friend jumped out a window."

Vicky was shocked. It was even worse than she had thought. "I'm sorry. Do you have any idea who Alfred Ching's backers were?"

"I heard his money came from New York."

"Americans?"

"Chinese-Americans."

"Who?"

"No one knows."

"American-born Chinese?"

"I doubt that. It's a front."

"PRC?"

"Oh, no. No, not PRC. Listen, Victoria, considerable cash has left Hong Kong the last ten years. Alfred seemed to have coaxed some back."

"Secret money?"

"Shall we say 'private'?"

"But not enough."

"Apparently," Ng agreed, "his well ran dry."

Vicky telephoned Alfred's office. The line was busy. She engaged an automatic dialer, and ten minutes later a harried-sounding secretary answered in Cantonese.

"Alfred Ching, please."

"He is not in office," she replied in English. "Maybe you call back tomorrow."

"This is Victoria Mackintosh. Mr. Ching will want to speak to me."

"Not here."

"Where?"

"Not sure. Maybe you call back tomorrow."

Vicky placed both hands on her father's desk and stared at the ship's clock that hung beside an oil painting of the Haig Line opium clipper it had come from. Past midnight.

She called the Regent Hotel. Steven was back. "Hey, the bed's empty."

"I need a little more time. What did you tell me you did those years in New York?"

"I don't even remember their names."

"Seriously. You worked, didn't you?"

"I told you, my old man set me up."

"Doing what?"

"He had me looking for investment opportunities."

"Did you run the office yourself?"

"Are you kidding? They start work early in New York. What's this about?"

"How did you know Alfred Ching was in trouble?"

"I heard it around," he said, as casually as he had claimed not to remember his girlfriends.

"In New York?"

"Jeez, Vicky, I don't remember. Is it important?"

"I'll explain later. Did the office make other investments, other than what you brought in?"

"I hope so," Steven laughed, "or they're broke by now. Vicky, I wasn't exactly a ball of fire, but they could count on me to play tennis with their clients and bring girls to parties."

"They?"

"My old man's friends."

"It wasn't his company?"

"Naw. He just got me the job. Listen, sweet, you coming soon?"

"I don't know. I'll try."

"Well, I gotta split early in the morning."

"Where are you going?"

"Old Man's sending me to Taiwan. I'm leaving about nine."

"Oh, no. When are you coming back?"

"When he tells me I'm coming back. Looks like weeks."

"No." She had fallen into a very happy routine of work and Steven. Even when they couldn't get together, they'd have long talks on the telephone, and she had begun to take for granted, she realized now, that he was always there when she wanted him. He would telephone her from the ship to say good night and good morning in the afternoon, and a day without at least one chat felt empty.

"Sorry. I'll miss you."

"Damn. That makes tonight even worse. Call me as soon as you know. . . . If I don't see you, sweet dreams."

"Sweet dreams on you."

Vicky cradled the telephone. She missed him already and almost

called him back to tell him that. There flashed before her eyes an
image of herself, ten years older, still running MacF between delirious afternoons at the Regent Hotel. She pushed it from her mind.
She'd be lucky to be running MacF ten days from now at the rate
prices were tumbling.

Steven's trip to Taiwan stretched to a week. He called every day,
sounding sad and lonely, usually at a moment when she was too
busy to talk. This evening was no exception.

"Oh, hon, I miss you. I'm going crazy," Vicky said.

"You broke yet?"

She was too tired to joke. "How are you doing?"

"Bored."

"When are you coming back?"

"When the Old Man says so. How'd you do in the riots?"

"The media made it seem worse than it was." There had been
small disturbances at Aberdeen, North Point, and on the Hennessy
Road in Causeway Bay where a British-owned department store had
burned. The police had prevailed, thanks to quick responses and the
fact that the stock market was holding its own, barely, after an initial
thirty-percent plunge. Small investors had been badly burned, but
not yet wiped out.

"Have you talked to your friend Ching yet?" Steven asked.

The property market was a grimmer story and getting worse.
"Not yet."

Peter ran into her office with bad news on his face.

"I'm sorry," Vicky said, "I really have to go."

"I love you."

"Back at you."

"Who was that?" asked Peter.

"Uncle Ng. What's wrong?"

"The Chartered Bank's getting really bolshy."

Later that night, while still at the office, she caught wind of a
rumor that Alfred Ching had been seen at the Yacht Club. She called
Chip at home. "Right. Popped in for a quick one and popped out."

"How did he look?"

"Like death warmed over."

"I've been trying to find him all week. Thanks, Chip."

"Find him soon. I'd not be surprised if he stepped off a building."

She tried Alfred's office, got a machine, tried his home and got his other machine. The Hong Kong Club and the Jockey Club hadn't seen him, or else they were covering, manfully. He liked drinking bitter at the Mandarin's Chinnery, but it had closed for the night.

Suddenly inspired, she started to telephone Ah Ping at the house, then changed her mind. This was no time to negotiate tense streets in an ancient Daimler that fairly shrieked British Empire. She called down to the lobby instead, ordered a taxi, and slipped quietly from the office.

"Do you know the Orchid Garden Restaurant?" she asked the driver.

"Kowloon side."

"Take me there, please."

"Take ferry. Tunnel stopped."

It would be faster on the subway. "MTR."

The driver turned around. He was a middle-aged, moon-faced Cantonese, with liver spots on his high brow. "Not safe for lady."

Vicky felt a chill. The city was on the brink. She could see it in his eyes. "All right. Take me to the ferry, then." She looked at her watch. A few minutes to the last boat. "Hurry."

Traffic was heavy, despite the hour, and they just made it. As she paid the driver, he said, "Kowloon street not safe."

"Old friend there," Vicky replied. "He might need me."

The driver shrugged. They had moved beyond his range of English, and if the gweipo still felt an urge to brave the far reaches of Kowloon, foreign devils did all sorts of strange things.

The boat to Kowloon was half empty, the terminal across the harbor strangely deserted. Police guarded the gates. She saw four Land Rovers full of backup constables parked nearby. First off the ferry, she snared the only cab on line. "Orchid Garden Restaurant. Haiphong Lane."

She watched the streets ahead, vowing to turn back if it looked dangerous. People were crowding around bars and clubs, and the usual gangs of tourists were wandering around the all-night shops. But Alfred's parents' restaurant was well above the brilliantly lit tourist section. The neon vines had been switched off.

"You get out here," said the taxi driver.

"Wait."

She knocked on the plate-glass door. No one came. The foyer was dark, but some light spilled down the stairs. Steven had given her a heavy gold ring of entwining dragons, which were lovely match mates for her dragon pendant. She clicked it sharply on the glass until eventually a shadow shuffled down the steps, shouting Cantonese.

"He say closed," called the driver.

Vicky banged harder.

"He say he call cops."

"Would you please get out of that car and come up here and tell him I'm an old friend?"

The driver glanced up and down the deserted street, climbed out of the cab, and loosed a torrent of Cantonese at the door, which eventually opened a crack. "He want know name of old friend."

"Alfred Ching."

"Alfred Ching?"

"Ching Chu-ming."

"He say wait." The man closed the door and went back upstairs. The driver asked, "Is that the Alfred Ching who blew the Cathay Tower deal?"

"Different one."

"Good. That guy oughta be shot."

Through the glass door Vicky saw Alfred's father come down. He poked his head out with a quizzical expression, saw Vicky, and nodded recognition.

"May I come in?"

The old cook nodded again. Vicky paid her driver and followed Alfred's father upstairs. He led her through the darkened dining room, past chairs upended on tables, and through a bead curtain into the kitchen. Alfred sat at a scarred worktable, his jacket off, his tie loosened, and his head in his hands. He was staring at the table, wringing his fingers and twisting his rings, and did not raise his face when Vicky entered.

"Come to see the fuck-up?"

"What happened? Where have you been?"

"If you didn't know by now you wouldn't be here."

"I want to know exactly what happened."

"I appreciate your coming, Vicky. But I am in no mood for sympathy."

"This is not a sympathy call, Alfred."

Alfred looked up at last. Vicky almost gasped at the fear in his eyes. His mouth set in a grim, bitter line. "Nor, from what I hear about your new boyfriend, have you come seeking love."

"Alfred, this isn't my fault. And my personal life does not concern you."

A slow glance from Alfred suggested he thought otherwise. "What do you want?" he asked, dropping his head and fiddling with his rings again.

"Information, Alfred. Dammit, what happened?"

"I got screwed is what happened."

"Somebody reneged?"

"Somebody set me up."

Vicky sat down across the table. "I thought so."

Alfred looked up. "You did?" Closer, she saw that his eyes were red and she realized with a shock that he had been crying. She reached for him and took his hands. They were cold. He couldn't look her in the face. "Who set you up?"

"I am so fucking naïve. I can't believe I let this happen to me."

"Even optimists are wrong sometimes, Alfred."

"I'm a jerk and the whole Colony knows it."

"Alfred, stop it."

"Stop what? Everyone in Hong Kong knows I screwed up."

"My father used to say if you don't take risks now and then, you're just cruising."

"I didn't take a risk!" he shouted with sudden vehemence. "I just put together a normal deal. There was no risk."

"So what went wrong?"

"I told you. I was so stupid I didn't realize what they were doing to me."

"Who?"

"My loyal backers," Alfred said bitterly. His eyes glazed over, and his voice sank to a mumble. "The trusting little Chinese boy from Kowloon. Vicky, I always did everything right. I got the best marks in school. I speak the best English. I play straight. I work hard. I followed the rules, Vicky. I followed every rule." A wan smile crossed his face. "Well, every rule but one."

"Which one?" she prompted.

"Fell in love with a gweipo from the Peak."

"Go on, Alfred, that's years ago."

"Turned off people, Chinese people. Closed some doors. I figure, fuck 'em. The great thing about Hong Kong is there's so many doors. They can't all shut in your face. But . . . they're shut now."

"What does that have to do with missing your payment?"

"I'm trying to figure out how I could be so naïve. I never saw it coming."

"What?"

"Do you remember when we met?"

"Of course."

"You liked me, right away."

"Yes, Alfred. We were simpatico."

"We were explorers. You were like a diver, checking out the depths. I was like an astronaut."

"It was just a tea dance at the Jockey Club."

Alfred didn't grin back. "You know what I mean."

"So what does it have to do with now?" Vicky asked gently.

But Alfred was drifting. "We were so young."

Trying again to make him laugh, she said, "I'm not sure I can deal with a sentimental Alfred, and I know I can't bear a maudlin one. It's not your way."

"And it certainly isn't yours."

"What is that supposed to mean?"

"You didn't come here to help me. You came for something."

"I told you straight out I didn't bring sympathy. I didn't think you wanted it." She wondered if there was something wrong with her, some missing link of feeling. For in actual fact it had never occurred to her that Alfred Ching would need sympathy.

"You're pumping me for some reason. What is it?"

"I want to know who set you up. You're not naïve. How could you screw up so badly?"

"I never saw it coming. They got the right dummy, didn't they?"

"Who?"

Alfred shrugged, beyond caring. Helpless to stop him, Vicky watched her old friend slip deeper and deeper into himself, his handsome face turning blank, his gaze fading inward, his mind escaping.

"Alfred?"

"What do you care?" he mumbled.

"If you're right, then whoever used you, set up the entire Colony for a fall."

She held his hands, which he didn't appear to notice. She sat with him, worrying about him, and worrying what would happen in the morning, fearing there was nothing she could do to stop the worst.

The hours crept by. Now and then he stirred, mumbled an incoherent sentence or two, and went silent again. He slept, his head on her hands, woke with a start, and stared some more.

Vicky fell asleep sitting up.

When it was still dark, she heard noise downstairs. Some cooks climbed the stairs and came into the kitchen, chattering sleepily, brewing tea and gathering around the other end of the long worktable as if she and Alfred didn't exist. Alfred's mother came in next and cast an anxious glance at her silent son, and an unreadable look at Vicky. She began shaping hundreds of thin dumpling skins, which the group stuffed with fillings from a dozen pots. Dim sum, Vicky realized blearily, still holding Alfred's hands and thinking she would die soon if she didn't lie down in a real bed.

"Alfred?" She yawned, freeing her hands.

"Yes?" He blinked.

He looked at her, oblivious to the others, who were talking quietly in Cantonese as they worked. "Hey, you're wearing my dragon."

"Always," said Vicky, touching the pendant he had given her out of his first big bonus. "I love it. . . . Feel better?"

"It just never made sense," Alfred replied, picking up last night's conversation where it had ended. "Even when I wondered why they were willing to pay so much for the tower, it never occurred to me they would deliberately throw the money away. I figured they had to have some other reason. I even figured maybe they were laundering money and so they didn't care how much the building cost. I figured: Okay, I can deal with *hei shi hui* money—gangster money—this one time, my foot in the door. The bulk of the money was going to be up to me to raise. So it would be mostly straight money, clean money, even if they were laundering. I could live with a little dirty money."

"Did you ever wonder why they picked you?"

"I figured I deserved it. . . . I got what I deserved. . . . What I still can't figure out is why they would deliberately throw money away unless they intended to cause a crash. Who would do that?"

"You tell me."

" 'Cause that's what he's done."

"Who?" For the first time, Alfred had referred to the backers as "he" instead of "they."

"It's only a guess. I don't know for sure."

"Who?"

"This is just between us. I could get sued for slander." He laughed. "Not that they would win much, that's for sure. I'm busted, broke. Wiped out."

"I won't quote you. Who?"

"Couldn't prove it in a million years."

"Who?"

"Forget it." He closed his eyes and let his head sink back on his chest.

"Two-Way Wong."

Alfred's eyes popped open. "How do you figure that?"

"I used to suspect that the PRC had to be your mystery backer. It was certainly to China's advantage to thrill the markets and make the business community rich and happy in Hong Kong. But obviously I was wrong. The PRC would not deliberately destabilize the Colony."

"Right. Unless they want to buy it up real cheap."

"It's not worth bankruptcy. The last thing China needs is six million broke mouths to feed. So if your backer wasn't the PRC, it had to be someone with pretty heavy funds. Two-Way fits that description."

"So do a dozen other guys in Central."

"Most of them have made low-ball offers to pick up my disasters cheap. Not World Oceans."

"Maybe he knows the crash is going to keep crashing."

"Also, the word is, your money originated in New York. Am I right?"

"Essentially. That's where the checks come from. Came from."

"So what were you doing in Canada?"

"I was trying to get new investors. I kind of sensed this coming."

"So you weren't totally naïve."

"Not totally."

"That's good. I hate to think of you as totally dumb."

Alfred grinned wanly. His first smile since she had walked into the kitchen.

"New York," Vicky said, "is where Two-Way sent Steven Wong. Did you deal with Steven?"

Alfred grinned again. "No way I dealt with No-Way."

"But you saw him in New York?"

"Ran into him last autumn."

"And you guessed the connection with your generous backer."

He squirmed, and his grin vanished. "Vicky, maybe I did guess. But I didn't want to know. I leave guessing to the other guy."

"But you agree," Vicky insisted, "that Two-Way Wong is probably your secret backer on the Cathay Tower deal and deliberately set you up so the deal fell through and the property market collapsed? Don't you?"

"Possibly. Not probably. I'm only guessing from these little pieces."

"Good guess, Alfred."

"But what does he want? Why isn't he buying cheap? Isn't that the point of breaking a market?"

Vicky said nothing. She was gazing past Alfred at the black iron gas woks. From below flickered the blue flames of pilot lights.

"What does he want?" Alfred asked again.

"Chaos."

"Why?"

"I don't really know." But she stood up from the table and stretched with the pleasure of feeling slightly more on top of things. Dawn had broken and a watery gray light was seeping through a window on the alley. "What are you going to do, Alfred?"

"Emigrate, I guess. I'm through in this town."

"Get back on your horse and go kill something."

"Easy for you to say, Taipaness. I've got nothing. Nothing left. And with my new reputation, I doubt my own mother would give me a job chopping scallions."

"You still import rooster testicles, don't you?"

Alfred gave her a bleak look. "I don't want to go back."

"Well, that's okay, except for one thing, Alfred. You and I have a deal."

"What deal?"

"Expat-Emigrants, which you've done damn-all for. Now that you've got some time on your hands, let's get moving."

"Are you kidding? Nobody in his right mind would emigrate

back to Hong Kong, now. The city's gone to hell. You said it yourself. Chaos."

"Alfred, we made a deal. I really hope you're not going to sit in
your mother's kitchen and disappoint me."

Alfred Ching looked up from the table.

"Me? Disappoint you? That's a laugh."

"Sarcasm does not suit you, Alfred, and I'm not laughing. You
say you're broke? I'll make up the difference. We'll call it Mackintosh-Ching."

Alfred stood up. "There isn't a Chinese in the world who'd re-
turn to Hong Kong on the recommendation of gweilos. Ching-
Mackintosh. And we'll instruct our receptionists to mumble the
Mackintosh."

"Alfred—" But her mind was long past helping Alfred back on
the horse. "All right. Is there a phone I could use?"

She called Wally Hearst. Wally's wife, Ling-Ling, answered in
a sleepy, little-girl voice. Vicky asked for Wally. He came on, quick
and clear-headed. "Yeah, boss."

"Find Vivian Loh."

"Where should I start?"

"Shanghai."

"What should I tell her?" Wally asked.

"She'll know what I want."

Back in the kitchen, she said goodbye.

"You're looking determined," said Alfred, who was looking determined himself. "Thanks for the help." He took her hand, kissed
it, entwining fingers. "Where are you going?"

Vicky patted his cheek and headed out the door. "First I'm going
to get an hour's sleep and a shower. Then I'll spend several days
begging from truly horrible bankers—thanks to your screw-up—and
the nights thinking over what you've told me. Then, if it all keeps
unfolding like it has been, I'm going to visit my mother."

"Your mother? What for?"

"To collect my inheritance."

26

*B*LINDFOLDED, A SLIGHT figure with a cocky swagger was hustled out of a windowless van. Broad-shouldered laborers shielded him from view as he was led through a parking garage and bundled into a freight elevator. A muscle-guy held his elbow and assured him politely, "Almost there."

The Fax Cracker—as Shaw Sin was known to the Royal Hong Kong Police—was a warped electronics genius whose young life had taken a surprising turn for the better when he was arrested for gypping Hong Kong Cable and Wireless out of facsimile machine telephone charges. He had invented a method to send faxes free, and had been caught the previous month peddling the service to small businesses. But instead of being hauled off to court, a speedy trial, and a long term pounding rocks at Stanley Prison, Shaw Sin had found himself released into the custody of a Chinese lawyer in an iridescent suit who had taken him up to Mong Kok. There a low-ranking Chiu Chau Triad officer had warned him that if he was ever caught again, he would have his hands chopped off.

Shaw Sin was not easily awed. He knew he was a genius and he also knew that Triads did not punish people for defrauding Hong Kong Cable and Wireless, which meant that the Chiu Chau wanted something, as the sons of that exceptionally larcenous province usually did.

"Then how in hell," he had asked, "am I supposed to make a living?"

The Triad officer had handed him $30,000 in a slim briefcase and told him to go enjoy himself.

"What's it for?"

"Consider it a retainer. Just don't leave the Colony before July first."

Shaw Sin had nowhere to go before or after July 1. He had used a portion of his new wealth to buy a stolen miniature computer, which he secreted under his clothing and took to Happy Valley Racecourse. There he had experimented with a horse-betting system he had invented to crack the Six-Up. He was down to his last five hundred when the Triad picked him up again and told Shaw Sin what they wanted. They wanted to be able to broadcast to every facsimile machine in every office, store, and restaurant in Hong Kong, simultaneously.

Interesting problem, Shaw Sin had thought. Various electronic guards and locks and shunts had been devised to shield fax machines from unwanted messages. The Hong Kong and Shanghai Bank, for instance, did not desire unsolicited advertisements from Henry Wong's Lotus Garden Restaurant spilling out of facsimile machines reserved for international wire transfer confirmations.

The Triad had been adamant: *every* fax machine in Hong Kong. Shaw Sin had run a basic scheme through the computer in an evening, then had done a random test. Some of the police faxes were tough to crack, and the international corporations' machines were locked like missionary legs. Back to the drawing board. He had ended up spending the entire week of the Ching-Cathay Tower crash staring at a computer screen, but at last it was done, and after another long week of tests he delivered a neat snatch of coded software on a disk.

"You sure it work?"

"It work." He was back in Mong Kok in the guy's grimy office. The Triad was fondling the disk as if it came from Mars.

"You sure?"

"I bet my life on it," said Shaw Sin, just to hear the corny answer he knew he'd get back.

"You just did."

"Right."

"Okay. There's someone you gotta meet and tell him what you done."

"Am I getting paid more for this, or was it just the thirty thou?" Never hurt to ask.

"This guy'll pay you."

"Who is he?"

In answer, the Triad took out a silk scarf and tied it around Shaw Sin's eyes. "I don't know. And the guy I hand you to don't know, and the guy he hand you to, who don't know me, he don't know either."

He was led outdoors, through alleys, in and out of vans, up some stairs, down some stairs, more vans, and finally up a freight elevator. At least it smelled like a freight elevator. It would have been scary except that they wanted something from him. He had fun estimating how high up the criminal chain they were taking him by the smell of their cologne, starting with something that smelled like sweat, then Old Spice, then counterfeit Chanel, then Aramis, and finally something kind of South-Sea exotic and expensive-smelling. Then the freight elevator. Then cool air and thick carpets and the most expensive sound in all of Hong Kong—sheer and utter silence.

Gradually, as he stood, still blindfolded, on an amazing-feeling rug, he realized he was hearing a single clock tick somewhere in the distance, across an enormous room. "Excuse me," said a cultured voice speaking Cantonese with a Shanghai accent, and the scarf was removed gently from his eyes.

Shaw Sin blinked and swallowed hard. He was in the top floor office of World Oceans House; the view alone told him that. There were no buildings out there. Just sky. And the man sitting behind the gigantic teak log he used for a desk was none other than Two-Way Wong.

Shaw Sin's smirk faded, to be replaced by a look he hoped was respectful, but which his host recognized as calculating.

"Good afternoon," said Two-Way Wong.

"Good afternoon . . ." What should he call him? Sir John? Wong Li? Damned sure not Two-Way. "Good afternoon, Lao Yeh." *Lao Yeh* could mean grandfather or master. Let Two-Way choose. What a chance! He wanted to pound his fists on his chest. The biggest of the big time. The Main Chance!

"Sit down, young fellow."

Shaw Sin scrambled to the chair offered. He was quickly recovering his equilibrium and felt almost at home when Two-Way asked, "Shall we have tea?"

"Don't mind if I do. Yes, Lao Yeh. Thank you. Tea would be fine." Shut up, he told himself. Stop running like a sewer. And whatever you do, no stupid questions. He was burning to know what Two-Way Wong wanted with a citywide fax broadcast.

Two-Way stabbed a button in the teak. Servants glided in with green tea in covered porcelain cups. "I am told that you performed superbly."

Hey, I'm the best, thought Shaw Sin. The best. I belong here. He said, "I did what was asked. Sure hope it works."

Something cold and dark as the space between the stars grew large in Two-Way's eyes. "I am told you guaranteed it would work."

"Guaranteed," Shaw Sin agreed quickly. The old guy was a little slow on the uptake. But it would probably not be a great idea to explain that he was joking. "It will work, Lao Yeh. Have no fear."

"Explain how it works, please."

"It's a little complicated, Lao Yeh."

"I prefer personal explanations from men who do important work for me. Explain it, please."

Shaw Sin explained. Whether Two-Way Wong understood, he would never know. But Wong's eyes never left the young man's face, and Shaw Sin was damned glad he was not faking it. At last, the Taipan seemed satisfied.

"There are rewards and there are rewards," Two-Way intoned

magisterially. "You deserve money, of course"—his eyes flickered toward a briefcase a lot thicker than the last one—"and it is yours. But money alone cannot fully repay special efforts. Therefore, may I offer you something money can't buy?"

"You've been too kind already," Shaw Sin demurred. Laying it on with a trowel, he thought. Careful you don't overdo it. The main thing is to be invited back.

"Not at all. I've barely managed to keep even with your efforts."

Two-Way stabbed another button in the teak log. Eighty feet away, another door opened and an extremely good-looking girl came in, smiling. She had a roundness that Shaw Sin associated with Fukienese women. In his experience, you could keep your Shanghai and Suzhou beautifuls. Great to look at, to be sure, but for sheer eagerness in the sack, give him a Fukienese any night. They smoldered. Also, they were nuts about numerology, which gave a guy in the numbers business yet another way to turn them on.

"I know what you're thinking," said Two-Way. "With the money you've earned you can buy anything. But I promise you there are certain women with certain skills money cannot buy, unless you know where to look for them. I recommend a massage. She's been trained by masters."

Shaw Sin sat up straight as the girl drew near. She was something special, even for a Fukienese. She had blue eyes. And she looked a little crazy, in a promising way.

27

AH CHI WAS squatting on the sampan dock, staring at the water, his sunbrowned face blank, his muscular shoulders hunched unhappily. He reminded Vicky of Alfred Ching folding into himself at the kitchen table last week. His girlfriend with the pretty smile watched anxiously from her boat, which lay alongside.

"Good morning, Hua. Good morning, Ah Chi. Could you run me out to the boat, please?"

The boatboy returned a morose stare.

"What's the matter, Ah Chi?"

"Tai-Tai go England."

"*What?* When?"

"Now."

Vicky was hurt, and a little mystified. There'd been no talk about visiting the U.K., and it was strange that her mother would leave on such a long trip without a goodbye. "Did Tai-Tai say when she come back?"

"Not come back."

"Oh, my God," she whispered, wondering sadly what had finally stirred her to leave Hong Kong. An awful picture formed in her mind of her mother stepping off the plane drunk and utterly alone in Heathrow Airport. She had to fly to England herself to see what shape she was in.

"Would you run me out to *Whirlwind*, please. There's something I've got to pick up."

"Tai-Tai go to England."

"I know, but I need something from *Whirlwind.*"

Ah Chi stared, mute. Vicky looked at Hua. Hua murmured, "*Whirrwin'* go Englan'!"

"I beg your pardon?"

"Tai-Tai sail England."

"My mother is *sailing* to England?"

Ah Chi nodded. Vicky, feeling a sudden need to sit down, knelt between them. "Was she drunk?"

Eventually she elicited from Ah Chi and Hua what her mother had done. It was not exactly spur-of-the-moment. She had provisioned the boat over the past several weeks, had directed Ah Chi to make some repairs, and had, this morning, ordered him to motor her out of the typhoon shelter. Then she put him off on his girlfriend's sampan and simply sailed east.

"*East?*"

"No pirates, east," Ah Chi explained.

Vicky shook her head, stunned. Ah Chi knew every inch of the South China Sea, from Sumatra to Taiwan, but had a somewhat murkier concept of the rest of the world. While it might make sense to avoid pirates on the Strait of Malacca—Indian Ocean—Suez Canal route, sailing east to England necessitated crossing both the Pacific and Atlantic oceans—a six- or eight-month voyage well within the capacity of a boat like *Whirlwind* if it were crewed by several strong young sailors.

"Drunk?" she asked again, but again Ah Chi just shrugged, refusing to speak ill of Tai-Tai. He looked as if he had lost his best friend, and his girlfriend looked ready to cry.

"Don't worry. I'll get her back." She stood up, wondering how. "Is Chip working on his boat?" Chip had sailed in from Manila, and had mentioned when he told her about Alfred that he planned to devote the rest of his holiday to getting his new home in shape. "Run me out to him."

Hua snaked her little sampan through the tangled moorings. The shelter was jampacked, and virtually every vessel over twenty feet looked recently fitted for ocean passage. Ah Chi indicated a sleek diesel junk with enormous exhaust ports. "Huang's," he said, with mingled envy and pride.

They found Chip disassembling a winch on a sturdy little sloop. He was directing a spray of WD-40 into its guts and had the happiest smile Vicky had ever seen on his face. The sloop, while obviously neglected, was a pretty little thing. Fiona, she feared, had acquired a serious rival.

"*Tasmanian Devil*?" she called as Hua's sampan glided to its stern. "You've got to change that name."

"Got to change a lot," he called back. "The blokes who named her were of the floating gin palace persuasion, as you can see. Ruddy lucky to bring her back alive. Sails like a lady, though. Come aboard. Have a look 'round."

Vicky stood on the sampan, holding onto *Tasmanian Devil*'s backstay. "Chip, you're not going to believe this, but Mum just took off for England."

"Rather sudden."

"On *Whirlwind.*"

Chip put down the WD-40. "You're not serious."

"She can't have gotten far. I wonder, could you lay on a search helicopter? I've got to stop her."

"Ah Chi, run us in to the club. I'll phone a chap in the Marine Police, Victoria. Then we'll nip down to the Old Queens Pier."

Vicky telephoned the office to have her secretary cancel her meetings and to alert Peter. "Brace yourself, but Mum's sailing to England."

After a long silence, he said, "Good Christ, I knew she was up to something. Damn! She asked me to stop by last night, but I didn't have time. Oh, God, Vicky. I'll bet she wanted to tell me. I could have stopped her."

Vicky doubted that and told him not to blame himself.

"What are we going to do?"

"I'm already doing it. I'll get her back. Chip's got a helicopter."

"Oh, I wish I had gone to her."

"I'll see you later. Don't worry. It'll be fine."

She found Chip in the car park, standing in an empty parking space between a Mercedes and a Land Rover and scratching his head. "Somebody pinched my ruddy car."

"You're joking. Are you insured?"

"Of course not."

"Sorry, Chip. Come on, I've got mine."

"Who would steal a copper's car? There's a sticker on it."

"Maybe a pirate needed an anchor. Come on, let's go."

"Very funny, Victoria. With the money I've saved on fancy motorcars, I bought my boat."

He reported the theft by radio after the helicopter took off. Vicky, swallowing hard as the land dropped away, heard the muffled laughter in the earphones the pilot had given her. "They nicked *that* car. Right, Chip-Chip. We'll keep an eye peeled for a mob of blind car thieves."

Vicky and Chip conferred with the Chinese pilot and drew a circle on the chart centering on the typhoon shelter. "Six knots, tops," they agreed. "Six hours since dawn. Thirty-six miles." With no idea whether she was hugging the coast or heading far south to avoid the shipping lanes, a thirty-six-mile half-circle amounted to an enormous stretch of ocean.

They searched for hours.

The pilot insisted on buzzing everything with two masts, even when Vicky or Chip knew it was not *Whirlwind*. The late spring haze glared white on the water. Sometimes it thickened into fog banks, which were penetrable only by radar. The shipping channels were remarkably busy as incoming freighters lined up on the Eastern Approaches, and outgoing steamed away. Fishing boats plied the water, but even near the coast, the sea was astonishingly broad and empty.

Vicky strained for sight of her mother, brooding how she had already lost Hugo and her father in these waters, the South China Sea, their playground and their workshop. Her eyes were burning, and every wavetop looked like a yacht driving east.

While they swept the water for *Whirlwind*'s distinctively ragged spread of schooner staysails, the pilot scanned the radio channels, querying whether any boats had seen the yacht. The radio was as barren as the sea.

"Not much more fuel," Chip warned.

"Twenty minutes," said the pilot.

Ten minutes raced past. Vicky grew frantic. It hadn't occurred to her they wouldn't find *Whirlwind*. Now the possibility had grown strong that not only would her mother sail to an almost certain death alone at sea, but she would take with her the evidence against Two-Way Wong. Two-Way would be free to sow chaos in the Hong Kong markets and prepare his own peculiar welcome to the Mainlanders on July 1, 1997. She didn't understand the shipowner's goal yet, but she was sure that using Alfred Ching to collapse the property market was only his opening gun.

Suddenly Vicky remembered that Ah Chi had never admitted her mother was drunk. What if by a miracle she was sober and sailing at the top of her form?

"Go farther out," she told the pilot, showing Chip the chart. They were flying the rim of the circle, extended now by two more hours to forty-eight miles. "Chip, if she was racing, where would she go? Where are the best currents and winds, right now?"

"There. We've got ten minutes." Chip sketched a narrow slot for the pilot. The helicopter forged into it.

The sea yawned ahead, still empty.

•   •   •

It was a sweltering afternoon even on the garden-draped Peak. The boys in Lady McGeddy's Dancing School had been particularly loathsome — wet-palmed, smelly beasts — which was the only subject upon which Millicent and Melissa Mackintosh agreed while they waited at the end of the McGeddy drive for their mother or Ah Ping or someone to take them home. Muggy haze had risen from the sea. A thick fog had descended from above. There was nothing to see. Mosquitoes had begun to bite, and their dancing frocks offered little protection to bare legs and arms.

"Cow," Millicent said moodily.

Little Melissa raised the eyebrow she was teaching herself to manipulate and said, with quiet authority, "Cows are dull and chunky, like you."

"*Where* is Mum?" They were the last children left and while neither said it aloud, they knew that yet another catastrophe had rocked the Mackintosh household. Grandmama had gone sailing without telling anyone, Auntie Vicky had gone tearing after her, Uncle Peter had fallen off the wagon, and Mum was in a state.

"Oh, there's Chip!" Millicent cried, miseries banished by the sight of his little Toyota laboring up the slope. "Mum sent Chip."

"Don't be daft," said Melissa in a perfect imitation of Auntie Vicky. "It's too hot to ride in that shambles."

"The windows are closed. He got the air conditioner working again."

The girls exchanged covetous glances.

"*I'm sitting in front!*"

"I'm sitting with Chip," said Millicent.

"It's cooler in front," said Melissa.

They ran full-tilt to Chip's car.

"Sorry," said the pilot. "Maybe we refuel and come out again." He banked to turn back. In that last second, Vicky saw the sails. "*Whirlwind,*" she cried, urging the pilot closer. "That's *Whirlwind.*"

The navy-blue hull carved a creamy track through the turquoise sea as it raced before the southeast monsoon.

"Dear God, she's streaking," said Chip.

"Hot boat?" asked the pilot.

"Hot skipper. Chip, you've got to get me down there."

"We're almost empty."

"Please. I've got to get her back."

Chip glanced at the pilot, who looked worried. "I drop you if she stream sampan at back. I not get near those masts."

He swooped down on the speeding schooner, circled it.

Vicky's heart jumped. Her mother was sprawled facedown on the stern deck, half-over the transom. "She's fallen!"

Chip had her in the binoculars. "She's all right. She's mucking about with the self-steering. Even wearing her harness." Sally looked up at the noise, shielding her eyes from the sun, and climbed back into the cockpit.

Vicky hung out the door, straining against her seat belt. When her mother saw her blond hair, she waved. Chip switched on the bullhorn.

"Sally, it's Chip." His voice echoed through the roar of the helicopter. "Stream your dinghy aft. Vicky wants a natter."

Sally bent a longer line onto the dinghy painter and let the little boat drift astern until the helicopter had room to descend over it.

"Pick you up in an hour?" asked Chip, as Vicky shrugged into a life vest.

"No, that's all right. I'll sail her back."

"Maybe we'll swing by just in case. That boat's not been to sea in a year."

He helped Vicky into a simple sling and swung her out the door and down twenty feet to the dinghy, which stopped bouncing as the helicopter downdraft flattened the chop. She touched her feet to the Fiberglas floor, swallowed her fear, and let go. The helicopter soared away, taking its noise with it, as she pulled the line hand over hand to catch up with *Whirlwind*. Her mother opened the lifelines and lowered a ladder.

"Welcome aboard."

She was high, Vicky thought. But not drunk.

"Where do you think you're going?"

"Home."

"Home? Home is back there."

"Scotland is home. Hong Kong was fun while it lasted. The party's over."

"For God's sake, Mother, you were born in Hong Kong."

"Schooled in Britain. Summered in Scotland." Sally trimmed a sheet and disengaged the self-steering, and the big schooner seemed to drive harder. "There's nothing here for me anymore."

"I'm here."

"You're young. You have a life. I'm old. . . . I think I'll have a beer. Would you care for one?"

"Why didn't you say goodbye?"

"Because you'd interfere."

"Mother, you can't sail to Scotland."

Sally Farquhar Mackintosh looked up from the ice chest she had lashed to the steering post. "The devil I can't. She's my boat. I'll sail her where I ruddy please."

"Mother, you haven't the strength. You can't drive this boat for eight months. You said it yourself: You're old."

"Chichester was older when he circumnavigated. I'm only going two-thirds 'round."

"But eight months, alone."

"I've plotted it rather more like six months. Prefer not to arrive at the North Atlantic in winter. Soon as I'm through the Bashi Channel, I'll shoot for Hawaii, lay over and rest up, then down to the Galapagos, through the Panama Canal—"

"Why not round Cape Horn while you're at it?"

Her mother gave her a severe look. "Sarcasm is neither a pleasant trait nor that amusing in a younger woman, Victoria."

"Mother, you will kill yourself. You'll brush the Atlantic hurricane season."

"I want you to go below and tell me what you see above the chart table. . . . Now, please."

Vicky went down the companionway to the chart table, which was tucked between the main salon and the aft passage. Wired clumsily, but securely, to a hook screwed in the teak above the table was the silver cup that Sally Farquhar Mackintosh had won in her last China Sea Race in 1962. Two years before Vicky was born. On the table were the charts and the courses her mother had drawn, Admiralty *Sailing Directions*, and a copy of Cornell's *World Cruising Routes*.

Shaking her head, Vicky punched up the Sat Nav, found it working, then discovered two sextants, both recently certified in alignment by the instrument shop. Checking the charts for the second half of the voyage, she found her mother had plotted a course from the Panama Canal across the vast Caribbean Sea to the windward island of Antigua, where old friends owned a boatyard, then up to Bermuda, and a final leg to Southampton—from which seaport, family lore had it, Haigs and Farquhars had set sail for China in 1839.

She looked around the cabins. The yacht was stuffed with provisions, including an ample store of Migs and Boodles. The sail lockers were in good order, tackle and repair materials in abundance. The digital tank gauges showed water and fuel topped up. The batteries were all new and the fire extinguishers in place and recently tested.

Vicky went up and found her mother at the helm, her eyes restless on the sails. All she could say was, "She's a big boat, Mother."

"She's a staysail schooner. There's no sail too big for me to handle."

"Are you going to fly a spinnaker?"

"I'm not daft." Sally smiled. "But I did have Ah Chi's people fashion an ultralight whisker pole. I can lift it, barely, to pole out a light air drifter. Bamboo, no less. Have a look. It's on the foredeck."

"I can't talk you out of this, can I?"

"You've had your beady gaze below. Is she seaworthy?"

"You or *Whirlwind*?"

"Both."

"Yes, Mother," Vicky conceded reluctantly. "She's seaworthy. And so are you, I suppose."

"Care to join me?"

•   •   •

"You're joking." The next thought rocketing through her mind was *escape.*

"You're more than welcome, Victoria. As you say, she's a big boat. We shan't get in each other's hair."

She was tempted. "Mother, that's so lovely of you."

"Not at all," said Sally. "I'd enjoy the company."

"I can't leave."

"Whyever not?"

"You know. The hong. MacF. Everyone's counting on me."

"Bosh. You've got scads of managers and Peter's there and the redoubtable Mary Lee will lend him a hand, I'm sure. Not to mention your father's Chinese girl. Come along. We'll have a great time of it."

"I can't, Mother, thank you."

"Suit yourself," Sally said airily, but Vicky could see she was disappointed.

She looked at her watch, checked the sky to the west, then gestured toward the toilet below decks. "Right back, Mum. The head."

"It's in the foremast," said her mother.

"I beg your pardon."

"What your father hid there. I found it while I was hiding some gold and diamonds. Go on, take it. That's what you've come for, isn't it? Lift the floorboards just aft of the galley and you'll find a little door in the mast foot."

Vicky went below, pulled up the carpet in the salon, and raised the floor. The mast resonated with the strain of the sails. She found a neat little door cut in the thick aluminum, pried it open with a butter knife, and shone a flashlight inside. A plastic envelope lay among the cloth bags her mother had stashed.

She opened the envelope and found what appeared to be another jewel. It was a green plastic sphere smaller than a marble — an optical computer storage disk which could easily store documents as large as the Bible. The Japanese had been making them smaller every year and were promising "pinheads" for the year 2000.

Closing the cache, she joined her mother on deck.

"Got it?"

"Thank you."

"Business?"

"Very much so." She was suddenly very anxious to see what her father had recorded on it. She glanced again at her watch. A while to wait.

"Well, good luck," said her mother.

"Mummy?"

"Yes, dear?"

"Why was Daddy . . . the way he was?"

"What way?"

"You know."

Sally shrugged. "Driven?"

"I used to think he was always running about after something. Now, when I look back and think about him, it's more like he was being chased. Do you mind awfully my asking?"

"Not at all. It's rather pertinent. You're so damned much like him, sometimes, I don't want you to ruin your life the way he did."

Vicky recalled their last talk as he lay dying. She doubted that he thought he had ruined his life. He had, despite defeat, died a man in love.

Her mother bent the empty Mig can back and forth until she could tear the thin metal, and tossed it overboard, where it instantly sank. Then she pulled a fresh one from the cooler, touched the beaded can to her cheek, and popped it open.

"What chased him, Mother?"

"That depends on whose theory you subscribe to. Fiona, God bless her psycho-hocus-pocus, claims Daddy felt insecure because he was the son of a clerk and grew up at the bottom of the heap in British Shanghai and so had to prove his worth to everyone he met. If you ask George Ng, he'll tell you Daddy was driven mad trying to hold MacF together—you know the bit: last British family-held trading hong beset by the new Asian hordes." She snorted and swigged her beer.

"And you, Mummy? What's your theory?"

"All I know, darling, is you can give your heart to a man as best you can and still never know why he's unhappy. In other words, I don't know. Do you want my advice?"

"Please."

"Marry a cheery soul—some chap who doesn't take things too seriously."

Like Steven, Vicky thought. He's a cheery soul.

"And I don't mean a layabout like No-Way Wong."

Vicky felt her mouth pop open. "I didn't know you knew."

"Good God, dear, your taste in men is appalling."

"He loves me, and I love him."

"Men do not change, is the point I'm trying to make. Find a cheery soul who's manly. Don't make a face—I said manly; I meant manly. A fellow who enjoys being a man out of the kip as well as in, the sort of chap who takes responsibility for the fact that women and children are happiest when their men act differently from women and children."

"Mother, really—"

"When they act big," her mother went on, "gruff, but gentle, decisive but not bullying, active, determined. They can even be remote, now and again, so long as they're not cold. Strong sometimes, but not all the time. Easy. Everything you want in bed—out of bed too. Manly. Chip, for example, or better, your brother Hugo. I know Hugo wasn't a mountain-mover like your father. But my God, look at those children. They're treasures. Dead, Hugo's still a better father than most of their school chums have alive. And remember the smiles on Fiona? The man enjoyed more than his business. He enjoyed his family and his sailing and just being a man. . . . Those wee girls knew that when they were with Daddy, he *was* Daddy and not just Mummy with pants on." Sally's gaze advanced to the foredeck, where she had finally had the safety lines repaired.

"Mother?"

Sally Farquhar Mackintosh looked her daughter in the eye. "No. I will not tell you who Peter's father was."

"But . . . All right, but what was he like?"

Her mother laughed softly. "Smashing in the kip, for a

while. . . . Ultimately, just another dull businessman. Otherwise, all I will say is I know exactly where you inherited your appalling taste in men."

Her eyes darted over the sails and she cranked a notch on the genoa winch. "Not to worry. If there's one advantage women have it's that we're adaptable. You can change. You really can, Vicky. You can allow some manly fellow like Chip in your life. And I don't mean Chip himself, by the way. I suspect Fiona's already got him. But a fellow like him. Manly . . ." She cocked her ear to a distant buzz. "I think I hear your ride home."

"Wait. How did Dad find out?"

"The ruddy fool I was sleeping with blurted it one night at the club in a burst of misguided romanticism."

"He must have been crazy over you."

"Maybe he was, but it wasn't his decision to make alone. Too many people were hurt. In my limited experience, I believe that lovers have a certain obligation to share in major decisions like spilling the beans."

"What happened?"

"Well, what the devil do you think happened?"

"I mean, you got back together with Dad. How?"

"I lied like a lady."

"You denied it?"

"What else did your father want to hear? What else would have worked? Of course, I suppose if you were poor Peter you'd wonder how well it worked. At any rate, I denied it, claimed the ruddy fool was drunk, which he was, and pushed on. Your father had damned little choice, as my father was still Taipan. Divorcing me meant leaving Farquhar and Company, which Duncan Mackintosh was not prepared to give up. . . . The things your poor father went through. Ambition is a cruel master, Vicky. And it never lets go."

She looked out over the silver sea, then back at Vicky. "I'm sorry you can't come with me."

The distant buzz became a thud and a roar, and the helicopter grew large in the sky. Vicky hugged her mother, kissed her hard, and climbed down to the dinghy. "Will you radio once a week?"

"If you like."

"I'd like to know you're alive."

"I'm alive. . . . Vicky, your father was a magnificent man."

Vicky's heart filled at the compliment. She wanted to think of him that way. "Thank you for saying that, Mother."

"When he came to Hong Kong he was like a typhoon that scours the city. So different from the complacent chaps I'd grown up with. He wanted everything. It was so exciting to be with him. I'd see his eyes linger on a big motorcar, or caress a yacht. No apologies, none of your casual born-to-the-manor airs for Duncan Mackintosh. He wanted. And he took. My father thought him too brash. Mother called him grasping. I wouldn't listen. I loved the action."

Releasing the closely snubbed line, Sally let the dinghy drift astern until the line fetched up. Vicky waved. Then Chip was lowering the sling, and moments later she was airborne, and her mother's boat a speck on the ocean.

On the way to the office, Vicky stopped at a jeweler in the Diamond Building, just off the Hennessy Road. The owner came out of his workroom, "hoping," as he put it politely, that her nieces had enjoyed their latest birthday gifts — a handworked bracelet for Millicent and monkey earrings he had made personally for Melissa.

"Happy small ladies," she assured him. He inquired about her mother, and she asked about his children who were moving to Canada. Over a cup of tea they got down to business, and an hour later she was back at her desk.

Vicky saw as soon as she loaded the optical storage disk into her TIC that her father had fed hundreds of sheets of paper through a scanner that stored text and pictures. The screen introduced a menu of topics: COPY ONE OF ONE COPY. Hong Kong bank statements and Swiss numbered accounts were correlated with lists of PRC officials' names and titles. Most of the myriad details could be loved only by

accountants or prosecutors, but some fairly jumped out of the screen—
proof of Two-Way's schemes to defraud the PRC.

She traced, in one particularly damning instance, an invoice for
steel plate from a Tianjin mill managed by a nephew of Premier
Chen, destined for a Nanjing shipyard, transshipped instead to Hong
Kong, trailed by plaintive letters from the shipyard seeking to discover the whereabouts of the missing materials. A letter dismissed
the persistent letter writer, and a newspaper clipping reported his
funeral in his native Ningbo.

Vicky wondered where Vivian's hand showed. Her father seemed
unusually well organized, but then again, she supposed, the computer could have done a lot for him. Few executives his age had
embraced the new technology as avidly. He knew enough to have
entered his material on the optical storage disk himself, and wiped
the computer clean.

Two things were obvious: Over the years her father had cultivated officials connected to dozens of low-level bureaucrats who had
mustered the courage to pass on information; and what had started
as a sideline—the slow accumulation of evidence against Two-Way
Wong—had become Duncan Mackintosh's obsession.

He had compiled a biography of Two-Way that included the
well-known story about his start as a crippled street beggar, and
made a much bolder assertion: Shipowner Two-Way Wong had made
his first fortune as a leader of the Green Gang, the criminal Triad
Society that had ruled Shanghai by terror and extortion until they
were routed by the Communists in 1949.

Two-Way Wong had bought the first vessels in the World
Oceans Red Ship Line with the profits of brothels and opium dens.
After the Korean War shipping boom, there had been no stopping
World Oceans, and when the remnants of the Green Gang fared
badly in Hong Kong, Two-Way re-aligned with the Triads that still
dominated the Crown Colony: the 14K, the Wo, and the Sun Yee
On Society.

The telephone rang, and Vicky jumped. She had been lost in
the material for hours. It was late, dark. Her private line was blink-

ing. *Steven.* She lunged for it. At last she was alone with a moment free to talk. She snatched it off the desk, her heart pounding with joy. "Hello."

"Ah, Ms. Mackintosh." A soft, insinuating Chinese voice.

"Who is this?"

"It is of no consequence."

"Who are you—how'd you get this number?"

"From small nieces."

28

"DO NOT WORRY. The children enjoy excellent health."

Vicky stopped breathing, as if she were watching something precious fall beyond her reach.

"Most imprudent young missies to stand alone in the road in such dangerous times, Ms. Mackintosh. Hong Kong no longer safe city you were child in. Very imprudent. Fortunately, we came upon them before others less respectful of young missies."

"Yes?" She was shaking with terror. She knew what they meant.

"They have been escorted to a safe place."

"Where?"

"Where no one intending harm will ever find them."

"You kidnapped them."

"Such an unpleasant word could be dangerously misunderstood by the police."

"What do you want?"

"Something as valuable to us as they are to you."

"I don't understand." But she did. She knew exactly what they wanted. It was staring at her on the screen. And she had been a fool to think that Two-Way wouldn't try again.

"We will call, later, to make appropriate arrangements," the voice concluded blandly.

Trembling, she put the telephone down. She remembered Two-

Way's child-servants, and her mind squeezed out a horrible image
of a barred room hidden in World Oceans House where the children were trained like animals. Shivering now, she tried to think of
a way out, but all she could think about was how frightened Millicent must be. Melissa would be defiant, for which they might hurt
her.

Her line rang again, Fiona in a rush of words.

"Vicky, I'm frantic. I can't find the girls. I had a puncture. Did
you pick them up from dancing class?"

"Is Chip there?"

"Yes, he was telling me about your mother, but—"

"Bring Chip and come here immediately."

"What is— Are they all right?"

"Fiona. Darling, brace yourself. They've been kidnapped."

"*What?*"

"We'll get them back, I promise you. Just come here, *now.*"

She pulled the optical storage disk from her computer and paced
the office, fingering her dragon pendant. She buzzed Peter, but he
had gone home. She thought a moment, then, wondering if Vivian
was back from Shanghai, knocked reluctantly on the door to Vivian's office. Vivian opened it.

"Another midnight oiler," the China trader greeted her politely.
"How are you, Vicky?" She was beginning to show, just a little, and
looked more radiant than ever. "Are you all right? You're white as
a ghost."

Vicky heard her own voice as if in another room, hollow and
detached, and miles from the terror gripping her. "I need some advice concerning the Chinese mind. I wonder if you could help me."

Vivian looked her over, wondering whether Vicky was putting
her on. But Vicky's lips were trembling, her eyes wide and staring.
Something terrible had happened. Vivian nodded gravely. "Of course.
Would you like me to come into your office?"

"Yes, please."

Vicky sat down at her desk. Vivian closed the door and took the
side chair.

"I've just had a telephone call from a Chinese person who claims to have kidnapped Millicent and Melissa."

Vivian's hand flew to her mouth. "Oh, Vicky—"

"My question is, if I give them what they ask and keep the police out of it, will they honor their side of the bargain and return the girls unharmed?"

"That depends upon who kidnapped them."

"I think you can guess."

"God and heaven."

"It must be him. They didn't want money. It must be my father's evidence."

"Do you have it?"

"Of course I have it. My father left it for me."

"Of course," Vivian echoed, wondering how Vicky could ever think her father had treated her shabbily—he had left her half the hong, and all his secrets.

"I have to assume it's Two-Way," Vicky said.

"Will you give it to him?"

"Would you? You're the one with the baby. Would you?"

Vivian bowed her head. "Yes."

"They're children. Frightened. I have no choice. Two-Way has won."

"Yes."

Vicky's hands were shaking violently. "Can I trust him? Will Two-Way give them back even if I do give him the evidence?"

"He leaves you no choice. You have to trust him."

"But will he keep the bargain?" Vicky whispered. "That's all I want to know."

"I can't tell you. . . . But . . ."

"What?"

"As I understand it, the way these things happen—"

"What things?" Vicky snapped harshly. She was losing control, paralyzed by helpless fear. Vivian answered her in measured tones, as if explaining the horror would calm them both.

"My mother told me stories of Shanghai. Kidnapping was com-

mon before Liberation. Ransom payments were honored to keep the
practice viable. But sometimes a criminal has partners or agents and
they . . ." Her voice trailed off. "I can't promise you anything,
Vicky."

"Then the way we do the trade is most important."

"Yes, build in protection."

"That's what I'll negotiate. I won't let my father's material out
of my sight until I have the children."

They sat silently, waiting for the telephone to ring. Vicky couldn't
stop thinking about Melissa. Would she have the sense not to provoke her captors? Vivian thought of Duncan. Could he have dreamed
of the fate to which he had delivered his family?

Lobby security reported that Fiona and Chip had arrived. Fiona
ran in looking wild, her red hair a tangle, her eyes round, her mouth
and cheeks rigid. "Vicky, get them back. Please."

"I'll get them back. I promise. I'll get them back."

Chip asked for the details. Vicky related them as thoroughly as
she could.

Security buzzed again. "There's a Tanka down here, Ms. Mackintosh. Demands to see you. Name of Ah Chi."

"Find out what he wants. Tell him I'll get back to him."

The guard buzzed back sounding panicked. "He's got a friend
with him threatening to drive his car through the door. Do you
know him or should I call the police?"

Vicky reckoned that Ah Chi, upset about her mother's leaving,
had gotten drunk. She remembered one party night, hauling his in-
ert form up a Philippine beach, pursued by the tide. "No. Send him
up. I'll straighten him out."

She waited, staring at the telephone.

Ah Chi burst in, gaping like a man who had never seen the
inside of an office building before, but not at all drunk. He was
trailed by a wary-looking Huang, dressed in a tight silk suit. Chip
took one look at Huang and stood up, his face blooming with interest in the transformation of Duncan Mackintosh's former assistant
boatboy.

"What is it, Ah Chi? I'm terribly busy here."

"Huang say all Two-Way children gone, Missy."

"What are you talking about?"

"Two-Way take Number-One Son's missies."

"How did you know—"

"Of course he knows," Chip interrupted. "The entire Chinese underground knows by now, and it looks like our friend Huang has become connected to it."

"But what—"

"All Two-Way Wong children away from Colony," Ah Chi repeated.

"But what does that mean?" She looked at Vivian.

Chip answered: "Standard operating procedure. Before you kidnap your enemy's children, you send your own family to safety. Ah Chi is right. Two-Way's your man." He turned to Ah Chi.

"Why Two-Way kidnap?"

Ah Chi shrugged. "No know."

"Old Son, why Huang tell Missy?"

"Huang third cousin Back Door Ping. When Taipan and Ping killed, Tai-Tai give Ping's wife gold."

Chip nodded his understanding. "Tell Huang that Missy will inform Tai-Tai of his respect and generosity." Ah Chi translated. Huang beamed.

Fiona was turning frantically from face to face. "But why?" she wailed. "Why would Two-Way Wong do such a thing? Vicky?"

"Yes, why?" Chip asked.

"There was bad blood between him and Dad."

"But they're children."

"I know that, Fiona. I'll get them back." She suddenly missed her father so badly. This was so far beyond her.

"Any reckoning what Two-Way might want, Victoria?" Chip asked mildly.

Vicky thought how her father would answer in such a way as to seem in charge. Sound certain and change the subject. "I'm sure he'll get around to asking. Chip, can you honestly advise us to ask for police help?"

Chip shook his head. "I'm sorry, but with '97 a month off, we're riddled top to bottom with all sorts of elements. I cannot tell an old friend to take the chance. It might get back to the kidnappers, and if it did . . . Besides, just because we know—or suspect—it's Two-Way, we can't prove it. He's insulated by dozens of layers. He can't be threatened by the law."

"What do you advise?"

"Wait to see what the kidnappers want and give it to them. I'm sorry, Victoria. Fiona. I wish I could perform some magic, but I can't."

"Ah Chi. Can Huang find the children?"

"No, Missy."

"Vivian?"

Vivian shook her head. "Give them what they want, Victoria."

Vicky stared at the Chinese woman. No one else in the room knew what Vivian had meant, though Chip looked as curious as a wolfhound sniffing the wind. Vivian said, "There is no other way to save the children."

"Fiona? Do you want the police or do you want me to try to negotiate with them?"

"You're the boss, Vicky. Do something. Get them back."

The telephone rang. Everyone jumped. It was her personal line again. She reached for it, fearfully. "Hello?"

His butterscotch voice. "I'm in Room Seventeen-seventeen."

Vicky spun her chair, turning her back on the others, stood up, and took the handset to the windows. "You're back!" she whispered. "When—"

"Don't tell anybody. If the Old Man finds out he'll kill me."

"What—"

"I figure we can have tonight and I'll sneak back out tomorrow. I got a buddy in Taiwan covering for me in case he calls."

"Oh, God." Her mind had already raced in a terrible direction.

"I love you. I missed you so bad I thought I'd die."

"Back at you," she whispered.

"Oh, I get it. You got an office full of long-face business types?"

"Right."

"How soon can you get here?"

Vicky's heart felt dry in her breast. "I . . . I . . . Give me an hour."

"Love you," said Steven. "Can't wait."

Her breath caught. "Oh . . . I love you, too," she whispered. "Always—Wait!"

"What, babe?"

". . . Forgive me . . ."

"For what, babe?"

"Forgive me if I'm a little late."

Steven laughed. "I'll find some way for you to make it up to me."

She softly cradled the phone and waited as long as she dared before turning back to the others. Fiona misinterpreted her tears. "What happened?"

"Nothing, nothing. Just a banker . . ."

They were all still hanging on the hope her call had meant something, all staring at the tears on her face. "I'm sorry." She brushed them away. "I'm so upset. . . . Chip, do me a favor, please. Take Fiona home."

"No, I'm staying here," Fiona protested.

"One of us should be at the telephone at Peak House. Go on, dear. Don't worry, we'll get them back."

"How do you know?"

"I promise I will get them back," Vicky said coldly. "I guarantee it."

Chip wrapped his arm around Fiona, and the Englishwoman collapsed against him as if her legs had melted. "Call us immediately, Victoria," he said. "The instant you hear."

"And you're absolutely sure about not using the police?" Vicky asked him.

"Only as a last resort. If we've no better hope."

As Fiona and Chip headed out, Ah Chi nudged Huang to follow. Vicky stopped them with a shake of her head. Vivian, who had remained curled, almost shrunken in her chair, noticed. Vicky shut the door and leaned her back against it. This was a terrible thing that a man like Hugo would never have dreamed of. But her father would have. And she knew beyond any doubt at this moment that she was cursed to be Duncan Mackintosh's daughter.

"They are not all gone."

"Who?" Vivian asked.

"Ah Chi. Tell Huang that one of Two-Way's children came back to Hong Kong."

Ah Chi translated. Huang shook his head. "He say they all gone, Missy."

"Steven Wong is at the Regent Hotel. He just checked into Room Seventeen-seventeen. I want you and Huang to kidnap him."

29

"*HAI!*" AH CHI turned to Huang and translated excitedly.

"*What?*" Vivian jumped to her feet.

"A trade," said Vicky. "Two-Way's firstborn son for my nieces."

"They'll kill him!" Vivian protested. "You can't do that. They'll kill him."

"No, not kill him. A trade. No one's going to kill anyone. Ah Chi, no kill him. No hurt. Just kidnap. Yes?"

"Yes, Missy." Ah Chi was grinning ear to ear and Huang looked as happy as a bear in honey. "We kidnap. No hurt. After, everyone still friends."

"Good. Call me when you get him. Do you have a place to hold him?"

"Oh, yes, Missy. Many place."

"They will kill him," Vivian repeated. She had gone white and was trembling, even as a bitter calm settled over Vicky. "You don't understand, Victoria. If Steven defied his father and came back and if that ruins his father's plan, he will be killed."

"By his own father? Don't be ridiculous."

"By someone involved. Mark my words. Steven will die and his death will be on your hands."

"He will not die."

"Who are you to say? What do you know of these things?"

"How else can I guarantee I get the children back?"

"Give Two-Way the evidence. Give him what he wants."

"You yourself said I can't be one hundred percent sure he will return them alive."

"No. You heard the boatboy. Everyone knows it's Two-Way. He'll have to return them in trade or lose face."

"I'm not taking that chance."

Vivian eyed her appraisingly. "Perhaps you are seizing a chance."

"What does that mean?"

"You're seizing this chance to keep your father's evidence."

"I am not," Vicky said quickly.

"You're betraying your lover to keep it."

"I'm guaranteeing the lives of my nieces."

"How convenient that you'll not give up the evidence. I hope you've made your goodbyes. You'll never see Steven again."

"You don't understand. His father loves him. That monster loves Steven. He would never hurt him."

"*You* don't understand," Vivian shot back. "All foreigners make the same mistake about Chinese people. You revere individualism. You assume we do too. We do not. Two-Way Wong doesn't stand alone. By thwarting him, you've thwarted others who depend upon his success. They will take their revenge. Not against you, not against Ah Chi and Huang, but against the man who betrayed his own father by disobeying him."

"If that's true, then Two-Way will protect him."

"What if he *can't* protect him?"

"Then he will send him away to somewhere safe."

"I hope you're right. And if you are, I hope Steven stays there. Either way, you've sacrificed your lover for the sake of your hong. You must be very proud."

"I am not proud," Vicky whispered. Beneath the calm of a decision made, she felt sick with grief, knowing she had lost him already: He would never trust her again. "I want you to tell Party Leader Tang that I've got the evidence."

"Never!"

"What?"

"I'll have no part of this."

Was Vivian right? Was she sacrificing Steven to carry out her father's plan against Steven's father? Were the children her excuse? But even Vivian had agreed, originally, that her only guarantee to get them back unharmed was to negotiate a foolproof trade.

She dried her cheeks and sat back behind her desk.

"How can you not help? What about my father?"

"Your father is dead. You were right—it was a clumsy plan. Enough people have died for it. Don't sacrifice Steven."

"But you supported my father. You believed in his plan. You told me it was the only way to save Hong Kong."

"China is more complicated than your father and I knew," Vivian answered deliberately. "I've come to see it differently. We will not change China in a single, dramatic sweep. What has happened to-night is a sign: This is how all things will be resolved if we allow it. Kidnapping children, killing innocents. There must be a better way."

"You're surrendering everything you worked for and, may I re-mind you, my father died for."

Vivian did not deny it. "I think pregnancy has perhaps cleared my eyes. At any rate, I was a teacher's daughter long before I be-came a taipan's concubine."

"Your word, not mine. Well, when you get a sign explaining another way, tell me about it. Until then, I'll fight this my way. Ah Chi, go get him."

"Yes, Missy."

"You can't do this," Vivian pleaded. "I won't help you!"

"I'll find another way. Two-Way Wong is a monster," Vicky said grimly. "I will not let him do this."

"Then Steven will die and you will be the monster."

"Steven will not die. Call me when you have him, Ah Chi."

"Yes, Missy." He spoke to Huang, and the young smuggler showed his respect. "*Hai*, Taipan."

•   •   •

Steven Wong prepared their room with his own hands. The last thing he wanted was houseboys reporting to floor managers who reported to higher managers who reported to people who would eventually report to his father that No-Way was back in town. He turned down the bed and lowered the air conditioning and arranged the flowers he'd bought on the way in and set a bottle of wine in ice. He laid out sushi and made a fan pattern of the soy-sauce packets.

Then he sat down to watch her shadow fall on the polished marble saddle of the door. The telephone rang. A meeting, he thought as he picked it up. More long-faced business types invading her office.

"Yes, doll. Where are you?"

"Get away."

"What? Who is this?"

"It's Vivian. Run. They're going to kidnap you."

"Who?"

"Run," she said again, and hung up.

He dropped the phone and ran for his clothes.

That's why Father had sent everyone away. He should have known. Cursing himself for the fool he knew he was, he fought into his suit, stuffed his necktie in his pocket, grabbed his wallet and his watch, and bolted out the door.

Four hallboys were approaching with a laundry hamper.

"Gangway!"

They pressed against the wall, bowing their heads. "Sorry, sir."

"Wait. Boy, take me down the back elevator."

"Yes, sir."

They led him, wheeling their hamper, through a swinging door into a service area and rang the elevator for him. "Great. Thanks." He peeled off a few bills. "You can go now."

"We ride down this way too."

Tanka accent, he thought. Sad hearing Tanka in the Regent

Hotel. Whole world was going to hell if the fishermen were turning into houseboys.

They crowded in with him, apologizing profusely. The door shut. They pulled the top sheet off their cart, threw a pillowcase over his head, pinning his arms and wrapping him in sheets and upending him into the cart. He fell on his head, nearly breaking his neck, and was so startled that the elevator was halfway down before he started kicking. Powerful hands held his legs.

He felt the elevator stop. The door opened on a garbage smell that mingled with the scent of the sea. The cart rolled down a ramp and he panicked, smelling the water and thinking they were going to drown him.

Somehow he got his head out of the pillowcase. He opened his mouth to yell. A callused hand rammed a towel between his teeth, and another tugged the bag over his head again. He caught a glimpse of a junk bobbing at the end of a corridor and realized they were smuggling him out the Regent's service entrance, which ran like a pirate tunnel under the harbor walk. The laundry cart trundled down a ramp and across the gangway. An unmuffled diesel started banging and the junk dug in its stern and sped into the harbor with him and the hotel's garbage.

At midnight, Vicky telephoned Ping at Peak House and asked him to pick her up in the Daimler. Then she spoke to Peter, who sounded so bombed that she told him to put Mary on instead.

"Mary, I want you to do me a favor. Call one of Peter's contacts at World Oceans and tell him I'm coming to see Sir John."

"Now?"

"Can you do that for me?"

"Is this about the children?"

"I can't talk now. Can you do that?"

"Of course, Vicky. May I do anything else for you?"

"No."

"Would you like me to come with you?"

"No. But thank you."

When the car arrived, she got in alone and sat readying herself in silence while Ping drove the near-empty streets from Causeway Bay to Central. World Oceans House was dark but for some lights in the lobby and a glow on top that indicated Two-Way Wong was still up and about. Her mind reached for Steven. She tore the thought away.

She waited in the car until Ping got the lobby guards to open the door. Only then did she step out of the car and into the office building. Mary had done her job. She was expected. A polite, heavily built young man in a dark suit walked her to the private elevators and rode up with her. He was the translator who had served Two-Way Wong at his New Year's party. They stopped on Two-Way's office level. The translator walked her through a maze of reception rooms and endless corridors, through locked doors that opened to his voice command, and finally to a solid teak door that he knocked on softly. It slid open. Before her lay an enormous room decorated with Chinese carpets and display cases of antique porcelain. In the distance, some eighty feet from the door, Two-Way Wong sat behind a huge slab of blackened teak that looked as if it had spent many years in the sea.

"Forgive me if I don't rise." His deep voice carried across the room. "Come in, Taipan's Daughter. What do you want from me?"

Vicky crossed the several carpets, deep into the silence of his office. The translator went ahead and took up a position beside and one step behind his Taipan. Vicky heard the door close. She was forcibly struck by the resemblance Steven bore to his father. Subtract the ruthless, empty eyes and the hard, determined mouth, and he could be Steven. But such a subtraction was not possible, for the ruthlessness and the emptiness were the essence of the man sitting before her.

"What do you want of me?" he repeated.

"I've come to trade," she answered.

"Trade what? You've already rebuffed my offer of a fine position at McGlynn and Kerry. What could I possibly have that you would want instead?"

"My nieces, Millicent and Melissa Mackintosh, the daughters of my father's firstborn son."

Two-Way Wong exchanged a baffled look with the translator, and Vicky thought If I didn't have what I have, I would run screaming from this room.

"I don't have your nieces."

"Then I suggest you get them."

"I'm afraid I don't understand."

"I have your son. And I will trade your son for my nieces."

Two-Way's face betrayed nothing. The silent translator was listening as expressionlessly as if Vicky had come to discuss the price of gold in Tokyo.

"Now I truly am even more confused. How could you possibly have my son? The way I hear it, my son has 'had' you."

"Telephone Taiwan. A friend of his will claim he is there, but he is not. I have him. I will trade him alive and well for my nieces, alive and well. Do you understand me?"

Something unknowable moved in the back of his eyes.

"He enjoys excellent health," Vicky mimicked the earlier threat. "But it was most imprudent of him to wait alone in a hotel room in such a dangerous city as Hong Kong. Fortunately I had him escorted to a safe place."

As vicious an expression as she had ever seen crossed Two-Way's face. "Shall we exchange fingers?" he asked coldly. "Two small girl fingers for one man's?"

Vicky had braced for this, knowing she had one chance to terrorize Steven's father. She drew strength from the only reservoir of cruelty she possessed, the memory of her own father's hand growing heavy in hers.

"I will send you his heart."

30

THE NIGHT PASSED, long and horrible with anticipation, then a full day. Fiona was frantic, crying, screaming, demanding Vicky do more, bolting for the telephone to call the police, only to be stopped by Chip, who repeated over and over that to involve the police officially would be to kill her daughters.

At Chip's insistence, the entire family retreated to the executive floor of Mackintosh Farquhar House, where a dozen off-duty senior expat officers began quietly hanging about the doors and elevators. The streets around the building, Peter reported, seemed unusually crowded with Tanka lurking in the doors and watching from taxis. He had taken three bodyguards with him to an unmissable meeting at the Hong Kong and Shanghai Bank.

The adrenaline rush of standing up to Two-Way had long faded and Vicky spent the hours in terror that she had miscalculated. Every telephone call, every messenger's arrival had her heart pounding: Would the Chinese tycoon deliver a child's fingers? She tried not to think of Steven, and when that proved impossible, she reminded herself that Ah Chi was a gentle soul. But Huang had seemed a gentle soul, too, and if there was one thing she had learned it was that she knew absolutely nothing for sure about the Chinese.

Late the second night, the telephone rang.

A Chinese voice, perhaps that of the first man who had called, said, "Let me speak with John Chypwood-Chipworth."

"They know you're here," Vicky said, handing Chip the phone.

"Of course."

"He used your name, not your title."

"Good. He knows why I'm here. Chypwood-Chipworth here . . . Yes . . . Yes . . . No. Absolutely not. Choose another place. . . . That's better." He covered the phone and whispered, "We'll exchange in the lobby of the Peninsula." He turned back to the phone and spoke in a low, cold voice Vicky had never heard from him before. "One more thing, old chap. I'll have three lads with me. We've all served in Belfast at one time or another. We will hunt you to the end of the earth if a hair of either of those children is out of place."

He hung up and immediately dialed Ah Chi. "We're on. Peninsula Hotel. One hour."

"I'm coming," said Vicky.

"No. And neither are you, Fiona. Don't worry, they're as good as back. No one's going to be silly this far in the game. We'll telephone as soon as we have them."

Then he was out the door.

Vicky sat at her desk, Fiona in the side chair. Neither woman said much for the hour, and when the telephone rang, Vicky picked up, dreading the worst.

"Your nieces are safe," said a tired-sounding Steven Wong. "I think I still love you, but the odds on trust are real low."

"I'm so sorry."

"Me too. Gotta go. They tell me I've got some explaining to do at home."

Vicky cradled the silent phone.

Fiona was watching, frozen.

"Steven Wong says the children are safe."

"Thank God. But Chip—"

The phone rang again. "Take it," Vicky said. "I'm sure it's for you. I've had mine."

Fiona lunged for the phone. "Yes . . . Oh. Oh, sweetheart, are you all right? . . . All all right? Put your sister on. . . . Yes, dear, Mum's here. Yes . . . That's all right, sweetheart. It's good to cry. . . . What? . . . No, Melissa, I did not mean to suggest you were a baby. Put your sister back on the line, please." Happily, she rolled tear-filled eyes at Vicky.

Vicky walked to the window and stared at the buildings across the road until Fiona finally hung up. "They're coming here."

"Good."

"I better call down for tea."

"Yes, do that." Vicky picked up another telephone and dialed MacF Golden Air. "Victoria Mackintosh here. Get on to Cathay or BA and book three seats to London. Mackintosh. Fiona, Millicent, and Melissa. . . . Immediately."

"What?" asked Fiona. "What are you doing?"

"You're going home, Fiona. Take the girls. Hong Kong isn't safe."

"But this is home. I can't just uproot them."

"I can't go through this again," Vicky said, but what she meant was that she could not go through with everything she had to if she were so vulnerable.

"But you'll be all alone."

"More than you know. But that's my fault. My mistake, my penalty."

"You disobeyed me."

"Yes, Father."

Steven Wong hung his head.

He had had two weeks to practice a pose of contrition—downcast eyes, humbly bent neck, guiltily slumped shoulders—but his heart wasn't in it. For despite fourteen long days of confinement to the family quarters atop World Oceans House, he was still reeling from Vicky's betrayal.

It stung as if she had done it to him an hour ago. Which made it difficult to get in the mood for what promised to be an extended fatherly lecture, on the priceless carpet in front of the Taipan's desk. Steven hid a wry smile. As near as he could recall, this was the first time in his life a woman had hurt him, with the exception of his mother, whom he could no longer seriously blame for dying.

Nor, for that matter, could he blame Vicky all that much. She had sacrificed him for her brother's children. A fair trade, he supposed: two little redheaded *gweiluis* for one aging girl-chaser. But it still hurt.

How his father had gotten into the little-girl-kidnapping business didn't bear thinking about. Nor would asking get an answer. Suffice it to assume that Vicky's nieces had been pawns in some bigger deal the Old Man had going down. And whatever that deal was, Number-One Son had stepped in it for sure.

"Have I asked too much of you?"

"No, Father."

"I feel a sick grief unlike any since your mother died."

"I'm sorry, Father. I wish I could change what happened."

Two-Way Wong touched his long fingers tip to tip and stared into the cage they formed. Great ambitions provoked powerful enemies and cost dear. It was fitting, he thought, that his last adversary should be British. Not any Brit, but the daughter of Duncan Mackintosh. Fitting, too, that thanks to her, the price of his highest goal would probably be his son by his first wife. He sensed a certain closing of the circle, events moving beyond even his control.

"If I have not asked too much of you, why did you disobey?"

"I didn't realize how important it was."

Two-Way stirred, his anger rising. "Is there some law—some custom I don't know—that requires a man to confide in his son before he will obey?"

"No, Father."

"How can a man make his way in the world if he cannot trust the family behind him? Have you any idea what damage you've inflicted?"

"No, Father. I did not know it was so important."

"A proper son would have assumed it was important."

"Forgive me, Father. I am not a proper son."

"Your brothers quake in fear of me," Two-Way mused. "Your sisters tremble. Why is that?"

Steven pushed Vicky from his mind. This was beginning to sound more serious than he had imagined. He gambled on his answer, which was no less truthful for its arrogance. "You love me differently from my half-brothers and half-sisters."

"I did," his father conceded, and Steven's blood ran cold.

"I love Victoria Mackintosh, Father. I went out of control."

"Love is a privilege you must earn," his father shot back. "First you put your house in order, so you can defend that love. It is the privilege of a man, not of a willful child."

"What have I done?"

His father held his hands together, like a man praying, and was silent for many minutes. "You may perform me a service," he said at last.

"Anything," said Steven, ignoring the thought that "anything" could be a dangerous promise to a man like his father.

Two-Way Wong pulled a single sheet of paper from his desk and handed it to his son. It was a brief typewritten memorandum from "Governor" Chief Executive Allen Wei, stamped TOP SECRET.

Next he passed him a blank sheet of the governor's official stationery, which bore Hong Kong's seal of the British lion and the Chinese dragon.

"Would you please translate this into Chinese?"

Steven looked at his father.

"Is there a problem?"

"Just, anyone could do this," Steven said.

"Anyone," his father agreed. "Anyone who's attended the finest schools, had the best tutors, had every door opened for him. I want *you* to do it. I want you to complete one simple task for me, so that when I go to bed and look at the dark I can remember that my Number-One Son did at least serve me once and exactly as I asked. Can you do it?"

"Of course, Father."

"Go ahead then."

"Now?"

"I would like to watch. There is brush and inkstone at that small desk over there. Bring it back to me when you're done."

Steven sat with the memo, scanned it for the overall meaning. "I don't understand, Father. What is 'Hong Kong Gold'?"

"Make that read like an official name. Like 'British Sterling.' "

While his father watched, Steven translated, pausing occasionally to choose a more artful character. When he had finished, he read it over with a certain pleasure. The language flowed, conveying both the sense of the original and its meaning. He looked across the office and saw his father watching.

"All done," he said, rising and bearing it to him. Two-Way Wong placed it reverently on his desk, donned his reading glasses, and read it over. "I've always admired your skill with the brush. You could have been a scholar. . . ."

"I could have been a lot of things."

His father opened a drawer and handed him a thin, beautifully made eelskin wallet. "Here is a ticket for today's Cathay flight to Vancouver. Credit cards, Canadian gold certificates, and cash. Goodbye."

"When can I come home?"

"Never."

"But—"

"If you do, the Societies will chop you."

"The Societies?" Steven echoed. "What do the Triads . . ." His voice trailed off as shock, fear, and understanding melded into a knot that engorged his throat. His father was not operating alone. Whatever the kidnapping had been about, he had employed Triad help. It would not be the first time he had used them. And they probably had a part in the memo about "Hong Kong Gold."

"What about your protection?"

His father shook his head. "I can't protect you this time. You've broken too many rice bowls."

How stupid he had been. If his disobedience had blown a deal

his father had going with the Triads, then the Societies would claim
the right to punish him.

Triad criminals, ironically, were great preservers of Chinese tradition, particularly when the defense of old values suited their pur-
poses. In the days of the emperors, death had been the penalty for
violating filial piety, which would give them a great excuse to kill
him. He shivered, violently, remembering how he had lorded it over
them. He could name a dozen Triad killers who would enjoy chopping the Taipan's arrogant son like some vegetable hawker behind
on his payments.

"You'll just let them chop me?"

"They have agreed to accept your exile to Canada as penalty.
To protect you here in Hong Kong would cost me energy I have
better uses for."

Better uses for rang in Steven's ears. Shocked, disbelieving, Steven Wong could not accept that his father had, at last, denied him.
"Better uses? What better uses? This?" Dropping all pretense of
respect, he snatched up the paper he had translated and read it aloud,
his voice heavy with scorn:

" 'Her Majesty's Government desires the transfer of all Hong
Kong Gold to the Bank of England in the City of London. Accord-
ingly the Hong Kong and Shanghai Bank and the Standard Chartered Bank are instructed to provide the Government with access to
their vaults.' What is this? There's no such thing as 'Hong Kong
Gold.' Gold is privately owned in banks and deposit boxes. Allen
Wei has no power to move gold."

"Chinese people have a great reverence for gold," his father
answered.

"And why'd you want it translated? English is the official language. Certainly in a memo to the banks."

"So Hong Kong Chinese can read it as it spills from their fax
machines."

"Fax machines?" Steven echoed. It took him another moment
to get it. "You're going to fax this? To whom?"

"Everyone."

"Everyone?"

"Broadcast to every business office, every restaurant, every tailor shop, every wholesaler, every agent, every shipper, every police station, every newspaper, every hotel, and every factory. It will appear to be an accidental leak of a secret transmission. An electronic mistake . . ."

"Who's going to believe the Brits are stealing their gold?"

"Everyone." The color had risen to Two-Way's face. It struck Steven that he had never before seen his father truly excited. "Last July, before you came home, half of Hong Kong believed that I would fill in the Causeway Bay Typhoon Shelter. Property prices near the shelter doubled, while Aberdeen and Yau Ma Tei were besieged by people trying to move their boats from Causeway Bay."

"That was a rumor."

"A profitable rumor. And now how do you think they'll react to this rumor?"

"They'll go nuts."

"Like mad dogs," his father agreed. "People who hold gold certificates will storm their banks demanding the metal. The banks are bound to be caught short. People with private safe-deposit boxes will carry their gold home to stuff in mattresses. There will be robberies. And there will be a run on the banks, which, I assure you, are hurt far worse than the media has reported by the property and stock crashes."

Suddenly a lot of things made sense, including his no-show job in New York. Emboldened by his father's unusual candor, and gratified by his trust, Steven asked, "Did you engineer the Cathay Tower crash?"

Two-Way Wong regarded him coolly. "Everything would have gone more easily had you not disobeyed me. By coming back from Taiwan against my wishes and forcing me to ransom your life, you've made me vulnerable. By destroying my plan to protect myself you have forced me to accelerate and intensify the chaos. So when you read of Hong Kong burning in your Canadian newspapers, you and you alone will know why the flames are so high and the heat so intense."

"There'll be riots."

"And whom do you suppose the people will riot against?"

"Allen Wei."

"The governor who's stealing their gold for the British."

"It's true, isn't it, what they say, Father? The Mainlanders will make you governor."

Again, the chairman of World Oceans ignored his son's blunt question and answered obliquely. "I cannot change, or even affect, certain events that will happen on July first. China is vast, Hong Kong small. I didn't negotiate the Joint Declaration. The British did, with the PRC government. Some events, however, I can bend to my will. . . . After the rioters have sacked Government House, they'll mob the gweilos."

Steven had a terrible picture of Vicky's blond head disappearing in a flailing sea of arms. "But you'll be governor of nothing," he protested. "The gweilos will pour out of town for good."

"They'll come back."

"Why?"

"Ah, you miss the point. Wong Li will not be the scourge of Hong Kong, but her savior."

"Who'll believe that?"

"The only ones that matter—the Mainlanders."

"You mean the PRC will appoint you governor in order to stop the riots."

"Very good." Two-Way smiled. "A Chinese governor of a Chinese city. Not a banana like Allen Wei. A Chinese governor the mob will stand in fear of, and obey."

Steven Wong shook his head. He wondered if his father had gone 'round the bend. "But why would the gweilos come back?"

"Businessmen will know that Governor Sir John is their sort of fellow. I am, after all, the ultimate capitalist."

Stability, Steven had to concede, was the main thing the global business-types yearned for. But they were not the only consideration.

"What will Beijing think of the ultimate capitalist?"

Instead of bridling at his son's temerity, Two-Way Wong laughed out loud. "You're such a child. Exactly like your mother. 'What will Beijing think?' " he echoed mockingly.

The Taipan pulled himself erect, leaning on his desk for support. Chuckling still, even as the pain sent a tremor across his face, he proceeded slowly across the office with the aid of his cane. Steven followed, knowing that if he tried to help, his father's bony frame would freeze like ice in his hands. He watched him limp to an old cabinet, which he opened, causing the interior to light up.

Steven gasped. Hanging by a silk cord was a Chou musical bell.

"Is it real?"

In answer, his father picked up a bamboo gong and struck it sharply. It rang pure and sweet. His father handed him the gong. Steven knew how they worked and aimed for the exact spot his father had struck. He missed. The bell rang again, a fine note, but different. His father laughed at him.

"What will Beijing think? Those who matter in Beijing—my 'old friends'—will receive their cut. They'll think themselves damned lucky and thank God and heaven that their 'real good friend' Wong Li is looking after their interests on the China Coast."

His father was not 'round the bend, not at all. His eye was on the prize, and the prize was nothing less than total control of Hong Kong. He'd be like an emperor, or a king. Which would make his son a prince, of sorts. Steven started to smile. Instead, he was overwhelmed by emotion. Trembling, he spoke from the heart. "I'm so grateful that you would confide in such an unworthy son."

"I believe you will never disobey me again."

"Can I come back when you've . . . when you've won?"

"We will see," Two-Way Wong answered vaguely. "Go. My men will see you safely to the plane."

Waiting at the elevator were a pair of guys who looked as if they could take the entire People's Liberation Army barehanded.

Steven got frightened, thinking they would dump him in the harbor. But that was absurd. If his father did want to hurt him, Steven knew for a fact that behind one of the silk screens in the chairman's top-floor office was an ordinary paneled door that opened on an empty shaft — sort of an express elevator minus the elevator car — providing a simpler way to dispose of a body than lugging it to the harbor.

"After you, gentlemen."

They plummeted uneventfully to the garage, where they crowded into the red "1997" Rolls and headed for Causeway Bay and the Cross Harbour Tunnel. Steven looked out the back window, up at the crown of World Oceans House, and wondered if his father was watching. Or had he gone on to his next piece of business? It had been the strangest conversation they had ever had. He could not recall his father ever confiding anything of real importance before.

As they neared Causeway Bay, he kept seeing glimpses of the gold Mackintosh Farquhar House, squeezed between its taller neighbors.

"I've got to make a quick stop."

"No stops," the bodyguard in the front seat said.

"This'll take five minutes." Steven pulled some money from his wallet.

"Taipan say no stops."

"He won't mind this one," Steven said, smoothly opening the door and hitting the road running. "I'll see you at the airport," he yelled as they tried to scramble after him. "I'll be there. I promise."

He sprinted across three lanes of moving traffic and rolled over a low barrier and found himself on the edge of the typhoon shelter. Some yachtsmen were just exiting the under-highway tunnel and he bounded past them, raced through it, and came up in the streets of Causeway Bay, panting in the humid heat. He ran the blocks to Mackintosh Farquhar House, burst into the frigid lobby, and combed his hair and straightened his clothes in the elevator.

The executive-floor receptionist was a cute Cantonese. She pushed a button that unlocked the door, but her expression said he had better have an appointment. Steven gave her his best smile.

"Please tell Ms. Mackintosh that Steven Wong would like to see her for five minutes."

"Taipan not here. Maybe you call later."

Steven switched to Cantonese. "Is she here or not here? I'm leaving town. I've got to see her."

"I can't tell."

"Please," he begged. "It's so important. I've just got to see her for one second. Please." He held the girl's eyes. "Please. We had a terrible row. I've got to apologize."

Despite Vicky's mania for privacy, there wasn't a Chinese in the city who didn't know they were lovers.

"Don't say I told you."

"Of course not. Where is she?"

"Airport. She take delivery new freight plane."

"Oh, fuck! I was just going there. Thanks." He whirled and ran to the elevator. "Wait. If I miss her, would you tell her something for me?"

"What?"

"Tell her it's okay. I'm not mad."

He tore into the street looking for a cab, saw none, and figured he'd have better luck on the Hennessy Road. Halfway there, he noticed two kids in loose white shirts and blue jeans following him.

Their baggy shirts were the giveaway—room to hide their choppers. They were pacing him easily, not bothering to hide it, and casually shortening the distance. He'd be dead in ten seconds in the crowds on the Hennessy—a bloody heap on the pavement.

Steven Wong saw his entire life narrow to one small fact—the wild and free spirit, the rule breaker, was as predictable as the monsoon. That bitter truth cut deeper than the fear, for now he knew why his father had confided so generously. Two-Way Wong had expected his son to disobey him again and had appointed him his own executioner.

He doubled back, crossing the narrow street and bolting for the waterfront. Much safer in the open until he found a cab and got the hell away from them.

The move caught them by surprise, as did his speed. Maybe the little monsters hadn't played pro tennis. He slowed down to save his energy when he reached the Lockhart Road. The heat was killing. Still no sign of their partners, which meant nothing. They could have twenty watching from doorways and rooftops, and old men in windows he'd never see.

He had been stupid. Stupid again. Of course they had staked out MacF House. There'd be others around World Oceans, in case he was dumb enough to take a stroll from his father's building, and others at every place he was known to hang out. A few at the pier for the launch that ran him out to the gambling boats. There'd be some at the Regent, even. They could have saved a lot of trouble; this was one guy dumb enough to visit his girlfriend when the Triads were on his tail.

No cabs. The kids rounded a corner, nonchalantly scanning the street. God, if he could get to the launch and take it to the airport. But the pier was back in Central. Then he saw his chance. Across the road was the Yacht Club and the Police Officers Club. He'd like to see them pull their choppers in front of a bunch of off-duty cops quaffing English ale. He ran to the nearest overpass walkway and started up, only to whirl and retreat in stomach-wrenching fear. Two of them were already on the overpass, waiting for him. The traffic was too heavy to cross on foot. He ran for the pedestrian tunnel.

Again his speed caught them off balance and he gained on all four who were streaming after him. He found the gray entrance door, yanked it open, and ran down the stairs. His footsteps made barely more sound than the light tap-tap-tap of fine Italian leather ghosting over the pavement. He opened up with all the speed he had left.

He was almost through when two kung-fu fighters came down the far steps and blocked his way. No room for choppers on these guys; muscle shirts. The choppers were behind him. Trapped, he turned to his fate.

Chinese punishment fit both the crime and the criminal. Death was the penalty for betraying an elder. The manner of execution depended upon the criminal. They had their razor-edged blades out now, gleaming in the fluorescent light. He was a tennis player, so they would cut the tendons in his legs. They glided closer, slowly, savoring the suspense. He was a gambler. They would take his hands. But when they spoke, he knew it would be worse.

"Hello, lover boy."

31

TWO-WAY WONG'S spy inside Mackintosh Farquhar trembled at the Taipan's anger. The death of his son had obliterated even the pretense of humanity. Thank every god in the universe that someone else was to blame. The Taipan's face was harsh, his eyes bleak, his mouth hard and dark. Even his voice had changed, deep and hollow as the Shanghai gutters.

His long, tapered hands, normally still, played incessantly with a crude knife that lay on his desk. It appeared to be made from a sliver of sharpened metal with a handle formed by a wrapping of grass or rattan. The spy had heard it was the knife with which Two-Way Wong had eviscerated the beggar who had broken his legs when he was a child.

"I want," he said, "what her father gave her."

"We still don't know that he gave her anything, Taipan."

"At least one of her safe-deposit boxes contains rubbish. She would not think to fool me if she had nothing to hide."

"Yes, Taipan." How the old man had breached even one bank vault, the spy would never know.

A sudden inspiration leaped like fire in Two-Way's eyes. His savage expression hardened into satisfaction. "What I want you to do—what you will do—is persuade her that you can lead her to Party Leader Tang."

"Forgive me, Lao Yeh, but I can't."

"Victoria Mackintosh won't know that."

Hong Kong's last month of British rule had begun—although the
word *rule* had long been superseded in most minds by the equally
inaccurate term *protection*. The fear voiced among the expats was
that the Mainland might use the chaotic atmosphere as an excuse to
billet the People's Liberation Army in the city as a preventive mea-
sure. Allen Wei had been quoted repeatedly to the effect that Beijing had promised him no occupation, but the Colony was rife with
rumors that Premier Chen would order Wei to step down. The
name heard most often as his appointed successor was Sir John Wong
Li, who, it was joked in the clubs, would presumably drop the *Sir*.

"How's the headache?" asked Mary, tiptoeing into Vicky's darkened
bedroom.

Vicky, curled beneath the sheets with her hands between her
knees, sat up and turned on the light, wincing at the glare. "I'm all
right. I've got to get to work." It was midafternoon. She had lain
awake an hour, attempting to nap away a headache. "Oh, God, it's
actually worse than before. What's that you're holding?"

Mary flourished her treasure box of antique acupuncture needles.
"I thought maybe you'd want a massage or something. What's that
you're holding?"

Vicky closed her hand around the slip of paper she had carried
everywhere since Steven was killed. *Steven Wong say it okay*, her
Cantonese receptionist had printed. *He say he not mad.*

"Nothing."

Mary said, "Your neck hurts, too, doesn't it?"

"Yes, Doctor."

Her physician from Matilda Hospital had paid a visit to Peak
House. Gordon had examined her thoroughly, but his prescrip-
tion—"Get away from Hong Kong a while, dear; try Bali, or London,
or the North Pole"—indicated that he had diagnosed her condition

from the tabloid headlines. PLAYBOY CHOPPED had driven PROPERTY PANIC, STOCK CRASH, and LAST MONTH TO TURNOVER off the front pages. The shrill retellings of Steven's gruesome death had lasted three days until the collapse of several famous hongs and a small but exceptionally violent riot at lunch hour on Exchange Square reclaimed the media's attention.

Mary had come to the rescue. With Fiona and the girls gone, and Chip serving on riot duty, Peter's fiancée was suddenly her only friend. And quite a good friend at that. Now Vicky understood what she did for Peter, for Mary could refocus her hard ambition into an attentiveness almost maternal.

"I keep telling you, Vicky. You blame headaches on your concussion, but they're really from that awful tension. Lie down. Relax. Let Mary fix."

"There's nothing that needle can change for me." She wanted to read his message again. It was the closest she could come to the last moments of his life, and she replayed in her imagination Steven bursting off the elevator and turning on his charm to persuade MacF's receptionist to break the rules and act against her better judgment.

"You don't know what happened to him. You don't know why and you never will. Steven Wong played with the Triads for years. No one will ever know what went wrong."

"I went wrong," she said bleakly. "Vivian warned me and I didn't listen."

Mary, who had lent a sympathetic ear for days, suddenly fixed her with a hard stare. "Hey. You rather the mistake went the other way? You rather explain to Fiona where are her children?"

"No," Vicky whispered.

"You did the right thing. Sometimes I think you're Chinese. Forget him, Vicky. It's over. The little girls are safe in London and you've got a business to run." She drew a needle from her box. "Turn over. I want to try something new on your neck. I've only studied this. I've never done it with someone before."

"That's reassuring."

The needle, nine inches long—frightfully long—reminded her

of something. Mary hitched up her skirt to kneel over her. "Turn over and lie very still."

Vicky's gaze locked on the needle. Suddenly she got it.

"The picador!"

"What?"

"My father took me to the bullfights in Spain. I was eighteen. Mother went to the Ritz for tea and we went to the bullfights." She stopped. Mary was staring. "Madrid," Vicky explained. "We were in Madrid. In fact, we were staying at the Wellington, the bull-fighters' hotel. It's owned by the bull breeders. Anyway, we went to the bullring. Daddy knew someone, so we had just the right seats, not too far and definitely not too near. You don't want to sit too near. You see too much. The tourists always get seated too near, but Daddy knew someone."

"I never heard you refer to your father as Daddy."

"Well, that's what I called him, particularly when I was younger. What did you call yours?"

"Mine was killed when I was young."

"He was? I'm sorry . . . Peter never made that clear. . . . You see, the picadors weaken the bull by stabbing it from horseback with this long lance, like your needle. Only much longer, of course. It's really horrible. And seems so unfair. The matador doing all his fancy stuff—doing it to a wounded animal . . ." Vicky paused in mid-thought, her mind shuttling between past and present, as it had been since Steven had been killed. She thought of her father's boat sinking, drifting down to the sea bottom.

". . . We were stopping at the Wellington, where the bull-fighters stay. I got a terrible crush on this new young fighter. Suddenly, that evening after the fight, while Mummy and Daddy were having cocktails in the lobby, he walked in. Mary, he shone. He was so tall and skinny, with this great steel profile, and I was gone, head over heels. I would have run away with him to some mountain vil-lage and stayed there my whole life. Daddy noticed.

"Right away, he asked the hotel owner to introduce me to the matador. And . . . well, the guy, you know, shook my hand. And then he looked away, smiled at some girl who just walked in, and went over and chatted her up. I just stood there, feeling less than nothing. And my father saw the whole thing. . . . It was so embarrassing. Daddy didn't know what to say, I guess, and I certainly didn't. . . ."

"Turn over," said Mary.

"No. I'm fine. I want to go to work. Funny, haven't thought about that in years . . . Not true. I remembered it when Daddy died. It was so awful, his seeing me get totally rejected. I could have handled it if he hadn't been there to see. . . ."

"Let me do your neck."

"Were you always pretty, Mary?"

"I'm not pretty."

Vicky jumped off the bed, went to the window, and cracked the curtain on a hazy, murky day. She had felt tears coming, and didn't want Mary to see. But instead, a curious relief washed over her. "I suppose it could have been worse." She laughed softly. "It would have been even more humiliating if Hugo had been there."

She dabbed a knuckle at her eyes. "Oh, God, I miss Hugo. . . . If only Peter hadn't gone forward first, he'd have stayed snapped to the jackline." She climbed back onto her bed.

"It was not Peter's fault," Mary said firmly.

"Of course not. Just one of a million ifs. If Daddy hadn't stayed that course. If we hadn't gone at all. If we'd been sixty seconds earlier or later we'd have missed that rogue wave. . . ."

Her mind was jumping faster, going out of control. Where was Vivian? Vicky was now totally convinced that her father had been right, that Two-Way Wong and Premier Chen could and ought to be brought down by the evidence of their corruption. But Vivian Loh—her only contact with Party Leader Tang—had pulled another of her disappearing acts. She had not come to the office since the kidnappings. Nor had she returned Vicky's calls. Desperate, Vicky had gone three times to her apartment, but if Vivian was hiding at home, she was not answering her door.

"You know, Mary, I distinctly recall Peter talking about your father as if he were alive."

"I have a stepfather," Mary answered.

"In Sydney?"

"No. Los Angeles."

"What do you call him?"

"Lao Yeh."

"Doesn't that mean grandfather?"

"Or master. He's much older and we're a big family."

"Right," said Vicky, mindful of what Peter had called Mary's fantasy life. She wondered, still, about the diaphragm he had found. But Peter seemed at peace lately, so maybe they had worked something out they could both live with. And yet, all the deception did not sit well with Vicky.

"Have many more gone to Sydney?"

"We're taking another look at Singapore. Sydney is so far."

"From what?"

"China trade."

"I never understood, exactly, how your family trades in China if your grandfather was a Kuomintang general with a price on his head."

Mary stared hard. "There are ways. We're all Chinese, after all. In fact, since you mention it, I've been wondering if perhaps you would want our help in making contact with Party Leader Tang."

"I beg your pardon?" How did Mary know about her connection to Tang?

"We have people in Fukien Province who might be able to help."

"I'll keep that in mind, thank you. Right. Well, I'm getting up."

"No acupuncture?"

"No."

Mary waved her needle. "One minute. I'll have you back to work in a flash."

"So you can listen to my conversations from Peter's desk?"

Mary flushed. "What is that supposed to mean?"

"You're spying on me. You're using Peter as cover."

"Spying?" Mary Lee looked baffled. "For whom am I spying, may I ask?"

"Your family. How did you know I'm trying to meet Tang?"

"I swear to you, Vicky, I am not spying on you for my family."

"Then how did you know?"

"Peter told me you had some crazy idea about enlisting Tang's help to get the water turned on at Golden Expo."

"Peter's got a big mouth," Vicky snapped, feeling like a fool for trusting him to keep quiet. Thank God she had concocted the drinking-water excuse.

"And I'll tell you something else. You've just had your last massage." Mary opened the needle box, slipped the needle she was holding into it, and snapped it shut. "You're quite something, Vicky. I've propped your brother up for a year, delivered him back as a man who can help you run your hong, and you insult me. I know you're under a lot of pressure, but so am I. And I'm damned sorry you can't handle it, because you're tearing up what little there is left of this family. Shall I leave your brother to your tender care? Shall I retreat to Sydney too? Would you like that?"

"I'm sorry."

"Till next time. You're worse than your father. You think nothing of lashing out."

"I feel like a total fool. I'm really sorry. Can you accept my apology, Mary?"

Fukienese women were known to be both sensitive and proud, and Mary was no exception. "Screw you," she said, and stormed out. Her heels clattered down the stairs. The front door banged. Her Mercedes flung gravel as it tore through the gate and down the Peak.

Hating herself, Vicky got up and dressed. She had been so sure that someone in their circle had betrayed her father to Two-Way Wong. Someone must have told him he was meeting the red junk.

Vivian's neighbors, the Chins, across the hall in 17F, had moved out Monday. The Lis, below, were looking to sublet. Mr. Tong upstairs had posted a sign in the elevator that he had furniture for sale. If her building was any example, it seemed that every person who could was getting out, while those who couldn't, despaired.

She heard a sharp click in the wall—Nancy the bar girl, switching on her bathroom light. Nancy had developed some special relationships with PRC ministry officials and was staying.

Vivian was not. It was quite dismaying—and impossible to comprehend fully—but her soon-to-be-born child had undermined her resolve to stick with Hong Kong. Sharpening her mind in interesting times suddenly seemed an indulgence. She felt herself buffeted by conflicting emotions. She blamed biology for her fear, and the cloying sense of practicality that accompanied it. But she sensed that something deeper she could not yet put her finger on was driving her from her home.

She owned her apartment, which had been a secure feeling until the Ching-Cathay crash. Now it was a drag on her. Even selling at a loss was no longer an option; there were no buyers. She would simply have to walk away from it and hope some PRC cadre made a decent offer in a few years. She had decided to leave her furnishings intact. The spirit walls and mirrors and door guards would be desecrated, disassembled. Perhaps her ying bik and her altars would snare a Communist buyer who had somehow regained traditional values. She would leave Tin Hau for him. But she would take the little porcelain statue of the goddess of mercy. Auntie Chen had given it to her, and she would someday want to pass it on to the daughter who had grown heavy in her body. She was rolling Kuan Yin in bubble plastic when they buzzed from the lobby. A little stab of anxiety invaded her belly.

Ordinarily she would ignore the call, but she was expecting the shippers to pick up her clothing, her Fragrant Harbor silk screen, and her office gear. Or it might even be her car to the airport, early. It was neither.

"The yellow-haired gweipo has come again," the doorman informed her in Cantonese. "Should I send her away?"

"I'm not at home."

A moment later, the doorman buzzed again.

"A thousand pardons, but the yellow-haired gweipo has given me one hundred dollars to ask again. And so I am asking."

"Tell her—"

Thinly, through the phone, she heard Vicky: "Please, Vivian. Just please talk to me."

Vivian imagined her in the foyer, straining over the doorman's shoulder, jostled by people coming and going. "Please." Then, miracle of miracles: "I want to apologize."

Vivian was astonished.

"What I tell her? Home or not home?"

"Home," Vivian sighed. "Send her up."

Thank God she hadn't packed up the kitchen. She could offer tea. She filled the kettle and put it on the stove to boil. Then she opened the draperies. If she was letting Vicky Mackintosh in, she might as well admit the rest of the city. There was smoke over North Point. More street fighting, she assumed.

She opened the door when she heard the elevator *ding* in the hall. "This way," she called.

Duncan's daughter looked sad and weary. Closer, passing under an overhead light, her cheeks appeared gaunt, which made her startling blue eyes look as big as the sea. She had been crying.

They exchanged thin smiles.

"Come in."

Vicky entered like a cat, alert and tentative, clearing the traditional high sill of the inner door with a daintiness Vivian envied. For a month she had been waddling like a goose. Vicky's quick gaze flickered over the furniture, then came to a halt on the packing boxes.

"You're moving?"

"Canada."

"You're not serious. When?"

"This afternoon. Would you care for green tea?"

Vicky looked stunned. "Yes, thank you."

Vivian went to brew it. Vicky followed, trailing close behind her. "Vivian. I've come for your help."

Vivian was suddenly tired of pushy gweilos.

"I thought you said you had come to apologize."

●   ●   ●

Vicky felt the spirit slide out of her like a falling tide.

If talented, proud, and ambitious Chinese like Vivian Loh abandoned Hong Kong, then the British Crown Colony would degenerate into just another overcrowded Asian city. What, she was about to ask, had ever happened to "sharpen the mind"?

Before she could, she remembered the hurt that preceded the anger on Mary's face. Bold and forthright, Vicky had been dead wrong, and it would be a long time before Peter's girlfriend forgave her.

She took a second look at Vivian. Beneath the flat calm — above her air of resignation — the woman was suffering. For if she, a gweipo, was shocked that Vivian had decided to give up and emigrate, Vivian had to be in a sea of pain, regret, and confusion.

"I'm sorry you're leaving. It must have been a hard decision."

"Forgive me, but I find your sorrow hard to believe."

Vicky took a deep breath, acutely aware that stifling the habit of a lifetime — an instinct to lash back — demanded moment-by-moment vigilance. She had learned from her father how to fight; she would have to teach herself how to listen.

"I *am* sorry you're leaving. Hong Kong needs people like you." She took another breath, counting heartbeats, while she gathered the courage to get nearer the truth. "And frankly, I suspect that in some weird way I'm going to miss you. I mean, you have a kind of . . . clarity." She smiled, pleased she had found the right word. "A clarity I envy. I hope that what I did . . . what I did to Steven, did not influence your decision."

Vivian forgave her, obliquely. "Perhaps what you did to Steven came from a sort of Hong Kong state of mind. We are all frightened and confused. And even a British taipan's daughter is not immune to chaos."

"But you've always fought against chaos. What changed your mind — if you don't mind my asking? Why are you leaving?"

Vivian scattered green tea leaves in two cups, closed the tin, and put it, after a moment's reflection, in the refrigerator. The water was taking the gods' own time to boil.

"For ten years — no, thirteen," she answered, "since the Joint

Declaration, I've argued with young couples who say that it's different with a child. That when you have children, you don't dare count
on the kindness of Beijing. Better to emigrate. The children can
always come back if things work out in a couple of decades. Every
time I heard that, I told them it was an excuse. I was wrong. It *is*
different with a child. Do you know why?"

Vicky shook her head.

"Here's how you think when you're pregnant, Vicky. Not only
the obvious fear—will my body be safe?—but this: What will I say
when she is twenty-one, and we're living in a slum like Shanghai
and the schools are a joke and there is no work and the boys she
meets are beaten down by the daily nothingness of a dying system,
and she asks, 'Mother, why didn't you get out when you could?' "

Vicky saw Vivian's eyes glisten with tears. She reached to comfort her, but Vivian retreated.

"I hate this," the Chinese woman wept. "I hate leaving my home.
But exciting times are for adults, Vicky. Not children. Would you
ask your sister to pay the price?"

"But she *will* be my sister. Her father *was* British. You can get
out any time, if things turn so bad."

"You're presuming a benevolent, rational Beijing."

"But my sister—your daughter—can be a British subject if you
want her to be."

"British protection is not quite what it used to be."

Vivian placed her hand on the kettle handle and waited silently
until the water bubbled. She poured it into the cups and covered
them. There were more reasons to abandon her home.

"It's not only Beijing I fear. My baby has a crueler enemy here
in Hong Kong."

"I don't understand."

"Two-Way Wong."

"What are you talking about?"

"He hated your father. And now—forgive me for saying this—
but in his mind, at least, you killed his son."

Vicky flinched.

"Two-Way Wong will do anything in his power to destroy Duncan Mackintosh's daughters. Both of them. Now do you understand why I cannot stay in Hong Kong?"

Vicky shook her head. "With all he's got going, and this daft dream of his to be the PRC's governor, do you really think he'll go to the trouble to kill a child?"

"He won't kill. He'll destroy by slow death. He'll see to it that Duncan Mackintosh's daughter grows up in misery. I can't let that happen."

She put the cups on a lacquered tray and carried them into the living room. Vicky followed. Vivian knelt on the floor and resumed rolling her statuette of Kuan Yin in bubble wrap.

Vicky said, "Forgive me, Vivian. But even with what happened to Steven—and I wish to God I had listened to you—I think that in this instance you're being awfully paranoid, awfully . . ."

"Chinese?" asked Vivian.

"All right, if that conveys the meaning of too much imagination."

"But you forget that so is Two-Way Wong 'awfully Chinese.' "

32

VICKY'S GAZE lingered on Vivian's rounded belly. The woman's vulnerability humbled her, for she doubted that, even unencumbered, she would have taken the chances on the Mainland that Vivian had already.

Vivian looked up, blinking tears. "I feel such a terrible sense of loss. I know I've given up, and I can't stop myself." She fumbled with the bubble wrap, her hands clumsy. Vicky knelt beside her with the cellotape, wondering how on earth she would ever get to Tang without Vivian's help.

"I'll take you to the airport."

"I've already ordered a car."

"Please, let me take you. Hey, we'll go on the new launch. Come on. By water is a much better way to leave Hong Kong. Fonder memories than a smelly car ride . . . Please, let me. You'll tell my sister we went together."

Vivian couldn't tear her eyes from the silver towers that rimmed the harbor. The buildings shone, even in the watery sunlight filtered by the thick, hot June haze. She suddenly recalled the first time she saw them from the Star Ferry while her mother chatted up an American sailor.

With blinding clarity, Vivian finally understood what was driving her from Hong Kong. Every word she had told Vicky was true, but not the whole truth. For she had a unique bond with her baby that transcended their biological knot, a bond forged in her promise that her child would never wake up wondering when she would see her mother again. She could not let her passionate pursuit of principle—her single-minded commitment to a free Hong Kong in a New China—scar her baby's life the way her mother's greedy passions had scarred hers.

Vicky was leaning on the rail beside her. "Beautiful, isn't it? Hard to believe things are so bad."

Vivian blinked at her tears. Great cities were always beautiful from a distance. Even Shanghai, spied up the river, looked enchanting. People like her father and grandfather and Ma Binyan and herself, who tried to change things for the better, were cursed with a peculiar nearsightedness. She felt like a traitor.

"Vivian? Is it possible for you—once you're in Canada—to put me in touch with Ma Binyan? Maybe he could help me get to Tang."

"I can, but he can't," she answered dully. "Ma Binyan is out of Tang's circle. He lost his place because he failed to deliver your father's evidence. Tang has moved on."

Vicky's last hope died. "Does that mean you . . ." Her voice trailed off.

"Ma Binyan was my original contact with Tang, but Tang developed a certain . . . appreciation for me. He calls me a Shanghai Woman."

"That's a serious compliment."

"Ordinarily, yes, but maybe not with Tang. He's begun to lose his taste for frankness from his supporters. I'm afraid he finds strength irritating when it questions him. I've lost my faith in leaders, Vicky. More important are systems to protect us from leaders."

"But how do you change things without leaders?"

"I don't know."

At the airport pier Vicky walked Vivian down the red-carpeted gangway and into the luxurious, but empty, hotel lobby. A Rolls-Royce waited to shuttle passengers to their airline terminal. By unspoken mutual consent, they shook hands. Having refused to bring Vicky to Tang, Vivian felt impelled to give her something. She offered to write letters of introduction to her many "old friends" in Shanghai factories, and promised to serve MacF as a consultant whenever Vicky wished.

Alone and lonely, Vicky tried to force her thoughts to business as the MacF Golden Airport Hotel launch sped her back across the harbor to Hong Kong Island.

The opulent *Inverness* was decked out in the red-and-gold house colors of the old Farquhar Line. Patterned after the long, sleek Chinese dragon boat, and decorated with an exuberant dragon-head bowsprit, it skimmed the water on nearly silent turbines. Ah Chi, whom Vicky had hired as number-one captain, was dripping in enough gold braid to shame the commodore of the *QE2*. His two mates, and the four anxious hostesses in red-and-gold cheongsams, looked relieved to be working at last.

Vicky was the only passenger; the government had still not granted a license to operate a Lantau-Central ferry service. Back at the pier the *Dundee* waited, similarly outfitted and fully crewed, ready to sail the instant Vicky managed to break the bureaucratic impasse, which was, of course, directly related to the PRC grab at the Expo Golden Hotel.

Any leverage she had hoped to secure by threatening to embarrass the Mainlanders with derelict buildings on Turnover Day had been lost in the property crash, because MacF—like countless other hongs—was so overextended with its creditors that banks controlled or influenced by the PRC could pressure MacF to accept any buyout terms Wu demanded.

The best Vicky could hope for was to close a bad deal within a week, surrendering Expo in exchange for the ferry permit. Meanwhile, the *Lewiston* and *Loch Inver* were undergoing final fit in an Apleichau junk builder, and when all four launches were joined by *Fort William*, *Invermoriston*, *Milton*, and *Glen Affric*, MacF would offer a boat between the airport hotel and Central or Kowloon every quarter hour.

The one bright spot in MacF's picture was Golden Air Freight. Having taken delivery of the first half-dozen Antropov 250s and secured landing rights and loading bays in the United States, Golden Air Freight had begun to ferry enormous cargoes out of Shanghai. And yet even here the price had been crushing debt, and Vicky was reminded of Hugo's apprehension that the PRC could shut them down with a phone call.

One of the young hostesses clustered around the boat's communications console, where telephones and market indexes were available to passengers, ripped a sheet from the fax machine, and brought it to her. The hostess looked panicked. Vicky scanned the sheet—several rows of artistically brushed Chinese characters under Allen Wei's official letterhead. "What is this? *Top Secret?* . . . This is daft."

"It say British take Hong Kong Gold, Taipan."

"What Hong Kong gold?"

Her beeper went off. She dialed her office. Peter answered. "Where are you?"

"In the harbor on *Inverness.*"

"Have you seen the fax?"

"It's some sort of forgery. It makes no sense."

"You'd better go to the airport. You're too late to make it home to the Peak."

Vicky felt a chill. Riots. But she was not about to flee to the airport. She thought quickly. The fact was, the launch had as complete a communications center as any building in the city. "Send the Chinese home," she ordered. "And bring our Brits to the Yacht Club. I'll meet you there. You're not safe in MacF House."

BOOK FIVE

The Hong Kong Woman

33

A NIGHT OF CARNAGE erupted simultaneously on either side of Victoria Harbour. The fraudulent fax "leak" had been timed exquisitely, after bank hours, promising all who feared for their savings a night of frustration and worry. Looters attacked the Golden Mile shopping stretch along the Nathan Road, while an angry mob, Hong Kong-side, marched on Government House, where Allen Wei was hosting a cocktail party for three dozen local chieftains of global corporations and their wives.

Chants echoed through the enclave of older buildings, churches, and gardens, as frantic office workers, shopgirls, and cooks' helpers climbed the steep and narrow roads from Central District demanding that the governor reopen the banks so they could cash gold certificates and empty safe-deposit boxes.

With the effects of the Ching-Cathay Tower crash still provoking unrest, security at Government House was intense. The gates were barricaded. And an awesome detachment of British Gurkha troops camped visibly on the lawn, part of a carefully rehearsed emergency plan for helicopter evacuation of the chief executive, his staff, and their defenders. An elderly Royal Navy helicopter carrier wallowed discreetly over the horizon in the South China Sea, with rescue craft and fresh Gurkhas. But the planners had not reckoned with forthright Allen Wei.

The chief executive stopped in the middle of an informal speech reminding his corporate guests that Hong Kong's International Exposition—due to open July 1 on Kai Tak under the banner "Hong Kong Shows The World"—could benefit from some additional cash contributions. The chants had been growing louder, and now it was obvious several thousand people were right outside.

"Excuse me a moment."

Wei pushed boldly past his guards and stomped across the grass to confront the crowd face-to-face through his iron fence. Snatching a portable megaphone from the anxious British officer trotting alongside, he let the mob have it in scornful gutter Cantonese.

"This rumor is pig-shit. The fax is a fake! The Brits don't want your fornicating gold, and if they did I wouldn't let them have it. Your gold and my gold is right here in Hong Kong, safe as the emperor's whore."

A full soda can sailed through the fence. It caught him square in the face and he toppled backward, falling hard and striking his temple on the butt of a Gurkha's assault rifle. For a second everyone was frozen, staring at his body sprawled on the grass with his jacket splayed open, his red tie tacked to his shirt like a wound.

Debby, his assistant, ran to him and knelt over him in her yellow cheongsam. Something in the tragic stillness of her bent shoulders was misinterpreted by the crowd: They believed he was dead. And when she kissed his lips with joy that he was only stunned, those at a distance saw a futile attempt to revive him by mouth-to-mouth resuscitation.

Shocked, the people simply walked away, trickling down the hill, leaving his teenage assailant alone and mute. The police arrested him, and Allen Wei was bundled into an ambulance, protesting mightily that all he had was a headache.

Things went much harder in the Nathan Road.

When he saw the first fax copy, Chip had predicted the trouble would center in the Golden Mile because of all the gold and jewelry shops. There was always an element, regardless of race, that would reason if someone was stealing their gold they had best steal someone else's gold. And many in the Colony who had no gold at all stood ready to seize unexpected good joss.

Three thugs commandeered a bus and rammed the shatterproof windows of the richest shop in the street. The honest and the timid ran for cover. Looters poured into the breached store, battling clerks, security guards, and one another for chains, rings, bracelets, and trendy gift ingots. In seconds, scores became hundreds became thousands — fanning out across the broad street, smashing windows and stealing the treasures inside. MTR trains delivered thousands more from the outlying New Towns. A torrent of the young and poor welled up from the Tsim Sha Tsui and Jordan stations, for the rumor had traveled far and fast.

The police had gone to "Force Standby" — a warning of a serious threat to law and order — the instant they received the gold fax. The commissioner upgraded it to "Force Mobilization." Chip and his mates in the Royal Hong Kong Police Tactical Unit were already on standby riot duty. He was second-in-command of his four-platoon company, the First Kowloon. Then, incredibly, in the middle of the company commander's briefing, while the radios were crackling out the first reports of looting and burning, a bunch of blokes from ICAC, the Independent Commission Against Corruption, marched into the briefing room and arrested the First Platoon commander on charges of masterminding a nightclub extortion scheme.

Jaws dropped, but no one, not even the company commander, balked when the bloody fool was carted off in handcuffs. The company commander — a recently promoted Chinese superintendent six years younger than Chip — "asked" whether Chip would mind filling in by stepping down to platoon command. Chip agreed, although taking charge of forty men in a street battle did not have the same appeal it had had when he was younger and routinely volunteered for that sort of work. There were less-senior Chinese chief inspectors the superintendent could have asked, and Chip once again congratulated himself on his decision to buy his boat.

•   •   •

Three whistle blasts accompanied the platoon sergeant's "Fall in!" Chip watched from the upstairs briefing room as his men lined up. They wore riot helmets, batons, holsters, and pouches, and each had a gas mask slung over his shoulder in a sack. The eight men of his First Section laid down their rattan shields and double-timed to the armory. Sections Two, Three, and Four followed, returning with Federal one-and-a-half-inch pistols, tear gas, wooden bullets, pump Remington shotguns, and three AR-15s, while the less heavily burdened First Section men—who had drawn only revolvers and twelve rounds—loaded reserve ammunition into the platoon's transport, a pair of dark-blue trucks and a Land Rover.

When they had done, Chip descended from the briefing room and gave the order to board. His men ran a prescribed route to their assigned seats—two sections per truck. Chip sat beside the Land Rover driver, with the platoon's sergeant and orderly behind him. The little column raced into the street, five minutes from the Nathan Road. The company's other platoons disappeared along different routes, swallowed up by the narrow streets.

Chip turned around for a look at the stolid sergeant, a Cantonese built like an armored train, and his gloomy platoon orderly—a man he would be depending upon when things heated up. "What's eating you, Mr. Lee?"

"The fornicating NYPD turned me down."

"New York's loss."

"Now I got nowhere to emigrate."

"Not to worry. You'll go far in Hong Kong."

"I don't want to go far in Hong Kong, Chief Inspector. My girl's got a translator job with the UN."

"I've seen her," growled the sergeant. "Girl like that'll grind your jade shaft into a Shanghai noodle. Much easier life with an ugly woman. Isn't that right, Chief Inspector?"

"Better grub, too," Chip agreed.

The orderly was unhappy enough to be rude. "Don't you miss your English widow, sir?"

The sergeant looked ready to slap Orderly Lee's teeth out, but

Chip just smiled. Try to keep a secret from the Chinese. "Yes. I sympathize."

"Well, that's how I feel about my girl. Not to mention the other drawbacks, stuck in Hong Kong."

The men fell silent. Chip knew what they were thinking. The orderly had raised the real issue troubling every Chinese on the force. The police were already outcasts among their own people, tending to cluster in PC-only housing estates. But where would they be if the Mainlanders purged the police force, as persistent rumor had that they would? Alone. Without a warrant card. On streets with long memories.

A steady stream of taxicabs raced out of the area as the column neared the Nathan Road. With blue lights flashing and sirens howling, they rounded the last corner. Good Christ, thought Chip. There must be ten thousand of them. From a distance the mass seemed to ripple like wind on a rice paddy.

"Stop there," he told the driver, indicating an intersection some 150 yards from the crowd. The other platoons would be approaching from side streets. "Here! Carry on, Orderly."

Mr. Lee jumped down with his automatic rifle and took his post forward of the door, facing the crowd, scanning the street and the rooftops. A great throng was surging in and out of gutted shops, blocking the road from sidewalk to sidewalk. Shouts, the crash of breaking glass, and a throaty drone rose from its midst.

When the orderly declared their position safe, Chip—following procedure to the letter—stepped down behind him, and faced the trucks. "De-bus."

"*Lok che.*" The platoon sergeant ran back, repeating the order in Cantonese and guarding the tail of the rear truck with a shotgun. The men scrambled down and formed up in front of the column in four lines of eight men each. The heavily armed Fourth Section loaded rifles and shotguns and faced the trucks, guarding their rear, while the first three sections faced the crowd.

Section One, in front, was the arrest section. Chip stood immediately behind those eight men. His height gave him a clear view over the heads of the Chinese PCs. He was flanked by his second-in-command and the unhappy Mr. Lee, both of whom carried rifles and scanned the rooftops—a crenellated maze half-hidden behind a forest of neon. Behind them were Sections Two and Three with tear gas and wooden bullets, and behind them, the firearms of Section Four, guarding their only means of escape.

The crowd had noticed them. In the half-minute the platoon had taken to get down from the trucks and form their lines, the drone had exploded into a full-throated roar.

Light was fading from the rainy evening sky. The huge over-head neon signs, suffused by drizzle and fog, painted the wet street red. Chip registered the strange absence of cars and taxis. Far back in the crowd he could see a bus angled into a building. Otherwise there were only people, a solid mass a hundred feet wide from build-ing to building, beginning to edge toward the platoon.

He lifted his battery-powered bullhorn, which hung from a lan-yard around his neck, and his amplified voice clattered off the build-ings. "Disperse! Disperse peacefully."

Orderly Lee raised a banner, which spelled the disperse order in large Chinese characters, and translated through his bullhorn, as he would each of Chip's English orders. *"Chin bin yan kwan wo! Ping saan hoi!"*

Chip had been a cop his entire adult life, and his training was rigorous and regularly updated. But it was still astonishing to see ten thousand people edging toward you, shouting bloody murder. He repeated the disperse order, and Orderly Lee translated again: *". . . Ping saan hoi."*

"By the center, quick march!"

Bearing their guns at high port, the platoon charged forward, stamping their boots on the pavement and appearing to cover more ground than they actually did. Chip let them go fifteen yards and called, "Halt!"

The crowd, recoiling at first, surged forward again as soon as the police had stopped. They were getting too close, catcalling, hurling bricks, feeding their fury. The daring of a Chinese mob was an awe-

some thing. Nor could one forget eight years ago in Peking that
this race had fought tanks with bare hands.

". . . *Ping saan hoi.*"

When Chip first came out to Hong Kong, an elderly British
police sergeant who had served the Queen in Rhodesia, Aden, and
Singapore, had addressed his class at the anti-riot training school.
He had probably been no older than forty-five, Chip realized now—
a big, bulky fellow with a Yorkshire roar, gin-bright cheeks, a crisp
uniform that somehow never wilted in the humid heat, and a scarred
baton with which he beat his palm for emphasis.

"Your mob," he'd thundered, "is distinguished from your lawful
crowd by the fact that its members have lost their sense of values"—
rap with the baton—"no longer respect the law"—*rap*—"nor fear
the law's consequences." *Rap*.

"Your mob's members go temporarily insane, together."

He had paused, looked out over the assembled sunburned young
faces, and continued in a conspiratorially modulated tone: "Isolated,
your average bloke—be he British or even Chinese—may be a cultivated individual. In your mob, he becomes a barbarian.

"The job of the police—your job, lads—is to remind this temporarily demented creature that he is an individual. Individuals know
they feel pain, bleed, and do not enjoy the night in jail. In a word,
lads, disperse." *Rap*. "Disperse the collective mind of the mob and
you will disperse the body." He'd paused again, caressed the baton
with his sausage fingers, and chuckled. "Of course, lads, sometimes
conditions force us to disperse the bodies first, in which event, their
minds will eventually follow. . . ."

"Fit gas masks," Chip ordered.

"*Daai fong kuk min gui.*"

Each constable in each section had a number, one to eight. Odd-
numbered men remained on guard. Even numbers put on their gas
masks, then guarded for odd. Orderly Lee covered Chip before don-
ning his own. Chip ordered up Section Two. On the command of
their section sergeant, they stepped beside the men of the arrest
section, loaded their Federal one-and-a-halves with tear gas, and
marched four paces ahead of the platoon.

"Disperse or we use smoke!"

A barrage of bricks and bottles greeted Orderly Lee's translation. The range was shorter, and the missiles fell close ahead in the road.

"Section Two, high angle. Pre*sent*!"

As the wind was in the platoon's face, Chip wanted the tear gas blown over the crowd from behind. It was equally important to disperse the back of the crowd so the people in front had somewhere to retreat. He and his second-in-command checked the elevations at which the Section Two men were aiming their pistols. "Get it up, Number Seven . . . Right . . . *Fire!*"

The guns banged, and the gas canisters arced high over the hanging neon and dropped lazily into the depths of the crowd. The constables reloaded. A truck guard ran forward and gathered the spent shells in a sack.

Columns of white smoke funneled up from the dense, dark mass. The brisk wind spread it rapidly, like clouds in quick time. Forming billows of cumulus in the center, thinning to mare's-tails at the edges, the tear gas pushed the crowd back nearly two hundred yards.

"Advance!"

The platoon broke into a dead run to make up the two hundred yards, faster and lighter-burdened men streaming ahead of the slower until the disciplined lines had become ragged.

"Halt!"

They stopped and re-formed perfect lines. Again Chip ordered the mob to disperse, and again Lee waved his banner and translated to Chinese. Another hail of thrown objects clattered onto the street.

"Look there, sir."

"I see it."

A missile had landed amid the bricks and stones, a paint can filled with concrete from which a short length of pipe protruded as a throwing handle. They were simple to make, but one didn't simply run up a batch and dash to the riot. The concrete had to cure overnight, which demanded some planning ahead.

They were getting too close, again.

"Section Two. By the high angle. Present . . . *Fire!*"

The smoke lofted through the neon, billowed, and spread too quickly. The wind was getting stronger. *"Fire."*

"Disperse."

"Chin bin yan kwan wo! Ping saan hoi!"

The mob roared its defiance.

"Fire! . . . Advance . . . Halt!" Fifty yards was the most he could take. Watching over the heads of his tear-gas section and his still-useless arrest section, Chip thought that if anything, the mob had grown denser. The other platoons ought to have reached the Nathan Road by now, which suggested they, too, had met resistance, and for some time each could expect to fight on its own.

"Shall we ring up for reinforcements, sir?" asked his heretofore silent second-in-command.

"We're all right for the moment," Chip answered casually, putting the man at ease. "Smoke section. By the high angle. Present. *Fire!"*

The Nathan Road looked as if a fog bank had rolled in from the sea. The gas hung over the crowd, rolled in front of it until Chip's platoon lost sight of them. When the wind dispersed it, the crowd was stumbling back, running fast to get away, dispersing down the many side streets and alleys.

"Advance!"

They belted forward again, Chip running full-out, megaphone banging his chest, holster flapping, and sweat pouring under the hot mask, through which enough tear gas had managed to seep to sting his eyes and burn his nose and throat.

"Halt!"

Chip ordered the smoke section back in line behind him. That put the arrest section in the lead again, positioned to nail the last hangers-on when the mob broke up, and ready to break into columns to send up alleys and into buildings to restore peace. The mob continued falling back.

He was about to order another short advance to put the fear of God in them without using more tear gas, when a rumor ran through the street that the Chinese governor, Allen Wei, had been killed by British troops. The story spread, embellished by provocateurs feeding on the crowd's deep sense of betrayal, and like any good fiction, it developed a rich logic of its own: The British had sent troops to guard a gold convoy which was to be loaded aboard a British destroyer at the Old Queens Pier. Allen Wei had had second thoughts about this thievery and ordered it stopped. "It is Chinese gold," he was heard to have protested, "not Britain's. Give it back to the Chinese people of Hong Kong." A tall blond gweilo officer struck him down, and the short, swarthy Gurkhas beat him with rifle butts. Allen Wei had died for his Chinese brethren.

"What are they chanting?"

"British killed Governor Wei."

"Tell them Governor Wei is alive and in hospital."

Lee translated, unheeded by the roaring crowd.

The wind brought sudden rain—great gusts of water that sluiced tear gas off the burning skin—and quite suddenly the mob was back in business.

"*Disperse.*"

"*Chin bin yan kwan wo!*"

"Smoke section forward. Low angle, present. *Fire . . . Fire.*"

"It's not holding them, sir."

"I ruddy well see that!" Chip snapped, and the second-in-command, who had known him ten years, was amazed to discover that the cool Englishman had blood in his veins. "Number Three section up!"

"*Daai saam!*" called the Section Three sergeant. "*Daai saam section yap daan.*" They loaded wooden bullets, and moved ahead of the tear-gas section. Chip, his second, and his orderly followed, maintaining their position directly behind the new front line.

Chip raised his bullhorn. "Disperse or we use greater force!"

Orderly Lee translated.

A hush descended on the riot-torn road. Faces glared from broken windows and gutted shops. "Tell 'em again. Disperse or we use greater force."

"*Saan hoi fau . . .*"

"Here they come."

A wall of running men, backed by another and another and another, charged the police. "Good Christ," muttered Chip, less afraid for himself than awed by their reckless courage. The old sergeant had had it right. Ten thousand people had gone insane and left fear behind.

"Number Three, low angle, present."

"Daai saam section, daai kok do, miu jun." Orderly Lee's voice rose to an hysterical high pitch.

Eight Chinese constables leveled their Federal one-and-a-halves at the charging mob.

"Fire."

A single loud retort as they fired at once, and a low moan shivered from the running mass. Eight holes appeared in the wall as if punched there by giant fists. Bodies fell and men fell over them, but the wall kept moving. Bricks and bottles and homemade concrete missiles began pelting the front line of the platoon. The police reloaded.

"Fire," Chip ordered.

Another single bang, a little ragged this time, and again a terrible moan as the front line absorbed the lead-weighted wooden bullets like a living sponge.

A barrage of bottles and rocks lofted into the police ranks. A Section Three man went down. The truck guard who had earlier collected spent tear-gas shells darted forward and dragged him away. Chip stepped into the breach for a better look.

"Sir! The roof."

He looked up. High atop a six-story building, just ahead of the platoon, a shadow leaned out and flared to life as he ignited the fuse of a Molotov cocktail.

"Shoot that man!"

The rifle leapt to Orderly Lee's shoulder. Chip waited for the crack of the gunshot and the man to fall. *"Go on, Lee. Shoot him!"*

It was impossible to tell exactly what was going through Orderly Lee's mind, but Chip could guess. A week from now, with a PRC purge of the formerly Royal Hong Kong Police in full swing, did Police Constable Lee want a dead Chinese rioter directly linked to his AR-15? It was one thing to fire wooden bullets at a faceless mob, quite another to stand alone and be counted.

"Number Two. Shoot him."

Chip's second-in-command, who was scanning the opposite roofs, as he should, whirled and snapped a wild shot. He missed, and the petrol bomb arced out of the sky with a flaming tail.

34

THE BOMB, a brandy bottle filled with gasoline and capped with a burning rag, exploded at Chip's feet and splashed liquid fire on him and the seven remaining men of the wooden-bullet section. The truck guards raced forward with fire extinguishers. Flames were leaping off Chip's uniform, blinding him. His men were screaming. He couldn't see, but he could hear and almost feel, through the hot pain, the press of the mob running at him.

"Number Four section up!" he cried, his voice barely audible. The flames were sucking the air out of his lungs.

He felt the firearms section brush past him. Someone tried to guide him back from the front line. He fought to stand, to keep his place. *"Fire!"*

The rifles crackled and then the pump shotguns opened up with an earsplitting roar. He couldn't see and he couldn't breathe. Fire seared his lungs. The shotguns boomed again, echoing like thunder against the gutted buildings of the Golden Mile. *"Fall back!"* he heard his second order. Too late. The mob was on them, their feet shaking the ground.

Two-Way Wong watched his city burn.

Columns of smoke rose each dawn from Tsim Sha Tsui, from North Point, from Mong Kok, blackened the sky and drifted north to China. The tourists fled first, emptying the hotels that had been enjoying a pre-Turnover curiosity boom. Extrapolating from figures at the many hotels he owned, Two-Way Wong estimated an exodus of 400,000, not counting the diverted cruise ships. Ocean Terminal was deserted. Longstanding room reservations for the last week in June and the first in July — Turnover Week, as the brochures had it — were unlikely to be honored, his managers reported, despite fifty-percent deposits.

The world media had focused relentlessly on the riot-torn city. No one near a television set could be unaware of the ferocity of the mobs, or the hopeless resignation of the law-abiding. Those Hong-kongers with any documentation to get aboard an aircraft, a ship, or even a train through China, wanted out. Those who couldn't get out wished they were dead. Every overseas newscast ended with the camera panning pathetic lines of people begging for visas from the U.S., Canadian, and Australian consulates, while a picture that would live in memory showed a young woman with children, kneeling in front of the fortified British consulate, praying in the midst of a crowd of people hurling stones.

Two-Way Wong took particular pleasure in the fact that Hong Kong's famous Noon Day Gun, the symbol of British culture, was flanked by heavy tripod-mounted machine guns manned by expat officers wearing flak vests. The space in front of the Police Officers Club was deep in coils of razor wire, all of which made irresistible television footage for the news teams cruising by on the Gloucester Road.

It was almost too easy. He suspected that had he done nothing, neither faked the gold fax nor employed Triads to foment anger, the anger would have exploded anyway. He might have saved the trouble. But the point, of course, had been to control the timing. And that he had.

By the third day, rumors swept Hong Kong that PRC troops were massing at the border. Twenty-four hours later the People's Liberation Army made it official. Northern regiments — not Cantonese — were poised to invade the Colony if the trouble didn't cease. At that point, expats who had lived and worked in Hong Kong for a lifetime began packing emergency bags. It had, after all, been only eight years since the Beijing massacre. Entrepreneurs, Two-Way Wong was informed, were selling stockpiled airline seats at triple price, provoking a sudden boom in counterfeit tickets.

Shuttling between his office windows, his Chou bell, and the telephones on his teak desk, Two-Way waited until he sensed the moment turning right. It was rather like cooking in a wok, he thought. The important thing was to ready the ingredients for the instant the oil was hottest. The cooking itself was done in a flash.

"Bring Mr. Wu of the Overseas Labor Committee."

Driving hard on his cane, he rushed back to the windows. He could see two typhoon shelters from his tower, Kowloon's Yau Ma Tei and the floating city the Tanka shared with the Royal Hong Kong Yacht Club at Causeway Bay. Every junk, yacht, and sampan, he was told, had provisioned for ocean passage.

Since the streets were not safe enough for gathering at a church, and John Chypwood-Chipworth's two clubs sat side by side on the heavily guarded little peninsula called Kellet Island, his friends at the Yacht Club trooped across the parking lot for a memorial service with his friends at the Police Officers Club. The police were grim, having lost others in the past three days and holding no guarantee they wouldn't lose more.

The sailors were stunned. Many were anxious for their homes and families, having been unable to go home since the fighting began, and few could quite grasp the extent of the chaos overwhelming the city. No one knew exactly what to say about Chip. Vicky rose to speak, listing his qualities of ease and steadiness, noting each had served him well as a sailor and a policeman, and finally quoting her father that Chip was "a hell of a foredeckman." It was singularly unsatisfying, but what was there to say about a man dying in the line of duty when the future had ended?

It was left to Mary Lee, of all people, to deliver a deep and feeling epitaph, after the ceremony, when they had returned to the Yacht Club verandah in the vain hope of finding a cooling breeze. "Chip was," Mary said, "the most courteous gweilo I've ever known."

An icy glance in Vicky's direction indicated where Mary placed the Taipan of MacF on that scale, but Vicky just nodded sad agreement. Chip had seemed such an innocent, despite his work. Grace, she thought, must be the ability to do what must be done without being hardened by the deed. She wished she had said that at the memorial.

"To Chip," said Peter, raising a glass of Coke. She had not seen him take a drink since the riots began, yet another reminder of how badly she had misjudged Mary. Vicky raised her own Coke, which was warm. The club's refrigeration and air conditioning were on the fritz and repairmen were scarce in Causeway Bay, where a pathetic crowd had laid siege to the typhoon shelter. So far, they were orderly, a gathering of men, women, and children pleading with Tanka fishermen for passage away from Hong Kong.

They offered gold, jade, computer software secrets, daughters, wives, small boys. No one knew where they wanted to go, other than far away before the Red Chinese Army took the streets. Rumors swept the Colony: Vietnam would refuse refugees in revenge for the treatment their own refugees received in Hong Kong in the late 1980s; Singapore would take skilled workers, provided they were younger than thirty and would give up speaking Cantonese for the government-mandated Mandarin, but old people would be pushed back to sea. Australia was sending ships, but the ships never came. In fact, few Tanka were interested in paying passengers. They had their own families to worry about.

The day Chip was killed, Vicky, already staggered by Steven's death, had thought she was ready to give up too. But Peter, prodded by Mary, had wangled government permission to fit MacF's air freighters with passenger seats, and the ensuing mad scramble to get the job done had derailed any thoughts of leaving. Overnight, everyone at MacF was working twenty-hour days, flying expatriates and foreign business people out of the beleaguered city.

Until yesterday, when a frightened mob of Chinese families with possessions on their backs, but neither visas nor tickets, had completely blocked the bridge to the airport. Then Vicky had learned firsthand how deeply alarmed the PRC was by the public-relations

disaster Hong Kong Turnover had become. Mr. Wu of the Overseas Labor Committee had telephoned personally to announce that
thanks to his intervention, Mackintosh Farquhar's Lantau-Central
ferry service had been approved to be licensed. Perhaps MacF could
begin service within the hour?

Vicky had stripped her communications gear from the *Inverness*,
commandeered a storeroom in the club, and pressed the launch into
evacuation duty, ferrying ticket and visa holders from Central and
Kowloon to the airport. The Tanka of Causeway Bay were profiting
similarly. Their junks and sampans were streaming past the Yacht
Club verandah, shuttling between the typhoon shelter and Lantau
Island.

HONG KONG'S DUNKIRK, roared the headline on the international edition of the London *Sun*, which was spread on the table
and spotted with wet-glass rings.

Vicky folded the soggy paper and fanned her face. Before air
conditioning and modern medicine, the gweilos of old Hong Kong
had built their homes high on Victoria Peak, seeking cool breezes
and elevation above unhealthy swampland. But in the last days of
June 1997, there was a definite comfort in being at sea level near a
boat. She sent Peter in search of the cabin keys to Chip's *Tasmanian
Devil*. Chip had had no relatives here in Hong Kong, and she and
Peter and Mary might have more immediate need of a sturdy little
sloop than his cousins back in England. Her mother, who had radioed twice, was safer in the middle of the Pacific Ocean.

The sun began to set, the sky turned lavender—except where
thick black columns of smoke smeared it—and the drinking picked
up. Vicky stuck to Coke. She had no doubt that Two-Way Wong
was behind the riots and she was raking through her memory for
some new scheme to connect with Tang's inner circle.

A Hakka junk from the Yau Ma Tei Typhoon Shelter in Kowloon motored into Causeway Bay and pulled up to the sampan dock.
"Good Christ," cried a drunken banker who had taken refuge in the
club, "it's the bloody twit who started this whole mess."

His host, a retired jurist, equally drunk, took the banker to task.
"If you're referring to that gentleman, sir, I must inform you that

he happens to be a winner of the Round the Island Race and a member in good standing of this club. Good evening, there, Alfred. Come have a drink."

Alfred Ching bounded onto the verandah in a cool-looking linen suit. "Thanks anyway, but I'm rather caught up. Have you seen Vicky Mackintosh?"

"Young fellows work too hard," grumbled the banker.

Vicky stood up. "Alfred. Over here."

The wind on the harbor had mussed his silky black hair. His dark eyes were lively. "Have you got a decent fax machine?"

"I'm set up in the cellar."

"I was operating out of my parents' restaurant, but we lost electricity. I figured I'd try the club." He glanced around, bent closer, kissed her cheek, and whispered, "I'm buying the Cathay Tower."

"Again?"

"I had investors committed to buy it for two billion. I can snap it up today for eight hundred million. It's worth a billion-six, at least."

"Alfred, they're killing people in the streets."

"Excellent time to swing a deal. I'm almost there."

"Who's backing you?"

"Canadian and New York banks. Turns out Two-Way Wong went behind me to undercut some of my deals. I'm putting 'em back together again."

"How the devil can you convince them when all they have to do is turn on the TV to watch us burn?"

"By persuading them to take a chance on doubling their money."

"What if you're wrong?"

"If I'm right, I'm made. Let me use the machine."

She led him through the bar and downstairs to a room lined with boxes of whisky and gin. "Mind if I listen in?"

"Be my guest. I just hope the ruddy phone lines hold."

Vicky stood behind his chair as he direct-dialed New York. It would be eight in the morning there. To her surprise, someone answered immediately, and Alfred, talking at machine-gun pace, picked up a conversation that had apparently been interrupted in the middle.

She listened less to his words than to his tone. By his third call, she concluded he was neither daft nor faking, but was still a long way from swinging a deal.

Dialing his fourth call, Alfred craned his neck to kiss the fingers she'd let rest on his shoulder. She squeezed back, a little surprised she had put them there, and ran her other hand through his hair.

"Wouldn't happen to know anyone in Tang's mob, would you?"

"Not offhand."

"Seriously, Alfred."

"Seriously, I don't. Sorry."

"Shall I have the waiter bring you a nosh?"

"Tea, thanks." Alfred winked and blew her a kiss. Vicky went back to the verandah. Peter was back, nursing another Coke. He tossed her Chip's keys. "Told the steward you were inventorying the boat for Chip's family. He looked like he wished he had thought of it himself."

"Thanks." Vicky sat down, feeling slightly uplifted by Alfred, but still stymied. She was sitting on dynamite with her father's kickback evidence. But it was useless if she couldn't deliver it directly to Tang.

"Where," Peter asked of no one in particular, "will we all be on Turnover Day?"

Wally Hearst stepped out of the bar and scanned the verandah, which was lit by orange hanging lanterns. "Here, Wally." Vicky waved to the China trader. "What are you doing here? I thought you were in Peking."

The American hurried over, shooting glances to either side, and knelt beside her chair so only she could hear.

"Thought you should know, Taipan. Tang's coming to town."

"*What?*"

"He's going to take a personal shot at quelling the riots. He's organizing an anti-riot rally for trade unionists in Mong Kok."

"How does he imagine he can pull that off?"

"Man of the people promises his fellow Cantonese that post-'97 life will stay peachy-keen in Hong Kong. He's got the credentials — you know, he's a fisherman's son, a genuine Old Hundred Names. The Cantonese love him."

"Peter, listen to this."

Wally, glancing around again to make sure his information did not travel beyond Peter and Mary, repeated what he had told Vicky. "Soon as Tang lands, he's going to try to placate those poor bastards camping on the airport bridge. Figures if he can send them home, and open the airport, we'll at least look orderly. Then the Mong Kok rally."

Peter and Mary exchanged glances. Peter said, "Unless Chen sent him on a last-ditch mission to save Turnover—which I doubt— this is most likely Tang's last-ditch effort to save himself. Reckons that Chen can't fire him if China sees him calming Hong Kong. The question is, how well has he covered his back in Peking?"

"Yes," said Vicky. "What's to stop Chen from firing him? They've bounced three party leaders in the last six years."

"The answer to that is: Yes, they can get rid of him and probably will, unless Tang has more irons in his fire," Hearst replied with a significant glance at Vicky, who was already wondering how to waylay Tang in Hong Kong. Wally seemed to read her thoughts. Very quietly he murmured, "You asked me to put you in touch with Tang a while back, but I couldn't. Now, maybe I can."

"You can? How?"

"I'm in touch with his security people. I can get you close to him in Mong Kok."

"How close?" she demanded, imagining the mob scene.

"In his lap. Guaranteed." Wally nodded toward the bar, where his beautiful Chinese wife had drawn the attention of a half-dozen men. She flashed Wally a smile, her eyes aglitter with blue contact lenses. "Ling-Ling, my wife," Wally said proudly. "She's got a cousin on Tang's security staff."

"Why didn't you tell me before?" Vicky exploded.

"I didn't know. I don't usually talk business at home. She's just a kid."

"Maybe you ought to start—she seems better connected than you. All right, when's Tang arriving?"

"Tomorrow. I'll get you to him. The rest is up to you, Taipan."

35

"PASSPORT."

Vivian had it ready, her Hong Kong British passport, a travel document that conferred no right of abode anywhere but Hong Kong.

"Where were you born?"

"China. Guangdong Province."

"This says Hong Kong."

"I was a refugee."

"Take a seat."

"Is there a problem?"

"You'll be called in turn."

"My visa is valid. I'm visiting my mother, who is a legal resident of Toronto."

"Wait your turn."

Her mind was reeling from the interminable flight. She'd hardly slept, reluctant to injure her baby's health with her customary trans-Pacific sleeping pill. Hoping the wait wouldn't be too long, she retreated to Vancouver's shabby transit lounge. It was jampacked with Chinese clutching their luggage. A weary old woman took pity and offered her own seat.

"When's the baby due?"

"Two weeks." She had prevailed on an old friend at Cathay Air to waive their long-distance flight restriction for very pregnant women. "How long have you been waiting?"

"Three days."

"Three *days*?"

"They're getting stricter. And they're not very pleasant. There are so many of us trying to get in, and many forged visas."

Vivian sagged in the plastic chair. MacF executives were expected to maintain certain standards while doing business, and it was some years since she had traveled rough. Nor had she ever been treated so rudely by Immigration, not even in London's Heathrow Airport, which was notorious for its hostility to Asian travelers. Her gaze met that of the old woman, who had perched on a suitcase. They exchanged helpless smiles, and suddenly she had never felt so Chinese, nor so far from home. It was one thing when you crossed borders for international business, quite another when home was a transit lounge, and God the official with a stamp.

Twelve mind-numbing hours later it occurred to her she was stateless.

Television sets had been scattered about the dreary room. At first they didn't work. Suddenly they all came on at once. She watched the late news from Hong Kong, and was shocked to discover how bad the rioting had become. Entire police units had been overrun and the death toll was rising. She spent the night staring helplessly at horrific CNN satellite pictures. But far more frightening than the riots was the official silence out of China.

When Beijing was quiet in crisis, she had learned over the years, the government of China was fighting itself. Silence meant Chen's hardliners and Tang's reformers were locked in secret combat within their walled compounds, waging clandestine political battle for control of the army and the Party. God and heaven help the people until one faction triumphed.

Exhausted, she slept on the floor under a blanket given her by a Salvation Army volunteer, who pressed a miniature prayer book into her hand. The next morning, the same fresh-faced young girl brought her a container of coffee, which she couldn't stomach.

When she overheard a sleazy immigration lawyer bribe his way into the holding area to canvass her fellow inmates for retainers, Vivian realized nothing would improve unless she took matters into her own hands. Lining up at the one working pay telephone, she opened her address book. By late that evening, she had hired a lawyer, who thought to expedite matters by pleading the imminence of her baby's arrival. That night, some thirty-six hours after she had landed in Vancouver, her lawyer ran in waving a paper. "You're in for at least a month. Whatever else happens, your baby will be born Canadian."

Canadian. No matter what, her baby had a home, now, separate and independent of her China and Duncan's Great Britain.

Wheeling her luggage into the cool night, she paused and gratefully inhaled crisp, free air. An enormous figure loomed out of the shadows, and she shrank back before she recognized Ma Binyan. Her old friend looked drained. In stark contrast to the smartly dressed people hurrying about the terminal, his clothes were shabby. But the fire still glowed in his eyes. Whatever his shortcomings, she thought wistfully, he would never give up the fight.

"What are you doing here?"

"We gotta go back."

"I can't go back."

"Tang's going to Hong Kong to stop the riots."

It was electrifying news—until she thought about it. "A hopeless gambit, don't you think?"

"He's desperate." The big Northerner leaned against a pillar, blocking her way, and said, "Two-Way Wong just made his move."

"What move?"

"Two-Way sent word to Chen through Wu of the Overseas Labor Committee that he will stop the riots if Chen appoints him governor of an autonomous Hong Kong city-state."

"That snake."

Ma Binyan cracked a weary smile. "Kind of ironic. We've hoped for a city-state for years. He'll run Hong Kong like his own private kingdom."

"How can he stop the riots?"

"Two-Way has a better shot at cooling the situation than Tang does, because he can mobilize the Societies. How many rioters will go up against the Triads?"

"Of course."

"What it comes down to is this, Vivian: If we can't stop Two-Way Wong, he'll turn Hong Kong into a cesspool like the Green Gang's Shanghai."

Vivian looked around her. It was just an ordinary small city airport like dozens around the world, but it was peaceful. All she had to do was have the baby in Canada, and they were safe for life. "You don't need me. Take Victoria Mackintosh to Tang, yourself."

"Do you think I'd have chased you all the way to Canada if I could do that? Tang's given up on me. But he might see you."

"I'm not so sure of that."

"You have your own routes to him."

She had the hunter in the Mong Kok wild-animal market. And the woman in Shanghai. "No," she said, her sense of duty warring with her vow to her child, and the awful fear behind it. If only she were still alone, beholden just to herself. "I'm not going back. I have a baby due any day. I won't risk her. I'm sorry." She tried to steer the luggage cart around him. "Let me go. You'll find some other way."

"There is no other way."

Her hands crept protectively to her belly. She wondered if in trying to be a better mother than her mother had been, she was repeating another dismal pattern instead. Her father had fled China for a better life for her. Now she was fleeing for a better life for her child. Had they both deserted China when she needed them most?

Her heart rose to her father's defense. He had had no choice. There was no fighting the Red Guards. But she . . . she had some power, some place in the world. She had left on a jet plane, not swimming in shark-infested waters. That had to mean something.

Her baby chose that moment to stir. Guilty, torn, she affirmed her choice.

"Goodbye, old friend. I cannot help you." She tried again to push past him.

Ma Binyan held the cart. "You know," he said softly, "Tang

might appoint you governor of Hong Kong if you help him oust Premier Chen."

"You're daft," she blurted in English.

"Tang spoke of it the last time I saw him in Shanghai. On the red junk, right after you went ashore. He said his choice for the next Hong Kong chief executive would be startling, to dramatize China's intention to turn her back on the old, corrupt, empty promises we've so often given the West. The appointment of an accomplished businesswoman with China trader connections to Beijing and Shanghai, as well as the new premier's ear, would tell the West it's safe to invest in Hong Kong."

"Nonsense." The idea was absurd. "He would never choose a woman, and even if he did, not one as young as I. Perhaps some grand figure like Dame Lydia or Selina Chow," she ventured, naming two mature women who had made enduring marks in Hong Kong politics and business. "Not a pregnant unwed woman in her thirties."

"But Tang is very young himself, remember. And Hong Kong is a very young city. Past forty you're old there. Tang said that his governor would have to be a business person, which you are; a longtime Hong Kong resident, which you are; young and bright and tough, which—"

"You don't have to bribe me to help China."

"I'm only telling you what I heard."

"You of all people should know that about me," she protested. She felt betrayed by Ma. It sounded as if he were denying every fight she had fought for China, every risk taken. "You should know how hard it was to quit. And I resent your implication that I'm ambitious."

"I'm just telling you what I heard Tang say. As for ambition, I've never doubted you were ambitious—for China."

Stung, she said, "My father wasn't a high Party official like yours, Binyan. You've never known what it's like at the bottom. You have no right to remind me of commitment. It's always been a game to you."

Ma smiled. "My father was not a man of principle like yours,

Vivian. I had to discover commitment by myself. You take for granted treasures most have never owned."

Vivian hung her head. "I'm sorry. I can't. Besides, I'm not suitable to be governor. I'm not qualified. I've no administrative skills and no real political skills. The business community would see China's appointment of me as a terrible omen."

"Tang checked you out," Ma persisted. "He was impressed with how you handled Allen Wei's Legco campaign."

"Well, you tell Tang that keeping Allen Wei—belly or no belly—is his best bet to reassure the international business community. As for this governor talk, you're making it up. Tang might appoint a woman like me to a Legislative Council seat, but not governor. Not chief executive."

Ma Binyan sprang the trap that Vivian had been too distracted to see. "Why not ask him for a Legco seat, then?"

She knew that the aging student leader would say anything to persuade her to go back. He was a clever, accomplished liar to have survived as long as he had. And she was his last opportunity to regain Tang's confidence. She knew all that. Her difficulty was how badly she wanted to believe him.

"What exactly did Tang say?"

"Tang said, and I quote, 'I'll give Hong Kong a Shanghai Woman.' "

Her heart started pounding with the possibilities. The things she could do . . . firmly ensconced in the government, supported by direct, personal ties to the highest councils in Beijing . . . the things they *all* could do . . . what changes in the new century that lay ahead of China . . .

"Of course," said Ma Binyan, "first Tang must displace Chen as premier. And to do that he'll need all the help he can get."

"Of course."

36

WALLY HEARST WAS perspiring heavily in the afternoon heat, exuding a rank odor of fear as he strained to distinguish MacF's *Inverness* among the junks and sampans streaming in and out of Causeway Bay Typhoon Shelter.

"Got the stuff?"

"What stuff?"

"Whatever it is you want to give Tang," he stammered. "You said you were trying to get the Expo hotel open, I figured you must have something to give him, right?" He glanced at her shoulder bag.

Vicky fingered her necklace. The China trader was making her nervous with his fidgeting.

"Relax, Wally. We won't get off the boat if it isn't safe."

"Sorry. Crowds make me nervous."

"Tough on a China hand, I'd think."

"Very." He laughed anxiously. "Sometimes I wonder how I got into this business."

His wife rolled her creepily tinted eyes like a petulant child. Vicky thought that her father's assessment of Ling-Ling's mind had been uncharacteristically generous. She wondered if Hearst had any inkling how ready the girl appeared to be to dump him.

She had been driving Vicky mad, chattering endlessly about Tang's bravery, the opulence of the motor yachts maneuvering in the shelter, rumors of a People's Liberation Army invasion, and the cowardice of the rioters, who, she said, deserved to be shot, with the exception of their leaders, who should be tortured first. All this was delivered with a certain naïve wit and ebullience which might have been briefly charming on a less momentous day. But with smoke rising around the harbor and the *Inverness* late, and an ominous jockeying of boats toward the mouth of the typhoon shelter, Vicky could have cheerfully shoved Ling-Ling off the sampan dock, were it not for her cousin in Tang's bodyguard.

"There's the boat!" cried Ling-Ling, with a happy squeal and a kiss on Wally's ear that appeared to melt the middle-aged China trader's knees.

Vicky had diverted the *Inverness* from the airport shuttle to take her and Wally and Ling-Ling across to Kowloon, up to the Yau Ma Tei Typhoon Shelter, where they would try to intercept Tang Shande on his way to the Mong Kok rally. The long dragon boat came slicing a path among the junks, glided into the shelter, and maneuvered gingerly up to the sampan dock, Ah Chi backing and filling into the tight space while the mates traded the latest rumors with the sampan drivers.

"Don't tie up," Vicky yelled as he drew near.

She had seen something they hadn't: the sudden start of a movement of junks en masse toward the shelter mouth. She had been fearing it all day, for there were only two narrow exits through the sea wall, one at either end, and no way all the boats could get out quickly if a rumor panicked their owners.

"Jump, Wally! Let's go!" The mates hauled the overweight Wally aboard. The athletic Ling-Ling spurned the hands offered, as did Vicky, who jumped, shouting, "Go, Ah Chi! Full astern! Chop-chop!"

Ah Chi reverse-throttled full speed astern toward the shelter mouth, which was fast clogging with junks. The sight of the needle-thin *Inverness* lunging between two broad-bottomed junks frightened a third out of the way. Ah Chi sideswiped a speeding motor yacht and burst through the opening in the sea wall. His boat's helm spinning in a blur of spokes, he careened into forward gear. The

next second the turbine launch was whining across the harbor for
Kowloon.

"Hello, Vicky."

She whirled about, astonished. "Vivian!"

Behind her father's mistress loomed Ma Binyan. "How's your
head?" He grinned.

Vicky ignored the student leader. "Vivian, what are you doing
back?"

"I was just coming in from the airport. I hopped the boat to
meet you at the club."

"Why?"

"I've come to bring you to Tang."

"Wally's already taking me."

"Wally?"

"That's right," said Hearst. "We're gonna intercept him at the
Yau Ma Tei Typhoon Shelter. Ling-Ling's arranged to walk us
through security."

Vivian glanced at Ling-Ling and back to Vicky. "I want to help."

"I understand. But I've already made arrangements. Besides,
Tang's trailing a mob everywhere he goes. You really shouldn't be
caught in that."

"They loved him on the bridge," Wally explained. "He's addressing the trade union anti-riot demonstration next."

"I'll take the chance," Vivian said coolly.

Vicky tried and failed to meet the Chinese woman's gaze. They
were thinking the same thing: If Vivian brought her to Tang, Vivian
would reap the credit and Tang's gratitude; but if Vicky delivered
her father's evidence on her own, Tang would regard Vicky as the
instrument of Chen's downfall and Tang's salvation. It was, for Vicky,
a once-in-a-lifetime chance to become an "old friend" of the new
premier—a connection that would smooth a hundred negotiations
for MacF, and virtually eliminate any British-gweipo stigma.

Wally Hearst sounded fully aware that he had plenty to gain
too. Shooting unfriendly looks at Ma Binyan, he said, "It's all set,
Viv. The Party leader's expecting me and Ling-Ling to do the introductions and vouch for the Taipan."

"Forgive me, but I dare say that Party Leader Tang would accept my vouching for the Taipan, as he has asked me repeatedly to introduce her to him."

"Trouble is," said Hearst, "you've got to get through security to reach Tang, and Ling-Ling's the only one who can get us through."

"We'll have no trouble getting through once Tang sees me," Vivian insisted.

"But how will he see you at all," Hearst retorted, "in a mob of construction workers? Trust me on this, Viv. We've got the better in."

"Vicky, may I join you?" Vivian asked.

"Why did you come back?" Vicky asked.

Vivian glanced at Wally and Ling-Ling, who were watching closely. "Two-Way Wong has made his move. Stopping him is more important than anything else."

Again, Vivian glanced at Wally and his wife. But when it was clear they would not leave and Vicky would not order them to leave, she answered, speaking only to Vicky. She was a blunter Vivian than Vicky had known before, and keyed to a high pitch of excitement.

"Two-Way got our old friend Mr. Wu and some others to approach some 'real good friend' of Premier Chen with a deal."

"What deal?" Vicky asked. The launch was approaching Kowloon fast, circling the deserted Ocean Terminal to dart up the west shore of the peninsula.

"Missy!" Ah Chi called from the helm. "Taipan!" He was holding the radiophone. "Tang not go Yau Ma Tei."

"Bloody hell. Where is he?"

"Mong Kok rally."

"Tell the car to meet us on the quay. What deal?" she asked Vivian again.

"Two-Way offered to stop the riots."

"How can *he* stop the riots? No one's sure even Tang can."

"He probably started most of them," interjected Ma Binyan. "And who in Hong Kong would defy him if the Triads put the word out that they back Two-Way? The Secret Societies are glad to help. They'll flourish under Two-Way."

"What do you mean *under* Two-Way?"

"In exchange for stopping the riots," answered Vivian, "he demands to be appointed governor of Hong Kong as an independent city-state."

Vivian had used the term *city-state* the day they met on *Whirlwind*, Vicky recalled — July, a long year ago.

"A totally autonomous Hong Kong, except for foreign policy," Vivian explained. "Two-Way would be sole ruler; his word would be law, the police his private army, the entire city his."

"Chen will never agree to that," Wally interrupted. "China won't give up Hong Kong."

"China has closed every door to the outside since the Beijing massacre," Vivian countered hotly. "Every door but Hong Kong. Chen and his hard-liners won't accept real change, but they know they need Hong Kong to continue being China's door to the West. Two-Way has convinced the hard-liners that he'll bring back the gweilo businessmen China needs for Western investment."

"Never happen."

"It's like Shanghai all over again. In Shanghai the gangs corrupted the police and intimidated the workers for foreign businessmen. He'll do the same here. Hong Kong will be a wide-open city. Everyone will pay him protection. And the gweilos will permit it, so long as they can do business."

"Bullshit!" Hearst retorted. "Beijing has promised one China since Liberation. How can Chen let Hong Kong go?"

"They will cloak it in traditional language. Remember, Vicky, I told you that Vietnam and Korea were vassal states of the Middle Kingdom? They'll make the arrangement look like that. Two-Way will 'kowtow' to the 'emperor.' He'll pay his respects to the Party and the Beijing government, but in reality he'll be free to run this town as his personal kingdom."

Vicky nodded, remembering that her father thought Two-Way was part of the Green Gang that ran Shanghai. "I can see how that might seem attractive to Western corporations."

"Before you get too attracted," Vivian replied acidly, "do not forget the place *you* hold in his heart. MacF might as well close its doors and leave the key in the latch. I hope you enjoy the weather in Britain more than I did."

"I'm not forgetting," said Vicky. "But I'm afraid if what you say is true, we're all too late. What I've got for Tang can't help him anymore. Two-Way's stolen our thunder. Tang won't have time to get my father's evidence to enough Chinese officials to pressure Chen to resign. And he'll appoint Two-Way governor the instant the riots stop."

"Chen can't outrun the mob."

"But you just told me Two-Way will stop the mob."

"Not Hong Kong's mob. Beijing's mob. Canton's mob. Shanghai's mob. Chongqing's mob. Chengdu's mob. All Tang has to do is fax your evidence to the Party elders in the Politburo Committee of Five—proof that Chen and his gang have bled China for years. That will destroy him in the court of the street. The Party elders will know instantly that Chen has to go or China will explode. Don't forget, the 1989 Tiananmen student rebellion erupted into a national democracy movement when people learned the government clique had profited from giving away Hainan Island commercial rights to the Japanese. They were so angry they lost their fear. Conditions are worse today. They will rise against *any* target that becomes really visible. The Party elders will be terrified that with the example of Hong Kong already burning, the Chinese people will go mad."

"Chen will slaughter them."

"We don't think so," Vivian replied. "The army still hasn't recovered from the last time. The Committee of Five knows he'll find it harder than Deng and Li Peng did to convince the generals that 'stability' is more in their interest than the support of the Chinese people."

"The Chinese people will bleed again if you're wrong," Wally said gravely.

"Hong Kong is already bleeding. Let us apply the tourniquet. . . . Again I ask, Vicky, may I come with you? You may need my help."

"The Taipan's fine with us," said Wally. "Right, Ling-Ling?"

"Maybe too many people scare Tang," said Ling-Ling. "Maybe pregnant lady safer at home."

The speeding *Inverness* heeled sharply into the Yau Ma Tei Typhoon Shelter. Junks were milling as chaotically as they had back in Causeway Bay. Vicky directed Ah Chi toward a Land Rover waiting on the quay. It was plastered with big character decals and flags that identified it as a press car. She had wangled it from Allen Wei, along with passes to cross police lines, just in case. Wally had wanted to arrange transport but she had preferred to control what little she could, herself.

"Tang's either brave or a fool," she said, re-joining Vivian as the launch maneuvered toward the Land Rover. "What if Two-Way tries to turn the rally into another riot?"

"Hong Kong is Tang's last chance," said Vivian. "He figures he has nothing to lose."

"How about his life?" Vicky asked, wondering what about their lives, too, if the mob went crazy.

"Whatever else his shortcomings, Tang doesn't think that way. Besides, the police have had time to prepare. It's their last chance too. Have you decided, Vicky? May I come with you?"

"Too many people," Ling-Ling protested. "Not safe."

"Going to be a mob scene," Wally agreed. "I'd sit this one out, Viv."

Vicky could not think of what she would gain by bringing her. But Wally and Ling-Ling were both just too anxious to screw Vivian. In China, at least, it was wrong to side with strangers against family, and Vivian Loh, for better or for worse, was about to become family—any minute, by the look of her belly. As for earning credit in Tang's eyes, perhaps she would do better to arrive with an entourage of both Wally and Vivian, and let Tang draw his own conclusions when she, and she alone, personally handed over her father's optical storage disk.

"Vivian is coming with us."

Ling-Ling rushed off angrily to telephone and returned with the information that Tang had skipped the Yau Ma Tei visit for security reasons. The Party leader was scheduled to speak next at the construction-worker rally at the site of a new housing estate near the Kowloon-Canton railroad, a half mile inland.

"He'll meet you in a police command bus after he speaks," she finished.

"If we can get there," Vicky said.

They climbed into the Land Rover.

"I suggest," said Ma Binyan, "that the gweilos sit between us."

Vicky sat between him and Vivian. Wally hunkered in the front between the Chinese driver—a nephew of old Ping—and Ling-Ling. As the Land Rover nosed into heavy traffic outside the typhoon shelter, Vicky again had second thoughts. It seemed impossible that they would get as close to Tang as Ling-Ling promised. Vivian helped Vicky stuff her bright blond hair under a scarf. "No point in provoking the natives," Vicky cracked nervously, eliciting from Vivian the thinnest of smiles.

Tens of thousands of Chinese workmen were converging on the Waterloo Road, which cut between the Mong Kok and Yau Ma Tei districts. The broad street was a moving sea of white T-shirts and thin, hard muscle. There was a police lane open for emergency vehicles and press—for the entire Hong Kong government was gambling on good publicity—but it still took the Land Rover a half hour to negotiate seven or eight blocks.

Finally the Waterloo Road angled past an enormous construction site, where tenements had been leveled to make room for new public housing next to Kwong Wah Hospital. Vicky guessed that easily a hundred thousand people had crammed into the pit to hear Tang speak.

The air lay heavy with anticipation. Emotions could swing, quite suddenly, either way. The police were everywhere in heavily armed forty-man companies like the one Chip had led. The constables looked grim, for they were truly caught between the mob they could see and the Chinese Army they knew would invade if they couldn't handle the situation themselves.

Marksmen with rifles peered down from rooftops, and helicopters darted overhead. As on the Waterloo Road, a lane was kept open in the north-south Nathan Road for police and ambulances. It appeared that Tang would arrive either by the Nathan Road or by helicopter.

He came instead, quite suddenly and unexpectedly, by the Kowloon-Canton Railway, a fact that became obvious when a police column poured down the Waterloo Road from the east. Sitting high in the Land Rover, which was stuck a few yards from the Nathan Road, Vicky saw a white Hong Kong Police van flying the Chinese flag. Tang jumped out, and spurned help as he scrambled up a ladder onto the roof of the van. He picked up a microphone and surveyed the roaring crowd.

The Party leader was wearing his trademark open shirt and sport jacket, sweat-drenched in the sweltering heat. He raised both hands, flashing his hand with the famous missing finger, and uttered a single sentence that drew thunderous cheers.

"What did he say?" Vicky asked Vivian.

"He greeted them: 'Hello, Old Hundred Names.'" The cheering got louder, and for many minutes Tang could only wait.

"Brilliant," breathed Ma Binyan, his face shining.

"How the devil are we going to get to him?"

Ling-Ling spoke to Wally. Wally turned to Vicky. "There's the police bus."

A big blue bus with POLICE COMMAND on the side was idling next to the emergency lane on the Nathan Road, less than fifty feet away. "That's our guys. Let's get over there. They'll bring Tang to us when he's done talking."

"I'll go first," said Ma Binyan.

"Good idea," said Wally. "Break trail. Ling-Ling, stick close to the big guy. All right, everybody, let's go."

A face sprang into Vicky's range of vision—broad, hard, flatnosed, with a familiar madness in the eyes—and just as suddenly fell back into the crowd.

"Wait."

"Taipan, we gotta go for it. Tang's only talking long enough to get face."

Hearst's words rocketed Vicky back to the Canton Club. The Triad gangster chugging brandy, demanding she do the same. *You no give me face?* The Triad gangster Steven had stared down with a chilly smile. She strained for another glimpse of the man, but he had disappeared in the densely packed mob.

"Come on," said Hearst. "He's not going to wait for us."

"Must go now!" said Ling-Ling.

Vicky hesitated, her mind churning possibilities. Throughout the entire discussion with Vivian and Ma Binyan, neither Wally nor his wife had questioned what all the talk about her father's evidence had to do with getting water for a hotel. Did they already know?

"Now!" Ling-Ling demanded. Her eyes were flickering back and forth like caged animals. Wally was gripping the door handle so hard his fingers were white.

They couldn't possibly know what she was bringing Tang. Unless Wally had betrayed her father to Two-Way Wong.

She hesitated, recalling how stupidly she had attacked Mary Lee. She strained for another glimpse of the Triad gangster, but the crowd had absorbed him as thoroughly as a drop of water on a dry pavement.

"Tang is finishing up," said Vivian. "He's begging them to disperse peacefully."

The crowd broke into another happy roar.

If Wally Hearst had betrayed her father, then this meeting was a setup of some sort to get her to bring the evidence so Two-Way Wong could steal it. That was why the Triad was waiting. Only the unexpected presence of Ma Binyan and Vivian had saved her so far—that and the fact that she had arranged her own transport. But she was on her own the instant she stepped out of the Land Rover. And even if she did miraculously make it to Tang with Vivian's help, the Triads probably had a hundred men ready to launch a suicidal attack to stop him from using it.

"Let's go," Wally shouted.

"Wait!"

She had to protect both Tang and the evidence. That meant

getting the evidence to Tang while appearing not to, and drawing the Triads away from him. But the only way she could do that was to surrender the chance to give it to Tang herself. A new thought whizzed through her mind. Would she have challenged Mary Lee as she had if Mary were not Chinese? After a life in the Orient, did she still play by different rules that allowed her to mistreat people who were not Westerners? Denying it mightily, she looked at Vivian.

Ma Binyan reached for the door.

Vicky stopped him.

"Vivian, you and Ma Binyan stay in the car. It's too crazy out there. I'll go with Wally and Ling-Ling."

Vivian looked stricken. "You promised—"

Vicky slipped off her dragon necklace and looped it over Vivian's head. "Just in case I get killed out there, this is for the baby."

"You promised—"

"Only if it's a girl. If you have a boy, then you wear it."

Vivian looked confused.

Ma Binyan started to protest. Vicky laid a hand on his. "Take care of Vivian. She's so big she looks ready to drop twins."

Vivian closed her hand around the pendant with a puzzled half-smile. No one knew better than Vicky Mackintosh that she had been named in Duncan's will because every test known to medical science said her baby was Duncan's. And the tests equally guaranteed one child, a girl. What secret did Vicky's favorite pendant hold?

"Quote the poet to the child," said Vicky, nudging Wally to open the car door.

"Which poet?"

"Lao-tzu. 'She who is clear-eyed . . . is immortal.' "

Vicky watched Vivian's fingers trace the dragon to its green eye, the optical storage disk with which her jeweler had replaced the jade. She gave a cautious nod. Ling-Ling stiffened, sensing something between them.

"Why?" Vivian asked. "You love it."

"It should stay in the family," Vicky replied. "Go on, Wally.

Right behind you, Ling-Ling." Hearst forced open the door and Vicky stepped after them into the crowd. It felt like falling into hot sand.

Ling-Ling had waited for Vicky and now fell in close behind her as Wally "broke trail," as he had put it, through the smaller Cantonese, who were surging toward Tang. It took five minutes to cover the fifty feet to the police bus.

She looked in vain for the Triad gangster. But she noticed others who looked like the tough young gangsters in the Canton Bar.

"Almost there." Wally shoved into the lee of some police constables guarding the bus. He rapped on the door. It swung open instantly. Vicky followed him and Ling-Ling up the steps. Inside, when the door closed, the noise of the mob faded a little and the air conditioning felt like heaven.

"This way," said a clipped British voice. Good Christ, what if she was wrong and she was suddenly facing Tang with nothing to give him? They were led in past the uniformed driver and down the aisle between the seats. Halfway back, the seats had been removed. Guns and gas masks and water casks were stacked in the space. A siren growled, the bus started rolling, and seconds later they were spinning down a cleared lane of the Nathan Road.

"Where are we going?"

"World Oceans House."

"I beg your pardon?"

"Sit down, Vicky," said Hearst. "I'm sorry about this, but life's not simple."

"You're taking me to Two-Way Wong?"

"Sit down," said Ling-Ling, and something in her voice was just scary enough to make Vicky sit.

"What about the cops?"

"I don't see any cops."

•   •   •

She sat quietly as the bus headed for and then inched through the crowded Cross Harbour Tunnel and then west toward Central District.

What were Chip's words about the police? "Riddled top to bottom"? Apparently it was a simple matter to procure a bus and a few constable uniforms. She saw no chance to resist, what with Hearst and Ling-Ling, the driver, and the men she sensed rather than saw sitting in the back. When the bus finally pulled into the shadows of the World Oceans House garage, she did as she was told, and followed Hearst and Ling-Ling off the vehicle and aboard an elevator. The same elevator, she recalled, that she had ridden to Two-Way Wong's office the night she had beaten him by kidnapping Steven. She shivered.

A look at Wally Hearst erased her fear momentarily. "You killed my father."

Hearst wet his lips. "Your father killed himself. I was just a guy in the middle."

"Shut the fuck up," said Ling-Ling.

Hearst went red, wet his lips again, and glanced in embarrassment at Vicky, who said, "Is she great in the kip or are you just awful?"

Ling-Ling seized her hair and yanked it, slamming Vicky into the jade walls of the elevator. When she let go, Vicky was totally disoriented, with tears in her eyes. Her heart was pounding wildly. She fought to regain her poise before they reached the top floor. When the door opened, she frantically discarded Vivian's scarf and combed her fingers over her aching scalp, as if by neatening the mess she would bring order to her predicament and corral her fear. Somehow she had to buy time for Vivian to reach Tang.

The deep voice of Two-Way Wong rolled across his enormous office, resonant with satisfaction. "Whose heart do you bring me this time, Taipan's Daughter?"

37

THE HEAVY SILENCE, the priceless carpets, the jealously hidden art, all conspired to threaten that events endured in this sealed lair above the city would never be known. Ling-Ling prodded her. Wally took her arm. Vicky shrugged him off and stole a glance at her watch. Less than an hour since she had slipped Vivian the dragon pendant.

They marched her to the teak desk, where Two-Way Wong waited. He watched her, gauging her fear. She spoke first, addressing the translator who stood beside the seated Taipan.

"Ask your Taipan if he knew my father in Shanghai."

Two-Way Wong interrupted the translation, replying directly in English.

"Colonial masters did not consort with street boys in old Shanghai."

"My father's father was a clerk."

"One does not take a taxi to the moon because it's closer than the sun."

"It's just that you were about the same age, both from the same city, and you so obviously hated each other."

Two-Way gave her a long look. "Had I known Duncan Mackintosh for what he was, in Shanghai, he would never have reached Hong Kong alive."

"What—"

He cut her off savagely. "Give me the material your father left you."

"What material?"

"I will have you stripped naked and searched. Ling-Ling would be more than pleased to perform the task."

Vicky felt the girl stir beside her.

"Your father gathered evidence to use against me. I want it."

"I have no evidence," she protested, ransacking her mind for some way to steer him back to Shanghai.

"Ling-Ling."

"Yes, Lao Yeh."

"Find it."

"What did you mean, had you known what my father was? What was he to you?"

"A thief."

"A thief? Duncan Mackintosh? I think not."

"Ask your mother."

"I beg your pardon?"

Ling-Ling reached for her. Two-Way Wong signaled her to wait. He seemed intrigued by Vicky's puzzlement. "Ask my mother?"

"She knew the thief."

"Thief of what? What was stolen? I can't ask my mother. You tell me." She was as baffled as she was relieved by this temporary shift in his interest.

Two-Way Wong regarded her with a chilly smile. "These are things of the past that mean nothing to you. Our struggle is of the present. Ling-Ling, remove her clothing and find it."

"Find what?"

"I have recently learned that it is very likely that your father reduced his documents—the evidence I want—onto a computer optical storage disk. I am informed these disks are quite small. You could easily have secreted it in your body."

Vicky's legs began to shake. He was invading her with his eyes. The quiet room seemed to grow even more still. A clock ticked somewhere behind her. Ling-Ling closed a strong hand around her

arm, her fingers pressing the bare skin. Wally Hearst shifted uncomfortably from one foot to the other and cleared his throat.

Two-Way Wong's black eyes flickered to the China trader for
a portion of a second. Wally froze in place and Vicky knew she
would find no help there. The China trader was the slave of his
young wife, who was, it was obvious, Two-Way's slave.

"I have the evidence."

"Give it to me."

"I'll tell you where it is if you tell me why you call my father a
thief."

At her apparent surrender, all feeling had drained from Two-
Way Wong's eyes, and he regarded the young Taipan of Mackintosh Farquhar as if she had ceased to exist. Her offer to trade drew
his contempt. "I'd rather watch Ling-Ling search for it," he said
scornfully.

"It's not on me."

"You had to bring it to give Tang."

"Nor is it 'in' me, to use your disgusting phrase."

"Ah . . . The British grande dame rises to the occasion. Have
the natives annoyed you, Taipan's Daughter? Has the 'Chinaman'
been impertinent? Will you have him flogged, or steal more of his
land?"

She had gotten to him, she reveled, in the last way she would
have expected of a man dubbed "Sir John Wong Li, CBE" by the
Queen of England.

"I said 'disgusting' and I meant disgusting."

Ling-Ling wrenched Vicky's arm and it hurt. "On the couch,
Taipan's Daughter." She started to drag Vicky away. Two-Way Wong
snapped his fingers. Ling-Ling let go, her animated face suddenly
stiff with terror. Her master turned smoldering eyes on Vicky.

Vicky spoke first. "You shame your race."

"Shame? Shame my race? How dare you? *You* should be ashamed.
You abandoned Hong Kong, threw it away when you were done
with it. Surrendered us, so you could make deals with the Communists."

Vicky bowed her head and let the silence grow slowly. "I'm

ashamed of Great Britain's behavior," she admitted. "But I am not
Great Britain. I am Victoria Mackintosh. And you know better than
anyone that Mackintosh Farquhar has risked ruin in order *not* to
abandon Hong Kong. Nor are we the only expatriates who've stood
our ground."

"Stolen our ground is more like it. You pillaged China. You
forced your ways on us." Two-Way Wong's face darkened with rage
as he began to rant in strangely measured tones about gweilos stealing China's art. His voice grew deeper, more sonorous, and his features collected into an expression that reminded Vicky of nothing
so much as a self-important PRC official demanding the kowtow
due his post. ". . . You looted," Two-Way concluded his diatribe.
"You oppressed. You destroyed."

"Helped for a hundred years by people like you, Wong Li. *You*
sold our opium; we just delivered it. *You* rounded up the coolies.
You filled the brothels." She would have given a year of her life for
another look at her watch.

"You dare to blame me for British colonialism?"

"People like you did the dirty work."

"You don't know, Taipan's Daughter, the things that were done
to China."

"But I know who did them. Corrupt Mandarins and Chinese
gangsters."

"And the British had nothing to do with it?"

"We reformed," Vicky shot back. "You didn't. We banned opium.
We banned slavery. We suppressed your pirates. We charted your
waters. We built your railroads, your shipping companies. We made
it possible for you to trade, to shift food to famines, to modernize
peacefully. But there was always a Chinese like you to find a way
around it, find a way to hold your fellows down."

"And being British," Two-Way replied with heavy sarcasm, "you
knew you were right."

Vicky finally stole another glimpse at her watch. He wouldn't
let her rattle on this way much longer.

"In 1880," she said, "my great-great-grandfather secured the
agency rights to a mechanical reaper. He loaded it onto a steamboat

and took it up the Pearl River to sell. Do you know what the Mandarins who ruled Guangdong Province told him?"

"They told him to take his bloody contraption home."

"Do you know why?"

"I can guess," said Two-Way. "It was a labor-saving device.
And the Mandarins no doubt asked, rightly, what the peasants would
have done with the free time they'd gain if they did not have to reap
by hand."

"They could have used the free time to educate their children,
grow more food, repair the dikes, expand their houses."

"But the Mandarins knew different," said Two-Way. "They knew
the peasants would have used their free time to revolt."

"It's thinking like that that makes a Brit—or any Westerner for
that matter—quite sure she is right. And quite happy she has had a
part in ridding Hong Kong of your sort of Chinese."

"Hong Kong," he repeated, savoring the name. "Your last surrender. British colonialism's last failure."

"Failure? Hong Kong is not our failure." Vicky felt an angry
pride rise in her breast. She had been talking, saying anything, to
fill time. But suddenly, this was something she could believe totally,
something her mother had said last year, the morning she came
home from New York.

"For more than a hundred and fifty years there has been one
small place in all of China—only one—where Chinese people have
worshiped their gods, fed their children, slept safe in their beds, and
honored their ancestors without the terror of knowing life could end
at the whim of a warlord, or a Green Gang boss, a revolutionary, or
a Communist bureaucrat. Hong Kong. British Hong Kong."

Two-Way's mouth started working. He gripped the edge of his desk,
shook with rage of a depth Vicky had never seen in a man or woman.
She thought she would never know how she had plumbed such
emotion in the most powerful Taipan in the city. But Two-Way
Wong told her in a voice that boiled with hate and pain.

"Your father stole my wife."

"*What?*"

But she knew instantly. Of course. Her father's first affair. A simple English girl. Steven's mother. A love of thirty years after she had died, said Steven. No wonder this monster kept loving his son.

"My son Steven's mother, whom I cherished. Your father stole her and used her and when he was done discarded her. I tried to take her back. She would not have me. She would have no one. He had ruined her heart and she died."

If there was any pleasure in this moment it was in denying Two-Way the knowledge of how her father had mourned his "discarded" love for the rest of his life. "Did my father know that you knew?"

"They thought that somehow they were above being caught."

"And you took your revenge."

"Slowly," said Two-Way Wong. "And profitably," he added with a grim smile. "The inevitable shift from West back to East worked for me, against him. It was a simple thing to create additional opportunities to make Duncan Mackintosh suffer."

"But you made a mistake when you tried to get him to kick back money for building your yacht."

"I have kept my bargain. I have told you of the thievery of Duncan Mackintosh. You will tell me where you've hidden the disk."

"Tang has it," she said, knowing she had stalled as long as she could.

Two-Way Wong laughed softly. "I've overrated you, Taipan's Daughter. You're a liar and a stupid one at that. *Ling-Ling.*"

"I gave it to Vivian Loh in the car and she gave it to Tang while I came here with Wally and his lovely wife."

"No," blurted Wally Hearst.

"Ling-Ling!" snapped Two-Way Wong.

Ling-Ling pawed frantically through Vicky's bag.

"No," Wally said again. "She didn't give—" He stopped talking abruptly.

"Yes, China trader?"

"Dear God, she gave Vivian her pendant."

"A gold dragon with a jade eye," said Vicky. "Only the eye isn't jade anymore."

Two-Way Wong turned white. "You're lying."

"I am not lying. It ought to be a simple matter to find out. Why don't you see what Tang is up to at the moment?"

Two-Way Wong snatched up a telephone, spoke briefly, hung up, and waited, casting a baleful eye upon Ling-Ling and Wally Hearst. Telephones began to ring. He picked them up, one by one, listened, spoke a word or two, and banged them down. After twenty minutes of cryptic exchanges, his cheekbones burned white in his skin. His gaze settled on Wally Hearst.

"Tang is holed up in the Peninsula Hotel. He's surrounded by Royal Hong Kong Police and PRC Public Security officers loyal to him. He is constantly in touch with Beijing by telephone, cable, and fax. An announcement is expected this evening in the Party organ."

"What announcement?" Wally breathed.

"Premier Chen will step aside immediately, for reasons of health. Next year he will retire. The Politburo Committee of Five has persuaded him that the Chinese people will accept nothing less."

"How could he give up so easily?"

"Easily?" Two-Way's voice dripped scorn. "Perhaps he didn't relish appearing at a televised trial in chains."

"But his friends—his whole network."

"Chen has been isolated. The fleeter-footed of his 'old friends' are making new friends. The members of the 'club' are realigning themselves. Power is an illusion, Mr. Hearst. Something an American ought to understand."

"What about Tang?"

"Premier, of course."

"What about Hong Kong?"

"An announcement is expected."

"What will it say?"

Two-Way Wong opened his desk and took out a crude knife with a rattan handle. It looked to Vicky as if it had been made by rubbing a sliver of metal against a stone. He rose from his chair, pushing off from the desk, hoisting himself on his cane. Once standing, breathing hard, he leaned on the cane and picked up the knife. The translator accompanied him as he shuffled around the desk.

"Come here, Mr. Hearst. I have acquired a lovely Sung screen that might interest you."

"What's the announcement about Hong Kong, Taipan?"

Two-Way Wong turned with glittering eyes. "How would I know what Premier Tang will announce, Mr. Hearst? My old friends are all gone. You can't expect me to make new ones overnight."

He started across the room again, heading toward the middle, where, beside his private elevator, a painted screen depicted the emperor's barges floating on the Grand Canal. "Ling-Ling, bring the Taipan's Daughter. She'll enjoy this too."

Ling-Ling took Vicky's arm. But her grip was a trifle less rough than before and Vicky could feel her trembling. For a moment they all stood in front of the screen like guests at a cocktail party waiting for their host to tell them an amusing story about the painter, or how the work had fallen into his hands.

Two-Way muttered to his translator, who moved the precious screen, revealing a second paneled elevator door. Two-Way lifted his cane and deftly pushed the call button. The door slid open on a dark, empty shaft. Air rushed up eighty stories with a warm stink of garbage.

Wally Hearst tried to turn away. Two-Way Wong stopped him by raising his knife and pointing it at his face.

"Ling-Ling."

Ling-Ling spun in a kick-fighter's half-circle, one leg pistoning off the carpet. Her foot flew at Wally, and the American China trader disappeared with a scream that trailed after him like a long rope.

"Next?" asked Two-Way Wong in a voice quiet as death.

Vicky was rooted to the carpet, gaping in shock at the empty space where Wally Hearst had been shuffling anxiously from one foot to the other like a puzzled panda. Ling-Ling reached for her.

Two-Way's cane leapt hard and fast and caught the Chinese girl in the face. A contact lens popped from her eye, glinting in the light. Toppling backward with an expression of total amazement, she whispered, "Lao Yeh," and fell silently down the shaft.

Vicky couldn't breathe. It had happened so fast, faster than the wave that had taken Hugo. She closed her eyes in terror, and suddenly there flashed into her mind an incongruous vision of her mother driving *Whirlwind*, plowing east, alone at sea. She seized the image, clung to it for strength.

Two-Way Wong had spoken again. She heard him as if from a distance, saying, "So much for fools and girls who know too much. And now you, Taipan's Daughter. What do you know?"

She opened her eyes and they were clear.

"I know that you will never kill me."

"In that case you know nothing."

"Let me amend that. I know you won't kill me for the next six months."

Two-Way looked puzzled and a little wary. "What are you talking about?"

"I'm carrying the firstborn of your firstborn."

38

"**Y**OU'RE LYING."

Like a lady.

"You said I lied about the disk, but I didn't. You'll be governor of hell before Hong Kong. Why would I lie now?"

"You'd say anything to save yourself."

Two-Way Wong raised his cane. The tip was steel, she saw. Beside and slightly behind her, from the empty shaft, the garbage smell wafted up from the subcellars of World Oceans House, warm and cloying. She glanced at the translator. No help there. His face was as expressionless as if she and Two-Way were negotiating a loan instead of her life. She felt her legs gather muscle, but there was nowhere to run. She had to stand for the lie.

"I *would* say or do anything to save my body. I can't expect you to understand, but it's instinctive when you're pregnant. I would lie to save this child. Your grandchild."

"There are tests."

"Get a doctor," she shot back. Time, she hoped, was on her side. With Premier Chen packing in Peking, the chairman of World Oceans had to hurl himself into damage control. He had defenses to prepare, new friends to cultivate, and trails to cover before the new Peking reformers took it in their heads to prosecute Hong Kong's leading capitalist. Vicky searched his eyes. Like her father, he gave nothing back.

"I have many grandchildren."

"Many children, too," said Vicky. "But you loved only one."

"Don't be so sure of that. I don't expect a British gweipo to understand a Chinese family."

Vicky glanced at the yawning shaft. "I think you've demonstrated your love for your orphans." She cast a look at the translator, surely another of them, but the young man's expression did not change.

Two-Way Wong's mouth, however, twisted in a sneer that skewed his handsome features. "Even if you are pregnant, how do I know it's his?"

"I doubt that Wally Hearst was your only spy. You know every second of my life since you killed my father. You know damned well there was no one else."

Two-Way raked her with his eyes. She stood still as death beside the silent translator, afraid to breathe. The cane tip flickered like a snake's tongue. Vicky watched, mesmerized, on shaking knees. Two-Way Wong jabbed at the wall switch, missed his first try and poked again. The door slid shut on the shaft.

He turned away and hobbled slowly to the windows. The journey seemed to take hours. There, at last, he tripodded himself on crippled legs and cane, catching his breath, silhouetted against the harbor and Kowloon. The city lights had begun to glow as evening fell. In the distant north, the Chinese hills stayed dark.

"Leave me."

Vicky headed for the door before he could change his mind. The translator overtook her, unlocked the door, and escorted her to the elevator. His soft voice was rich with insinuation. He could well have been the one who had telephoned about the kidnapped children.

"Unfounded rumors about a China trader who emigrated suddenly with his young wife could make confusion in the air-freight business."

"Tell your Taipan I don't give a damn about Hearst or that sick child. Tell him they were his. I've already lost enough of my own. Tell him my only regret is that my father didn't live to see him destroyed."

For the first time, the translator displayed emotion. It looked a little like pity. "Destroyed? Forgive me, miss, but I fear you dream. Two-Way Wong will always have a place on the China Coast."

"So will wharf rats, but not in Government House."

One of the Peninsula Hotel's green Rolls-Royces was parked at the front door of World Oceans House, nose to nose with a police car. Three Chinese inspectors sat in it, listening to their expat superintendent argue with Ma Binyan and Vivian Loh on the pavement.

". . . And I will tell you once again, madam, that the Royal Hong Kong Police do not break down doors without a proper search warrant. I've had all sorts of telephone calls from your friends in high places, but until I am issued a proper warrant, I am not about to violate the law. This is still British Hong Kong and will be for the next"—he glanced at his watch—"sixty-eight hours. Not bloody Peking. Ah! There's the young lady now, and apparently not a damsel in distress." He touched his cap. "Good evening, Taipan."

"Evening, Superintendent."

"Vicky? Are you all right?"

"I want a drink." She got in the car and collapsed on the soft leather seat. Vivian climbed in awkwardly after her. Ma Binyan took the jump seat. "There's a bar here. Maybe I can find you a glass of wine."

"Whisky."

"We got the police as soon as we could," said Vivian. "How'd you get away?"

"Informed him I was preggers by Steven."

"You *are*?"

"Lied like a lady. Ma Binyan, *that's* whisky. Open that. Thank you. There's a glass. No ice. Thank you." She tipped it to her lips.

"Oh, God . . . he killed Wally Hearst. Made Ling-Ling kick him down an elevator shaft. Pushed her after him." She took a second long pull of the whisky and shoved the glass at Ma Binyan. "More."

She didn't drink again but swirled the whisky around the glass, thinking and trying not to think. Vivian was watching her closely.

"Are you all right?"

"I am alive. Right now, that rates pretty high. . . . What's happening with the riots?"

"Over. Tang was a hit. The rumors have already started that the Committee of Five will make him premier."

"Is it true? Chen's stepping down?"

They traded notes, Vicky relating what she had learned from Two-Way Wong, and Vivian and Ma Binyan what they had gleaned in the outer rooms of Tang's suite at the Pen.

"Chen lost the army."

"Are you sure?"

"Tang's on top. It'll be a long night, but the cadres will fall into place."

"Hand me that phone."

"Who are you calling?"

"I want to be the first to congratulate Allen Wei." She dialed his private line. "Debby? Vicky Mackintosh. May I speak with him? . . . Allen, I am very happy and I want you to know my father would be too. . . . Right. Time to move ahead . . . What's that? *Vivian?* You're not serious. . . . Right. Talk to you soon." She hung up the phone, eyeing the Chinese woman speculatively.

"Vivian? Allen says Tang's ordered him to appoint you to Legco."

Vivian looked embarrassed. "It was entirely Tang's idea. I'm still astonished."

"So you knew. Good Lord . . . Well, congratulations. I'm sure you'll be good at it. And I must say it won't hurt MacF having its half-owner's Mum in the government." Vicky laughed. "We'll have to look out the ICAC doesn't charge us with loose talk in the nursery. Congratulations, Vivian. This is wonderful. . . . What's wrong? You don't look happy. Is the baby—"

"Vicky."

"What?"

"I'm not sure how to say this."

"Try directly. What's the matter?"

"Tang is grooming me to serve Hong Kong in the future. He wants me to be very visible in the business community as well as the government, to show foreign business people that China encourages free enterprise in Hong Kong."

"As well you should be. We'll cobble up some grander title for you at MacF and I'll arrange some directorships for you on British companies and I'll tell Alfred Ching—if he buys Cathay Tower—to put you on his board. Tang is absolutely right. You're young, proven in business, and a woman. You symbolize the best kind of change."

"He wants me to be a director of MacF."

"What? That's daft. He can't have you made a director of MacF. We'll come up with some title that sounds good and businessy, but not a directorship. We are a closely held company with a family-only board. You'll already have a vote for the baby. Your own direc-torship would give you too much power, to put it bluntly. I will work with you, I will heed your advice, but I am taipan and I intend to stay taipan. My father never had to debate his leadership with his directors and I won't either."

"Tang insists."

"Tang can insist until he's blue in the face. What's he going to do, send me to Mongolia? That would do wonders for the new im-age. Chinese leader imprisons British businesswoman who resists robbery of her company. Smashing. Tang can screw off."

"It's not that simple."

"It *is* that simple. MacF is a Mackintosh Farquhar family hong. My little sister, your child, will be a member of the family. Tang is not. Nor are you, in that sense. You have half. But my father set me up as taipan. I'm taipan until I step down, and I am *not* stepping down."

"Vicky, I'm sorry. I didn't ask Tang for this. It was his idea."

"Where did he get the idea to set you up in this particular struggling Scots trading hong? No one can take it away from me, Vivian. You don't seem to understand. The premier of China itself doesn't have that power unless he's willing to see every Western businessman in Hong Kong leave."

"If you want to keep MacF's Expo Golden Hotel, you need drinking water. If you want to operate the airport hotel, you need a permanent license to run the airport ferry."

"Of course. Without them, we're dead. But now that Chen's out it won't be a problem. So what are you saying?"

"Do you want access to Chinese labor?"

"You know I do."

"MacF will receive water and ferry permits when I'm appointed director. And Mr. Wu will end our labor problems."

"Mr. Wu? Mr. Wu is going to jail, isn't he? He'll be Tang's corruption exhibit Number One."

"No, Wu and Tang will come to some accommodation."

"What?" Vicky looked at Ma Binyan, who looked suddenly weary.

"Tang had to make certain concessions to get support in the Committee of Five. I don't like it any more than you, and one day, I hope, Wu will get his comeuppance. But the important thing now is stability."

Vicky shook her head in disgust. "Nothing's changed."

"Nothing changes completely," said Vivian. "But we have edged out of the darkness."

"What if I refuse?" Vicky asked. But she knew the derelict hotels would fall into receivership. The banks would get scared and call in her other debts. And MacF would go under.

"This way," said Vivian, "you protect your equity."

"And Fiona keeps her earnings," Vicky mused aloud, as the enormity sank in. "And my mother. Even Peter and Mary lose if I say no."

"I'm sorry. It wasn't my idea."

"Works out nicely for you, doesn't it?" Vicky tried to say, but her voice dissolved before she could finish.

"Forgive me," Vivian whispered. "But it's not so bad as you're making it. You're still Taipan."

"As long as you and Peter and Mary let me be."

Vivian looked away. In truth, the hong would fare better if Vicky eventually stepped down. She had no illusions about the defeat handed Two-Way Wong. He would remain a powerful enemy and was sure to blame Vicky for dashing his dreams.

"I thought so," Vicky murmured. She blamed herself bitterly. Old Friend Tang and Old Friend Vivian. How foolish she had been not to see it coming. Tang was working the same sort of scam Mr. Wu had worked, and she was as powerless to stop him. She might as well try to fight all China. Hot tears ran down her face, and she was too broken to hide them. She had lost everything.

"There are two things I ought to tell you, Vivian . . . two things my father told me. He told me you made him feel alive. And he warned me to look out for you. I wish I had listened. Both times."

When she could speak again, she said, "I'm tired. I'm going home."

"We'll drive you," said Ma Binyan, turning to speak to the chauffeur.

"To New York?"

"No, no, no," said Vivian. "Stay. We need gweilos to stay."

"This gweipo needs a long holiday. I'm going to take a year or so off. I'm going home."

"This is home."

"I don't feel that way anymore. Goodbye, Vivian. Good luck with the baby."

"You can't leave now. This first year is crucial."

"Will you drop me at the club? I've got to get my boat ready."

"Boat?" Vivian and Ma Binyan exchanged puzzled looks, as if wondering whether Vicky had come unhinged.

"If my mother can sail to England, I suppose I can make it to New York."

"You're daft. Vicky, you're shaken by what you saw up there. It's just now sinking in."

"Actually, I feel wonderful. Rather free." She sat quietly as the car trundled from glittering Central to Wanchai. Approaching Causeway Bay, a glimpse of the gold MacF House would have put new tears in her eyes if she had let it.

Old Friends

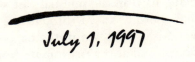

July 1, 1997

WHEN THE NOON Day gun went off for the last time under a British sun, Vicky Mackintosh was still in Causeway Bay, repacking food and bottled water. Chip's little sloop—less than half the length of *Whirlwind* and barely a fifth the tonnage—reacted tenderly to the distribution of weight and had developed a starboard list when she topped up the diesel tanks.

At last she got under way, motoring out of the typhoon shelter, waving goodbye to Ah Chi and Hua and some morose drinkers on the Yacht Club verandah. Everyone else was at Kai Tak, at the Turnover ceremony, which was supposed to be a low-key affair for the benefit of the foreign press. Speeches were broadcast on the radio. But wanting no part of it, just to be away before the transfer was effected, she tuned in a Cantonese country-and-western station and raised her mainsail to the strains of Patsy Cline's "Faded Love."

A perverse east wind sprang up, forcing her to sail close to Kai Tak. For a few minutes she probably had the best seat in the house. She caught a glimpse of a handful of British officers with a squad of Gurkha troopers and thought for a second they had coerced Allen Wei into wearing a plumed hat. But then, luckily, she had to tack the other way while the Union Jack still stood stiff in the breeze.

•　　　　•　　　　•

The British flag descended to the mournful wail of Scottish pipers at precisely 3:07, a time deemed auspicious by the astrologers. But the Chinese flag, blowing hard in the unusual east wind, jammed partway up. An anxious murmur raced through the viewing stands. A terrible omen, though the fault was in the flagpole. It was a creaky old wooden mast borrowed at the last minute from the Royal Hong Kong Yacht Club, when it was discovered that each of the forty-five highly independent Hong Kong businessmen and women who built Expo had assumed someone else would install a flagpole.

Premier Tang and Hong Kong Special Administrative Region Chief Executive Allen Wei jumped up as one, firing orders. Hongkongers and Mainlanders ran to the pole and hoisted up the smallest of their number, who shook the halyard free. With that, the red flag rose crackling to the masthead, while CNN flashed pictures around the world of a human pyramid composed of a dozen overweight businessmen and bureaucrats in their Sunday best.

"We'll be a laughingstock," a Mainlander complained. He was silenced by a growl from Premier Tang. "Loosen up, Comrade. They'll laugh with us."

Vivian Loh sat with her fellow legislative councillors, two rows behind Premier Tang and Allen Wei. She hardly heard the speeches, for her head was filled with her father's dreams. *Hong Kong is China. Your China.*

When it was over, Vivian had her driver take her to her favorite Tin Hau Temple in Public Square Street. It bustled with worshippers. And if the women burning joss sticks or the old fishermen approaching the altar on their knees were any gauge, she thought, Hongkongers were going about their business much as they always had, a day at a time.

"How went Changeover?" she heard a woman ask another with a radio.

"Japanese battleship," came the reply, a common pun on *Yamamoto*, which sounded like the Cantonese word for *boring*.

Vivian lighted a joss stick and let her mind drift with the pungent smoke. Father had marveled at how swiftly events moved in China. Who knew how long her new mentor would reign, or how long he would let her enjoy her appointment to Legco? Lasting reform was a product of resistance, not compliance, so she vowed to be pragmatic but never craven. An easy vow, she knew, now that for the first time in her life, thanks to Duncan's baby and Tang's patronage, she held the power that came from ownership—a solid place in a great hong.

In a swiftly changing world, triumph should be savored while it lasted, and savor it she did. But doubts nagged. It was a shame about Vicky's leaving, she thought. She and Peter and Mary together could not equal the crazed, hard-driving power of a man like Duncan Mackintosh or a woman like his daughter. The hong of MacF was poorer for her loss.

She should have handled Vicky better, not left her feeling as if China had robbed her. What did Duncan think, watching from heaven? Had she disappointed her beautiful lover? Lighting more joss sticks, she put her question in a prayer to the sea goddess. She could have predicted the answer. The ever-practical Tin Hau told her not to worry. Vivian, like all mortals, would learn heaven's secrets soon enough. In the meantime, there were pressing matters here on earth.

The east wind dogged Vicky all afternoon. She was still getting used to the boat and was not sailing it especially well, and it took hours to round the island and finally get past Shek-O. The sky was growing dusky as she crossed the Lamma Channel, reaching on the now-helpful wind toward the open sea. She kept looking back. But now the wind shifted south, back to the normal July southwesterly, which carried with it humid heat and impenetrable haze.

The horizon grew dark ahead. Behind her, Hong Kong began to make the sky glow red. She switched on her running lights. The compass light was too bright, robbing her night vision. She opened the binnacle, removed the hot bulb, and painted it with nail polish.

Perfect. She settled down behind the helm and thought about having a beer. Clouds rolled in, covering the stars. The red glow astern faded to a soft line that barely skimmed the waves. The rest of the China coast was dark as always, while ahead the black night of the South China Sea reared as solid as a wall.

"*Vicky.*"

She thought she heard her name on the wind, a whisper floating from the dark, and she half-rose from the cockpit seat before she decided she must be conjuring voices from her loneliness. Already? She faced a long, long voyage. A frightened grin tugged her face. Time for a little mental geomancy, straighten out the *feng shui* in her brain. She got busy, trimming the mainsail to get in tune with the boat.

"*Vicky.*"

She jumped up, scalp prickling. That was real. Out of the dark she heard her name. She looked for a boat, saw no light, heard no engine.

"*Vickiiiiiiiiiii!*" Thin on the wind, urgent.

She turned on the work lights, flooding the sails in a silent white explosion, blinding herself to the dark beyond but lighting a beacon for whoever was calling. Straining to hear an engine, she heard only waves slushing past the hull. Then, at the extreme rim of the pool of light that surrounded her boat, she saw a tiny sail dart up a sea slope and burst the crest in a gleaming cloud of spray.

A windsurfer smacked down in a trough and ran up the next slope. Guiding this apparition, like a sturdy ghost in a yellow wetsuit, was the short, stocky figure of Alfred Ching.

The windsurfer banged against her hull and Alfred tumbled through the safety lines. Vicky caught a handful of sail, drew the little board alongside, and snubbed a line around a cleat. Alfred started to slide back under the safety line. Vicky tugged and pulled him into the cockpit, where he sprawled, breathing hard and grinning like a fool.

"We have to talk."

"Alfred." She looked at the dark circle beyond the work lights, glanced at her watch, and calculated how far he had come. "Alfred, are you crazy? We're *miles* offshore. You would have drowned if you hadn't found me."

"I found you."

"But if you hadn't you'd have never made it back."

"Do you have a beer, by any chance? I got so thirsty."

"How long were you out there?"

"Hours. I think I overshot you. Thought you'd be making better time. Could I have a beer?"

"A beer?" she repeated, awed by what he had done. "Sure." She went below in a daze, took a Mig out of the cooler, debated a moment, and opened two. Up on deck, Alfred still sprawled on his back, still grinning. His breathing was slowing and he tried to sit up.

"Thanks. Cheers."

"Cheers."

They sat silent a few minutes.

"All right, Alfred. What are you doing?"

"I want you to come home with me."

"Home?"

Alfred put his beer down and looked her straight in the eye. "Vicky. I want you."

"You want me," she said, dully aware she was echoing him like a parrot. She could not believe the risk he had taken to find her.

"I love you," Alfred said firmly. "You're the most beautiful woman I've ever seen and I want to see you every morning. The first time you said no. This time it's got to be yes."

"Yes? Why yes?"

"Because I love you, and now I can give you a home."

Vicky stared at him, shaking her head.

"I'm serious. I want a life with you. We go back a long way, Vicky. We have plenty going for us—always had—and you know it."

She could not deny their old friendship, nor their mutual attraction. Two people simply didn't stay friends so long if they didn't really admire each other. But she knew she was in no condition to make a go of marriage with anyone, friend or no.

"I've driven one husband and several boyfriends into the ground like tent pegs, Alfred. I don't want another divorce."

"I'm no tent peg, Vicky."

"Perhaps not," she admitted.

"Definitely not," Alfred fired back.

She wondered whether as a younger woman she had dodged Alfred because she instinctively feared he would try to dominate her as her father did. Moot question today, of course. She had grown strong enough to fend off several sure, strong Alfreds if need be.

Today, Alfred presented complications of an opposite sort. He had put her on a pedestal, in exactly the same way her father had elevated her mother to a fantasy status he could never achieve. It was almost as if these driven men had to choose some goal in their lives they could not win. If her father's experience was any example, such a losing contest played hell with love. And love, she thought, was not something she wanted halfway, not anymore. Not after Steven. No more wounded birds, no more struggling men to care for in the name of love, and no mindless adoration, either, thank you very much. She would rather do without.

"My father chased behind my mother most of their marriage, just trying to catch up. I don't want a man to feel that way about me—"

"I don't care who's on top. Jockeying for position is a waste of time. I don't have to be number one. If you want to be Taipan at home, fine with me."

Vicky shook her head.

Alfred said, "In other words, you're afraid I'll love you more than you love me?"

"I just want a more equal relationship. Emotionally equal."

"Is that what Steven Wong gave you?"

Vicky reflected on Steven. How much had he given her and how much, as Steven himself had insisted, had she finally been ready to accept?

"Among other things, yes. But marriage to Steven Wong was never on my agenda, Alfred. I couldn't live like that forever. If I ever do find someone, he'll be a man more like me, a man who works as hard as I do and enjoys making things happen. What are you grinning at, Alfred? I'm a Hong Kong woman. I like the action. *What* are you grinning at?"

Alfred slapped his chest. *"I'm* that guy."* He pointed astern. *"There's* Hong Kong. That red glow in the sky. Let's turn this stupid boat around and go home."

"That glow is all that's left."

"The hell it is. It's only gone if people like you and me leave. Vicky, we can do it."

"Can we? I don't think anyone can save Hong Kong, Alfred."

"You know any couple better qualified to try?"

Vicky could almost feel the excitement radiating from his body. She retreated, afraid he would infect her with empty hope. "You've always been an optimist — too much of one, I might add."

"What's the alternative?"

"That's how you let Two-Way Wong dupe you, Alfred."

"I don't mind making a mistake."

"Yes, well, I do," she said sullenly.

"Hey, beating yourself up about Vivian Loh goes nowhere, Vicky. I remember an old friend recently told me to get back on my horse and go kill something. Remember?"

Vicky remembered, but it had been a whole lot easier telling Alfred what to do than doing it herself. She was tired, she told herself, and more than happy to throw in the towel.

"Did I mention," Alfred asked casually, "that I closed the deal on Cathay Tower?"

"You did?"

Alfred grinned proudly. "I raised the money to buy the Tower and some adjoining properties too. All for seven hundred and eighty million."

Vicky was astonished, overwhelmed with admiration, and more than a little envious. What a coup. What an amazing deal to swing in the midst of chaos, even if it was the last big deal Hong Kong ever saw.

"Congratulations, Alfred. I am deeply impressed."

"You gave me the push to do it, that night at my parents'."

"That's awfully decent of you to say, but you did it."

"I'm not asking you to marry me out of nowhere, Vicky, or from the past. You helped me. We're a team. Now, here's what I'm thinking next. On the extra property, I'm going to build a head-quarters house. The land rises, so we'll have smashing views of the typhoon shelter and some of the older buildings, like MacF House. We'll be able to watch them sunbathing on the roof."

"Headquarters for what?"

"The umbrella company we form over the whole shebang. Ching-Mackintosh Expat-Emigrant and Ching-Cathay Property. Maybe even a vertical campus for Ching University—you know that Asian uni-versity I was telling you about? Also, I've got an idea I've been want-ing to discuss with you. If things keep growing, Hong Kong is going to need a separate industrial airport just for air freight. What do you think?"

"Alfred, do you realize you could have died tonight if you hadn't found me?"

"I did find you. If I live to be a hundred and twelve I will never understand this gweipo penchant for speculation. What if? What if? It's like sailing in the dark."

Vicky watched the helm turn in the ghostly hand of the self-steering. A jog to port, a jog to starboard. She couldn't get over the chance Alfred had taken with his life. He might have drowned, just to ask her to come back. She wondered whether her mother would have considered it a "manly" act, or just plain reckless. But Alfred Ching loved life too much to be a reckless man. He was brave. He had risked his life. And his heart.

She touched his face. He looked so tired. "Next year or so I'll come back to Hong Kong, if it works out. Come back and fight for my hong. Ask me then."

"You're taking the worst-timed holiday in history, Vicky. What-ever happens in this town is going to happen in the next twelve months, while the timid wait on the sidelines."

Vicky turned off the work lights to escape him, but she could still hear his little windsurfer thumping impatiently against the hull.

Alfred gave an exasperated snort. "I'll tell you why you're leaving," he said. "You want to know why you're leaving? You're leaving because you're exactly like your father used to be. You refuse to share MacF and now you're refusing to share with me. You have to run the whole bloody show yourself."

"What's wrong with that? Committees don't work."

"Even if that's true, it's empty. Do you want to wait till you're your father's age to really give yourself to somebody? You deserve better. You're actually a very generous woman."

"You don't know me, Alfred."

"Once upon a time, very long ago, I was in bed with you. The memory lingers."

"Bed's not life," Vicky shot back. "But thank you for saying that." She shivered, hugged herself, and looked back at the red horizon. "Actually, you're terribly sweet to say that—did you mean it?"

"They don't make women like you every day."

If *she* lived to be a hundred and twelve she would never forget his bursting over that wave in a cloud of spray. Until tonight, she had never thought of Alfred as romantic. But he was. More than brave, more than "manly," as her mother put it, he was deeply romantic. He brimmed with hope, and what could be more romantic than hope?

". . . You know, Alfred, all those projects you're dreaming up are going to take money."

"Lots of money," he agreed patiently, as if he routinely mingled love and high finance in the same breath.

"Hongkongers are going to be extremely cautious investing locally for a few years."

"Extremely cautious."

"And China's broke."

"Stone broke. No loans from China."

"So we're talking about foreign investment."

"Gweilo money," Alfred agreed. "The only investments we'll see for the next five years will come out of Britain, Europe, and the United States."

"They won't come easy."

"Very hard. But we can do it, Vicky. We can."

"You'd have to put up everything you've got to convince people—rooster testicles, and especially any equity you've managed to
keep in Cathay Tower."

"*Ching*-Cathay Tower."

"This is no joke, Alfred. You're talking about risking everything
to save a city that's not necessarily savable."

"But worth a try."

She stretched her legs and hooked her toes on the bench across
the cockpit. Alfred reached out in the dark. His short, blunt fingers
had always known the precise spot where her instep ached to be
squeezed.

"God, that feels good."

"Give me the other."

Vicky looked back at the red glow astern. Somehow, as the night
grew darker, the light seemed to pulse higher into the sky. Alfred
saw her smile. "What's funny?"

"Exciting times," she mused, thinking that she could raise London and New York money for a Hong Kong air freight port if she
could persuade Premier Tang to make the Chinese government
guarantee the bonds. Tang owed her that much, at least. "I could
give you a hand with the gweilos."

"I'd certainly appreciate it if you would talk to people in New
York."

"No, no, no. I don't want to be a broker."

"Perhaps form an investment company?" Alfred ventured.

"That would be the way to go."

"Here in Hong Kong."

"Of course, Hong Kong, Alfred. This is where the action is."
She started tapping her free foot. ". . . So long as it's solid, old-
line Hong Kong, if you know what I mean."

"Like a Scots trading hong?"

"We will call it Mackintosh-Ching Investment. Instruct the receptionists to mumble the Ching so it sounds like China."

"Ching-Mackintosh might better convey the sense of the new order."

"Don't underestimate the value of the past, Alfred. Hong Kong's the only piece of China that's ever gotten better— How's that for a slogan? Would you risk money for a shot at the best of China?" Fiona and the girls could ride home on that one, she thought, while she engineered a way to regain full control of MacF.

"Smashing slogan. Still, Ching-Mackintosh has a certain—"

She took her foot back. Alfred seized the other. Vicky took that foot back too.

"Dammit, Alfred, my family settled Hong Kong while yours was still frying monkey brains in Canton. You just got here. It's Mack-intosh-Ching and that's ruddy final."

"Is that a yes, or not yes?"

"I want to build a railroad."

"*What?*"

"Your air freight port is a good idea, but I've got a better one. A high-velocity train between Hong Kong and Peking. It will pull China together and put Hong Kong right in the catbird seat."

"Vicky! Yes or not yes?"

Vicky kicked the self-steering release and freed the helm. "Coming about!" Alfred helped with the sheets as she turned the boat back to the red glow.

"I'll get Tang to back us in Peking and Vivian to push it through Legco. She owes me. Take the helm a sec."

She snapped the work lights on again, ran below for her satellite phone, and scrambled back to the cockpit, punching Vivian's number into the keypad. Alfred, she finally noticed, looked sad enough to cry. Vicky flung her arm around him and pulled him close as she pressed the phone to her ear. "Wish me luck. . . .

"Vivian? Vicky Mackintosh. I've got an idea."

Acknowledgments

Christine M. Loh illuminated the issues of 1997 with a sharp mind, a generous spirit, and an awesome patriotism that proved interesting times breed interesting people. I am also especially indebted to Frank and Anna Ching, John Chetwynd-Chatwin, Samantha and Nigel Stevens, and Manny and Avic Ticzon.

As to the Hong Kong promise that "Anyone in this town will give you twenty minutes," my wife and I found it usually extended to hours, generous evenings, and wonderful weekends. Those who shared information and hospitality were: Denis Bray; Vivien Chou Chen; Raymond Chow; Jennie Edwards; Janet Golden; Katherine Hart; Rolf Heiniger; Robert A. Ho, Jr.; Frank and Cynthia Hydes; Eric T. Kalkhurst; Akber Khan; Allen Lee; Helen Lin; Hugh and Helen Livingstone; Leo C. H. Ma; Peter Moss; John R. Newnam; Linda Ho McAfee; Simon Murray; Dr. Anthony Ng; Susie and Richard Sayes; Pat Sephton; Shaw Sin-ming; Kitty Sit; Michael Somerville; Peter Thompson; Betty and Tuon Van Hong; John Wei; Henry Wong; Wong Luk Kan; and Irene Yau.

In New York, William Dorward, Kerry and Jennie McGlynn, Jay Tunney and Dan Gattis provided invaluable introductions and helpful insights, as did Greg and Sally Ann Gray, and Robert Gray in London. And I saw a Shanghai I never could have seen without John Huang.

JUSTIN SCOTT

Newtown
January 1991